VLAD DRACULA

VLAD DRACULA

THE DRAGON PRINCE

A HISTORICAL NOVEL

Michael Augustyn

iUniverse, Inc.

New York Lincoln Shanghai

Vlad Dracula

THE DRAGON PRINCE

iUniverse, Inc.

For information address:
iUniverse, Inc.
2021 Pine Lake Road, Suite 100
Lincoln, NE 68512
www.iuniverse.com

ISBN: 0-595-33271-4 (pbk)
ISBN: 0-595-78084-9 (cloth)

Printed in the United States of America

To Patricia

For all the help and support,

and so much more.

To John Burke
St. Joseph's University

For correcting every comma on every theme,

and for all of the encouragement.

With special thanks to

Carole and Dom Roberti

for the design and composition of this book,

and to my parents and brothers,

Michael Mallowe,

Jack "the Greek" Xenakes,

Tom Hinchcliffe,

Robert Smith,

Rick Barnes,

Jill Galper, and

Barbara Kelly,

all of whom helped with this work

in various ways.

CONTENTS

▼

Foreword

Though this book is a novel, it attempts to follow actual history as much as possible. With the subject of Vlad Dracula, that is not easy. While much is claimed as fact regarding his life, one of his biographers explained it to me best: *East Europe, Fifteenth Century*...Few records survived the turmoil of the region.

To illustrate the problem, regarding one battle, I found two sources, each claiming a different victor. Turning to what should have been a good third source—the records of one of the combatants—I found no mention of the battle at all—at least not in texts printed in English. Further, for many of the historical characters—though fortunately not Dracula himself—there is no documentation to support accurate physical descriptions.

Still, I tried to capture the flavor of Dracula's life. He was a fugitive, a prince, and a prisoner, pretty much as described. Many of the other characters are also presented in their actual historical context, including Radu, Stephen, Bogdan, Hunyadi, Matthias, the sultans, Toma Catavolinos, Skanderbeg, Gales, Ilona, and Jan Jiskraz. Prasha, too, is presented in context, though her actual name and origins are uncertain. Much about Dracula's sons is also uncertain, other than that he fathered at least three—two by his second wife, Ilona. Other characters—like Balt'zar, Wilk, Ibrahim, the spy, the priests—are composites; their types have some basis in fact in Dracula's life. For example, there are historical references to his employing foreigners in his service, just as foreigners also served the sultan.

Regarding battles, I tried to give accurate numbers of the respective sides. Regarding Dracula's major campaign, though much of the route is uncertain, his tactics are described in both history and lore. Also, where I specifically mention something as historical fact, I believe it to be so, based on at least one reference. And yet this book is intended as fiction, an author's interpretation of the characters' motives.

A Note on Pronunciation

Generally, "s," as in Gales, is pronounced like "sh"—Ga-lesh. "J" is like "y"—Jan Jiskraz/Yan Yiskraz; Janos Hunyadi/Yanoosh Hunyadi. As noted in the text, "Wilk" sounds like "Veelk."

P R O L O G U E

▼

October 1448. He was a month shy of his seventeenth birth-day when he led a column of cavalry two thousand strong to the wooden walls of Tirgoviste. He had already attained a man's average height, with the scrubbed complexion and lean build of a junior officer fresh from training. The build, like that of most soldiers of his day, thickened at the neck and shoulders from the constant wielding of lance and sword. His hair showed as a wavy black fringe under the crown and nape of his open-faced helmet. His eyes were dark emerald.

He halted the column at the edge of the broad field opposite the main gates. As it spread behind him in attack formation, he dismounted, walked his horse forward, and knelt. His men thought that he was merely offering a Christian prayer, just as they, in their own tradition, were offering Muslim prayers. But he had taken a handful of earth—his native soil—and, squeezing it dearly, drank in its scent. After a long moment, he rose.

Tirgoviste was the capital of Wallachia, a small country in southeastern Europe wedged between the Roman Catholic kingdom of Hungary and the western edge of the Islamic Turkish empire. Yet, even as the capital, the city's main defense was its wooden walls, a mere palisade of hewn logs—and the last obstacle between him and his destiny.

Destiny. Though his life had been short, the years to him had seemed long, long indeed. But they had finally brought him to this spot. He was at last poised to reclaim the throne that had been held by his father as *voevode*, or, as the word translated in Wallachia's Romanian tongue, "prince."

At the very thought of his father, his mind raced, and a glaze settled in his eyes. It was a glaze of pain and anger—*rage*—the glassy-eyed look of a wounded animal. With it, his hands tightened till they paled, and his head felt light, as though he were drunk on strong spirits. He was conscious of both sensations—the tightness and mock intoxication—but neither fazed him anymore. They always came with the glaze, and the glaze had come, on and off, since he had crossed the threshold to manhood. In the past year especially, it had been with him more often than not.

Through the swirl of images and emotions that the memory of his father conjured, he seized a single thought and thrust it to the fore of his mind: He would be his father's son in every way that he possibly could. They already shared the same first name: Vlad. And he would soon have the throne behind the walls. Then, in time, he would also take the name that his father had earned: *Dracul,* or "Dragon." He would have done so already, except that the troops behind him, Turks, held the name as anathema. But he would free himself of the Turks in due course, and then...then he would declare himself "Son of the Dragon": *Dracula.*

A horse trotted to a stop behind him, and he turned. Smiling slightly in the saddle was the column's native commander, Balt'zar-bey. At twice Vlad's age, he was a warrior in his prime. He had the bronze skin of his race, and his eyes and hair, with trim beard and moustache, were dark. Like Vlad, he had the active soldier's build.

The commander was a *sipahi,* one of the Turkish sultan's own vassal knights. As such, he was one of the Turks' heavy cavalrymen. His armor consisted of turbaned, open-faced helmet, round shield, and long, chain-mail shirt. His mount was also protected by mail on head and torso. The sipahi hefted a lance—not the jousting lance of romanticized tournaments, but a fighting spear some ten feet long. On his belt, he wore the Oriental curved saber, the *scimitar.* In Balt'zar's case, he was not only a knight, but a *bey,* a Turkish feudal lord. In the name of the sultan, he served the local *pasha,* or overlord, the infamous commander, Hamza. Now, simply as a matter of good form, he addressed Vlad as a lord and spoke in Romanian, though his manner was somewhat casual.

"So, Vlad-bey, what are your orders?"

Vlad had known him for only a few weeks, from the time that the column had been "borrowed" from Hamza Pasha. He found this Balt'zar to be like most knights he knew, both Muslim and Christian. He talked chivalry—duty, prayer, fasting, charity, mercy, justice—but he practiced something else.

As a matter of pride, to show that he needed no deference, Vlad answered the commander in flawless Turkish. "Send a rider. Tell them to open the gates and ride away free. If they refuse, no mercy—none. Tell them."

It amused Balt'zar. The rider who carried such a message might not live through its last word. Among most peoples who at the time claimed to be civilized—save perhaps for the Tartars—messengers were sacrosanct, untouchable. At least, most of the time. They merely carried the words of their masters. They had nothing to do with the content. So they were not to be harmed.

But history testified that enemies were the most bitter when separated by race, religion, or culture. And, in Vlad's time and place, they were often divided by all three: European vs. Turk; Christian sect vs. sect vs. Muslim; Occident vs. Orient.

So messengers were sometimes used—as the Tartars casually used them—to make a point about hatred.

Balt'zar would not waste a native Turk on such an errand. But no matter. He would send another. He called: "Ibra-him'!"

The man spurred forward promptly. He stood out from all the rest by the very color of his skin: the darkest ebony. He was lean and slightly taller than average. His short beard ran in tight, dark curls from under his turban. His African tribe had only recently converted to Islam. Politically the tribe was independent of the Turkish empire. But the empire called itself the Porte—the *Divine* Porte—the empire at the very gates of heaven itself. And Ibrahim had been sent by his sultan, as so many provincials were, to learn the ways of this great empire—the newest "Shining Light" of all Islam.

Ibrahim took the message and galloped for the gates. Eagerly. As always. So eager to do his duty for the Faith. Even as he made the first strides toward Tirgoviste, he was erased from Balt'zar's thoughts.

The bey instead glanced to Vlad and his smile twisted wryly. Among his people, there were many stories and whispers about this young "Lord." Everyone knew that the sultan had tried to humble him in the ancient way of breaking a captive's spirit: rape. Some said that the sultan had succeeded. But others swore that Vlad had thwarted the attempt, with the help of some angel, or even the help of an evil *jin,* one of the devil's own genies.

But whatever had happened with the sultan there were many now who feared Vlad, who called him brutal and cruel—and mad, as witnessed by the passing glaze in the green eyes. And there were many who said, too, that, despite all appearances, Vlad hid a bitter hatred for *all* Turks.

But to Balt'zar it was gibberish. Nonsense. Not worth thinking about. Of course the sultan had taken his way with Vlad. For how could a mere boy—jin or no jin—have resisted the great sultan? And "brutal and cruel"? What true soldier—what Turkish soldier especially—could not see through such things? They had one purpose: terrorize an enemy. They frightened only the weak-hearted. Balt'zar was not weak-hearted.

Further, as Balt'zar saw it, if Vlad was mad—and admittedly he probably was—it was not the wild-dog madness, the dangerous madness, that people thought. It was the madness of delusion, of bold orders in clipped phrases: "...no mercy—none." The madness of a mere boy who thought himself a great prince.

As for hatred...Balt'zar laughed heartily inside. All provincials, especially Christians like the Serbs and these Wallachians, hated the sultan and the empire. But greater peoples—like the Mongols and Tartars—also hated the empire. It made no difference. It was the way of the world. The empire simply hated them back. In the grand scheme, provincials had one purpose: to bow. Not love. Just bow. Obey.

But Balt'zar turned his mind back to the task at hand, to Tirgoviste. "They are your people, Vlad-bey. What do you think? Will they run or fight?"

"Run," Vlad said. "At least, they should."

"Yes," the commander agreed. "Better for them if they run." With a note of concern, he added, "And better for us."

Vlad said only, "Aye."

They shared the same worry. It was not the walls themselves, though walls were usually enough to stop cavalry in its tracks. To breach walls, one typically needed infantry equipped for assault and siege. But Vlad's cavalry were Turks, and *Osmanli*, or, as the west called them, "Ottoman," Turks at that. The tribe had risen from slaves on the far eastern steppes to carve an empire that straddled Europe and Asia. From four years of training with them, Vlad knew not to worry about the wooden palisade.

Nor was he particularly worried about the troops manning the walls. They numbered only a few hundred and were led by some *boyars*, Wallachian noblemen. The boyars were part of the faction of the current voevode, Vladislav. But boyars were notoriously self-serving, and their voevode was gone.

A few weeks before, Vladislav had led the bulk of his army in yet another Christian "crusade," or holy war, against the Muslim Turks. His family, the Danestis, were cousins to Vlad's family, which, from Vlad's father, Dracul, had come to be called the Draculas. By Wallachian law, since both families had the blood of voevodes in their veins, both could claim the princely throne. Both in fact did and so became bitter rivals. In the shifting politics of the day, the Danestis had allied with Hungary, leaving the Draculas—by necessity—to ally with the Turks.

The most recent crusade had been called by the great Hungarian baron, Janos Hunyadi. For him, fighting the Turks had become his destiny. Sometimes, he had won incredible victories; and sometimes he had lost, barely escaping with his life. But even in defeat he had risen from the ashes like the phoenix, and, for his efforts, Christendom had dubbed him "The White Knight." As the Danestis' patron, when he had called the last crusade, Vladislav had dutifully joined him. They crossed the Danube river riding south and met the Turkish sultan, Murad, on a Serbian field called *Kossovo,* the field of the "Crows."

At the time, though Vlad had been trained as a Turkish officer, he was left well behind the lines. His real value to Murad was as a candidate to Wallachia's throne. For, though small, Wallachia was fanatic—even to the point of national suicide—in upholding its customs. And one of those customs was that its voevode be of native blood.

The great sultan, of course, could have conquered the land outright. But then Wallachia would have rebelled, and kept on rebelling, until the sultan's conquest was a wasteland. It was far more practical for Murad to rule Wallachia through a puppet prince—and the Osmanli were an eminently practical people. Vlad was Murad's candidate, just as the Danestis were Hungary's candidates. So Vlad had been left safely behind the lines.

The battle at the Crows had raged for three full days. It was the second battle on the same field between Muslim and Christian; the first had been in 1389. And both ended with God—in His name as Allah—smiling on Islam.

In the aftermath of the second Crows, Vlad's time had finally come. Both Hunyadi and Vladislav were among the missing. All that Vlad needed was the sultan's permission—and the troops—to march on Tirgoviste. He got the first, and the second naturally followed.

The column that he was "lent" consisted of five hundred sipahis, supported by fifteen hundred lighter troops, the *akinjis.* The akinjis were the sipahis' own vassals. As a distinct form of cavalry, they dated back eight centuries, to when the Turks had first risen from slaves to raiders and rustlers on the steppes.

They were essentially horse-archers. Like their masters, they wore the turbaned helmet, but the rest of their armor was little more than thick, quilted shirt and small, target-like shield. Where the sipahis, as the Osmanli heavy cavalry, blended shock and speed, the akinjis blended speed and maneuverability. They screened the sipahis' charge; sprung hit-and-run strikes; and rained arrows on the enemy from running formations. But, once a battle was joined, once their masters engaged, they could also draw scimitar and lock with the enemy.

At his very word, Vlad knew, the column would lunge at Tirgoviste's walls. The akinjis would lead, raking the ramparts with arrows. Under that cover, the sipahis would streak through the ranks, massing in separate contingents here and there under the walls. When the defenders rushed to repel them, another contingent would suddenly spring from among the akinjis where the ramparts were left sparsely defended. They would jump from the saddle with scaling hooks. And once the sipahis got a foothold on the walls, the akinjis and all the rest would converge and follow. A fortress with high stone battlements would surely stop them. But Tirgoviste's poor palisade would surely not. To its shame, Vlad thought, the city's walls were like those of some mere garrison town. And he had seen the Osmanli, even with only cavalry, take many garrison towns.

What troubled Vlad and Balt'zar were the small, round, black mouths spaced along the ramparts: Tirgoviste's artillery. There were only a few guns of medium caliber, but, three decades before, gunpowder weapons had been refined by a Christian sect called the Hussites.

Ironically, the sect began as part of the Protestant, or Reformist, religious movement; their first conflict was strictly spiritual, against the leader of the Roman Catholic Church, the pope. But most of the feudal lords remained loyal to the pope, and they sent armies of knights—trained soldiers—against the mostly peasant Hussites.

At first, as could be expected, the Hussites were driven from field after field. But then they adapted and refined gunpowder weapons, and they came to drive the knights from the field. Already men were imitating the Hussites, loading cannon with canister and chain-shot for a scatter-gun effect, as well as with stone and iron balls for distance and penetration.

There was a fair chance now that the boyars—though the odds were against them—would choose to fight. They knew that Vlad hated them—and not just because they served a rival voevode. His hatred burned much hotter. And, if they chose to fight, they would do so with desperation, the desperation of condemned men. As Vlad had vowed, *No Mercy*. So the boyars would unleash their cannon, and, though they would lose in the end, Vlad could picture his troops savaged by canister and chain-shot.

Balt'zar, in fact, was now wishing that Vlad had allowed time to recruit a swarm of the Turkish irregular infantry, the *baji-bazouks*. They were irregular indeed; the Turks themselves called them horse-thieves and scavengers. And they fought like thieves and scavengers: for plunder. They hardly had the "stuff" for real combat. But bazouks made good cannon-fodder. With the akinjis' bows aimed at their backs to give them courage, they could have been driven to Tirgoviste's walls, taking the brunt of the cannons' barrage to clear the way for the cavalry. But Vlad had not waited for any bazouks. In fact, the commander knew, if Vlad could have found wings, he would have flown to Tirgoviste.

At the city walls now, Ibrahim turned his mount and set spur. He galloped back to his bey and Vlad and reported: The boyars had given no answer to Vlad's ultimatum. At the gaping mouths on the ramparts, thin spirals of smoke began to rise; the tapers were being lit to fire the guns.

While Vlad's face betrayed no emotion, he cursed inside. As Balt'zar had a wish, he, too, had one: *If only he had artillery!* Even one gun could turn the tide, smashing the wooden gates to pulp. But artillery—guns and the mysterious powder that fired them—was ungodly expensive—so much so that the pasha, Hamza, in "lending" Vlad *two thousand* men, had refused to part with even one gun.

Vlad mounted his horse and drew sword. From a hitch on his saddle, he took the kite-shaped shield preferred by western, Christian cavalrymen.

Balt'zar was aghast. "Vlad-bey! Surely you don't mean to lead the charge!"

"I do," Vlad said.

He knew what the commander meant. There was a time for officers—even sultans—to ride into battle. But there was also a time when they had to refrain.

Balt'zar argued, "Today, you are the head, not the hands! Your place is here, as our general!"

"And today," Vlad countered, flashing his own wry smile, "the head's order is simple: Take that city!"

As Vlad walked his horse forward, Balt'zar cursed. Indeed the boy was mad; he thought he was still on the drill field. And Balt'zar had no choice. Hamza's orders had been clear. The sultan wanted Wallachia; Vlad was the key to Tirgoviste. Balt'zar hefted his lance and followed.

Vlad was about to raise his sword when the gates opened, just enough to spring a single rider. He carried no weapons and galloped across the field, stopping short just a few feet from Vlad. He was a burly man with full beard. Like Vlad's, his eyes were glazed. But his was the glaze of pure fear. He had to strain to keep his voice steady.

"Vlad, I am sent to ask you—"

Vlad quietly cut him short. "You will address me as 'lord'. I am voevode here."

The man bowed his head, but with eyes ever on Vlad. He began again, "Lord Vlad, I am sent to ask you: are you still a son of the True Faith?"

"I am," Vlad said.

As the messenger meant it, the Christian Orthodox faith, as opposed to Islam or any other Christian sect. Since another of Wallachia's strict customs was that its voevode be Orthodox, Murad had let Vlad keep his faith. And Vlad, for the sake of appearance, professed it.

"And, Lord Vlad," the man continued, "will you swear on that faith—on your very soul—that your terms of surrender are true?"

"I swear it," Vlad said.

It was the holiest of oaths. In those days, most men—even hard-bitten warriors—believed in souls. And they believed that a soul lost on a broken oath would burn forever in hell.

The man studied the green eyes and seemed assured. He could not know that it had been quite some time since Vlad had given a care about souls.

The man reined about and galloped to the walls. He did not even wait for the gates to open, but shouted his message and spurred away—skirting the field as far from the Turks as possible. A moment later, the gates swung wide, and a stream of riders galloped in his path.

Again Balt'zar smiled. "Vlad-bey," he tempted, "they could be yours for the taking." He knew the hatred in Vlad's heart for Vladislav's boyars.

But even Vlad was a bit stunned. "We gave our word."

"No," the commander said. "*You* gave *your* word. My duty on this day is to follow your orders. As Allah is my witness, if you give the word, I can attack with clear conscience."

And yes, Vlad noted, he was still learning about the Osmanli—and it was like dealing with the devil. And the devil's temptation here was great. For, even aside from his hatred for the boyars, the Osmanli had taught Vlad that—first and foremost—a prince had to be feared.

But he sheathed his sword. For he had also vowed to himself that his word as voevode—at least to his own people—would be iron-clad. And, in truth, long after his death, the peasants of his land would testify: Prince Dracula struck terror in men's hearts…but his word was a bond with even the lowest of his people.

Watching the boyars disappear, Vlad's heart took wing. If it did not soar, it at least rose, taking a great burden with it. Surely a long way had yet to be travelled. But a long way had already been crossed. He was—finally—voevode.

He ordered the column to walk behind him in parade formation. Slowly. Stately. Not like a wild rabble. He hardly cared when Balt'zar smirked in passing the order.

Inside the main gate, Vlad was promptly met by a delegation of the city's leading citizens: merchants, shopkeepers, the heads of the tradesmen's guilds…and, of course, a priest who spoke for the metropolitan, the Orthodox bishop of the country.

None of the delegation were soldiers or the voevode Vladislav's men. They were civilians, "neutrals." With the boyars gone, the lot fell to them to come to terms with Vlad. They would bow to him, as they had to Vladislav and Dracul—and to the long line of voevodes that each decade seemed to bring to their land. And they—or nearly all of them—would bow *gladly* if the voevode were reasonable.

But Balt'zar began giving orders. He barked for half the column to secure the city. The other half he loosed to dash through the streets with the shouts of conquerors. And with the shouts spread cries as bolted doors were smashed.

Even before the delegation could fall to its knees for mercy, Vlad gave Balt'zar a low but hard command: "Stop this. Now."

"The city is ours," Balt'zar said.

"The city is mine."

Balt'zar sneered outright. "You forget whom we serve. Whom we *all* serve."

Vlad knew. There was no arguing. It would do no good. The Turks would take what they wanted. Only then would the city be let to stand, to go on as it had, more or less. Neither Hamza nor the sultan would object to a little looting and "sport."

The delegation turned from Vlad to grovel now to the Turkish bey, who obviously held the real power here. Their begging grew as the cries from the city also grew.

Balt'zar told them, "Bring gold. Bring it here. One chest. Only one. But a large chest."

The delegation implored. There was no gold. At least, not so much. What Vladislav had left, his boyars had just taken.

"Am I a fool?" Balt'zar said. "Bring what I know you have buried." He told Vlad, "Come. Let us see your new 'palace.'"

But Vlad did not follow. He only stared as his "allies" went on manning the walls...stared as both maidens and mothers were raped in the streets and then slung across saddles to be carried to wherever the conquerors chose to spend the night.

He was straining to keep his lone sword sheathed when he glimpsed a small band of Turks standing aloof from the pillage and rape. Among them was Ibrahim.

Vlad spat, "Don't worry. I'm sure you'll get your share. It's a large city."

Ibrahim came forward. "Lord, we could take our 'share' now if we choose. We are free to join them."

"Then what holds you? Don't you like helpless girls? Or do you prefer pretty boys?"

One of the Turks answered. "Lord, you wrong us. This—" He gestured to the chaos. "This is not Allah's way."

Vlad was struck dumb.

The Turk continued, "This is not why we took the oath as soldiers of Islam."

"Then why did you?"

Ibrahim spoke, "To spread the Faith, lord. And the True Faith is not spread by hatred. It *cannot* be."

"Aye," the Turk agreed. "The great holy warriors, the *ghazis* of old, understood this. They raised sword only against sword. Not against the meek."

"You talk like priests," Vlad said.

Ibrahim replied, "Your own book says, lord: 'What does it profit a man to gain the world…?'"

"To gain the world" but lose his soul.

Vlad looked back to the city. He told Ibrahim and the others, "In truth, you ride with the wrong company."

FUGITIVE

1

DECEMBER 1448. TIRGOVISTE. Vlad leaned back on the throne and let his eyes drift over the court. "Throne," he thought. And "court." Wallachia's throne was nothing more than an oversized wooden chair raised on a small, low platform. The court was a rectangle of stone and wood. On holidays and feast days, the Church's holy days, it might hold a hundred comfortably, or two hundred crowded at tightly packed tables. Even the tapestries on the walls had almost faded into the gray stone.

Vlad ignored the noise from the courtyard: the loot of a city being culled for what could easily be carried. Nor did he listen to the harsh echoes from the inner wall behind him: the ecstatic groans of men and the whimpering of women as the Turks had their last way with their young "ally's" city. He paid no mind to the crackle of the hearth at his back or the advance of the chill as the heat of the dying embers retreated.

He lifted his face to the high, narrow windows overlooking the courtyard, to the clear sky and sharp rays of the sun. Their light and warmth were among the few things still left to him in his own capital. But even his slight reverie was shattered by a stomp and scuffle of footsteps forcing their way into the court from the inner rooms: the bey—Balt'zar. He led a young girl by the arm, almost as a father might lead a recalcitrant daughter. But she was naked behind the crumpled bundle of her clothes, which she struggled to hold as he dragged her along. He pushed her toward Vlad: "She's still almost a virgin." He strode out the thick double-doors leading to the courtyard.

It was a long moment before Vlad's eyes left the doors. He turned to the girl, but she recoiled. He averted his stare. "Dress, lady. In peace."

Another long moment passed before he heard the rustle of the clothes. He asked her name and she gave it haltingly: Alma. The simple syllables alone were enough to shake her voice into quiet sobs. When she was dressed and he turned to her, her hands clearly trembled as she vainly tried to straighten her long, brown hair.

Vlad spoke almost to himself. "I can at least let you go home."

Her words slashed through her weeping. "Home? What home now?"

Vlad understood. She had been violated. Shamed. Through no fault of her own. But to some families it did not matter.

And yet what else could he do? He went to a window and saw the man he wanted. He called to him: "Ibrahim!"

When Ibrahim came, Vlad told the girl, "He will take you safely." Even as Ibrahim gave a nod, Vlad told him, "See that her family takes her in." As Alma hesitated, he gestured to the inner rooms. "Would you rather they have you back?"

Ibrahim had the girl veil her face with her cloak—the Muslim sign of a modest woman. As they left, Vlad watched from the window. Watched as the Turks saw the African with the girl...as they cat-called him with lewd jibes...as Ibrahim merely pushed his way through them—even across the path of a smirking Balt'zar-bey sitting regally in the saddle.

Ibrahim had just crossed that path when a pack of Turks were at his back. Vlad's hand was on his sword when he saw...The pack was not closing on the girl. They had new prey: a lone man. He was about Vlad's own age, with fair, ruddy skin and dusty blond hair. His build had gone a bit thin for his ample chain-mail shirt, thick boots, and plain, worn doublet. A gleam in his blue eyes and a cynical twist to his slightly cupid-bowed lips belied the obvious fact that he was a soldier—an alien soldier now trying to argue in accented Turkish with the pack growing around him.

He led a charger still in his prime but also gone somewhat lanky, and a donkey laden with a large, cloth bundle. As the Turks picked at the bundle, he poked a hand to hold them at bay, as he also poked to keep them from the large broadsword and small purse on his belt.

Vlad flung open the window. "Leave that man alone!"

The Turks looked at him, stopped, then looked to their bey. Balt'zar nudged his horse, ambled to his men, and looked at Vlad. With a smile he drew his sword and cut the bundle from the donkey's back. Its contents spilled with a clank and clatter: an assortment of arms and armor...mostly old—to the Turks, junk.

Balt'zar extended a hand for the purse. The man gave it. The bey held it aloft and emptied it in the dirt. He and his men laughed. For all the fuss the stranger had caused, there was nothing worth taking. As the Turks melted back to their looting, the man recovered his few small coins and called to the window. His Wallachian, like his Turkish, was accented. "Thank you, sir. I am looking for Prince Vlad."

Vlad motioned him in, and the man guessed as he entered, "*You* are Prince Vlad." He knelt and was let to rise.

Vlad said only, "State your business."

The man was taken for a moment by the grunts of lust from the inner rooms. He said through them, "I would join you, lord."

Vlad mused, "As what?"

"A soldier."

Vlad smirked. "Are you sure?"

"I am here, lord. And I've come a long way."

"Perhaps. But others, too, have come a long way. And they'll be here soon: the Danestis. Do you know who they are?"

"Your enemies, lord. They come from the Crows, Kossovo. In a roundabout way. They should be here tomorrow. So I was told."

"Told by whom?"

"Your own people," the man answered. "Refugees." His lips twisted in a smile again. "Those from the north head south. Those from the south head north. They all know a war's coming. But they don't seem to know much else. At least, they don't know which way to run. In truth, they're like a flood. They almost blocked my way here."

"And still you came. To join me. To fight."

"Yes, lord."

"Do you know who rides with the Danestis?"

"Janos Hunyadi's men. Or what's left of them from the Crows."

"There's enough of them left," Vlad said. "Trust me. I have it on good authority: a threat from Hungary itself. My enemy, Vladislav, escaped Kossovo. But the king's 'hero,' Hunyadi, is still missing. The king wants him back. And he thinks I might have him. So he's taken all the stragglers from Kossovo, put them in new units, and given them to Vladislav."

"Despite the fact, lord, that they say Vladislav deserted Hunyadi at the Crows. Ran and left him on the field."

Vlad shrugged. "The king doesn't know that for sure. Besides, Vladislav is Hungary's only candidate for my throne—and the king can always settle with him later. So tomorrow, you see, I think I'll be facing, say...five thousand men."

The man threw a nod toward the courtyard, to the Turks. "With only them? No more help from the sultan?" He explained, "At least, no one on the road claimed to see any more Turks."

The man seemed to know much. Vlad challenged, "Your accent is Polish. Who are you?"

The man pronounced his name: Veel-kov'-skee. As it was spelled, Wilkowski. But he was called by something shorter, he said: the root of his name, Wilk, spoken "Veelk."

Vlad noted, "In your language that means wolf."

"Aye, lord. And not so long ago this doublet would have been rich—and embroidered with a wolf. A snarling wolf. My father earned a title by the sword. This broadsword."

Vlad posed, "But now it's lost? Was that by the sword as well?"

Wilk answered, "No, lord. Neither Tartar nor Mongol nor Hussite nor German nor Turk could take it from him. He lost it on the way to Varna."

Four years before. On the great Varna crusade. Which history would call the "Last Crusade," the last real crusade. Led by a young Polish king—and Janos Hunyadi.

Wilk explained, "My father told the king and Hunyadi the truth: their 'crusade' was folly. He joined your own father, in fact, in urging the king to turn back. His words offended the pope's cardinal. He was excommunicated."

Cast out of the Church. His soul condemned. And with no soul to swear on, he could neither give nor accept oaths, neither hold nor grant titles and estates.

Vlad gave a low laugh. "The power of 'the Cloth.'"

Wilk continued, "Eventually, of course, my father asked for absolution. Of course, it was granted. Of course, it cost dearly. It took what money he had. In the end it did no good. He was stained. Shunned. The lords didn't need him. They passed him over for other men."

"An object lesson."

"Aye. Living proof that you can't challenge the Church. Though in my father's case the proof didn't live very long. He was born to fight. Idleness killed him."

"And you, Wilk," Vlad asked. "Are you now reconciled with your Church?"

Wilk answered, "At the risk of offending you, lord—a Christian prince...I have no quarrel with pious men—of any faith. I simply make an effort not to think about the Church—any Church." He quickly added, "But you don't need heaven or hell to bind my oaths. I live by my word. As my father lived by his."

He went further, "My father's few possessions were divided among us. My older brother got the house and land—just enough, as it is, to keep him behind his own plow. My sister was married off—a step down, of course, what with the family's 'stain.' Me..." His smile broke through again. "I got the noble beast— the horse—that you saw outside. As I hope you also saw, I've doubled that. Almost."

"By the sword?"

"Aye, lord. A Lithuanian magnate had a quarrel with some Cossacks. Poor folk, the Cossacks. My share of the 'conquest' was the donkey. That, and one silver mark for each month I served the magnate."

"And now you come to me. Again I ask: Why?"

"Fate, maybe. Destiny. It just feels right. After all, lord, our fathers' fortunes fell together."

"So you say."

"I am not staking a claim, lord. Your father did not cause mine to fall. My father advised his king as to what he thought best. That the advice was the same given by your father made no difference. It simply seems to me that, since our families' fortunes fell together, they might also be destined to rise together."

"And again I say, how do I know your tale is true?"

Wilk shrugged. "You don't. Unless it was something that your father also shared with you."

He regretted it as soon as he said it. Of course Vlad's father had told him nothing of Varna. The tale of the Dracula clan was well known. It was long before Varna that Vlad had last seen his father, Dracul. Dracul had left two of his sons, Vlad and his younger brother, Radu, in pawn on his oath to the sultan, Murad. An oath of loyalty. An oath broken at Varna. Dracul had been afraid that the crusade—at Hunyadi's urging—would turn on him if he did not join. So he sent his last son, Mircea, Vlad's older brother, to ride with the king.

In the end it did no good. At Varna—just as later at Kossovo—Murad had crushed the Christians, killing the young Polish king in the process. But Hunyadi had survived. Three years later he attacked Dracul. He put Vladislav on Wallachia's throne. Mircea was captured in Tirgoviste, tortured, and murdered—murdered horribly. Dracul was caught fleeing far to the south, on a nameless marsh. He was beheaded.

And Vlad and Radu were left with Murad as forfeit pawns.

Wilk offered, "You know, I once cursed the Church in front of my father. After the excommunication. He beat me unmercifully. Had the penance for his absolution been to sacrifice a son, I would not be here now. I am sure of it."

"And yet," Vlad said, "if you still had his wolf's doublet, you would wear it."

"Aye. And proudly. Whatever he did—or would have done—was for the family. The entire family. The 'line.' It's the case with us nobles, eh?"

Vlad gave a slow nod then spoke. "Well, Wilk, let me answer your former question. You were right. There are no more Turks coming. My 'army' is what you saw outside. Do they look ready to face Vladislav?"

Wilk protested, "But the Turk just took this land." He caught himself. "I mean—"

"I know what you mean. It is true. I am the sultan's puppet."

"That is not what I meant, lord. My point is that the Turk should want to keep you on your throne."

"Yes. He should. But he sends no more men. Why? Why indeed? He calls Wallachia a 'piss-land,' you know. Hardly worth his trouble. So maybe he shies from fighting for it. At least, so soon after Kossovo. He won the battle but was pounded. Pounded by Janos Hunyadi's cannons. Just as he won at Varna but was pounded."

"What about your Wallachians?" Wilk asked. "How many are with you?"

Vlad forced a laugh.

Wilk was stunned. "So that's it? That's all? A handful of Turks? You'll lose your land without a fight?"

"Oh, no!" Vlad said. "There's going to be a fight. The bey—the one who spilled your purse—has assured me. In truth, though, it won't be much of a fight. More of a show, I think. For Murad. Reinforcements or not, the bey can't simply run without the sultan's orders. But, as it is, the bey doesn't like me much anyway. And who can say who will die in battle?"

"You're saying he'll try to kill you. Would he dare it?"

"Best for me, I think, that I assume so."

"But you are Murad's candidate. If the bey loses you—"

"But you know," Vlad said. "Murad has another candidate. One that he's very *fond* of."

Wilk blushed. That part of Vlad's tale was known, too. His brother, Radu, had become the sultan's lover.

"Murad will be angry," Vlad said. "But not wildly so. The bey knows it. And he also knows that he is all he is ever going to be: a bey. The dog of his pasha, Hamza. So what does he really lose if he comes back without me?"

"We can run," Wilk said. "Leave tonight."

"'We'?" Vlad asked. "You would still join me?"

"Aye."

"Are you a lunatic?"

Wilk smiled. "No, lord. I am simply...so to speak...a 'free lance.'"

"And 'free' you would be," Vlad said. "I have only what you see: an empty court. And soon to lose that. What could I pay you?"

"Whatever piece of your fortune—good or bad—that you choose to give."

"I can't even make you a boyar, you know. Assuming, that is, that we live. And assuming that I'm ever in a position to make boyars."

Wilk understood. Some lands, like Hungary or his own Poland, bowed to aristocratic blood. As long as a man could prove his pedigree, that he was of the better classes, regardless of national origin, he could aspire to noble office or even the crown. But Wallachia bowed only to its native sons. Native blood. Native Orthodox faith. Wilk acknowledged, "Your people would never accept a foreign boyar."

Dracula posed, "Then why not serve Austria or the Italians? They pay well. They grant titles. And they have hundreds—thousands—of men like you."

"Aye, lord. And I'd rather not be one of thousands. How did the Roman say it: 'Better the chief of a village than second man in Rome.' How many men did you say you have?"

Vlad answered, "As of now it seems...one."

Wilk made to kneel but Vlad took his hand. "No. Save the kneeling and 'lord' for court—when we have a court. For now...we must live past tomorrow. We have to find a way."

Wilk offered, "Who can say who will die in battle?"

"Aye," Vlad said. "We could kill the bey before he kills us—*if* we can get close enough to strike a blow. A hidden, lethal blow."

Wilk raised a finger to give pause. He left the room for the courtyard. When he returned he wore his shield—and a somewhat bewildered look; another man was with him. He was of middle age, but hard-used: creased, weathered skin...balding...slightly stooped. His skeletal frame wore a coarse monk's robe that hung like a shroud. The robe was stamped with dusty footprints—especially at the rump. It was flecked with fresh phlegm and spit. The monk's mouth bled where a tooth had just been lost...another gap in a mouth of gaps.

At the sight of Vlad he raised a fist, but Wilk's dagger appeared to stifle his tongue.

Wilk stated the obvious. "He's a priest." He added, "A madman, I think. He was raving at the Turks. I couldn't just leave him to be killed."

Vlad waved the dagger down. "Are you indeed a madman, father?"

The monk sneered, "You should be cursed! Damned with the worst curse of Mother Church!"

"Why so, father?"

The monk exploded, "Why!? Do you have eyes!? Do you have ears!?" He jerked his head to the inner rooms, to the sound of degradation. "*Your* Turks! *Your* sin!" He made to say more but was stifled by his own rage.

"*My* sin, father? And what of my enemies, the Danestis? Did they keep the Hungarian papists from our women?"

The monk spat. "Turks, voevodes, and papists: the scourge of mankind!"

"No, father. Just get me some Wallachians. I will drive the Turks out. And the papists. I will rule our land as it should be ruled. Go, father. Right now. Ask your bishop. As I have been asking. As I pledged to him. He will not even answer."

"This is not the bishop's doing."

"But it is, father. As much as mine or any man's. The bishop can call the faithful to arms. Call from every pulpit in the land! And I swore to him: I would lead whatever men heeded his call. Even a rabble. Even to certain death. But the bishop—the Church—will take no such risk. No, father. The Church lacks courage—faith!"

"Blasphemy!"

"Truth. You bow to all voevodes—to any who do your bidding—and so bow to none. You—like the boyars—keep the voevode weak. But when foreigners treat you like slaves you rail at the voevode. Truth, father. Else go bring me men. Bring them now. Right now. And I will drive out the Turk."

The monk's rage still seethed, but in circles, confounded from its target. Vlad went to him and, with his own sleeve, wiped the blood from the monk's mouth. With his own hand, he brushed away the dust left by the Turks' feet.

"What is your name, father?"

"Tibor."

Vlad walked to a window, beckoning Tibor and Wilk to follow. He asked the monk, "Do you see that corpse?"

Father Tibor squinted at the courtyard. "What corpse? I see only living men—the devil's own!"

Vlad corrected, "No, father. He in the saddle. The bey. Hamza Pasha's dog. He is already a corpse."

"He looks live enough."

"Aye," Vlad said. "But tomorrow he will be dead." He looked to Wilk. "But how will we kill him?"

Wilk turned from the window and studied the far wall at the hearth. He considered, then pointed. "The dark board. There." He peered. "About midway down…"

The edge of his shield turned toward it. A snap. A thud. A bolt appeared in the board. Midway down.

As Vlad raised an eyebrow, Wilk showed him the weapon: a small crossbow. Almost comical in size. Small enough to be hidden flush against the inside of the shield.

Vlad was impressed. "Some archer must have worked long to contrive that."

Wilk sneered. "Archer? What soldier do you know makes such devious weapons? It was made by a tinker. For his son. Like a toy, I think." He walked to the wall and grimaced.

"Why frown?" Vlad said. He could not help grinning. "A lethal blow. And quiet."

"But I missed my mark. I wanted the *center* of this knot."

Vlad rolled his eyes. "It will do." He turned to the monk. "So bear witness, Father Tibor." The green eyes also took Wilk into their stare. "Do justice to my name: *Dracula*—as my father was Dracul. Tomorrow we go into battle. We kill the bey or he kills us. But, even if we survive the bey and the battle, the Hungarians will come again to drive us from this land."

The emerald stare hardened at the next words: "But I mean to return. As no man's puppet."

It took a moment for Father Tibor to shake the stare. He bowed. "Aye…lord. I hear you."

"Then go. Go quietly and quickly. Weather the storm. Wait. Bear witness, Father Tibor. Bear witness to Dracula."

The monk hurried from the court into the city. When he was safely away, Wilk noted, "But until we can stand on our own we still need the sultan."

"No," Dracula said. "You heard what I told the priest. Those who serve everyone serve no one—least of all themselves. That is especially so for a prince. Sooner or later, I must declare myself…let the world know where my heart lies. Only then will my people know where to follow."

Wilk chuckled. "Then where will we go? Hungary? The king?"

"We will go back to the sultan. For now. But at the first chance we will leave. For Moldavia."

Wilk nodded. He knew his world, knew of the small country just northeast of Wallachia. "Your uncle Bogdan and cousin Stephen fight to hold their throne."

"Yes," Dracula said. "Perhaps we can help them. Some day, in turn, perhaps they can help us."

2

ONE YEAR LATER. SUCEAVA. CAPITAL OF MOLDAVIA. Dracula told Stephen, "In truth, cousin, it wasn't much of a battle."

"From the sound of it," Bogdan said, "you were lucky to escape alive."

"Lucky indeed, uncle. Once the bey went down we had only that one thought: escape. But the Turks looked to me as their only leader."

Wilk laughed. "Aye, lord. Unbeknownst to us."

"I dashed right," Dracula said. "They followed. And Vladislav thought we were trying to outflank him. He spread his line in our path. So I went left. The Turks followed again. Again Vladislav spread. There was no point in turning back. The Turks were packed so thick at our backs that we would have tripped on them. So we charged the middle. It was so thin that we broke through. And kept on riding. I don't think we stopped till we reached the sultan's door in Adrianople."

They all laughed as they entered the court hall. It was much like Tirgoviste's: stone and wood. On this night, it was set with two tables, a longer abutted by a shorter, like a "T." Bogdan stood at the head at the very tip of the T, with his son on his right and his nephew and Wilk on the left.

He was a big man, taller than average and stout. His face was a ruddy oval centered by a narrow, bridged nose. His bushy brown hair and beard were streaked generously with gray. His brown eyes were lively…lit, it seemed, by a constant, amused curiosity.

Stephen shared his father's height and eyes but little else. He was about Dracula's age, lean, and beardless. His hairline was already highly receded.

Bogdan offered a short prayer to thank God for the feast. His quiet words were assailed by a frigid wind whipping the windows with fallen snow. He motioned for all to sit and dug promptly into his meat with a knife. He frowned at his nephew's simply settling back in his chair. "Eat," he told him. "Look at you." He included Wilk. "Look at you both. You're hardly slivers of living men."

The long roads had indeed kept Dracula thin. But gone were the outward signs of his years with the Osmanli. He wore the suit of a Wallachian noble, with felt cap and a richly embroidered felt coat newly given him by his uncle. From under the cap, his wavy hair fell to above the shoulders. He wore a moustache turned down at the ends.

Settled in his chair, he looked over the room with eyes clear of any glaze. He assured Bogdan, "But I am eating, uncle. Eating heartily. Not food. Something else. Something much more satisfying."

Bogdan knew. "Contentment. Peace."

"Yes. As though I am...home. Or at least very near it. It's been a long time since I haven't kept an eye over my shoulder."

Still eating, Bogdan said, "Unfortunately, to be a prince in this world, you will always be looking over your shoulder."

Stephen agreed, "It seems to be part of the price demanded by God."

A mutter escaped Dracula's lips: "God."

He regretted the slip even before Stephen noted, "You are bitter. At God."

Dracula blushed. "I mean no offense. But, yes. I am bitter."

Stephen pressed, "At God?"

"If He exists."

Bogdan assured, "I take no offense. Your faith has been tested. Sorely. And it is still being tested. And it always will be. Especially when you are prince."

"So it is," Stephen said. "It is the lot of a man who would be prince: *Dare great things. Risk great loss.*"

For a moment, Bogdan ignored his plate to turn to nephew and son. "Still you would be voevode. Both of you. You can choose a quieter life, you know."

Stephen countered, "As you could have."

Dracula added, "Or my father."

"But you didn't," Stephen said. "So it simply seems that we sons are cut of the same mold."

Bogdan went back to his plate. "Just so you choose your course with open eyes."

Stephen added wryly, "And constantly looking over our shoulders." He raised his cup to his cousin in a toast. "To the choice we make—whatever it costs."

Dracula was quick to accept the toast. From over the rim of his cup, he noticed a face at the other table. A lady. His own age...perhaps even younger. Her face was framed by the crescent of her chin and the thick line of her long, raven hair set straight across her brow. Her eyes were hazel, her nose petite. Her lips were thin but very red and slightly arched. It was hard to say if they caught the eye more than her porcelain skin. Each alone was enough to draw a stare, only to have it drawn in turn by the other.

She met his eye straight-on and only released it when her companions beck-oned her back into conversation.

Stephen followed his cousin's stare. "Smitten already? Which one?"

Dracula was unabashed. "The dark goddess with the white dress."

"Elizabeth," Stephen said. "She is not yet spoken for. But not because she hasn't been asked."

Bogdan eased back to sip his wine. "Her faith, too, has been tested. She is not to be dallied with."

Stephen moved to keep the talk light, suggesting to Wilk, "I'm told the Turk-ish ladies are a fair sight."

"Fair?" Wilk repeated. He reflected. "Lord, they have skin like dark honey. They veil their faces then glide under the veil like spirits whose feet are above touching the gross earth. And wherever those spirits pass they lace the air with spice. And you wonder: Can such a bouquet really be only perfume, or is it the natural scent of the dark honey?"

Stephen's youthfulness was piqued. "Is it?"

"In truth, lord, I wouldn't know. I wouldn't be caught dead trying to touch one."

"Why not?"

"Let me rephrase, lord. 'Dead' is the only way that you would touch an Osmanli lady. The Osmanli men would see to it."

"But what of the harem? Surely those women can be 'touched.' They say the sultan keeps the flower of his empire. It is a large empire. They say, too, that he sometimes shares the harem with…noble guests…like yourself."

Dracula answered. "The harem's a brothel. An *elaborate* brothel. But a brothel none the less. Most of the women are mindless. Slaves. Only slaves."

"Cousin," Stephen jibed. "You seem so serious. Is it the delicacy of the sub-ject?"

"The subject?" Dracula said. "Debauchery? No. I can appreciate debauch-ery—as a vice. Believe me I can. But as a way of life…as the sultan makes it?" He shrugged. He added teasingly, "But for one who looks to God, cousin, your blood seems awfully hot."

Stephen confessed to set them laughing, "Aye, cousin. Awfully."

Bogdan returned to weightier things. "Why didn't the sultan set you back on your throne? Why doesn't he challenge the Hungarians and this Vladislav? Did Kossovo leave him so wounded?"

"I thought so," Dracula said. "But now I think it's something else, something simpler: He's a sot."

"He's been a sot for some time," Bogdan said.

History would affirm it. It was said that Murad's consumption of wine was *six quarts* a day. He had been chastised for it by an *ulama*, an Islamic holy man, who reminded the great sultan that strong drink went against the Book, the *Quran*. Murad had simply had the man banished from his sight.

"But now," Dracula said, "his drinking gets worse. The wine's stolen his sense. He shakes. His face tics. If he wasn't the sultan he'd be in the gutter."

Stephen suggested, "Even so, perhaps there's something else keeping Murad from Wallachia: Hunyadi. The way he cheats death has to have the Turk wondering."

Hunyadi. Just as after Varna, he had cheated death again after Kossovo. As the dust of the battle settled, the Turks were looking so hard for him that he knew he would be captured. So he disguised himself as a common foot soldier. When the Turks took him with hundreds of others they did not know who they had. He escaped and made a roundabout way back to Hungary.

"Yes," Dracula said. "Hunyadi keeps the Turk wondering. And afraid. If Murad doesn't believe Hunyadi's the devil himself, he at least believes he's in league with the devil. I myself heard him muttering in his cups."

The green eyes looked to heaven. "May my father and brother forgive me, but I am glad that Janos Hunyadi is still alive."

Bogdan asked, "Then you hate the Turk more than you hate him?"

Dracula declared, "Infinitely more. Perhaps some day I will kill Janos Hunyadi. Or he will kill me. But I...I *feel*...We might yet ride together against the Turk."

"Perhaps," Bogdan said. "But let me give you counsel, as uncle to nephew. You might do best going back to the Turk, and going fast. Convince him—plead with him—to give you troops now. Even a few troops. Hunyadi's all but sure that the Danestis deserted him at the Crows."

Dracula pressed, "'All but sure?'"

"If he was sure, Vladislav would be dead. As it is, Hunyadi's cooled toward his 'ally.' I don't think he would do much to support him."

"Then perhaps, uncle, he seeks a new ally."

"Not you. At least not yet."

"We already asked, cousin," Stephen said. "Discreetly. He wants no parts of the Draculas. He simply cannot—"

Dracula finished the thought. "—cannot trust me. How could he? He killed my father. And brother. But *need* makes strange allies. Surely he knows that."

"Surely so," Bogdan said. "But he is not yet ready to embrace a Dracula."

Dracula mused, "Even so, things are better between us. If he is not ready to move toward me, he has at least moved a step from Vladislav." He drank as though to toast it.

"Still," Bogdan said, "you might be best going back to the Turk. If he knew that Hungary has cooled toward Vladislav, he might give you troops."

"He might," Dracula said. "But I don't think so."

Stephen questioned, "Because of his stupors, or his fear of Hunyadi?"

"Because of either...or both. Or even because of something else: my own brother."

Bogdan nodded. "Radu."

"Yes, uncle. Our own blood. He sleeps with the sultan. *Sleeps* with him."

"He must have been forced," Bogdan said.

"He was, uncle. At first. But now Radu makes his own choice. He's found that he likes the harem. All of it. Men and women alike. The sultan most of all. And between trysts he begs for my throne. When he's not begging the sultan, he's begging the sultan-to-be."

The sultan-to-be: Murad's son—Mohammed.

Bogdan nodded. "If Murad is as sick as you say, how long can it be before Mohammed is sultan?"

"They say this Mohammed is brash," Stephen said. "Hot-tempered. Reckless."

"Hot-tempered, yes," Dracula said. "Reckless? No. They call him reckless because they don't understand. He's...He's like us, cousin. *Hungry.*"

Bogdan said heavily, "Then the Turk has set your own brother against you."

"Let me put it this way, uncle. The Turk might not be ready to support Radu yet. But, as Hunyadi has cooled to Vladislav, Murad seems to have cooled to me."

Bogdan asked, "Then what will you do for troops?"

"Wait," Dracula said. "Bide time. For now, uncle—if you would—let me stay here. Can you do that much?"

"I can, I think. Neither the Turk nor Hunyadi seem to be paying you much mind. So stay here. In Limbo."

"There is a condition," Dracula said. "I would join you in your war. Because your brother—as mine with me—has been set against you."

The Moldavian civil war was even more bitter than Wallachia's. Bogdan indeed was fighting his own brother, Petru Aaron.

Bogdan noted to Dracula, "Petru is also your uncle. Why fight for me?"

"I hardly know him."

"You hardly know *me.*"

"Aye. But you would be my patron."

Bogdan's voice hardened. "You mean...*I* have the throne. So if Petru Aaron were prince you would serve him."

"No. You fight for yourself. For Moldavia. My good Uncle Petru, I believe, has allied with the Poles. He would be their puppet."

"But you yourself just said that you might some day serve Hungary."

"No, uncle. I said that I hated the Turk more than Hungary. When I am prince I will serve Wallachia."

Bogdan grunted. "Perhaps—for as long as the powers-that-be let you." He softened. "Take no offense, nephew. I tell my son the same thing."

"He does," Stephen said. "And I agree. As you also said, cousin: *Need* makes strange allies. We are small states. We need the larger."

Dracula repeated to Bogdan, "If I stay, I would join you."

Bogdan asked Wilk, "What of you, sir? You are a Pole. Poles would put my brother on my throne."

"Lord," Wilk answered, "My 'brother' Poles ruined my father. I serve Dracula."

"So, uncle," Dracula said, "you now have a Wallachian contingent—all two of us."

But Bogdan remained serious. "No. Before I agree I would have you think. I owe you—and your father—nothing less. The Poles are hot to put Petru on my throne. They will send an army in the new year. A *large* army. I will meet them with what I have—*all* I have: a *small* army."

Stephen added, "We are in much the same position as your father was. You saw the city gates. Closed. Closed, locked, and guarded—heavily guarded. Like the gates to this fortress. There are too few men we can trust."

"Aye, nephew. Even our *own* boyars are not our own. So this is what you would join: *Enemies without. Enemies within.* Think on it."

Dracula made to answer but Bogdan insisted: "Think on it."

Turning back to the feast, Bogdan invited certain of his guests to entertain the rest. Some recited verse. Some posed riddles. Some sang. The songs were mixed: soft ballads; bawdy ditties—very graphic—with loud, lewd choruses sung eagerly and cheerfully by men and women alike.

After a few good laughs, Bogdan ushered the company into the brisk night air to walk the walls of the palace battlements. Dracula lagged behind the others with his uncle and cousin, leaving Wilk free to join a group of the young gentlemen trying to join a group of the young ladies. As was proper, some older women were chaperons, holding the thin line between the groups. Elizabeth was with the crowd but not of it; she walked alone a pace ahead.

Noting Dracula's eye on her, Stephen offered, "She is Wallachian. Her father was a boyar—one of your father's own."

Dracula guessed, "Dead?"

Bogdan answered. "A cruel death. Torture. At the hands of the Danestis. Their henchmen made the father watch while they made sport of the whole family—wife, daughters…and the sons. Then they killed them all. Elizabeth—thank God for His mercy—was here at the time."

Dracula asked, "Will she stay?"

"She is more than welcome," Bogdan said. "But her mother—like yours—was Transylvanian. She thinks she might find family there to take her in."

As the wind gusted, Dracula seized the opportunity. With a smile to his hosts, he ran to join Elizabeth. "My lady. I thought you might be cold." Before she could answer, he slung his cloak over hers. As he did he noticed that hers was embroidered with two initials. "The first 'E' I know," he said. "Elizabeth. But what is the second?"

"Eupraxia," she answered. "My second given name. My Baptismal."

"It is beautiful, lady. And you do it justice."

She turned from his look—but not before he glimpsed her smile.

"If I may, lady…I have asked about you. I know the hardship you have seen."

The smile faded and steps passed before she replied flatly, "Vlad Dracula, you were prince."

"Aye. I was. For a whole month!"

"But they say you would be prince again, that you are here to ask your kinsmen for help."

"In time I will ask. Just now there is no help to give."

Her voice remained quiet but her words were suddenly sharp. "I hope you do take your throne."

He responded to the tone. "Yes. Revenge."

But she seemed to recoil from the word. "No. I mean…"

"There is no need to smooth it. We want the same thing. Justice. Revenge."

Her next words were not rhetorical. "But doesn't that belong to God?"

"Doesn't the Bible say 'An eye for an eye…'? But even if it did not, can we deny what we feel? Our own blood…murdered…mocked with torture."

Her lips quivered. She gave a long sigh to calm her trembling breath. "I would rather not speak of it."

"Nor would I, lady. Nor would I think of it anymore…or let it haunt my dreams. But it is there. Always. And it will be. Until…until the ledger is set right."

As she huddled in the cloaks he noticed her face in close view. Porcelain, yes. A gift of nature and youth. But it was worn. Wan.

She said, "You dream of them, too…your family? My dreams give me the melancholia. Like…"

"I know what it's like, lady. Very sad. Very heavy."

"They are dead. But I live."

"Aye, lady. For a purpose."

"What purpose?"

Dracula answered only, "As you said, lady…Let us not speak of it. Let it wait." A step later he asked, "May I hold your hand?"

When she smiled now she turned to him then back to the chaperons. As she offered her hand, they gave their own smiles and nodded.

Dracula gestured to the night. "We have so much before us. The moon. The stars." He gave an exaggerated shiver. "This damn frost!"

She laughed and—with only a nod to put the older women on notice—took him under the cloaks.

She told him, "I have come to like such nights. Cold and dark. The earth covered and quiet."

"Aye," he said. "Peaceful." He quickly continued, "But just now I have a problem."

"A problem?"

"Aye. Which do I like better? Elizabeth? Eupraxia?"

"In truth," she prompted, "I have always liked the second."

"So be it," he said. "It is beautiful." He teased, "But it is also so…saintly." He repeated the name: Eupraxia. Eu-prax'-ia. Prax'-i-a. He rolled the sound to one of familiar affection: *"Prasha."*

3

THE NEW YEAR. JUNE 1450. MOLDAVIA'S VASLUI FOREST. As Bogdan had predicted, the Poles had sent an army. A large army. Twenty thousand strong.

Bogdan waited relaxed in the saddle, like a traveller at rest, or a pilgrim in reverie. To honor his silence, his son and nephew waited a short distance behind him. At another distance were Wilk and the Moldavian officers with the voevode's army: eight thousand.

Around them, the notorious Vaslui forest echoed with the myriad voices of its own mid-morning affairs. The damp air hummed with swarms of tiny insects, the hums and swarms occasionally roiled by the heavy buzz of a plump bee on its errant but purposed course. Birds called and answered. A boar snorted in a hidden glen. From the swampy trails between the trees came croaks and splashes. From near and far, tangled brush would snap and whip, and the carpet of leaves would hiss with a rush, all at the dart and scurry of things unseen.

Far from stifling the forest's sounds, the tramp and clatter of Bogdan's eight thousand men only seemed to stir them more. The woods breathed as they always breathed in summer: sweet honeysuckle, sour marsh... The Vaslui was unafraid of massed men.

Just in front of Bogdan, the road narrowed between steep hills. The slopes were so thick with tall trees that they actually blocked the sun, making a separate, twilight world of the land below. Bogdan straightened. There was movement in the distant shadows along the road. Slight movement. A stirring of the brush at the foot of the slopes. It moved toward him in on-again off-again steps, appearing and disappearing until a ragged line of men scrambled onto the road.

They came at a trot, barefoot and streaked with dust-dried sweat. Their tattered leggings were caked with black mud, especially at the knees, from stalking and crawling. They gave their voevode a quick bow and reported in hurried whispers. Then they trotted to the rear to take their place with the infantry.

Bogdan waved the officers forward and set them to deploying. Half the army would block the invaders' path: infantry in the hills; cavalry squared across the road behind the army's few cannon. The other half of the army disappeared into the woods on the left.

Watching with his uncle and cousin, Dracula was skeptical. "Do you really think they'll engage us here? I wouldn't."

Bogdan declared, "They're the invaders. If they want my throne so badly, let them come to me."

"They'll come," *Stephen said. He called the Poles by their own word for nobleman: Pan. Pahn.* "As it is, the Pans don't think much of us. Remember, they call their land 'The Commonwealth.' We are only a poor principality." *He gestured to the infantry. Peasants. Their "armor" was padded clothing, their "weapons" mostly farm tools and clubs—though many were proficient with the bow.* "When the Pans see them especially," *Stephen said,* "they'll come—to show their contempt."

Dracula still did not believe. "But they'll see cannon in their face. And cavalry."

"A few guns," *Stephen said.* "What little we can afford. They won't scare the Pans. And our cavalry...The Poles have cavalry like Hungary: knights."

Dracula understood. Moldavia's cavalry was like Wallachia's. A "medium" cavalry. Something of a cross between the Turk's sipahi and akinji. Only a few—the greater nobles—like his uncle, cousin, and some boyars, wore full armor. The rest could not afford it. They were protected only by breastplate, helmet, and shield. They fought with lance, saber, and bow.

But the Poles…Their armor for man and horse weighed to *three hundred pounds*. And they were trained to carry the weight, to fight for hours at a stretch. In close combat against lighter foes they were nearly invincible.

"So they'll come," Stephen said. "They'll expect a single charge to send us running."

Bogdan declared, "But it won't. Not if we use the land—the hills. Then, when they can't break us, they'll try to outflank us. But there—" He pointed right. "—swamp and marsh. Impassable to heavy knights. So they'll come there." He pointed left.

"Where half your men hide," Dracula noted.

"Aye," Bogdan affirmed. "Where the track is narrow and tangled. Where even the boldest knight is only a slow-moving target. Where numbers can't be brought to bear."

Still, as Bogdan moved forward, Dracula frowned.

"You're unconvinced," Stephen said.

"I believe in walls. *Strong* walls."

"What walls do you know can withstand all enemies?"

Dracula answered in a word: "Constantinople."

The capital of the Byzantine empire. The city lay on the Bosphorus, the hair of a strait separating Europe from Asia—at the very heart of the Osmanlis' own empire. The Byzantines had once been mighty, but they had fallen. The Osmanli had stripped them of virtually everything, save for their capital. And it stood, a Christian bastion, surrounded by its walls: inner walls, outer walls, walls in between…They ran in a rough double ring, each ring about sixteen miles long. In any one spot, in the aggregate, the walls were more than *thirty feet* thick.

"Byzantium's walls have stood for a thousand years," Dracula said.

Stephen countered, "They won't make another hundred. Have you seen the big cannons? The *bombards*? They hurl shot the size of boulders. No wall in the world can stand against them. It is a new age, cousin."

"The Poles don't have bombards," Dracula said. He flicked a hand to the Vaslui. "Even if they did, they would never get them through this. Suceava's walls are stone. You could hold them from there."

"So you envy our walls?"

"I do. When I am prince I will have the same for Tirgoviste."

Stephen shook his head. "Then you'll be doomed. And I can tell you why in a breath: the janissaries."

The Osmanlis' infantry shock-troops. Ironically, they were the sons of captured peoples—mostly Christians. They were taken as a form of "child-tribute," converted to Islam, and nominally "adopted" by the sultan as his personal guard.

"The Turk will have bombards soon enough," Stephen said. "And the janissaries will haul them to wherever they must, wherever their sultan commands. And you know them better than I do."

Dracula did. He had seen the janissaries' training firsthand. They were molded into a crack corps. Ten thousand strong. Trained in all aspects of war.

Stephen lamented, "Fanatics. And they seem to forget their native lands and religion. They are so fiercely loyal to their sultan."

"Most," Dracula agreed. "But not all. But is it a wonder? The children the Turk takes are mostly peasants. And how do we—Christian lords—treat our peasants?"

In truth, history would dub the peasants the "mules" of Christian society. There were a few called "free," who earned some rights by service to their lords— mostly war service. But most were tied to their masters' estates. They were taxed thrice over: by their landlord, his overlord, and the Church. They could not travel or even marry without permission.

So, for some families, when the sultan's agents came, they *volunteered* their sons to the corps. The sultan would at least raise them in status to soldiers, his own household guard. They would be respected. And paid. They might even become lords themselves.

So if the rare janissary remembered his roots—that he had been virtually kidnapped—the great majority of the corps was indeed fiercely loyal.

"But you see," Dracula said. "You fall into the Turk's trap. A trap for the mind. His best weapon is not a cannon or a janissary. It is your own mind. You are afraid of him."

Stephen confessed, "I am."

"And he plays on that," Dracula said. "Like Murad's 'feast' at Kossovo."

The tale had spread throughout Europe—just as Murad had intended. After his victory at the Crows, the sultan had ordered a banquet spread on the field. Right among the enemy dead: rotting corpses. So the world had to wonder: *What kind of men—or monsters—were these Osmanli?*

Dracula continued, "And before he sent me to Tirgoviste the sultan tried to give me a private lesson: the fate of those who betray him—Impalement. Have you ever seen one?"

As Stephen had not, Dracula described it. "He condemned a man for treason. They stripped him and pinned him to the ground. Face down. His arms and legs were tied with small ropes. A man sat at each rope. Sat in the dirt and pulled. Spreading the victim…"

The victim's anus was greased. A long stake was tapered, then the point rounded and also greased. It was inserted into the anus. Slowly. Very slowly. It was tapped with a small mallet…an inch at a time.

"It took hours to move through the body," Dracula said. "They were careful not to pierce vital organs."

After each tap, the executioner would wait. If the victim's skin turned purple, there was too much internal bleeding. The stake would be withdrawn a bit and rerouted.

"With luck," Dracula said, "—grim luck—the stake would have exited the mouth. But it came through the shoulder."

It usually did. No matter. It was even better; the victim would live surprisingly long. The stake was then raised and planted in the ground. The victim was let to hang…for days…somewhere between earth and hell. Living death.

"And the whole time," Dracula said, "a mob mocked the victim. Insults. Spit. While the sultan—and his son, Mohammed—blandly watched. In fact, they ate while they watched." He told Stephen with a chuckle, "I got their point—so to speak."

"Point indeed," Stephen said. "Betray them and that would be your fate. Casual and cold. So brutal."

"Yes," Dracula said. "That is the Turk's best weapon: *Terror*. Fear. Nothing more."

Stephen countered, "Nothing less."

Dracula laughed. "You have been polite, cousin. You and your father. You have not even asked."

"Asked what?"

"If the sultan indeed raped me," Dracula said. As Stephen blushed, he waved it off. "He did not. I would not let him."

"But how—?"

"Aye," Dracula said. "How could a mere boy resist the great sultan?" He tapped his breast. "Here, at my heart, is a scar. Murad took me to the harem. He enticed me with women. Then he made to take me. I resisted. He threatened. I ran. He set his guards after me. He threatened again: torture. So I broke a lattice and took a piece of the wood. Like a stake. I put it to my own heart. I pushed. But rather than see me dead, he freed me."

He continued, "He needed me. As a puppet. A Wallachian candidate. I knew it. So, when he tried to 'get into' my head, I got into his instead. Do not let the Turk—or any enemy—ever cow you with plain fear."

But again Stephen shook his head. "Still, if I had to fight the Turk, it would be from the land rather than walls. And I would rather not fight him at all. I said before, cousin…we are small states. In the end we need the larger."

"But today," Dracula said, "you stand against the Poles."

"Only because they offer no compromise."

"Then let us see, cousin," Dracula said. "Let us see if your Vaslui can hold back the Pans."

From under his doublet, he took a black cloth—a pennant—and affixed it to his lance. On the black field was his father's, Dracul's, old insignia: a dragon. A dragon impaled by a cross, a Christian cross—a symbol of good over evil. It was from the insignia that Dracul had gotten his name. He had been inducted into an order, the *Societas Draconis*, "Society of The Dragon." The Dragons were sworn to fight the Turk—and Islam—which is why the Osmanli found the name anathema.

Dracula beamed at the pennant. "It was Prasha's idea. My own 'banner.' And she insisted that my own hand go into it."

Stephen laughed. "She had you sewing!"

Dracula shrugged. "Only a bit. There, in fact…where the stitch runs foul."

Stephen grew quiet. "You really love her."

"Madly. She is my angel on earth."

Stephen perked again. "'Angel?' That's a strange word for a man who doesn't believe in God."

"A figure of speech."

Stephen was serious. "Then you really don't believe?"

"That disturbs you?"

"Yes, cousin. I don't want to see you lose your soul."

"Then put it this way," Dracula said. "I believe in God as much as He believes in me."

"But He does believe in you."

Dracula sneered. "You jest."

His cousin's eyes dropped. "You *have* had it hard."

"Forget my case," Dracula said. "I *chose* a hard path. I still choose it. I want to be voevode. But what of Prasha? How could such terrible things happen to one so innocent? Then again, they happen to the whole human race."

"I have no answer," Stephen said. "At least not in words."

Dracula challenged, "'Not in words.' But still you think you have one."

Stephen answered with a question. "Do you know the story of Scipio?"

"What soldier doesn't?"

"Aye. We all know the story. At least the part we like to remember. Scipio Africanus. Victor of the great battle of Zama. Conqueror of Hannibal. Savior of ancient Rome. But what of another part of the story, that he spent long hours in the temple?"

Dracula remembered: long hours in the temple.

"It stays with me," Stephen said. "Think. He was a soldier. He saw hardship. Great hardship. Yet the 'long hours' strengthened him. And he prayed only to God in a lesser form—a pagan God. We pray to the true God. So how much richer should be our prayers—and the answers?"

Dracula also remembered, "I did pray."

Stephen repeated, "'Long hours...'"

Dracula countered, "How long? How long is needed to save us...from death and torture?"

"Prayer will not do that," Stephen said. "God will not. He cannot. He cannot block men's evil without leaving us less than men. Prayer is to save the soul. To give the mind peace." He affirmed in a word: "Faith."

"And still," Dracula said, "I see the innocent. Prasha. You know, cousin, she suffers from the melancholia. She says it's only spells. Only sadness. But it's more. Melancholia. The black bile. Nothing less. It runs thick in her. She sheds it sometimes. We laugh much. But always it returns. It seized her again just before we rode."

Stephen knew, "You will marry her."

Dracula's smile returned. "I will. We would be like husband and wife now except...except for those damned old women! She has more guards than the pope!"

Stephen shared his laugh. "My father was serious. She is not to be dallied with."

"She is no dalliance. I will marry her."

Stephen noted, "Take no offense, cousin, but...You would be prince. You could find the daughter of an ambitious family. A rich family. One that could buy you an army."

"I will get my own army."

"With all respect—how?"

Dracula chuckled and tossed back a word: "Faith."

"I envy you," Stephen said. "You will marry for love."

"Yes. I have nothing, no one. No one to push me. My poverty is my luxury."

"And me...I will fight, live, die—and marry—for my throne."

Dracula seized the one word. "Die. If I do, cousin...if I die today...promise me..."

Stephen pledged, "Eupraxia will be cared for." He added, "In fact, I owe you more."

"You owe me nothing."

Stephen insisted, "But I do. Today you risk your life to help us hold our throne. So I owe you much. Some day I hope to be able to repay you."

He offered his hand as though in a pact. Dracula leaned in the saddle to take it. They embraced. Then Dracula started forward. But Stephen stopped him.

"No, cousin. Not at the front. You are needed here."

"Here? At least send me into the woods then. There will be no fighting here."

"There will," Stephen said, "if the Poles break our line."

"But I can serve better elsewhere!"

"You don't know the Pans."

"You don't know *me*, cousin. If you think I'll sit safely back here—"

"Here you'll sit," Stephen said. "With them." He threw a hand toward a small reserve, a few horse and a gang of peasants. "It's all we can spare. You lead them. Believe me, we might need you. You might get more than you think. If not, I won't cheat you out of the battle. That I can promise."

He set spur to make the words final. Dracula slumped in the saddle and waved for Wilk. Seeing the Pole's broadsword still strapped on his saddle, he advised, "You'd better put that on."

Wilk grinned. From under his shield he showed another weapon: a flail—a spiked iron ball on a length of chain with a short, iron handle.

Dracula snapped, "Junk. Worthless. Who uses them anymore?"

Wilk whined, "The sword's too damned heavy. I want something lighter...quicker."

Dracula showed his own weapon. "Then use a saber."

Wilk looked down his nose. "Too common."

Dracula threw up his hands.

In short order the Pans came. They were arrogant. Stubborn. Brave. At the sight of the defiant Moldavians, they spread along the hills in a thick wave that washed both the road and the slopes.

Their infantry engaged on the hills, but they were moving targets to the Moldavian archers, who were dug in along the line. On the road, the Poles set their own cannon against Bogdan's. But again, as the invaders gained a foothold, they were moving targets, while the defenders were set and waiting—aimed.

After losing a few guns, the Poles simply stormed the pass, using infantry for fodder to exhaust the volleys of Bogdan's artillery. Before the Moldavian guns could reload, the Polish knights charged. Before they, in turn, could close, the Moldavians sprang more archers from the slopes and jammed the road with logs and flaming brush. The Moldavian guns reloaded and resumed work.

The morning passed. The Polish guns rejoined the fray, lobbing shot over the lines, exchanging volleys with Bogdan's. Behind them on the road the Pan knights seemed to be waiting, just as their infantry also seemed content to hold a static line on the slopes.

Just past noon, the forest itself—on the left—exploded with a shout. The Polish regiments waiting on the road had been a ruse. The rest of their army had snaked into the woods to outflank the defenders. But it had been caught in Bogdan's own ruse. On the road the Pans stirred at the realization. Then they sprang. Head-on. Do-or-die.

The roar of guns from both sides withered and finally fell silent. The Poles had bought the road to Bogdan's lines with mounds of shredded flesh. The carnage stymied the charge of knights. War showed its most primitive face: man-to-man.

Dracula knew. His cousin had been right. His own men crouched at the ready as Bogdan's square heaved. Heaved. Heaved again. Then disgorged a band of knights. The Pans had broken through.

Dracula charged. He looked to engage a single foe, as noblemen did in feudal warfare, a foe whose defeat would bring him honor: a knight. He found one alone, but only briefly. Dracula's lance shattered on a shield; his shield shattered a lance. After that, there were only faces in a mass, a press of beasts and men.

Dracula found himself hammering with his saber. Hammering metal like an anvil, a shifting anvil, one that moved to wherever he turned. He was adrift in a sea of men, friend and foe alike. Time passed. Minutes? Hours? Had his sinews ever been pulled so taut? He saw Prasha. He went on hammering.

Finally he found his second single foe. They found each other. The Pole was massive, a small wall of iron on a huge charger. He pushed through the ranks with no more trouble than a plow rending the earth. Behind him Polish footmen swarmed, shouting in all but triumph at being led by such a champion. Dracula tried to back away, to find room for a glancing attack, but his Moldavians were just as frenzied as the Poles. Packed at his back, they were holding him fast.

The mouth-slit of the Pole's visor seemed like a grin. Dracula's saber swung in an overhead arc. The knight's broadsword swung upward to meet it. Dracula's lighter blade went flying. The Pole's sword swirled in a fast circle. Once. Twice. It zipped through the air, gathering space and speed for a blow. Dracula braced his shield with both arms. The knight's mouth-slit leered. The sword rose. A spiked iron ball crashed over the rim of the Pole's shield. The shield flicked it away. The Pole turned on his new opponent: Wilk. The flail swung. The sword caught its chain and flung it away again, this time clear through the air.

The knight turned back to his first prey. A Moldavian footman had just tossed back Dracula's saber. It was still pointed earthward while the Pole's huge blade was already poised. But another huge blade struck. A broadsword. Wilk's. It struck the Pole on the mail bib just below the helmet. The sword's serrated blade pulled. The mail parted. The air rained red.

The sight of their Goliath toppling doused the Poles' ardor just as it inflamed the Moldavians. As they surged forward to plug the breech in Bogdan's square, Dracula found himself swept to the front of the line.

The Vaslui joined the battle with a loud, distant rush—men running through the woods—and thin but swelling shouts. The forest began spewing Moldavians, who quickly rushed to bolster their voevode's line. The Poles saw. The woods had devoured half their army. They themselves might now be outflanked. Their wave—much dissipated—ebbed from the road and slopes just as quickly as it had flowed. The very sight of the Vaslui kept it running.

When the Moldavians' victory cry, too, finally ebbed, Dracula made to leave the saddle. It took an effort. As he had hammered the enemy, he also had been hammered: cut, bruised, jolted…Pain stabbed his movements. His dried blood stuck his armor to his skin. He could hardly walk—and certainly not upright.

He found Wilk bent over a corpse. When the flail had been flung away by the Pole's sword it had landed in this now dead man's skull. The ball trailed only a few links of chain. The rest of the links and handle lay nearby. Wilk inspected them. "Damn! The Pan cut it clean through. Chain!"

Dracula snarled, "I told you that thing was worthless."

"Well," Wilk said, "at least I saved this."

He gave Dracula the dragon pennant.

4

AUTUMN. SUCEAVA. The slanting rays of the setting sun poured through the open windows, tinting the entire court with a soft, golden hue. The cool breeze carried the breath of the land: a heady odor of the juices of freshly cut crops, heavily laced with the earthy smell of leaves going to rust. The court basked in the effect. There were no songs, no poems or riddles, only light conversation to the hiss of meat on the spit and the clatter of plates and cups.

A young page approached Dracula. To his whispered message, Dracula rose, his eye lingering regretfully on his unfinished meal.

"Eat," Bogdan said.

"I will, uncle, but Wilk wants me. It seems his rheum has lifted. I would see him now, before he dozes again."

Bogdan noted almost in question, "He's been sick a lot of late."

"Just a chill," Dracula said. "A stubborn chill. The change of season perhaps. I'll take him something warm."

"Here," Eupraxia said, "let me help."

As she rose, Bogdan gave a jaundiced eye, a look of suspicion. But it was smoothed some by another woman's voice: "I shall go with them."

Her name was Felicia. She was tall, blonde, and not un-fair, though she kept herself unadorned: hair pulled straight back...very little of the paints, powder, and perfumes generally favored by the women of her noble class. She was hardly old, but time had taken her youth and left her unmarried, left her in the imminent role of court spinster. She accepted the role with grace, like the demure "older sister" to her younger peers. Sewing, reading, prayer...she guided them in all.

Her offer to chaperon was enough for Bogdan, but not for her mother, who suggested, "Perhaps others should go as well."

The etiquette of court: It would not do for two single men to be alone with two single women; it was just not proper.

Felicia turned to two other women like herself. They, too, it seemed, were unadorned by choice, despite the constant prompting of the older women that they primp themselves to lay the expected snares for marriage.

As the women rose, decorum was served; the party was large enough for propriety. Felicia's mother even beamed some as her daughter supervised the making of the sickbed tray. Felicia was proficient in the corporal works of mercy.

In the hall outside of Wilk's room, Felicia the chaperon gave a last glance back. The party was alone. She went to Wilk while the others took the adjacent rooms. Three couples. Three rooms. Three locked doors.

Alone, Prasha and Dracula fell to the floor even as they began kissing—hungry kissing stoked by groping hands and tongues. They pulled free laughing. The laughter melted as they stood again. They began shedding their clothes, carefully, so as not to create telltale wrinkles. In truth, the slow undressing was a boon to them, a gift that each gave and took in turn.

She helped him remove his tunic and shirt, then stepped back as he slipped from shoes and leggings. She always insisted that he go first. She would watch his muscled form stripped down to the last, to the codpiece, the pouch of cloth tied tightly to harness his manhood. She liked to watch the pouch strain as she, in turn, unveiled herself from her dress and layers of petticoats.

Always, at the last of the petticoats, he would stop her. He would dwell on the shadow of the hair of her loins. He would slide the strings of the petticoat from her shoulders. That last veil would drop to her feet, leaving her only in a cinch that raised her full breasts, pert nipples riding high.

His eyes would meet hers. Her smile would draw his sigh and locking embrace. Their kiss would hold fast even as they melted again to the floor.

It was easier for her to take him now. She had endured the sting of her first opening weeks before, just after Fate had taunted them that Dracula might never return from the Vaslui. They had vowed then to damn the "never." Pledged it with their eyes in their first glance on his return. Felicia had seen them exchange the glance. She had confided in Prasha that she was the "spinster" by choice. Though without a husband, she was not without heat. She took—and left—lovers at will. Discreetly. She would gladly help Prasha take her own, without the lengthy delay of formal courtship.

So Dracula and Prasha had consummated their love—over and again. They learned when to grasp, when to probe, and when to merely touch…when to embrace slowly and when to wrestle and cling. They came to know each other. Thoroughly. So if their passion ran unbridled it ran within bounds—the generous bounds of the familiarity that they both eagerly sought.

Now, they were still panting from passion spent, when Prasha began giggling. "I think we've exhausted this 'sickbed' excuse. Did you see your uncle's look?"

Dracula turned her on her side and held her close from behind. He buried his face in her hair. "It's so good to see you like this. Happy. Laughing. The melancholia gone."

She almost shivered at the word. "I hope it is gone. She added in turn, "You seem happy, too, love. Very."

"I am. I have you. I have the spoils from the battle—enough money for a small army. My uncle was generous. And I have more. I thank God for it."

She was brightly surprised: "God?"

"God."

"But I thought you lost Him."

"It was I who was lost, not God."

"And you found yourself again?"

"Yes."

"Where? When?"

"In the Vaslui."

"Ah! In battle. In the face of death."

"No. In some words of my cousin."

Dracula related the story of Scipio, the "long hours in the temple."

"Since then," he said, "I've spent my own 'long hours.'"

"But you're only in chapel on Sunday, with me."

"The chapel is only one temple. I have found others. In walking…riding…in just sitting alone."

"You pray?"

"Aye. But not by rote. Not the drone of the priests' verse. I talk to God."

"And you think He answers."

"He does. In His own way. With patience you can hear Him—as I am just starting to hear Him now. A little more each day."

"And what do you hear?"

Dracula answered, "The prince is the shepherd. The people are the flock. It is as simple as that."

She turned to him to question, "That gives you such comfort?"

"Oh, yes," he affirmed. "Think of it, love. I was torn by so many things. My hardships. Your hardships. The misery of our people. I hated the men who put my father's head on the block. I hated the boyars who tortured my brother in such a cruel way and tamped his grave—as he surely heard in his last gasps—with mocking insults."

Prasha consoled, "Such hatred is hard to shed."

"Yes, love. You know that all too well. In my prayers—at first—I heard it: *Forgive! Forget!*"

"As we must."

"No, love. Hear me. I cannot forget. I will not. And so I prayed. I wrestled with it, wrestled as with the devil. And my prayer smoothed the way."

He went on, "My prayer reminded me of what I learned after my father left me with the Turk: A prince cannot be pampered. His life is hard for a purpose. He would be shepherd. A shepherd must be hard. He must stand against wolves. So God hardens him."

Prasha asked, "But where is there room for hatred in this?"

Dracula told her, "Hatred of the wolves keeps the shepherd to task."

As though to herself, she slowly shook her head.

He urged her, "Think of it, love. It is the only way it can all be reconciled. Think of your enemies. Think of your feelings."

"I fear the men who killed my family. And I do hate them. Yet I loathe both the fear and the hatred."

"And yet such feelings have purpose."

"For you, perhaps, love. You would be prince—voevode. If what you say is true, you need such feelings to strengthen you. What purpose do they serve for me?"

Dracula answered, "That, you already know. Be my wife. Be with me in what I must do."

She turned from him again. She said hopefully, "Perhaps the worst of our trials are over. The Poles are gone. Perhaps we can live in peace."

"No, love. Uncle Bogdan's enemy, Petru, still lives. As long as he does Moldavia will know no peace. His Poles are gone—for now—so he schemes with the boyars. And after we are done with him...after Moldavia...we still have our own land...our own throne to take and hold."

As though from a chill, she pressed closer to him. "If I could, love, I would freeze time now. I would stay here forever. Just us."

He was content to let her linger in the fantasy.

But she burst it. "We can run, love. We can leave here. Leave it all."

"And go where?" he said. "Where would we be happy?"

"I could live anywhere with you. Anywhere away from...from the misery we have known."

Now it was he who slowly shook his head. He asked again, "Be my wife."

She loved him. She was afraid for him. She was afraid for herself. She said, "You need someone...stronger."

He declared, *"I need you."*

She welcomed a sudden noise from another room. Wilk's room. A groan. Pleasure. Felicia's. Another groan. Wilk's. They seemed to be answering each other—as it were—nip and tuck. And getting louder.

Prasha's laugh infected Dracula. "My God!" she said. "They'll get us caught!"

But neither she nor Dracula moved to stop them.

Through his grin, a thought struck him. His eye led toward the third room, that of the two women. "What do *they* do?"

"They read, they say. Poetry, I think."

"Behind closed doors?"

"Remember," she said, "they are supposed to be with us. All of us. Together. Proper. So they pass the time unseen."

But, as though on cue, other groans intruded. Also of pleasure. From the room of the two women.

"Well," Dracula said. "If it's poetry, it's Sappho."

Sappho. The woman. The great bard of ancient times. Of the isle of Lesbos.

But Dracula barely had time to smirk at his own jest. For he was quickly seized by Prasha—and the songs of satyr and sirens.

5

1451. THE OSMANLI COURT AT ADRIANOPLE. The women of the harem dutifully sat at the bedside as Murad slowly turned on his back. They immediately moved to straighten him, to untangle weak arms and legs. He made to talk but his speech was garbled. Half his face was dead, half twitched in spasms. His eyes were vacant. They saw only vague shapes. It made little difference; his mind could barely relate to whatever the eyes saw.

At the foot of the bed, the imperial physicians gathered around the sultan-to-be, Mohammed. At twenty-one he was of regal height and strong build. His nose was nobly aquiline. His dark eyes peered from the frame of a dark, close-cropped beard. The physicians around him hailed from every corner of the earth: Africa; Cathay; India; native Turkey—even the greater kingdoms of the Christian west. The best that money could buy. But that, too, made little difference. They had no hope to offer.

The great sultan had been felled. Felled, as most would later agree, by his excesses. By drunkenness and debauchery. By apoplexy. Stroke. But some—a few—would look deeper into the cause, to the very roots of the excesses themselves. Yes, they would conclude, he had been felled. By life. The great burdens of his life as sultan.

Mohammed went to a room off the court for the first of the private meetings he had called. He sat at a low table set with a chessboard. The board had been with him—almost always—since childhood. Chess was more than his favorite game; it was an obsession.

Murad's Grand Vizier, Chalil Pasha, was called into the room and left standing across the table. He was a wisp of a man with hair and thin beard gone gray. Mohammed was seemingly rapt in his game as he told Chalil what the vizier already knew and sorely lamented. "My father is dying. It might be a day, a week, a month...but he is dying."

"Yes, highness," Chalil said, "to the deep grief of us all."

Mohammed answered, "It is God's will. We must accept. Praise God." In another breath, he proceeded, "Twice my father abdicated. Twice he made me sultan. Twice you called him back."

Chalil blanched. It was a reckoning he had dreaded, one he had somehow hoped to avoid—and one he had tried vainly to prepare for from the moment Murad was stricken. He was being called to account for past acts. Twice Murad had tried to retire, had abdicated to Mohammed, who had eagerly taken the sultanate. But twice Chalil had begged Murad to return—a clear vote of no-confidence in Mohammed. Now the vizier answered haltingly, "You were younger then, highness."

"Yes," Mohammed agreed. "Then, I was younger."

Then. But no more.

Chalil dropped to his knees and bowed low. "Highness, I only did what I thought best. If you would show me mercy, I would fade with the passing of your father. I would retire to prayer."

"No," Mohammed said. "The whispers—yours among them—once called me the 'pup.' And so I am still—at least to an old dog like you. But an old dog is smart: Long of tooth, long of knowledge. So teach me. Guide me. As you once did my father."

To Chalil's incredulous look, Mohammed gave a nod.

The vizier rose with the pledge, "I accept, highness. With great honor. Use me as you will." As Mohammed's eyes returned to the chessboard, Chalil made a bow to leave.

Mohammed snapped, "Did I dismiss you?"

Chalil froze. "No, highness. Forgive me, highness. I only thought—"

"No," Mohammed said. "You did not think. You *presumed*. Do not presume with me." He uttered a quote repeated for later history: "If a hair of my beard knew my thoughts, I would surely pluck it out."

He moved a piece on the board. He told Chalil, "The janissaries robbed my father."

It had shocked the empire. Months before, with Murad showing the first signs of exhaustion, the usually obedient corps had, as it were, snapped at him. They had demanded a raise in pay. When he refused, they staged a riot until he gave in.

Mohammed strained to keep his voice even. "And they grow bolder still. Especially the stiff-necked Wallachians."

Chalil, of course, was aware of it. The janissaries had heard of Bogdan's victory over the Poles. With it they had heard the whispers about "Dracula," how he had helped his uncle to victory. On the scale of the empire it was a trivial affair, a piddling triumph. But some of the Wallachians in the ranks lent a pricked ear to it. There were rumors that some might even desert to find this Dracula, to serve him—to keep the Osmanli from their land.

Mohammed declared, "Before I even warm my throne, I want the janissaries to 'heel.' I want their commander replaced."

Chalil stiffened. The corps would protest. They might even riot again.

But Mohammed was not done. "I want him flogged. In public. And broken in rank. I will choose a new commander."

Chalil's face was pure ash. The corps would surely riot—or worse.

Still Mohammed was not done. "As vizier, you will carry out the order."

He moved another piece on the board. During his reign as sultan, he would move one with every decision he made, if not on a tangible board then on one in his mind. He often remarked, in fact, that the game was much like life.

He assured Chalil, "And yet I am not unsympathetic to our loyal soldiers' needs. Like anyone else, the janissaries want money. If not for themselves, for the mothers and fathers they left behind. So I will raise their pay. And that, I will tell them myself."

Chalil's mind was clicking. Clearly, he thought, there was more here than his teaching and guiding the sultan-to-be. Clearly, he already *was* being used. To the janissaries, the vizier would bring the "stick," the sultan the "carrot." So it was the vizier on whom the corps would focus its hatred.

Mohammed pressed on, "There is another group, too, that I would deal with: my father's hunting entourage."

As Mohammed was obsessed with chess, Murad had been obsessed with hunting. On some outings, he had commandeered entire provinces—whole countries—as his preserve. And he sometimes rode with upward of *ten thousand* retainers.

"I will disband them," Mohammed said. "We do not need thousands of men armed to the teeth to chase deer and small birds. If they are so brave, let them hunt my enemies. If they accept, I will form them into regiments in the army. My own personal regiments."

But, of course, he knew, the hunters were brave men. Most had already served in the army, and gladly. And, of course, they would accept his invitation to rejoin the ranks. They enjoyed the privilege of being in His Highness's close circle. It was not something they would lightly toss away. So he would put them in these "special" regiments...similar to, but separate from, the janissaries themselves. And if the janissaries ever did think to riot they would have something else to think about as well.

The "old dog" wondered. What was the "pup" really up to? He was settling an old score with the janissaries; he was vindictive. But what sultan—what *good* sultan—was not? Still, whole regiments of new troops...there were other ways to keep the janissaries in check. But those ways required tact. Did the pup have tact? He did not before. Which is why Chalil—the entire empire, in fact—had called Murad out of retirement. Twice.

Chalil wondered further: Had Mohammed suddenly learned tact? Or was he planning something bigger, something...reckless?

As though in answer, Mohammed said, "You should know...I am going to offer the Hungarians a three-year truce. And the rest of Europe—more or less—I am going to leave as it is. For now."

It gave Chalil pause. Relief: *Peace—for three years.* Perhaps the pup had indeed matured.

Mohammed gave Chalil leave, but the vizier hesitated, eager to show his new master his willingness. "Highness, perhaps there is something you should know. Something small really. I would hardly trouble you with it. It concerns the Greeks."

The very word lit Mohammed's face. The Greeks. Byzantium. Constantinople. He was eager to hear.

"They know your father is dying, highness. They harbor a claimant to your throne. They..."

As he hesitated, Mohammed had to prompt him. "They what?"

"Incredibly, highness, they demand a payment, a tribute. Else they threaten to turn the man loose—with enough money to hire an army."

Mohammed was struck. But pleasantly so. He fairly glowed. "So they think the pup has no bite. They think if they roar I will cower. Very interesting, these

Greeks. They intrigue me." He added as though in passing, "They have for some time." He chuckled. "I would like to read this demand for myself."

Chalil explained, "It is not yet in writing, highness."

"Then how do we know of it?"

"By word. To me."

Mohammed's eyes dropped to the chessboard, and he was grateful for the board. It sometimes hid his reactions when he wanted them hidden.

How was it, he thought, that the Greeks talked directly to Chalil? But he set the question aside. For now. As though still amused, he simply told Chalil to get the demand in writing and then sent him off.

The next man to enter was also a high lord, a pasha. Mohammed greeted him warmly and bade him to sit, telling him, "My father is dying. It could be a day, a week, a month…but he is dying."

"Yes, highness. A cloud hangs over the world."

"It is God's will. We must accept. Praise God. You are a most loyal vassal."

The pasha gave a nod of gratitude.

"I would have you do me a service. As you know, one of my father's wives has just borne him a son."

The pasha knew mother and infant. He had shared Murad's joy at the blessing of the birth.

Mohammed reflected on the babe, "My own half-brother. I should look forward to the day when I can teach him to ride and shoot…to hunt…to do all the things that brothers do. But…we must all make sacrifices for the empire."

The pasha understood. All too clearly. It made him squirm. But not visibly.

As though to soften the inevitable, Mohammed said, "Even now the Greeks threaten me with a claimant." He threw up his hands.

The pasha pledged, "Highness, for the good of the empire, your will is my own. What service can I offer?"

"When my father dies," Mohammed said, "marry the mother of this infant. Take her to your province. Keep her in God's mercy." As the pasha waited for more, he added, "That is all I ask."

That was all. Yet it left the pasha in turmoil. Inside. He was a God-fearing man. And this order…Marry the woman. Take her out of the way. Let her live out her life as a respectable wife, in the style befitting a sultan's widow. It was the civilized thing to do—and the easiest part of the plans Mohammed had made— for both mother and infant.

Yet the pasha wished that he had not been called for this. In truth. But he served the empire, and the sultan ruled the empire, and the very word, *Sultan,* meant "Authority."

When the pasha was dismissed, another man was called: Radu—Dracula's own brother. At eighteen, he was tall and lithe. His smooth skin was the color of milk. His hair was the rich color of henna. It was shaped close in front, long in back, almost like a short veil that swayed with his movements. His eyes, too, were rich—bright blue.

Mohammed repeated the greeting for the day: His father was dying...

"Yes, highness," Radu lamented. "Sad. Very sad."

Mohammed also repeated the rejoinder: It was the will of God...

"True, highness," Radu agreed. "We must accept. Still...I lost my own father even while he lived. I often thought I would see him again. I at least had hope. But death leaves no such hope." As his blue eyes met Mohammed's, he offered in sympathy, "I am very sorry, highness."

The stare unsettled Mohammed so that he glanced at his board and muttered, "I thank you." He gathered himself. "But we have other things to deal with. Things that do not wait even for death. Your brother is in Moldavia."

Radu said reflectively, "Vlad."

"He calls himself 'Dracula.'"

"And surely, highness, he knows the name offends you. Better for all of us, I think, that he stays in Moldavia."

"He will not."

"No, highness. He will not."

"He would be prince."

Radu replied bluntly, "Highness, you know that I, too, would be prince."

Mohammed quizzed, "Even if it sets you against your brother?"

Radu answered, "Yes, highness. He chose his path. I chose mine. Two men cannot sit the same throne." He plunged further, "Highness, what can I do to prove my worth as your candidate?"

Mohammed was rapt in thought, a jumble of thoughts. Could Radu really be prince? He was very close to being what a provincial vassal ought to be. He was no false fawn. He kept his noble bearing and most of the ways of his land—like the Orthodox religion that Wallachia demanded of its prince. Yet he blended those ways with those of the empire. And he saw things in the context of the empire. He knew his place in it. He accepted with both grace and gratitude.

More, if he was not accomplished in war—his only "battles" to date had been in maneuvers—he stayed within his limits; he often deferred to the Turkish officers. And he was no fop, no coward. He accepted the scars that drill demanded—even the few that marred the rare portrait that was his face. He did not brood over such things, these scars. He wore them. Almost like adornments.

But could he best his brother?

Mohammed remembered the brother: *Dracula,* as he dared call himself now…stubborn, arrogant…perhaps even mad.

Could Radu best him? And if he did would he remember his place? Would he remain loyal to the sultan? Only time could tell. But Radu seemed surprisingly determined to force the issue, and so Mohammed weighed him as a would-be prince.

But Mohammed's thoughts had another current. What was it about this boy? Was it the eyes? The smile? Was it the purse of the lips? They were all so…open…so…almost inviting.

"Highness?"

Radu was craning his head to recapture Mohammed's attention. The blue eyes were peering up. The smile was marked by the gleam of teeth on the lip. As their eyes met again Mohammed knew: all of it—eyes, lips, and smile…the tilt of the head—was indeed inviting. And Radu knew it.

But Radu's smile disappeared as he said intently, "Highness, I *would* be prince. I know you cannot answer me now. I will not ask. But I would be prince."

The serious tone of it somewhat settled Mohammed. "No, I cannot answer now. Wallachia must wait." He quickly added, "Now I must go to Asia. I must prepare my vassals for my ascension." And he offered, "Come with me."

Radu answered quietly, "If you insist, highness, I will. But…your father was very good to me. I would stay at his side now, if only to pray for him."

Mohammed sighed. "I understand. Perhaps when I return…"

If only for a glimpse, Radu's smile returned. "Highness, it would be my honor. And my pleasure."

Even as Radu left the room, he was followed by Mohammed's gaze.

6

THE SAME YEAR. MOLDAVIA. Prasha was vexed. "I thought the news would please you. It seems that he truly wants peace." "Yes, love," Dracula said. "It *seems* that he wants peace. But don't be so naive."

He led a few steps in silence as he gathered his thoughts. Around them the court basked in the bright warmth of the autumn day. The women did the things that would raise their worth as the present and future matrons of their households. They were expected to be more than "kept." In their struggling world, that was a luxury few households could afford. When the men were away, the women had to manage…manage estates, children, servants…They also had to support their households' cultured—*noble*—image.

Some now honed their skill at weaving, some at fine needlework. Some studied: keeping accounts, the basics of medicine, animal husbandry…Some read poetry and the classics. From a small group in a corner came giggles at their own missed notes as they practiced on various musical instruments.

The men talked business, especially about the harvest and profits from their estates. From the courtyard came the clank and clatter of weaponry and the stamp and snort of horses. Some of the younger nobles were at the drill, practicing at war. Some of the older were joining Bogdan and a troop of his regular guards on a sojourn around the city.

"You see, love," Dracula continued, "with the Turk, even a truce is a weapon. And the more terms on the truce, the sharper that weapon is. So consider…He offered the truce to Hungary and its vassals—including my own Wallachia. So he left much uncovered. Everything south of the Danube. Not by chance. He does nothing by chance. And he offered this truce for three years. Why three? Why not five or ten? Because somewhere—somewhere south of the Danube—Mohammed intends to strike—within three years."

He speculated, "But where? Serbia? He virtually owns the Serbs already. He has made their princes his puppets. Soon he will own the land outright."

He shook his head. Mohammed's target was not Serbia. There was one more logical: Albania. There, a rarity—a rebel janissary—Skanderbeg, was leading a rebellion against the Porte.

Skanderbeg's own father had once ruled Albania. When the Osmanli took it, they also took the son for the janissaries. He seemed a pliant cadet, loyal to his new religion, Islam, and his new master, the sultan. He proved, as well, to be a superb soldier.

When a group of Albanian partisans rebelled against the Porte, Skanderbeg himself was chosen to crush them. Instead, he betrayed and slaughtered his Osmanli garrison and became the partisans' leader. He was too smart to attack the empire head-on. He led his men in guerrilla warfare from the mountains. In effect, the Osmanli ruled the land by day, while Skanderbeg ruled by night.

"Aye," Dracula reflected. "Albania. When the sultan uses his terror-tactics there, Skanderbeg repays in kind. He plagues the sultan. And so it must be: Mohammed will attack Albania."

Prasha objected, "But surely he knows better. If he attacks Skanderbeg, Hungary will not stand idly by. It cannot. Skanderbeg is too valuable an ally."

"Exactly," Dracula said. "No doubt Mohammed is counting on just that. He has a three-year truce. He will spend two making ready. In the third, he will attack. All-out, full-scale war. Hungary will be sucked into it, forced to break its own truce to help Skanderbeg. Should it then turn to the west for help—as it did at Varna and Kossovo—the kings will have the excuse they always seek, a reason to steer clear of the Turk—as they did at Varna and Kossovo. They will blame Hungary for breaking the truce. They will turn their back on the whole affair—rather self-righteously—until they lose Hungary, too."

Prasha snapped, "That whole line of reasoning is so devious."

"And practical, love," Dracula said. "Logical. In fact, it's so logical that I can't believe *this*." He gestured to the court. "I'll wager it's the same in all Christendom. Everyone breathes easier because the Turk has offered 'peace.' They have nothing better to do now than tally their livestock and crops."

"Which obviously fills you with contempt."

Dracula said only, "*Delenda est Carthago...*"

The words that had guided ancient Rome in her war with her great African rival, Carthage: "*Carthage must be destroyed...*Or Rome would never be safe."

"All of us—" Dracula said, "Hungary, Poland, Wallachia, Moldavia—and every kingdom in the west—should be using Mohammed's own scheme against him. We should be getting ready for war. And when Mohammed comes..."

Prasha brushed past him. "And maybe the others are right. Maybe he really does want peace. Maybe the kings know better than you."

Dracula persisted, "No, love. Remember. I lived with the Turk. I dealt with him firsthand."

She challenged, "You were fast friends, then, his confidant?"

"He has no friends. He wants none. He needs none. He is sultan."

Prasha turned back to him. She said as though in pity, "Are you so afraid of him?"

Dracula answered only, "If our places were changed he would do well to fear *me*. Look what he has done already. He's brought the janissaries to heel and formed new regiments. And he murdered his own brother—an infant."

Prasha turned away again as though to flee from the words. History would indeed confirm what the world then whispered: Mohammed had killed his brother. He would brook no rivals to his throne. Not even the hint of a rival. Not even his own infant brother.

Some said that he had strangled the babe with his own hands. Some said that—more like an old tribal ritual—he had used a bowstring. History would dismiss both accounts as too dramatic. It would conclude that Mohammed had the babe drowned in his own bath by an assassin. He then had the assassin murdered for daring to harm a member of the imperial family—the same brother that the sultan himself had ordered killed. And he had closed the chapter by marrying the mother off to a pasha, to be kept in high style, as befitting a sultan's widow. It was the civilized thing to do.

Dracula's hand stopped Prasha. "Does he sound like a man of peace, love?"

Her eyes dropped. "I am sorry, love. I only hope—"

"I know. You only hope this peace is real. So do I. Truly. But the brutal fact is that our world—"

There was shouting in the courtyard, a mix of alarm and confusion as horses rushed through the gates. Fainter, like a deep, distant chorus, there was shouting in the city, punctuated by the occasional pop of another of the new gunpowder weapons: the prototype rifle—the *arquebus*.

The entire court was hurrying toward the yard when the doors burst open to a band of the younger nobles, still in their practice armor, propping a wounded man. He was one of Bogdan's troopers. As Stephen pushed through the crowd, the trooper pulled free of the others and delivered his news in a whisper. As the man staggered back in his own seeping blood, Dracula was at his cousin's side. Stephen was pale as he uttered what Dracula had already guessed: *Rebellion...Petru Aaron.*

Dracula started for the door but Stephen caught him. "No. Not yet. Not until we know..."

Dracula understood. It was common sense. It would not do for both father and son to be killed or captured. Before Stephen could chance saving his father, he had to know what he was up against.

And Stephen's look now was dark. He threw a nod to the trooper, who had been eased down to die on the floor. "His words were blunt: 'Save yourself.' Aaron's men are all over the city. They just...sprung!"

"Then I'll go now," Dracula said. "I'll learn what I can fast."

A third voice answered. "No. I will go." It was Wilk.

He was already in his armor. Stephen and Dracula both gave a nod and he rushed to the courtyard and gathered a troop of volunteers. The young nobles, if frightened, were still eager to save their prince.

Even as they streamed through the gates, Stephen was passing orders, each one bringing more color back to his face.

Every able-bodied man was to be mounted in the courtyard. Horses were even readied for the guards on the walls. The rest of the court were loaded into wagons along with the treasury and bare essentials. Men were stationed with oil and torches, ready to burn the rest. If Wilk reported that Bogdan had a chance, Stephen would dash to save him. If not, he would not be caught behind his walls. And, if he had to run, he would leave nothing for the enemy.

The shouting in the city suddenly swelled, along with the crisp echoes of metal stinging metal; Wilk's troop had found the enemy. In the courtyard, as the women took to the wagons, some prayed, wailing aloud. Some quietly passed daggers. In the voevodes' civil wars, one side tried to supplant—to *replace*—the other; a captive's life—especially a woman's—was only a brief nightmare.

Almost as quickly as he had left, Wilk was back. He had saved some of Bogdan's men but at a terrible cost to his own. Petru Aaron's coup had been thorough. He had spent his last gold on mercenaries and secreted them with his own men in and around the city. They had sprung as though from the woodwork and were now converging on the fortress from all sides.

Wilk offered only one hope: "They are still scattered."

"Then we go," Stephen said. His father would understand—as Stephen would if their roles were reversed. He cautioned Dracula, "But we have only one hope."

Dracula knew. Hungary. Hunyadi. It was a matter of politics. Both Poland and Hungary wanted Moldavia. Aaron was Poland's ally. Hungary would—should—want Stephen.

Stephen assured, "You are part of my household."

As such, even though Dracula's father had been Hunyadi's enemy, he would—should—be protected. *If* Hungary agreed to harbor Stephen.

Stephen gave the command. The gates opened. The train began to roll. Dark smoke poured from the buildings behind it.

Dracula waited to see Prasha into one of the wagons. Seeing the dagger in her hands, he pledged, "I will not leave you, love." He spurred ahead to join his cousin.

It was as Wilk had said: Aaron's men were still scattered. Some of the rebel boyar cavalry and mercenary infantry were winding toward the palace, the mercenaries especially pausing to loot along the way. Stephen's force, small, but concentrated and flying, cut many down in passing. Its last hurdle was a city gate that Aaron's men had taken and closed. But even there the enemy was thin; it took only a short skirmish for the train to clear the city.

What had been a familiar road was now treacherous. The estates nearest the city, those of Bogdan himself and his closest boyars, had already been ravaged.

From the smoking wasteland came the refugees—peasants, scattered men-at-arms, and the few surviving nobles—oozing slowly toward the road like the seeping blood of the land itself. And still more refugees ran from the city, unsure yet as to who the invaders were, hoping to cling to the fleeing prince for whatever protection he could give. Yet Stephen had no idea of what lay before him. How far had the rebels ranged? Were there more waiting along the road?

But what difference did it make? Stephen had only one way to go and he rode his course, as it were, as far as his eyes could see at a stretch, sending scouts dashing ahead, keeping his train rolling as fast as he could on the clear path. Even so, the wagons were slow, and stopping for refugees only made them slower. He had no choice but to give a hard order. If any were to escape, all had to move faster. The train would stop or slow for nothing...not for stragglers or the rugged jarring that would surely kill some of the wounded.

By dusk, there was hope. The train had reached land that the rebellion had not touched. Aaron had gone for his enemy's head, for Suceava and Bogdan and Stephen. But he had too few men for a general rebellion. The road to Hungary seemed clear. But having been thwarted at winning all in one fell swoop, Aaron was trying to make amends. More and more, refugees riding from the rear carried word of men in hot pursuit. And to show the urgency of the news they would simply give their reports as they fled past Stephen and his cumbersome train.

Stephen halted and called his officers. Men and beasts were exhausted. Should they run on or brace for a stand? They could run into the night. The darkness might save them. But how far would they get? And how much more spent would they be when the enemy finally caught them? Better to make a stand.

Still, Wilk had a suggestion. He had fought for pay himself. He knew how mercenaries thought. He would have the train go a little farther, scattering its valuables on the way. What soldier—least of all a mercenary—could resist? It would buy time.

It did. But finally some of Bogdan's men-at-arms, some of the last to escape the city, caught the tail of the train and gave a report. As the wagons were let to go ahead, Stephen gathered his men to catch their breath and hear the latest of the enemy. Aaron's men were very close. The sun was setting, but its last rays would surely see the sides clash.

Stephen asked the stragglers, "My father? Is there any word?"

To a man, they paled. None would even look at him. But one said quietly, "Dead, lord."

"In battle?"

"No, lord."

"How?"

At their hesitation, Stephen guessed. His father must have been executed, not as a nobleman, by beheading, but as a commoner, by hanging. A last insult from Petru. From Bogdan's own brother.

But someone uttered the word: "Impaled."

Stephen went white...almost pure white. His lips twisted and trembled. His body visibly shook. But in that very instant he was struck by something else. His eyes snapped wide. His twisted face hardened. He drew sword and charged down the road. The first of Aaron's men had appeared.

It was more butchery than a battle. It could have been that Aaron's men had ridden hard, too hard, in their lunge at certain victory. Or it could have been the respite—albeit brief—that Stephen had given his men, or the fact that Aaron's men had scattered to gather the booty jettisoned by the wagons. Or it could have been all of those things. Or just rage.

Impaled. Bogdan. Father. Uncle. Beloved prince. Impaled.

Stephen's men swept the road. No strategy. No tactics. No prisoners. The crawling enemy wounded were hacked to bits.

Yet the refugees waiting in Stephen's wagons neither saw nor heard any signs of victory. They only saw their men charge off. They heard the clash and screams. They saw a line of silent, ghostlike riders trotting back toward the wagons. In the fading light, the line was almost on them when they realized that it was their own men returning.

Dracula went straight to Prasha. She seemed entranced. It took a moment for her to look at him, to see him. In her hands a bared dagger was set to her own heart. He brushed it away and lifted her to his saddle. He found a priest and married her there and then.

7

CONSTANTINOPLE. Toma Catavolinos looked every bit the part of the Byzantine merchant. His tunic and breeches belied his modest wealth; they were plain—practical. His complexion, framed by the dark of his eyes and beard, was coarse. Not rough like a peasant's, but not pampered either. Weathered. Suited to the roles he played in plying his trade: overseer, traveller, gentleman. He was of average height and girth, but his muscles were distinct; he himself had worked the rigging of a few ships. He did not mind his colleagues calling him Volinos for short.

Already he was amused by the meeting. The "old blood" of Byzantium—the emperor, nobility, and patriarch of the Church—wore robes—the same ostentatious robes worn a thousand years before by the aristocracy of Rome. The emperor, in fact, still had himself announced as "Emperor of The Romans"—as though he ruled that grand empire of old. His chair at the head of the long, narrow table was raised on a low platform above the rest.

Indeed, Volinos thought, the emperor did look regal: tall; thin; sharp, aquiline nose; dark eyes; dark hair and short beard tinged with gray. He was the eleventh emperor to carry the name of Byzantium's founder: Constantine. He was the eighty-first man to sit the throne.

Constantine spoke quietly now; all in the assembly could hear—if they listened.

"The sultan has given his answer."

But the room—the entire city—already knew. Mohammed had intended it that way. He had spread his answer throughout the city before giving it to Constantine as a formal reply. So the "Emperor of The Romans" was the last to know the sultan's will—even behind the beggars of the street.

So Constantine could only tell the assembly what they already knew. When the young Mohammed had ascended his throne, Constantine had "tested" him, demanded a tribute on the threat of supporting a rival claimant to the sultanate. He had sent the threat through the old vizier, Chalil. Along with a little gold. For gold, Chalil had promised, he would do what he could to sway the new sultan.

Volinos—like the rest of Constantinople—had been shocked by the emperor's boldness. Yet he understood. When Constantine had treated the Turks kindly, they had pushed him, intimidated. He had simply tried the other tack.

And Mohammed had given his answer: no tribute. Further, he was, as it were, raising the stakes. The Turks already had a fortress on the Asian side of the Bosphorus, right across from Constantinople. Mohammed now announced that he would build another fortress. On the Greeks' side of the strait. In the very shadow of the city itself.

In truth, Volinos almost pitied Constantine. To the emperor, even voicing the sultan's answer was like drinking gall. But more...the Emperor of The Romans seemed confused...frustrated...like a man whose best efforts were falling short. And he could not understand why...why the Turk—in reply to his threat—had insulted him so.

Volinos's eyes passed over the room—not the men at the table, but the room itself. The walls rose high, like a shaft to heaven. They were decorated. Ornately: murals, filigree, icons. The Virgin Mary and child Jesus were at the apex.

The decorations, particularly those of Virgin and Child, were stylized. Not as simple holy figures with glowing halos and serene visages. They were like high aristocracy: crowns, robes…Like an emperor's own family. Like God molded in man's—the imperial family's—image.

As Constantine finished voicing the sultan's answer, the patriarch spoke: "It seems that Your Majesty underestimated the sultan."

It was impertinence—putting the blame on Constantine for rousing the Turk. It might have been taken as the mere "frankness" of the old, the cute blurt of one whose impending mortality has sapped his tact. The patriarch, after all, was old, and gray and bent. But between his long beard and tall, black, clerical hat, his eyes were still keen. His words—*Age be damned!*—were still always measured. He knew he was the only man in Constantinople who could speak so to the emperor. In the *twelve hundred* years of Byzantium's existence, Church and State were almost woven like one.

Yet Constantine bristled in reply: "Every one of you knew what I was doing. If you felt it ill-advised, you should have spoken then."

Volinos scanned the table. His fellow merchants were clearly troubled by the sultan's answer. But the nobility merely seemed…bored…*more tiresome news about the Turk.*

Constantine challenged, "It is time to choose. What will we do? We can no longer sit on our hands. The barbarian made his truce with Europe so he can focus on us."

The barbarian: the Turk. To the Byzantine Greeks, all the world beyond their walls was still "barbarian."

As the nobles smiled skeptically, the patriarch posed, "What would Your Majesty have us do?"

"Act, father! Prepare!"

"For what, majesty?"

"Invasion, father! Invasion!"

The nobles' smiles spread. Their thoughts were obvious: *What could the Turk do? Build a fortress outside the city? So what! Would he try to breach the walls? That had never been done!*

Constantine warned, "These are not the old days. Barbarians no longer need ladders and hooks."

The patriarch countered, "Then what will they do, majesty?"

"They will stand off with their gunpowder, their cannon, father. They will batter the walls down."

But the smiles still held. *What cannon could batter the great walls?*

"You have never seen the greatest guns," Constantine warned. "The 'bombards.' They are not the puny cannon of the field, nor even like those mounted on walls. They look like trees. Giant, hollowed-out trees. Like the 'Father Oak' trees. They do not simply throw shot. They hurl boulders!"

Smiles gave way to smirks, as though the emperor were some crank telling a tale.

Volinos spoke quietly: "His Majesty is right."

He blushed some at the attention he drew. He knew that he was as much a nuisance to the nobles—and the patriarch—as they were to him. In the grand days of the empire, a man of his class would never even have been invited to such a table.

The grand days…Then, Constantinople had a *million* people. A city of dreams indeed. Crown of an empire that stretched from Asia to Europe. Protected by a magnificent military machine. Its fleet ruled the waves. Its army had not lost a single major battle in *five hundred years!*

Aye, in those days, a man like Volinos was just another commoner, another hustling trader. In those days, the "old blood" triumvirate kept a foot on the neck of the lower classes.

But now they needed the "commoners." Men like Volinos. *Hungry* men. Men who worked and risked. The "fresh blood" that kept the ailing "empire" alive.

Even so, Volinos was now wary of what he said—and how he said it. These greater men, as it were, were really "small" men. Jealous. Treacherous. There was no profit in having them as enemies.

He continued quietly, "I have seen these bombards."

A noble challenged, "Are you saying they could breach *our* walls?"

"Yes, lord," Volinos said. "Given time…I think they could."

Heads shook. Some laughed. Someone proclaimed, "We still have the Fire!"

It was called "Greek Fire." Byzantium's invention, its secret weapon. A mixture of sulphur, pitch, naphtha, and…and whatever else indeed remained secret, lost to later history. The Fire could be hurled in balls from catapults or shot as a thick liquid through tubes—the prototype of later warfare's napalm and flamethrower. Water would not extinguish it. The Byzantine fleet, in particular, had made good use of it. But that particular fact was moot now; centuries before, the Byzantine admiral had *sold* the fleet.

Constantine stated flatly, "The Fire will not be enough. Not this time. The big guns can sit out of our range."

The patriarch argued, "Your Majesty speaks as though the Turk already has these 'bombards.' As though he already has our city! Yet we still have the greatest shield of all! Or do you forget, majesty? Our Lady!"

The Virgin Mary. The Mother of Jesus Christ. The Byzantines truly believed that she protected them. She was the patron of their city.

Constantine piously bowed his head. "Father, I would never forget Our Lady. But can we presume on her now? Have we been so faithful?"

Byzantium had not. It believed in Divine Protection. But it also hedged. It looked to other things for some sort of superstitious protection: seances, prophecy, dream interpretation.

The patriarch repeated his question: What would the emperor have them do?

"Defend *ourselves!* Hire men!"

The patriarch scoffed, "We have our own men, majesty."

Constantine would not even dignify the statement with an answer. Instead it was his turn to smirk. Over the centuries Constantinople had shrunk to sixty thousand inhabitants. Of those, nearly a third claimed to have taken religious vows: de facto noncombatants—a good example of religion as an occupation. Of the rest, only five thousand were willing to fight. But only four thousand were physically able.

Four thousand men. Thirty-two miles of wall.

"We need money," Constantine said.

For mercenaries. A lot of money. For a real army. Even the Church would have to contribute.

Volinos and the merchants waited in silence. They, of all, would be willing to fight for their city, their very livelihood. But the effort would be useless without the backing—the gold—of the nobility and Church. Men like Volinos would not waste hard-earned money on a mere *show* of defense.

"My own money is spent," Constantine said.

Spent on barely keeping his city alive. There were specters in the city now: shells of old houses and palaces...whole sections of rubble...Most of the people were unemployed and on the dole—welfare. In some quarters, gangs ruled. On some streets, the very paving stones had been stripped and sold to other cities as a "last gasp" for the treasury.

Again Volinos looked at the room. There was a time, he knew, when all of it—murals, filigree, icons—had been burnished in gold and jewels. A single picture on a single wall had been worth a fortune. Now the gold was only paint, the jewels paste.

The emperor prodded the assembly, "I need you. We need *one another.*"

Silence. He could not force them to join him. He did not have the raw power. He had only a small guard. And the nobles and patriarch had their own guards.

"Are you with me?" he asked.

Averted eyes.

He declared, "I am going to fight. So you are leaving me no choice. I will have to look elsewhere for help."

It meant only one thing: an alliance with the west. With papists! As the head of the western Church, the pope would be willing to help, to raise an army, a Christian crusade against the Turk, *if*...

The papacy had spelled out its conditions centuries before. It would help the ailing Byzantium if the Orthodox Christians would bow to Rome, to the pope. No longer would there be two sects. Only one. Under the "Holy Father" in Rome.

The patriarch bristled. "You would not dare!"

Constantine was not haughty. He knew the impact of his words. He offered, "At least the papists are Christians."

But an anonymous noble retorted, as history recorded: *Better a turban than the papal tiara!* Better to be conquered by Turkish Islam than concede anything to the pope.

Hatred. Between the Christian sects, Roman and Orthodox, it ran deep. Twelve hundred years before, Byzantium had been founded as the distinct eastern half of the Roman empire. Each half was supposed to help the other in times of need.

The east, anchored by impregnable Constantinople, grew. The west, centered in vulnerable Rome, was overrun by barbarians: Huns, Goths, Vandals, Franks, Magyars, Bulgars...Soon the only authority left in Rome was the spiritual: the pope. Popes called to the east for help and often received it. But eventually the east denied the west as a growing liability.

To save their "flock," popes tried to force Byzantium to come to the west's aid. The pope, they noted, was bishop of Rome, the first bishopric in all Christianity. Therefore, they claimed, the pope had spiritual authority over all Christians. He could order the east to help the west.

The eastern Christians never accepted the pope's argument. They simply formed their own True, or *Orthodox*, Church, led by the bishop of their grandest city, Constantinople. They called the bishop their "Father," their *patriarch*.

Through the centuries, as the west converted the barbarians to Christianity and so rose from its Dark Ages, the two sects feuded. The feud culminated with each side declaring the other heretic; with an Orthodox mob seizing a papal legate, beheading him, and tying the head to the tail of a dog; and with the westerners, in turn, seizing Constantinople by a shrewd strategy and setting a whore on the altar of the holiest Orthodox cathedral.

It had been centuries since the papists had been driven from the Orthodox capital. In those centuries, the Osmanli Turk rose to threaten the east, and the popes made their offer to Byzantium. Now it was they who were in a position to offer military aid. And they would. For the price: conversion. To Constantine, it was the only hope for his empire.

But the patriarch hissed, "You will be anathema. Excommunicated from the Church."

Constantine was calm. "Well then...We have no gold and no help from the pope. But we still have one hope: Janos Hunyadi. He has hinted that he might fight for us—his truce with Mohammed be damned! *If* our price is right: land, titles..."

Still the patriarch shook his head. "The pope and Janos Hunyadi are one and the same. One papist will only draw the rest."

Constantine posed, "So tell me, then, father. What *would* you have us do?"

"Keep faith! Trust Our Lady to help us!"

Constantine said nothing. He merely rose, gave a curt nod, and left. The patriarch and nobility could ponder their folly.

Volinos listened to the aftermath...the patriarch jabbering about faith, the nobles scoffing at the very idea of a Turkish invasion.

So Volinos began weighing...The emperor was right. War was coming. The city could yet save itself. To Volinos and the merchants it was worth saving—the best trade base in the world. If Constantinople merely survived, there would be profit enough to go around, enough for all. And better days for the "empire."

Yes, there was still time. As Volinos saw it, Mohammed had made his truce with the rest of Europe for three years. Three years to launch his invasion of Constantinople. A full two years were yet left. Time enough for the Church and nobility to come to their senses. Because without them there would be no real defense. Without them, as Volinos saw it, he would simply have to move on...elsewhere—anywhere—to find new opportunity.

8

January 1452. Hungary. Matthias Hunyadi stood with his father and older brother at a window overlooking their palace courtyard. He was barely nine years old, with dark brown, curly hair worn rounded across the brow and long at the sides and back. His eyes, too, were dark brown. His squared chin already showed the slight heaviness that would mark his visage as he grew older.

His brother, Laszlo, approaching twenty, was more like their father: light brown eyes; long, brown, wavy hair worn straight back; high forehead; and the solid beginnings of the father's bull-like build.

Janos Hunyadi gestured to the courtyard, to the train of wagons and horses just pulling rein. He said tersely, "Stephen of Moldavia."

Laszlo guessed, "He wants asylum."

Matthias cautioned, "But if we grant it won't we have trouble with the Poles? They supported Petru Aaron in Moldavia."

As his father smiled, Matthias understood: His own political instincts were good—even at nine years old. He also understood as his father said nothing, but only led the way to a table. There was no time for discourse. Already the footfalls of the Moldavian delegation could be heard on the stairs. They entered and were seated with little fanfare—men roughened and thinned by their weeks of fight-and-flight from Moldavia. Even the last of their "finery" was patched. And on the finery of one—who sat at Stephen's right hand—Matthias saw the symbol of his father's Wallachian enemy: the dragon. Dracula.

As the supplicant, Stephen began. He did not mince words: He had nowhere else to go. And Matthias was gratified when Stephen echoed his own thought: "Of course, if you accept me, there could be trouble with the Poles."

Hunyadi answered, "Poland will not war with Hungary over my granting you asylum. At least not now."

So, Matthias knew, there was something new to learn from this meeting...something bigger afoot in their world.

Hunyadi offered Stephen, "I am sorry about your father."

Impalement.

Even now it visibly stunned Stephen. He hardly heard Hunyadi finish, "Savagery. Something I'd expect of the heathen, not a Christian."

At Stephen's side, Dracula's lips thinned, but he caught himself. He could not help thinking of another act of savagery: his own father and brother murdered—by Janos Hunyadi.

Hunyadi shifted subjects, "You saved your court."

"I did," Stephen said. "Most of it." He took the point. In his wagons were many mouths to feed, people to cloth and house. But he had also saved some of his treasury. "I can pay for our keep."

Hunyadi waved it off. "You are welcome here as my guest." He added frankly, "And not just as a prince who would be in Hungary's debt. We need each other now." He gave the reason in a word: "Mohammed."

Now it was Dracula whose political instincts were gratified. *Mohammed. Need.* It could mean only one thing: war. No doubt, as he had predicted, against the rebel, Skanderbeg, in Albania.

But Hunyadi continued, "The new sultan is bold. Bolder than anyone thought. He wants no less than Constantinople."

The surprise in Stephen's voice answered for his whole delegation: "Folly!"

If so, Hunyadi explained, the folly was already under way. Mohammed, as he had threatened, had begun building a fortress right next to the Byzantine capital.

Stephen was still unconvinced. "All of Christendom will rise! Papist or Orthodox, it makes no difference now!"

Young Matthias felt the words. As he—as all Christendom—had been taught, Constantinople was more than just a city. It was indeed the bastion of Christianity at the very heart of Islam. It simply could not be let to fall.

But Hunyadi followed, "The Greeks are making it difficult. Their emperor has asked for help. The pope is willing to give it—as am I. But when the emperor even talks to us his people and Church threaten rebellion."

So Mohammed's plans seemed less and less folly.

Hunyadi told Stephen, "But in one sense you are right. Christendom will have to rise. Either with the Greeks—if they let us—or after they fall. The man who breaches the great walls will not stop there."

And Stephen had to ask, "But can they really be breached?"

Hunyadi gave the terse answer: "Bombards."

The Age of Gunpowder had come. The Age of Walls was over.

"So sooner or later," Hunyadi said, "we are going to fight the Turk. We will need every man we have. Every reliable man. I think you, Stephen, are such a man. Which is truly why you are welcome here. And which is why—" He finally acknowledged Dracula. "—he is not."

Stephen sprang to his cousin's defense. "He will be with us. I assure you."

Hunyadi was firm. "I can hardly depend on that. You know my reasons."

Dracula spoke, "I know them. My father and I were allied with the Turk. But—"

"I know," Hunyadi said. "'Not by choice.' My reasons stand."

Stephen laid a hand on Dracula's shoulder. "I know this man's heart. It is more than just the fact that we are cousins."

Dracula affirmed for Hunyadi, "And if you could see into this heart you would see this…The sultan has my brother. He will set him against me. And I will fight my own brother."

Hunyadi conceded only, "You are right. I cannot see into your heart. I only see what I see. You rode with the Turk." As Stephen made to protest he continued, "And there is another reason. My allies. The Danestis."

It was a point of honor that Stephen could not refute. He had presumed on the fact that Dracula, as things stood, was hardly a threat to the Danestis, was merely part of his own refugee household. But Hunyadi was setting it differently: Dracula's very presence in Hungary was an affront to the Danestis. An affront that Hunyadi challenged.

But Dracula dared, "If I may be so bold, I might yet make a better ally."

Better than the Danestis—who, as the whispers still held, had abandoned Hunyadi at Kossovo. In truth, Dracula admitted, as much as he hated Janos Hunyadi, he also respected him. The baron had risen from the lesser nobility by the sword—by fighting the Turks odds-be-damned. Clearly he would have his family—in the person of his two sons—rise even further—by fighting the Turk yet again.

But Hunyadi answered, "You *are* too bold. You insult my ally to my face."

It was Stephen who had to say, "No insult was intended."

Hunyadi was adamant: "He must go."

As Stephen was bewildered…embarrassed…Dracula rose. He stifled any protest from Stephen with a quiet, "You have to think of the others. And yourself."

Still Stephen protested to Hunyadi, "He has a wife."

Across the table, it gave young Matthias pause. He understood about the Danestis and Dracula…about allies and honor. But he also understood chivalry. Refusing a woman asylum now…a woman who was already a refugee…and with the Turk stirring…He was gladdened to hear his father offer, "She can stay."

But just as Matthias was relieved by his father's chivalry, he heard Dracula's reply: "She is my wife." He heard Dracula cite the Bible: "Whither I go…"

Into all the danger and uncertainty, Dracula would have Prasha go with him.

9

MAY 1453. Mohammed awoke in the dark of the tent to find his nakedness coated with sweat. His hands were cupped and extended before him. He was trembling. He whispered, "I have it!" Then seeing his hands empty his thoughts corrected: *I had it!*

He rolled on the silk sheets and shook Radu, who snapped from his sleep with eyes wide and hands frantically groping for his scabbard.

"No!" Mohammed told him. "No danger!" His strong hands stopped Radu's. "I had it! This time, I had it!"

The fear melted from Radu's body. He slumped forward and laughed. He listened to his friend's tale: the dream. Again. *The Jewel.* Constantinople.

"I had it," Mohammed declared. "As I shall surely have it soon. And I held it here, in front of me. *My* work. And men hailed me: *Greater than Murad! Greater even than Leg Breaker!*"

Leg Breaker. Osman. The steppe chieftain of centuries before. The very founder of their tribe.

Radu gave a faint smile. Indeed, the sultan who conquered Constantinople would be the greatest of them all. The Prophet Mohammed himself—praise his name!—had predicted centuries before that a great ghazi, a holy warrior, would take the Christian bastion. But Mohammed's siege was approaching its eighth week. The "Jewel" had been assailed by land and sea, surrounded on all sides. Yet, with only a handful of men on its walls, led by the stubborn Constantine, it had refused to surrender to the sultan. And there was no end in sight.

Radu tried to ease his friend back on the pillows. But Mohammed read the meaning of the touch: *Pity!* He swiped Radu's hands away, then just as quickly seized them and held.

Radu felt himself drawn close by the sheer strength of the grip. He felt the coarse hair of the sultan's body crumple against his own fair skin. He let the strength hold him, pliant. He raised his lips and offered them, and Mohammed's almost accepted, brushing close. But the sultan's lips burst with a grin as he playfully pushed Radu away: "There's no time now! The Jewel is mine! The dream said it!"

As the sultan rose and began dressing, Radu started to caution, "But why should—?"

Mohammed cut him short. "Why should the city fall now? Because of a dream?" He sneered. "Maybe I don't believe in dreams." He drew a breath to gather himself. "To take the Jewel, they said, I would need a huge army."

So he had gathered one: *seventy thousand picked troops; seventy thousand more baji-bazouks; the ten thousand janissaries.*

"And they said I would need a navy. But how could we Turks do that?"

How indeed! For all their conquests, the Osmanlis' roots were still on the Asian steppes. They were hardly sailors.

Mohammed grunted. "So I bought a navy."

Three hundred ships. Manned by only the best seamen: Europeans—Christians. Mercenaries. This was the *business* of war.

"And I bought bombards," Mohammed said. "And gunners."

And these, too, had been only the best: European Christians. They plied their trade like any other; they had formed guilds. They sold their skills—the secret of gunpowder and cannon—to anyone for a price. For Mohammed, they had forged and manned *sixty-five* siege guns. Nine were of the biggest: bombards. More than twenty feet long, they hurled half-ton shot for a range of a full mile.

Mohammed paused in his dressing as his mind showed him a chessboard. Across the board was a single castle: Constantinople. Ranged against it were his own varied and heavy pieces. "But today..." He laughed. "I add a mere pawn. And the dream said that the Jewel will be mine."

As he finished dressing, Radu followed his lead. And wondered: *A pawn?* What could his friend possibly mean? Why should the city fall now? Even the great bombards would take months to breach the legendary walls. But if Constantinople did fall...

Radu suddenly felt the excitement. He heard himself blurt, "Then Wallachia!"

Mohammed almost stopped in place, almost scoffed. *Wallachia?* This Radu was truly a provincial. A good provincial perhaps. A good vassal. And more: a pleasant diversion. He knew how to serve. Mohammed chuckled: *In more ways than one.* And yet...With Constantinople at stake, Radu was thinking only of Wallachia. Petty Wallachia. A mere piss-land. Truly.

Mohammed rubbed his friend's auburn hair. "Wallachia can wait."

Radu protested, "But my brother will—"

Mohammed spat the name: "Dracula? He will do nothing. My 'eyes' tell me..." Osmanli sultans had many eyes. "Your brother is a fugitive. Escaped from Moldavia. Driven from Hungary. He has only his new bride and some Pole. They travel like ghosts: on the wind and by night. They are seen and disappear. Living...but as good as dead. So your brother is no threat to you. Or to me."

Mohammed strode from the tent and Radu followed. The sultan ignored the glare of the morning sun, ignored the abject bow of the Grand Vizier, Chalil, and of the lesser pashas and beys. He gave a terse order that sent a runner to the artillery brigade a short distance away. He paused a moment to gaze across the expanse of open field—to Constantinople. His eyes seemed to look past the rubble ripped from the walls by his bombards. And they certainly did not lower themselves to the mounds of bodies—mostly bazouks—heaped around the rubble.

The moment passed. Mohammed moved on, skirting his lines, oblivious to the weary, vacant-eyed stares of his soldiers—the frustration of the bloody, two-month siege—and oblivious even to Radu at his side.

He stopped at the artillery, at the eight bombards centering the brigade. The twenty-foot barrels were laid bare on mounds of earth; the guns were aimed by shifting the dirt of the mounds to change trajectory. Each mound was protected by a wooden mantelet, a makeshift wall set on levers. The mantelet was raised to allow its gun to fire, then lowered again to protect the crew in reloading. Now, near the bombards, a crowd had been gathered by the sultan's order. They were not of the janissary gun crews, nor of the mercenary gunners who directed the crews. They were Byzantine Greeks. They bowed to the sultan as Osmanli custom demanded: face to the ground.

Mohammed bade them to rise and began, "You came here seeking my favor and you have found it."

Heads nodded eagerly. These were the Greeks who had deserted Constantinople. And why not? The capital was doomed. The emperor had tried to save it. But the patriarch and nobility had thwarted his efforts: no mercenaries; no alliance with the west—with papists. In the end, as Mohammed dropped his "noose" around the city, the nobility gathered its wealth and fled. The patriarch, left behind with the emperor, was, presumably, praying. Fervently.

The men with Mohammed now had simply accepted the inevitable. They fled to where they were welcome. By invitation. The sultan used deserters much as he did his "eyes," his spies. Even the smallest bit of intelligence they could offer was worth at least a few pieces of silver.

"But today," Mohammed told them, "you will see how generous I can be."

Behind him, the crews began loading each bombard: *three hundred* pounds of powder; *half-ton* granite ball. The janissaries did most of the work by rote now. They had learned well from the hired gunners.

Mohammed beckoned a man from the crowd. As he approached the sultan, a chest was also brought forward. A chest of respectable size. It was left unopened, but Mohammed told the man, "If what you said is true, this is yours."

He promptly led the crowd a good ways off. Already on firing, one of the bombards had exploded, erasing its crew—including the "expert" mercenary gunner. If gunnery was a guild science, it was as yet inexact.

The crew at the first bombard gave a signal. Everyone held his ears. A lit fuse was set to the gun. The air roared. The ground shook. The bombard jumped on its mound and spewed a long tongue of flame and an even longer tongue of smoke—thick, acrid smoke that drifted in a cloud far out onto the field. All along the line the troops cheered the marvel. Their hundred-thousand voices rose as one. The shot hit the city walls in an explosion of pulverized stone. But it was wide of its mark.

The first gun would be let to cool. On each shot, a bombard burned so hot that it could only be fired some seven times a day. The second gun corrected its trajectory by the error of the first. It fired and was also wide, but the third, fourth…each crept closer to the target. It was a groping, patient exercise. It was after dark and approaching midnight when a glare at the wall showed the first direct hit.

Still at Mohammed's side, Radu peered at the city. Where the shot had hit was a burning, gaping hole—more than could have been expected on the incredibly thick, solid walls by a single shot. Mohammed, too, saw it. He beamed as he called his informant to claim his reward.

As the man bounded to the chest, Radu felt a twinge, a pang. The man had just sold his city: the Jewel—legendary Byzantium. He had told the sultan of Constantinople's "Achilles' Heel": an ancient gate that had been bricked over. A single hollow abscess in the solid walls. Already the entire artillery brigade was tearing at it as waves of baji-bazouks swarmed the spot under the covering fire.

Radu gave pause: Was he any different than the man who had just sold his native city for gold? But he reassured himself…Yes, he would be Mohammed's candidate in Wallachia. He would deliver the land into the fold of the Porte. But not for gold. He *believed* in the Turkish empire. An irresistible force. A *civilizing* force. Beyond the sentiment of race and religion, the empire would bring Wallachia to order.

And more…it would do so in the name of this sultan, Mohammed, who had truly become his…friend.

The guns ripped the old gate apart, obliterated the whole section of wall, then fell silent to let the bazouks storm the breech. Their battle-cry was a shriek. Hysterical triumph! But it turned to agony as the city belched fire—Greek Fire.

From his place among the deserters, Toma Catavolinos thought of the raging flames: *the last gasp of a dying Dragon.* The distant flicker danced on the brim of the now-opened chest. So much gold! Volinos fairly gaped at the man who had claimed it. And he prayed to God to grant that he, too, might some day earn the sultan's great favor.

10

HUNGARY. Laszlo and Matthias Hunyadi watched in silence as their father pored over the map. It stretched nearly the length of the table, with the western kingdoms at one end and far Asia at the other. But Hunyadi's eyes, his hands, were focused on the center—Hungary itself and the Balkans—as he set each country with small, wooden figures...almost like children's toys...cavalrymen, foot soldiers, towers...

He finally commented, "The Turk was like a shark. But now he is like a whale. And he is hungry again."

Constantinople was now Istanbul. Or, as the Turks affectionately called it, 'Stambul. Constantine, the last Byzantine emperor, had been found among the dead. He was dressed like a commoner, apparently trying to make a quiet escape while the Turks poured through the breach. His corpse was identified by the feet; he had forgotten to remove the distinctive, purple imperial slippers.

Laszlo followed his father's thought. "So now Mohammed will come for us. Or Albania...Skanderbeg."

Hunyadi corrected, "Us. He can always backtrack on Skanderbeg."

The "toys" told the story. The Albanian guerrillas were marked on the map by a single soldier. On each of three sides it was faced by a pair: soldier and knight. Each pair stood for the Turks and their allies. Skanderbeg was firmly hemmed in. His options were simple. He could continue to fight as he was: hit-and-run from the mountains. Or he could run, quit his country. In any event, he was contained.

Matthias concluded, "Then the Turk will come for Buda." Hungary's own capital. "You said before that he wants Buda now. Now that he has Constantinople."

"He does," Hunyadi said. "But attacking our capital now would be too much, too soon."

He frowned in disgust. Even with the cataclysm of Constantinople, the western kings seemed content to pretend that the sultan himself was content. Rationalization. Delusion: *Mohammed had Constantinople! His people now hailed him as Fatih, "the Conqueror"! Greater even than Leg Breaker, Osman! What more could he want—at least so soon?*

But if Mohammed lunged at Buda even the west would have to admit: Buda, then Vienna, Rome...Surely the kings would unite against the sultan.

"So it is not Buda," Hunyadi counselled. "Not yet."

Matthias ventured, "Then he'll strike here." His finger touched one of the towers, a Hungarian fortress along the Danube.

Hunyadi shook his head. "For a whale, that's hardly a morsel. He needs more. More than a fortress—but less than Buda."

His sons got the point. Their fingers hit the map together: Belgrade.

It, too, was marked by a tower. It was a city protected by a fortress. It was not a particularly grand city, nor rich. But it was Hungary's "anchor" in the south. It lay on the Danube on the Serbian border, where the river forked into a tributary. The entire settlement consisted of three parts: the city proper on one bank; a fortress on another; and an island at the fork on the river. It was, depending of course on perspective, a southern door to Hungary, or a northern door to the Turkish empire. Hunyadi concurred: "Belgrade. Still," he warned, "you never know with the Turk."

At the thought, he sighed and stretched the stiffness from his joints. Since Constantinople, it seemed, he had been more alert, more on edge, than he could remember. The Turk—all his enemies—were always on his mind. They always had been. How many nights—thousands of nights—had he drifted into sleep putting his mind into theirs to anticipate their plots? Lately, though, his thoughts of the Turk weighed heavily. They literally hung about him, it seemed, and, though they let him sleep, they also left him tired, sorely worn. Or, Hunyadi thought, maybe he was just getting old.

He laughed to himself. "It's part of the heathen's charm, I suppose. Whenever you think you know his mind...tread carefully."

He had a decision to make. He could gamble. Put everything he had in Belgrade. But then...

He chose another tack. His finger slid along the Danube. "We'll strengthen the whole line, the larger forts. Forget the smaller. Else we'll be spread too thin."

He told Laszlo, "The job is yours. Use the requisition."

Requisition: the lord's right to strip the land. Food. Drink. Livestock. Mostly it hit the peasants. Their own supplies would be hauled off to stock the forts for siege.

Laszlo noted, "We will need more artillery."

There were, of course, no guns to be had in a requisition. They would have to be bought. With gold. Paid in advance. To the gunners' guild.

Matthias cautioned, "We don't have money like that on hand."

Hunyadi smiled. His young son managed well. An organizer. An overseer. One estate, two, three...It made no difference. He kept the accounts of a whole province in his mind. And he was still hardly more than a boy. Unfortunately, now, his grasp of the problem was right.

But Matthias also knew the single solution: "The Saxons."

Hungary's merchants. Two centuries before, the great Mongol invasion of Europe had stripped Hungary of nearly everything—including its population. To rebuild, the land especially needed a new economy: merchants. The Saxons of Germany were among the best. To attract them, Hungary's kings offered special privileges: low taxes, a monopoly on trade...So the Hungarian lords protected the Saxons. And the Saxons, in turn, supported the lords. They would lend Hunyadi money. It was simply good business.

Still, Laszlo grimaced. "Of course the Saxons will want another 'favor.'"

They would want something to add to their already generous privileges.

"Of course," Hunyadi said. "But I told you before—"

"I know, father, I know. We'll get the favor back. Some day."

Favors traded hands like coins. It only depended on who needed whom.

Yet it was bitter for Laszlo, the young noble. "Blackmail. We are the ones who risk our lives. But we have to go to them hat-in-hand."

Matthias laughed. "You are too proud, brother. We fight with the sword, true. But the Saxons fight with the purse."

"And more and more," Hunyadi counselled, "war is fought with the purse." Gunpowder and cannon. The ungodly expense. "And it's surely here to stay. So are the merchants. And—thank God—our Saxons are the best."

"Aye!" Matthias agreed. "So learn to live with them, brother." He cuffed Laszlo on the cheek. "And smile."

Laszlo retorted, "Just keep your own smile, brother. When I am lord here, I am going to leave the merchants to you."

"Aye," Matthias said. "And I dare say you'll be pleased with how I handle them."

Inside, Hunyadi glowed. Whether age was taking him or not made little difference. Not with such sons. They were not plagued by the jealousy that rent so many families. His line would be left in good hands. Blessed! The boys would inherit his estates and all the power he had built. Together, surely, they would add to it immensely. They would be men to be reckoned with.

He thanked God again for such sons.

But now they had business. He told Laszlo, "You know your task. Stock our forts."

"Aye," Laszlo affirmed. "And then I will join you in Belgrade."

Hunyadi said flatly, "No. You already have your spurs."

The spurs of knighthood.

Hunyadi looked to his second son, and Matthias was stunned...joyous: "My sword is sharp."

Hunyadi counselled, "I want you more for your head than your arm. Belgrade will be your baptism."

Matthias would be with his father in combat. He would take a step toward knighthood. He would learn the rudiments of command, firsthand, from Hungary's best general.

Hunyadi was delving further into his plans when the canter of hooves echoed from the courtyard. A small party. Some riders and a wagon. Hunyadi had been expecting them. His sons followed to the window.

Matthias was surprised at the lead rider: "Dracula?"

He was also surprised as his father explained, "He has asked for an audience."

And Hunyadi had granted it. His own men, in fact, had been Dracula's escort from the border.

And Matthias saw the beginnings of an answer to a question that had been pricking his mind. In his father's plans for the Turk, Wallachia—the Danestis—had not even been mentioned. Why? Why was his father not counting on their ally, the voevode, Vladislav?

Matthias begged the obvious conclusion. "Father, can you trust this Dracula?"

But Hunyadi knew that his son—both of them—already knew the answer. They *should* have known it. *He* had raised them. Still he stressed the lesson again. "Trust? Never. When blood goes sour between men..."

It never again runs sweet. Especially when one of the men has killed the other's kin.

"I can only use him as long as I need him—and he needs me."

Business.

Laszlo commented, "The Pole is still with him."

The Pole. Wilk. Wilkowski. Hunyadi remembered the road to the great battle of Varna. He remembered the old Polish knight with the wolf's doublet. How strange that the man's son was now in league with an enemy. And the son seemed like the father. Stiff-necked. At least he had the beginnings of it. This Wilk had followed Dracula on some long, hard roads. The Saxons—who often served as Hunyadi's own "eyes"—had seen it on their travels. Dracula and Wilk...and Prasha...

After Hunyadi had expelled them from Hungary, they lived like ghosts indeed. No land to call their own. Hunted by Moldavians and Wallachians...Yet they had survived. With Wilk, as it were, guarding Dracula's back.

So the Pole had to have some mettle. Like his father—who had suffered excommunication just to speak his mind.

Then again, Hunyadi thought begrudgingly, Dracula, too, had to have mettle.

As he watched, a small crowd rushed into the courtyard. Moldavians. Stephen. They were still Hunyadi's "guests." Now Stephen embraced his cousin and rushed to the wagon to embrace Dracula's wife. She shied a bit. He backed away. Prasha stood to show him. Her belly was large. Pregnant. Hunyadi noted the fact more than just in passing.

He sent his sons off. They had their work. They had best be at it. He would see Dracula alone.

So the baron and would-be voevode came to sit across the table. Dracula thanked Hunyadi for the audience, but no smiles, no small pleasantries, passed between them. They sat together by circumstance. Fate.

Both knew what would be said. That, too, was by circumstance. Hunyadi needed Dracula as much as Dracula needed Hunyadi. Still, it was Dracula who had been cast in the role of supplicant. He would have to speak first. But there was no need to mince words.

His purpose was plain: "Let me be your Wallachian ally." He added in deference, "I mean no offense to your present ally." He amended, "No *undue* offense."

But no offense would be taken. He knew how things stood between Hunyadi and the Danestis. And the map right under his eyes confirmed it.

The carved horseman marking Wallachia faced neither Hungary nor the Porte. It stood aloof. Set neither for nor against either side.

Constantinople had indeed changed things. If Mohammed, *the Conqueror*, could smash a legend, what could possibly stand against him? Or so the Wallachian voevode, Vladislav, apparently thought. He had cooled toward Hunyadi. Word had it that he was flirting with the sultan. Even if he did not join him outright, neither would he join Hungary in the face of a Turkish invasion. And Dracula knew as surely as Hunyadi that the invasion was coming.

So Dracula had made overtures to Hunyadi. And the baron had agreed to this second meeting.

Yet Hunyadi was cautious. As long as Vladislav did not break with Hungary outright, Hunyadi would try to keep him, keep Wallachia in the fold.

He offered Dracula, "You can serve me in another way. I need a captain in Transylvania."

Dracula was surprised. Pleasantly so. For his mind jumped at the implications. *Transylvania.* Right on Wallachia's border. Near—very near—to what he coveted. Near, too, to the man who kept it from him: Vladislav.

For Hunyadi's part, he was using Dracula as a reminder to Vladislav. If the voevode pushed the baron further, if he dared to join the Turk...

Dracula glanced at the map and spoke what he, like Hunyadi, had already concluded. "The Turk will strike at Belgrade. Belgrade first. Then Buda." At Hunyadi's tacit agreement he continued, "Can you stop him? Will you have the men?"

"I've asked the pope to call a crusade."

Holy War! All of Christendom under arms! *To Belgrade!*

Dracula asked, "Will he do it?"

A wry smile crossed the baron's lips. He called to a servant in the outer hall, "Bring the friar." He asked Dracula, "Have you heard of this priest, Capistrano?"

As Dracula only shrugged, Hunyadi explained. Capistrano was old. Ancient. One foot—and perhaps his mind—already in the next world. Some called him a saint. Others said he was simply mad. At seventy, he still served his Church. As an Inquisitor. Rooting out heretics. Holding court. Passing the death sentence. Without particular rancor. Or hesitation. He served "the Cause": the pope, the Church, God.

Capistrano was the pope's first reply to Hunyadi's call for Holy War. The friar had been ordered to preach crusade throughout eastern Europe.

As Capistrano entered the room, Dracula understood Hunyadi's wry smile. The friar's face was clear and ruddy. But it was also etched with the deep lines of God-knew-how-many vigils and far-flung quests. The flesh hung on his skeletal face above a body bent like a long-withering branch. His brown eyes seemed plain enough, except that they were lost somewhere on the wall over Hunyadi's shoulder. He ignored Hunyadi's invitation to sit.

"Father," Hunyadi asked, "how many men have you brought me?"

Capistrano's voice was as distracted as his eyes. As though softly from a distance, he answered, "It is not I who brings them, but God." Yet he followed promptly, "Five thousand. And more to come. Many more."

Dracula smiled. "You seem sure, father."

The brown eyes met the green. Met them as though to challenge the mocking smile. And Dracula flinched. What was it in those old eyes? Saintliness? Or evil? The blind evil of a mass-executioner Inquisitor.

But just as quickly as he had appeared, Capistrano left the room. Left without so much as a nod. As though suddenly called by another voice.

Hunyadi noted, "These 'crusaders' he finds are peasants. Nothing more."

Dracula noted in turn, "But five thousand. And more to come. Willing to stand against the Turk. After Constantinople."

He gave a nod; he was impressed. He told Hunyadi, "We should have a bit of time yet."

The baron agreed. Months. Months before the invasion. Which was good. Time to prepare. But was also bad. Because Mohammed, too, would declare Holy War. He would consume the time gathering troops. A *large* army.

And Hunyadi ruminated, "This 'Conqueror' is driven by single purpose. Witness what he did with his own Grand Vizier."

Dracula knew. The story had carried on the wind. Only days after taking Constantinople, Chalil Pasha was beheaded. Accused of treason. By the sultan himself. Accused of having taken the Byzantines' gold to use his influence with the sultan on their behalf.

Yet Hunyadi added hopefully. "In Belgrade I will have fifteen thousand men of my own. And I expect my king to join me. And maybe the kings of the west—when the pope calls the full crusade."

Belgrade would be packed with troops. Plus Capistrano's men—insignificant as those mere peasants would surely prove.

Dracula could see it, see Hunyadi's vision. A grand scheme. Indeed. Belgrade would be only the beginning.

But the vision also gave Dracula pause. "I will need your word. Witnessed. If—"

Hunyadi knew. "If the Danestis remain loyal to me, no harm will come to you. You will leave my land freely. You will have done me a service."

"Then when can I march?"

"When you have men. I have none to spare. You will have to hire your own."

So, Dracula knew, Hunyadi knew that he had some gold. Not much. What he had left with Stephen for safe keeping. Spoils from Crasna.

Hunyadi offered, "But my agents can help you find good soldiers."

Dracula gave a nod. A half-nod.

The baron rose. The audience was ended. As Dracula rose he noted Hunyadi's face...lines, new lines, to go with the old wrinkles and old scars. He wondered how many had been inscribed on his own account—in the baron's schemes about him.

At the door Hunyadi paused. "There is something I would say...about your father and brother. I had nothing to do with the way your brother died. He deserved better. Truly. He was a soldier. A good one. What was done was done by your own people. Boyars. As for your father...Only one of us could live."

He made his point even clearer: "I am not asking forgiveness. I just wanted you to know the truth."

Then his voice softened. "Your wife is pregnant. If you wish she can stay here. Transylvania has gotten rugged lately. Thieves. Highwaymen. They know my hands are full preparing for the Turk. They swarm. In large bands."

Even in the great baron's land, when brigands sniffed war...

"I will ask my wife," Dracula said. "At a time like this—" He patted his belly. "—the choice is hers." And, as they made to leave again, it was he who paused in seeming gratitude: "I thank you for the offer."

They parted. Dracula found Wilk, as ever, waiting. As they crossed the courtyard, knowing they were watched even by bare walls, they kept up their smiles. It was not difficult. Wilk, like Dracula, indeed found the prospect of Transylvania intriguing. He, too, appreciated the implications.

Dracula told him further, "He wants Prasha to stay here. He *offered* it."

Wilk laughed. By then, he knew his lord and friend. Dracula would never leave a hostage—let alone one so cherished—as he himself had once been left in the Turk's hands.

Even now Dracula muttered, "That is the second time he has offered to keep Prasha. I hope he really doesn't think I'm that stupid." But he reconsidered. "Or perhaps I should hope that he does think me stupid."

He continued, "And he wants me to use his agents to hire men. With *my* gold."

Wilk smirked at the thought. Hunyadi's agents would only hire men loyal to Hunyadi.

Wilk assured Dracula, "I will get you men."

Dracula cautioned, "He will insist that his agents go with you. So you will—"

"Aye. I'll have to be fast. I will. I'll have our men before they know it."

"You know what kind of men I want."

Wilk gave a nod. "Men who have seen blood. Their *own* blood."

As he and his lord Dracula had already seen their own blood.

11

BELGRADE. The sultan had been patient with his invasion. Patient in planning; it was July 1456 when his troops finally converged on Belgrade. And patient in the execution; it was the twentieth day of the siege when his artillery—*three hundred guns*—roared in a massed volley to finally obliterate a single target.

On the walls of Belgrade's fortress, Janos Hunyadi barely flinched; the fortress was not the guns' target. The concentrated fire destroyed the last of the city's outermost defense, a wall beyond the fortress. It had taken twenty days. But the wall was gone—along with the last of its garrison.

Matthias Hunyadi came to his father's side and peered from between the parapets. "They'll turn the guns on us now."

But Hunyadi shook his head. "If they come any closer they'll be in range of our own guns." He silently thanked God again for the Saxon merchants and their generous loan. Belgrade had a few cannon of respectable size, enough to keep the Turkish guns at bay.

Yet Mohammed was undaunted. He had come to Belgrade with sixty thousand troops and had hardly expended any; he had let his guns do the first work. The only thing between his troops and the fortress now was a broad, dry moat. And his army was like a machine. The same machine that had conquered Constantinople.

The invaders were deployed now in three lines, *en echelon.* The first, eye-to-eye with the fortress, bristled with the artillery, the janissaries, and a swarm of baji-bazouks. Twenty thousand men. With twenty thousand more each in the second and third lines, behind which Mohammed himself, *Fatih,* was perched at a raised, sprawling command pavilion.

At his signal, the first line lunged with the battle-cry of Islam: *Allahu akbar!* God is great! The janissaries led the way behind wooden mantelets, a moving wall spewing arrows, crossbow bolts, and the smoke and fire of arquebuses.

Hunyadi was content to let the fortress answer in kind, until the first of the mantelets parted to spring a horde of bazouks. They hauled timber, whole swaths of forest.

Hunyadi promptly told Matthias, "Bring anything that burns. *Anything.*"

In short order Matthias had lines of men stretched from the walls down to the bowels of the fortress, the storerooms. They began passing whatever they found, even as Mohammed's plan began to unfold. *Fatih,* the Conqueror, had breached the walls of Constantinople. He could fill Belgrade's moat. Fill it to ground level with timber, drop ramps across the wood, and roll siege towers right up to the walls. At the sight of such a feat, the defenders might even panic. They might abandon the walls before the towers were even needed.

The first timbers went into the moat. Hunyadi seemed content to watch. He would use the next minutes as a lull, simply leaning on the battlements, letting the stone help support the weight of his armor. He was tired. More so than the younger knights around him. *Twenty days.* But as the timber began creeping across the moat he straightened to guide the fire of his cannons.

From the courtyard behind him, the larger guns lobbed shot into the farther of the charging Osmanli lines. From the walls themselves, the smaller guns muzzled down to rake the moat point-blank with canister and chain. For each log dropped, it seemed, a bazouk fell. But Mohammed, the Conqueror, had as many bazouks as he had logs. And he had stripped the land of all the logs he needed to make his scheme work.

Hunyadi did not need to give orders. After twenty days, his men knew the regimen. They filled every gap in the battlements, with a second line and a third waiting as though in queue behind the first—living men, as it were, waiting to take the place of corpses.

The defenders fired as fast as they could, but the timbers fell almost as fast, the janissaries ever on point, at once returning fire and sidestepping the wood gangs. When a bazouk—or even one of their own brethren—fell, they kicked the corpse in with the wood. The moat *would* be filled.

Hunyadi wondered. How long could it keep up? On either side? His own body, truly, was moving on its own. A creature of habit. The habit of war. Sound a drum, give the cry, and it was up and into its dance, barking orders, directing fire...Joints throbbed, muscles burned, sweat poured. But arms and legs kept pumping. And so it was with his men. And the Osmanli Turks. Brave men, all. But...*Twenty days.* What held them up?

The first of the timbers hit the wall, hit with a crash that shook the stone even to the height of the battlements. Already the first ramps had been dropped across the timbers. Scaling hooks clawed at the parapets but were pried loose. The first siege tower lumbered to the walls. A gangway was thrust from it to the battlements but was staved off, plunging a line of janissaries down into the moat. But a second tower approached, a third...

For a moment, an eerie moment, nothing touched the walls. Not even an arrow or bolt. It seemed like the air itself was snatching a breath. Then all hell broke loose. Everything hit the walls, all at once. Hooks, gangways...Soon there was ample space for living defenders to replace the dead.

A janissary sprung over the parapet right in front of Hunyadi. It was the janissary technique: stop just below the wall; brace; swing over. And pray. A final prayer. Because, even with the surprise, the first over the wall almost always found paradise—as the first was now skewered on Hunyadi's own broadsword. But he served his purpose; he bought a moment for the men behind him. And they came fast, up and over. All along the wall they rose like a flood.

But the men around Hunyadi closed like a dam. They cleared the space around him and pushed the invaders from the walls. Even so, the janissary wave had filled the moat and was still rising on the battlements. And the Turks of the second line were rushing in a torrent behind it.

Fighting back to his father's side, Matthias christened his sword—the blood of his first "kill." But no haughty joy or boasts rang from his lips. He had seen death, had invoked it now with his own arm. The shock was still with him. He merely pointed with his bloody blade to where the stores were still being hauled up to the walls.

As his father gave a sharp nod of approval, Matthias urged further, "Call the reserves!"

The reserves. *Crusaders.* Men who had answered the call of the old friar, Capistrano. Hungarians, Poles, Germans, Bohemians, Serbs, Greeks…"Crusaders." But hardly soldiers. Commoners. Men who had lived in constant fear of Turkish invasion. They had nowhere to run. So better, they had thought, to get the inevitable—whatever it was—over with.

Their "commander-in-chief" was Capistrano himself, their "captains," lesser friars. Their "field officers" were whoever seemed qualified—usually the only man in each bunch who owned a sword. In the end, fifteen thousand had answered Capistrano's call.

But Hunyadi shook his head. No reserves. Not yet. Instead he told Matthias, "Pass the order. Let the Turks come to us. Let them get into the courtyard. You hold them there."

Matthias saw his father's purpose. The order was passed: Matthias formed a garrison in the courtyard; the knights on the battlements let the invaders come on, let them make a quick foothold on the walls and spill into the courtyard below. The Turks were ecstatic. Their cry swelled: *Allahu akbar!*

They could *feel* Belgrade teetering under their onslaught. The second wave was already at the moat, pushing at the janissaries' backs.

Hunyadi's next order was terse: "Wood burns!"

He showed what he meant by tossing a keg of oil into the moat. His men followed in kind, tossing everything that had been hauled from below. And Matthias had been thorough. He had brought everything that burned: tar, pitch, sulfur, cloth…even slabs of bacon.

All of it went into the moat with torches.

And the invaders, too, had been thorough. Too much so now for their own good. They had completely filled the moat and even smoothed the gaps with packed brush. Tons of willing fuel. The fire gorged itself and spread. The blaze dried the flood of invaders. Outside the walls, the heat itself drove them back to their lines. Inside, those in the courtyard were trapped. Alone. With arrows and bolts raining on their heads and armored knights wading into their midst, broad-swords drawn.

The last of the battle took mere minutes. The blaze in the moat lasted hours—through the day and into the night. With Hunyadi standing a vigil by its light. Watching. Praying. Hoping to see Mohammed finally packing to leave, to aban-don the siege. But the Turkish camp was only quiet. Resting.

As the next dawn approached, Hunyadi took what comfort he could. The invaders were still not stirring. So on that day, at least, there would be no fight-ing. Both sides were exhausted.

Before finally leaving the walls, Hunyadi called his son. There was work for the crusaders. Work suited to their station. Bury the dead. Then march out beyond the fortress to where the outer wall had been. Build a new wall of the rub-ble. Dig in. Dig deep. Stay put. The time would come soon enough when each would serve the cause. As battle-fodder. If they survived the next barrage of the Turkish guns, they could at least hamper the next assault. It was sad, Hunyadi thought. But there were not enough real soldiers left.

Soon the crusaders were streaming along Belgrade's streets, singing as they passed through the fortress, a hymn in Latin—the only echo of a common lan-guage among their motley tongues. Their chorus was ragged, gruff. As usual with such an "army," aside from the few with swords, only a few more had bows. The rest had only scythes and clubs.

And yet, when the hymn ended, laughing and banter carried over their ranks. Truly they believed: God was with them—as their "commander," Capistrano, had assured them. Else how could their soldiers have won the previous day's great victory?

As they passed through the fortress, Hunyadi found Capistrano. With his son, Matthias, as his witness, the baron repeated the order: *Dig in. Stay put.*

But watching the friar he had to wonder again: Was he really a living saint or just a madman?

Capistrano's eyes, as usual, were lost somewhere in the distance. Yet he nod-ded and said that he understood. He even repeated the order and promptly passed it to his "officers." He left the wall and blessed his men as they passed. They broke into another hymn. He promptly turned and walked counter to their line—back into the city—as though he had nothing more to do with the whole affair. But all along the line the hymn rose stronger as he passed.

It was only when he was gone that Hunyadi remembered the sun; it was only morning and he was baking in his armor. He left Matthias with a missive about the crusaders: "See to it that they stay put." Then he retreated to his quarters, a room deep in the fortress. It had been chosen specially—windowless, so as to shield it from the siege. It was cool. His servants had made it something of an oasis from the battle: candlelight...soft bed...

They helped him out of his armor and sponged his wounds. They brought a tub and helped him bathe. They dressed the wounds and wrapped him in a sheet. They set a table and brought breakfast. With bacon.

He gagged at the sight of it. He could smell the fire in the moat again. Smell it. Bacon and men frying together. He had the meal taken away. He could only drink some water. He lay on the bed and had the servants extinguish the candles as they left.

When the door closed the room was black. Cold now, it seemed. Dank. His thin sheet was hardly a cover. He was coated with sweat and yet shivering. He could still smell the bacon—and, somehow, the other, putrid smell that it brought with it. His head throbbed. His stomach churned. Spittle rose and fell in his throat.

Thoughts washed him like a wave: *What kind of a world was this? Useless. Madness. Was there really a God in heaven? Eternity was too long—dead or alive.*

But such thoughts, he knew, sprang from fatigue. He focused on his own breath, listened to it flow slower and slower, and he spoke silently to God and his patron saints. This—Belgrade—was just another trial. And what was a Christian knight's purpose if not to endure? Endure. Never be beaten. He took comfort in that. He would rest. Tomorrow was the Turk. Again.

He could almost see the army he had hoped for, called for. A crusade. A real crusade: all of Hungary, the western kings...Surely Mohammed had not scrimped for this campaign. He had declared *Jihad!*, Holy War. He had culled his sixty thousand troops from twice as many recruits. More, he had hired a contingent of the dreaded Mongols. And, to forge his huge artillery brigade, he had melted down the bells of Constantinople's captured churches.

Even now, lying in Belgrade in the dark, Hunyadi cursed. Crusade? No one had marched—except for the crazy friar and his peasants. The only soldiers in Belgrade were Hunyadi's own. Fifteen thousand. Or so they had been—twenty days before. The Hungarian king had not even *sent* any men, let alone ridden himself. At word of the Turks' marching, he had fled to Austria. By back roads. With him went the final hope of any crusade.

Hunyadi tossed on his bed. He. Matthias. And Capistrano. Alone. At first it seemed that God Himself might intervene. He sent a plague to ravage the Turkish camp. But Mohammed replaced his sick soldiers and settled in for the siege. With his three hundred guns.

Hunyadi could still hear them as though on the siege's first day. The Osmanli had learned at Constantinople, learned from their mercenary gunners. And they had learned more since. They put their artillery in the first line, right up front, and pounded away. Massed volley. Staggered volley. First bombards then smaller guns; smaller guns then bombards. For days on end. Pounding...pounding...

Hunyadi awoke with a start. He was actually hearing pounding. Not from cannon but from a fist on the door. A voice called. Hunyadi answered and heard the news: A skirmish was brewing. The crusaders were leaving the line and mixing it up with the Turks. It was spreading and no words could bring them back.

Hunyadi was beyond swearing. As he dressed, his hand moved in fits—tugging buckles, snapping belts...When he pulled on his boots, he stood and stamped the floor. Hard. He strode out to the battlements. He glared at Matthias. He wanted to hear no excuses. He called for Capistrano.

Waiting for the priest, he stared from the battlements at the antics on the field. As Matthias explained, the crusaders had at first followed orders, manning the old outer defense and rebuilding the wall from rubble. They even sang their hymns as they worked. But then a few noticed some Turks peeking from across the field. The crusaders hurled some insults. The Turks answered in kind, with a few gestures for good measure. Threats flew, then rocks, arrows...

A few crusaders—four or five at most—left the wall to get a better shot. A few of the Turks met the challenge. From the citadel, Matthias himself called to bring the crusaders back. They ignored him. A few more men from both sides trickled onto the field. They inched closer. Matthias had sent officers to stop the crusaders. But again the crusaders had ignored him.

Now, even as Hunyadi watched, scores of crusaders and Turks grappled between the lines. Despite himself, even Hunyadi had to chuckle at the sight. But, when Capistrano arrived, his mirth disappeared. He lectured the friar quietly but firmly about the need for discipline. Capistrano nodded profusely. And yet, as always, his eyes were off in the clouds.

Propped by a staff, the friar made a slow walk from the fortress onto the field. As his crusaders saw him they cheered. They flocked around him like children to escort him to their line. There, Hunyadi saw, the friar's bent frame straightened. His finger rose and shook. He was obviously chiding.

History itself—the accounts of both sides—witnessed what happened next.

What escaped the record were the specific words used by Capistrano. He apparently did call the men back and begin scolding them. But somewhere in the scolding he altered course. He spoke of the Cause, the Holy Cause. He extolled it. He harangued. The crusaders were inflamed. They began pointing to the enemy just across the field. Their own fingers, as it were, began to lead them on. They drifted onto the field. Capistrano—was it to keep from losing his audience?—drifted along with them.

Or perhaps the crusaders simply misunderstood the priest's intentions. After all, like the men at the biblical Babel, they did speak different languages. Perhaps they simply misread the friar's gestures.

The insults, rocks, and arrows flew again. Capistrano went on preaching. Hunyadi himself called him back. In vain. Before the call could reach the field, some Turks rushed from their line. The crusaders thought that Capistrano himself was threatened. Their whole line surged. Toward the priest. Like a mob. The mob chased the few Turks right back to the end of their line, where it found itself, as it were, with a snake by the tail.

Hunyadi was struck. *Mohammed's first line!* Even as he watched, the crusaders moved along the line, their mob of massed men matched to the Turk's pitiful single file. The Turks had no choice but to scatter in their path, to beat a retreat to their second line.

Hunyadi did not wait. He rushed every man he could out to the front. *Mohammed's first line!* Cannon! Powder! Shot! *Bombards!*

Even the peasant crusaders had sense enough to turn the guns on the enemy, while the first of Hunyadi's soldiers reached them and began directing fire. And Hunyadi was coming fast with the rest of the army.

At the Turkish third line, Mohammed had indeed been exhausted from the previous day's battle. He had to be roused from sleep. His officers were shamefaced. It had all happened so fast. They had not thought it would get that far.

The sultan rushed from his pavilion just in time to see the guns turning. *His guns!* His order was terse: Get them back!

But his men were exhausted. Drained. And now they were afraid as well. It had gone too far. They were being bombed...by their own guns...

As the Christians were finding strength in the sudden turn of events, the Turks' own juices were being sapped. They balked. Mohammed threatened. He had to lead the third line personally to push the second to attack.

It was a melee. A riot. The sultan pushed his men on. His stare, they knew, was making a list, etching faces in his mind—for future punishment. More than charging the enemy, they were fleeing their master's anger.

The sides hit. The lines shattered at the impact. They broke into small bands and broke again. Piece by piece the armies came apart. Even the disciplined janissaries, even the iron-willed Mongols—Mohammed's special contingent—came apart. In the swirling fray, the Mongol commander was killed, and Mohammed himself was wounded fighting hand-to-hand.

The Turkish chroniclers described it: "...even the dead climbed out of the breaches in the wall, swarmed out of the fortress and fell upon the army of Islam."

It must have seemed so.

Christian accounts would say that God had intervened, that He Himself had inspired the attack. They said, too, that leaden bolts had rained on the enemy—from Capistrano's eyes.

The Osmanli welcomed nightfall. Under its cover they fled. It was only after the hooves and feet faded into the black that Hunyadi lowered his sword. For a moment he pursued the enemy. But only in his mind. Never had his body felt so spent.

With the help of his men, he walked back to the fortress, indifferent even to the impassioned cheer that rose wherever he passed. In the distance, there were other cheers, as Capistrano, too, finally quit the field.

In his room, as his armor was peeled away, Hunyadi shivered slightly at a familiar sensation—a battle's sweat finally running cold. He waited for the chill to pass. But it lingered. Then again, he thought, it had been a long battle.

He knelt. He bowed his head and thanked God. Still in the grip of the chill, he took to his bed.

It would be another three months before his king mustered the courage to even set foot in Belgrade.

12

AUGUST 1456. When the news arrived, Dracula was at his business. As Hunyadi had warned, Transylvania was infested with thieves, the more so as the Turkish war had dragged on.

Dracula had cleared many of them from the roads. He had struck fast and hard, hoping to convince the survivors to run. They did not. They were brazen. They preyed on the roads and villages at whim, at night or in broad daylight. The few brave constables who tried to stop them were killed in mocking ways. Near rituals of cruelty. And the same it was for any citizens' vigilant groups who rose in their own defense.

So now Dracula was focused. He had devised a scheme. He chose the most notorious band of brigands in the most conspicuous spot. He baited them. He loaded wagons with goods and had them almost parade through the area. The

merchants who manned them bragged in taverns about both the goods and profits. They had only a few guards.

They were on the road again, just ambling through a forest in the afternoon
sun, when the brigands converged. They came as the rabble they really were, on
horse and foot from up and down the road and both sides of the woods. The bandits were stunned at first when the "merchants" joined the guards with sword and
bow, without so much as a moment's hesitation. Even as the brigands halted in
surprise, their ranks were already being thinned with cool precision by arrows and
bolts.

Dracula closed the trap from behind much as the bandits had closed their
own, from up and down the road and both sides of the woods. He did not bother
to close but just stood off. The brigands were caught front and rear in a cross-fire.
They did not dare try to break the ring. Men-at-arms were not their usual victims. And the men-at-arms facing them now were a bit different than most.
Strays. Mongrels. Curs who had been kicked but still showed teeth. These were
the men whom Wilk had found for Dracula.

For a time the brigands tried to return fire. But those who raised bows, it
seemed, were likely to draw two, three, even four arrows as warning to the rest.

Finally, one of their mounted number came forward under a shield. He was a
stout man, bearded, neither too young nor old. He was somewhat wild-eyed—
not madness, but a fury. He shouted: "Quarter! Quarter!"

He did not shout the word in the tone of its usual sense: a plea for mercy. He
was asking for respite, more of a truce.

Dracula gave it, raising a hand to cease fire. But the hand quickly flicked to the
ground and the bandit leader understood: *Dismount. Drop weapons.* He hesitated,
but not for long. What choice did he have? So he led his men in obeying Dracula's order. Still, he hardly showed fear. He wondered with some amusement
who this young nobleman was with the black, dragon-emblazoned doublet. With
a flamboyant bow and a grin, he addressed Dracula with an exaggerated, "My
lord." He made to go on, "You—"

Dracula trampled his words. "You wanted what was in the wagons. Take it."

The brigand showed his defiance by dragging his steps to the wagons and only
tugging at a parcel of cargo so that it fell to the ground. It was a cloth-wrapped
bundle. He tore the cloth and froze. Rope. Coarse rope. His wild eyes flashed on
Dracula with the hatred of an animal. An animal trapped.

"The wagons are full of it," Dracula said. "Enough to tie your men hand and
foot. Be about it. Fast."

In the words, the brigand seemed to see a reprieve. *Tie hands and feet.* Just tie. Tether. Enough rope on the feet to walk. To be led away. When he had first seen the rope he had thought of something quite different. And so, he thought, this pompous young ass of a lord was not as brazen—or bold—as he seemed. Perhaps, in fact, he could be challenged, frightened off.

But, for Dracula's taste, the man had hesitated too long. He threw a nod to Wilk. A crossbow appeared. A tiny one—one Wilk had used before. A bolt flew. One of the lesser thieves dropped. An example.

Whatever challenge had been rising in the brigand leader's throat died right there. He choked on it in rage. But, rage or no, he had his men tie one another, tightly, as Dracula's men watched.

As the leader himself bound the last of his men, Dracula's men also bound him and brought him forward.

Dracula said, "Well, 'My lord'…Pick your tree."

The man blanched. It was to be *hanging* after all. He snarled, "You would do well to think!"

"Truly," Dracula toyed. "Think of what?"

"Do you think we are alone?"

"Of course not. We are surrounded. By *my* men."

"That's not what I mean, my lord. Think of tomorrow. And the next day and the next. We thieves are a brotherhood. With a long memory. There's more to us than what you see here. Much more."

"I see," Dracula said. He made as if to consider. "What you are saying is that you are part of a…*society*. Like…like an order of knights, perhaps."

"Aye, my lord. Now you have it. And we own this road. All roads. And—"

"And I should deal with you gingerly. Lest I incur the wrath of your whole 'fraternity.'"

The brigand grinned. Now this pompous lord understood.

Dracula continued, "I suppose then that I should 'buy' this road from you. I suppose I could, aye?"

"Other lords have done so. Many lords."

Buy the road. Pay tribute to the thieves for their peace.

"Then I will," Dracula said. "And I will put the money in your own hand myself. I suppose this road is worth…"

He went into his purse and drew a coin. The smallest copper coin.

The brigand's mouth twisted at the mockery.

Dracula pronounced, "Bring me his hand."

It took a solid moment for the brigand to understand. By then, when he tried to bolt, he was in the firm hold of Dracula's men.

As one drew a saber, Wilk objected, "Wait!" He told Dracula, "Let me. I have just the thing, really."

He went to his horse and returned with a sword. A short sword. With a flat, very heavy, razor-sharp blade. Its handle was contoured, molded to the grip of individual fingers.

To Dracula's puzzled look, Wilk explained, "I had it made special."

"A waste of money," Dracula noted. "Too short for combat."

"Aye," Wilk said. "But not for cleaving meat."

All of the thieves stirred as he set hand firmly to handle and approached their leader, who himself raged and bucked to pull free of the men holding him.

"Let him go," Wilk said.

The man was freed. He ran—only to be tripped by Wilk. The short sword found the brigand's hand, touched the wrist, just touched it to hold it. Then Wilk pushed the blade—only pushed, not swung. The day exploded in a shriek that hid the crunch of wrenched bone.

Even as the brigand writhed and screamed, Wilk stooped, took the severed hand, and brought it to Dracula, who placed the coin inside and closed the fingers—though he did have to break some to keep them shut. He returned the hand to its owner. Tossed it to him. And still he was not done, was not satisfied.

"It was you," he told the brigand—told all of them—"who *mutilated* this province. Constables. Villagers. Good men all. You scum. As you gave, so now receive."

He gave Wilk a nod, and Wilk did according to the words. Not death. He raised the sword this time and hacked the bandit leader's shoulder. Tore it half away—but only half away.

The brigand was beyond screaming now. He was alive and aware, but his only movement was trembling. He dared not even look at his wound or at the soft warmth spreading around him: his blood.

There was moaning among the thieves now. A few vomited—fear and nausea mixed.

"Aye," Dracula told them. "But it was different, eh, when you were doing the carving?"

He was drawing his own sword when he was caught by a faint sound: hoof-beats. Distant but coming fast. With a shout.

Everyone turned to the flying wedge of riders: more of Dracula's men. As they galloped right to his feet, the lead rider pulled rein and swung from the saddle. He was grinning broadly as he gave Dracula a packet, a dispatch.

Dracula, too, grinned as he read. He commented as he passed the letter to Wilk, "We are indeed blessed."

Blessed by the news. Mohammed humbled, licking his wounds in Constantinople. And Janos Hunyadi dead.

Dead, it seemed, from a plague. A plague that had slithered into him from the rotting corpses of Belgrade. It took him in a shiver and left him in a fever. The great warrior had died in bed.

Something like it would also take the old friar, Capistrano, a few months later.

And Dracula read on. No one had counted the bodies at Belgrade, but it was said that a full third fell on both sides. More...Mohammed had lost his entire camp. All of his guns—captured or destroyed.

Dracula bellowed to the thieves, "Thank your stars! Go to the wagons and pick your ropes then pick your trees!"

There was no time now to repay their crimes as he had intended: mutilation and torture. They were, in a sense, lucky; they would all be hanged quickly.

Still, as Dracula's intention sunk in, a few tried to cheat even that death. They bolted, hoping for the lightning strike of the sword. Rather that than the agony of the rope. They regretted it. The swords that struck only left them, more or less, in the same mutilated state as their leader.

The lesson learned, the rest made a doleful procession to the wagons.

As they did, Dracula told Wilk his intentions in a word: "Wallachia."

There was nothing now between him and the throne. No Hunyadi to hold him back. No Turk to save the Danestis and their voevode, Vladislav.

"We'll finish here," Dracula said, "gather the men, and ride."

He could hit Wallachia within days. And there were other prospects, too. The Wallachian boyars knew well of his Transylvanian captainship. Knew he was with Hungary. As Vladislav was not. And Hungary had won at Belgrade. So the boyars would be with Dracula. At least—as always with the boyars—for now.

Even with these possibilities running through his mind, Dracula kept an eye on the thieves at the wagons. Many had soiled their breeches in fear and were weeping. Of those, one in particular struck him. A boy. How old could he be? Dracula approached and asked.

The answer came between sobs: twelve.

"How did you fall in with this...scum?"

The boy explained, "They took me in. I have no..." He shook his head: no family, no one.

Dracula took him aside. As he untied the boy's bonds, he said, "You know where their lair is."

The thieves' den. Hidden somewhere. To protect their loot. Money. Which Dracula would now use to his new purpose: more troops.

The boy nodded.

"And you will take me."

"Yes, lord. But will you..."

"No," Dracula said. "I will not kill you. In fact..."

He gave the boy a few silver coins. Not a fortune. But a start.

Then the green eyes held the boy's and Dracula spoke slowly: "Never break the law again."

He sent the boy to clean and compose himself. He commanded his men, "Hang them all." He pointed to the brigand leader lying in his oozing blood and still faintly breathing. "Except him."

And so the one was left on the road, with Dracula's tribute—the single copper coin—locked surely in his grip.

The rest of the thieves were hanged. Even the corpses sprouting arrows. Even the wounded without hands and arms. Hanged and left to hang as Dracula quickly rode on.

PRINCE

1

AUGUST 1456. TIRGOVISTE. *Tenui nec dimittam.* "I have attained it and will not let go."

So, in a breath, in the ancient Latin words, did Dracula declare to himself, Wilk, and Eupraxia—and the infant son she held—as they stood in his vacant court. He had attained it; he was voevode. For the second time. And this time he would not let go.

Indeed it seemed that heaven itself was celebrating Dracula's ascent. A great portent was seen in the sky: a comet. With a tail, it was said, that lit half the canopy of the night. Later centuries would name the comet: Halley's Comet. To the rest of Dracula's world, it was taken as an ill omen, a portent of great cataclysm. But to him it was surely a sign that heaven was with him. He would later inscribe its image on his first official coinage.

There was little in the foreseeable future to contradict his optimism. His descent from Transylvania had been as he had predicted: fortuitous. He had crossed the border with only his small band of men. But they were quickly joined by a large army of partisans.

Among them were many boyars. Of course. He was, after all, the ally of Hungary, the victor in the latest Turkish war. His opponent, the Danesti voevode, Vladislav, had forsaken his Hungarian alliance. So there was clearly more profit in the boyars supporting Dracula. At least for the time being.

Peasants, too, joined him, as though they had suddenly found deep affections for the Dracula clan—for this new prince of the line, whose black, dragon-emblazoned uniform recalled the days of his father, Vlad Dracul, himself. But the peasants, too, were just opportunistic, joining the sure victor to gain future favor.

Vladislav had ridden out to meet Dracula. The battle had been brief. Vladislav had been run down and killed in headlong flight.

"Maybe now," Prasha said, "we can have peace. Finally."

As Dracula turned to her, it was hard to say if she were cradling their son— Vlad, the Third—or if she herself were cradled in the infant. Her cheek was pressed as one with the tiny, sleeping bundle.

Dracula said gently, "Oh, love, how I wish it could be so." And, God, he thought, how he did wish it were so…if only for her sake alone. Even now, as he spoke, she seemed pained—wounded—by his very words: no peace. The birth of their son had left her wan, drained of color as well as strength. It also left her, as it often did new mothers, with the melancholia. Hers was worse because she had suffered from it before, and made worse still by the tensions of the past weeks, the war over the throne.

The doctors explained it as best they could: the Black Bile. The ill humor was spawned by the nerves and fear. It filled her system with dark fluids, which in turn darkened her thoughts. There was no quick cure for it. It would simply have to run its course. Its very slow course. But it would pass. Hopefully. A long spate of peace, Dracula knew, would certainly help the recovery.

But on the matter of peace he was compelled to speak frankly. "This is just the beginning, love. We have a long way to go to real peace."

He turned to Wilk for support.

"It's true, lady," Wilk said. He gestured to a pile of documents on the table near the throne. "Everyone wants something of the voevode. Everyone. Especially of a new voevode."

Dracula recited a list: "Hungary. The Turk. The Church. The boyars. They all have demands. And my cousin, Stephen. He needs help. And so many more."

Prasha blushed, as though a tinge of shame had been added to her melancholy. She spoke almost to herself. "Of course. Just the beginning. What else could it be, really? I was just—"

Dracula interrupted to console, "You were just thinking like a new mother. With hope. Great hope."

"I suppose," Prasha said. "Perhaps so."

Dracula assured her, "That's all it was, love. Perfectly natural. You want peace. For our son. For us. I want the same thing. And we will have it. In time. But we will have to work for it, love. And we will. Together."

As she managed a smile, he continued, ever gently, "Do you know what the Turk calls us, calls Wallachia? A 'piss-land.' Bumpkins. Wild. And, sadly, how can we argue? Look at us. But...I am going to change all that. Set things right. Civilize. Tame. Bring order."

He indicated the documents. "And I don't have much time. I am the shepherd. Wallachia is the flock. And the flock is plagued by wolves, inside and out. So I am going to need all the help I can get. High-born. Low-born. It makes no difference to me. I need everyone I can trust. But most of all, love, I need you."

She drew a breath that quivered slightly. "Then I'd better find strength, love."

"You will. But not in a day. You need rest."

He took her in his arms, wrapping their son in the same embrace. He walked her slowly to the door, still consoling, "It won't be all toil and trouble. We are going to rebuild this land. And I am going to start with the Church. Endowments. Monasteries and chapels. God's own work. And I want you to assist. So that what is done will be done in both our names: prince and princess. Will you do that for me, love? When you are ready?"

Her smile was a bit stronger. "I will."

"Aye," he assured her. "You will."

At the door he called a maidservant to walk with her. As she left he wore the look of a worried husband. But only for a moment. It quickly gave way to the look of a worried voevode, a new prince with much business at hand. He looked to the pile of documents. "Set the appeals and petitions aside."

They were the mundane, day-to-day legal business of the court.

"Aye," Wilk agreed. "They're just too many for one man alone. Let your judges and ministers hear them."

But Dracula corrected, "No. Just set them aside for now. I am going to hear them myself. Each and every one. In open court. This court. At least until Wallachia—judges and ministers included—comes to know me. And it better come to know me soon."

Wilk culled the documents. With the legal matters held, there were only four left: three letters and a map. One of the letters, Dracula already knew. It was from Stephen. That, too, he set aside. The remaining two were bound by ornate seals, the one of the king of Hungary, and the other of the sultan, Mohammed.

Before breaking the seals, Wilk tapped the king's letter. "You should know...With this one comes news. It seems that the king is full of himself. He has a new feud. With Janos Hunyadi's sons."

As Hunyadi himself had predicted—had wished and worked for all his life—his sons had indeed become men to be reckoned with. Rich. Powerful. And feared—especially by the king who had abandoned their father at Belgrade.

"This king," Dracula lamented, "lets Janos Hunyadi win his war. Then when the bastard's dead he feuds with his sons—when he should be staying at the Turk." He shook his head and moved on. "So what do they want, this king and the great 'Conqueror'?"

Wilk opened the letters and set them side by side. "To begin with, both want—*demand*—your loyalty. On oath. In public. Witnessed by their ambassadors."

"Done," Dracula said.

"But—?"

"But how can I swear to both? Because neither wants war right now. Both have wounds to lick from Belgrade. And the king has his new dalliance, his feud. Yes, they'll know that I've sworn to both. But neither will do anything about it. Not yet. So I'll give them their oaths. Bide time. What else do they want?"

"Well, the king is rather blunt. He wants only one other thing. *Only* one: concessions for his merchants, the Saxons."

"They already have most of our trade."

"They want it all. Monopoly."

Dracula echoed, "*Only* one other thing."

It was a not-so-subtle squeeze. What the king and his Saxons wanted, Wallachia's merchants also wanted. The king and the Saxons knew it, just as they also knew that Wallachia's merchants hated them. For good reason. In Wallachia, the Saxons already had several concessions—the voevodes' way of appeasing the king. But Hungary gave no such concessions to the Wallachians. It gave lip-service to the idea of free trade. But it often and without warning drove the Wallachian merchants from Hungary—even by the bloody sword.

And Dracula thought aloud to the heart of the matter. "What does a cannon cost—even a single, small gun? And powder? And shot? Where's a prince to find the money? Where do the king and sultan find it?"

As well as any, he understood: More than ever before, the gristle of war was money. And merchants made money for the realm. As it was, Wallachia's economy was not enough for what he had planned. He could not afford to weaken his merchants further.

Wilk posed, "But how can we refuse the king this? For this—for the Saxons—he might march."

"He might," Dracula said. "But he might not. Not if I don't refuse him outright. So I have to play Solomon. Split the baby in half."

He decreed: He would give the Saxons more concessions, more even than they already had. But no Wallachian monopoly. In exchange he would ask the king to confirm what Hungary already agreed to in principle: Wallachia's merchants could keep their foot, as it were, in Hungary's door. Further, Dracula would sweeten things for his own merchants by granting them certain exemptions from taxes and tariffs. He would give them the "seed," the money, to grow.

"But will they accept?" Wilk asked. "Either side? Only 'half the baby'?"

"They'd better," Dracula said. "Because it's fair. And it's all I have to give."

He pressed on, "And Mohammed? What does *he* want aside from my humble loyalty? Let me guess. Tribute. The same as my father paid: ten thousand gold ducats."

"Aye. Each year. Paid promptly. By you. In person. You are to come to his court—"

Dracula of course knew the Osmanli custom. "—and kiss the hem of his coat."

Literally kneel and kiss the sultan's coat.

"Aye," Wilk said. "And more. He wants janissary recruits."

"Anything else?"

Wilk shook his head. "But I'd say it's enough."

Dracula smirked. "He'll never see a Wallachian child. Not while I'm prince."

Wilk smirked in turn. "I'd like to see you kiss his coat."

"He'd better pray that I never get that close."

"But can we stall long enough?"

Dracula shrugged. "That is in the hands of God. But let's not waste the time we have."

He looked to Stephen's letter. That one, he had already read. More than once. It, too, seemed like the hand of God. Providence. Another sign. Like the great comet. Moldavia was war-torn again. Stephen saw opportunity. He was ready to leave his refuge in Hungary.

So it might be that both cousins reclaimed their thrones in the same year. Mere coincidence? Dracula thought not.

"All he needs are men," he said. "Just as we need men."

Men to hold the throne he had just won. Men to help his cousin. And men for what he had already planned for the future.

Wilk suggested, "We have the partisans."

Dracula's new-found allies. They would fight again for the voevode's favor, even if it meant in Moldavia.

"Aye," Dracula said. "For Stephen they might do. But they won't do for us. Not for the future. They blow with the wind. The *fair* wind."

When fortune shifted, so would the partisans.

Wilk brooded, "We can't afford more mercenaries."

As usual, in flight, the former voevode had taken the treasury. His death had not brought it back, only scattered it to God-knew-where. As the new voevode, Dracula had yet to collect a single tax. And even when he did it would not be enough. Not with what the Turk and Hungary—and even his own people—would extort in patronage and favors. Not enough for the army he needed.

"But," he said, "I don't think I want mercenaries either. I have something else in mind. Different men. Special men. Men who will fight for something dearer than pay. I want..." He called them by what he had already envisioned: "*Draguli.*"

Dragons. Men who would wear his name—the name of his father—with the same ardor that he wore it.

Wilk considered. "Some of the men we already have are such men. For you, they will fight without pay. Some."

"I think so, too," Dracula said. "But we need more than a handful. Can we find them?"

Wilk gave a slow nod. "Times like these—a land like this—breed such men. But we will have to train them. *Grow* these little dragons. Because they will not be soldiers. Not yet."

No, Dracula thought, they would not. Because they would have to be even more desperate than his desperate, destitute mercenaries. They would have to be...*victims.* Men waiting to be saved. And trained. And led. *Unleashed.*

And they would not even know it. Not yet.

"Find these men," Dracula said. "They will be the core of our army. The backbone. And the sooner you bring them the sooner I can send the partisans to Stephen."

Wilk offered, "When the time comes, I could lead our Moldavian contingents."

But Dracula reminded, "Wallachians are stubborn. They follow their own. Only their own. And I have one in mind. The boyar, Gales."

Wilk remembered. Gales had been one of the first to join the partisans. He was a young boyar. A lesser. He wanted to be a greater. And he seemed willing to take at least the usual risks. He had fought well against the Danestis.

Dracula took the map that he had kept with Stephen's letter. "And we'll take other steps as well."

He pointed northeast, to the very corner of Wallachia, to a fortress called Chilia. "It's like a gate on the Danube. We'll strengthen it. So it swings at our will. Protects both us and my cousin."

He pointed south, below Tirgoviste, to the fairly new city of Bucharest. That, too, he would strengthen, make a fortress in its own right.

The finger moved north-by-west to complete a triangle touching the edge of Transylvania, in the Carpathian mountains.

Wilk's brow wrinkled. "There's nothing there. It's God-forsaken."

Dracula corrected, "There's a fortress, a castle. A wreck. I want it salvaged."

"On those cliffs…It would take an army of workers."

"Aye," Dracula agreed. "Something like that."

"Where will we find them? How can we pay them?"

"I have something in mind," Dracula said.

Finally, he planted his finger south again, just inside the triangle near Bucharest, to a large lake. "There's a monastery here. On an island. Snagov. It would make a perfect fortress."

"Will the Church agree?"

Dracula left the table to take his throne. "Let's ask. The metropolitan's representative is waiting. Bring him in."

As Wilk went about it, Dracula wondered what the bishop's man would be like. He would be a priest, of course. And there were only two types of priests: the pious and the worldly. Many of the pious came from the lower classes, simple peasants and townsmen who took Holy Orders to serve God. But bishops' men were rarely like that. They were usually of the nobility, men who made religion a career. Learned. Glib. And ambitious. Doubly so: for their Church and themselves. Usually, too, they were older men, rather hardened to the task of wrangling at court.

But this one, Father Gregor, was younger, as young as the voevode himself. He was of average height and comfortably—prosperously—stout. His face was ruddy and squarish. His eyes and short hair were dark. From his neck hung a cross, a large, silver cross. A cross to show piety? Or silver to show wealth?

He gave a proper bow and with hardly a glance took the seat offered by Wilk, like one accustomed to taking a seat with a servant's mute assistance. As was also proper, he let Dracula guide the initial exchange of pleasantries, only then setting forth the metropolitan's business. "Lord, to the Church—to the whole country—you are still something of a mystery. Your family is well-known, but you yourself were born in Transylvania—papist Hungary—and it was from there that you rode."

Dracula acknowledged, "True, father." He had been born in Transylvania while his father was in exile. Exiled by his rivals for the throne. Dracula affirmed, "But I am Wallachian. And I can assure you…When it comes to our faith, our lord bishop's concerns are my own. We do not want our churches converted to mosques."

"Or, lord, to papist temples."

Dracula readily agreed, "Or to papist temples." He offered further, "So tell the bishop, father. What I do now with the heretics and pagans, I do only for expediency."

"But expediency, lord, should have limits."

"Mine does. It is merely a means to an end. An end that I think you'll appreciate soon enough."

"The bishop, too, has an end, lord. That of our holy Faith. He must govern our peoples' souls—with neither heathen nor heretic influence."

"Agreed," Dracula said. "Completely. The governance of souls belongs to the bishop. As the governance of the flesh belongs to me—to the prince. Like the story in the gospels, father. The centurion. As he told Our Lord, 'I, too, am a leader of men.' I, the voevode, father, am also a shepherd, like the bishop. Do you agree to that, father?"

The priest cited the Bible in turn, "'Render unto Caesar...'"

As the passage read: "...the things that are Caesar's, and to God the things that are God's."

The Church had its place. The State had its place. They could work together.

Father Gregor agreed, "The Church, lord, has always supported that principle."

"Then we have an understanding."

"We do, lord, but...The papists still have monasteries on our soil. Even the Turks do not demand that we have mosques."

"Not yet," Dracula reminded. "But what would you have me do with the papists, father?"

"Simply put, lord," the priest stated, "the bishop wants the monasteries removed."

"Aye, father. An expedient solution. But expediency, as you yourself just said, must have limits. Simply put, we cannot afford a war with Hungary. A move against its Church would certainly bring one. You understand that."

"I do, lord, but—"

"Father. Let me cut to the quick. For now, both the Church and I must tolerate foreigners. Hopefully that will change. Soon enough. Tell the bishop that. Tell him that his patience can hasten the day of change. Tell him what I said about our respective domains. He has his. I have mine. Tell him further that, at first, my methods might—will—seem unusual. But they will surely serve our mutual interests. Tell him that, father."

The priest caught the one word: "'Unusual?' In what sense, lord?"

"I will tell you, father. But rather than tell you in words I want you to bear witness. You yourself. Bear witness. Stay at my court. Observe. And tell the bishop what you see. Can you do that, father?"

Such an offer, Dracula knew, would tempt any bishop's representative. To be so close to the prince...

But if Father Gregor was tempted he did not show it. He answered only, "I would accept, lord, but the bishop would have to approve."

Dracula tempted further, "I could ask him, father. Personally. As a favor to me. As you said, I have been away from our land. I would appreciate close guidance in regard to our Church. These papists, for example. These monasteries. While I can't remove them, I can certainly help ours grow."

The priest nibbled, "Endowments?"

Dracula nodded. "My resources are limited right now. But I would like to give something. In fact, I just said as much to the princess. Some endowments would be appropriate. I would like her to plan them. And I would like you to help. If you could."

As the priest's hands began playing on his cross, the silver sent a glint of light into the prince's eyes. Seeing him wince, Father Gregor quickly slid the distraction under his cassock, hastening, "I think the bishop would be pleased, lord. Very pleased."

Aye, Dracula thought, just as Father Gregor himself would be pleased. Endowments not only enriched the Church, but also the boyars in whose lands they were made. The man who guided such endowments would certainly rise in influence. And the point was not lost on this particular bishop's representative.

Dracula continued, "Where is the need greatest, father? Which of our monasteries and churches have been run down? I know of one. But there must be more. Surely you can guide me."

Father Gregor was eager. "Which is the one you know of, lord?"

"In the south. On an island, I'm told."

The priest knew. "Snagov. Yes. And there are others, lord. Many. Like—"

"Hold the rest for now, father. Let us begin with this Snagov. Make it a veritable bastion, a beacon of our faith. I will even protect it with a garrison. Then, when you are here at court, you can help the princess make a list. Monasteries. Chapels. Whatever I can do."

As the priest's eyes were lost in the possibilities, the prince spoke again.

"There is one other thing, father. It is not easy to speak of. Something personal. Very personal."

Father Gregor glanced to Wilk. "Something you would tell me in private, lord?"

"No, father. Not a sin of conscience. Fortunately my conscience is quite clear. What I ask concerns my brother. Mircea."

Father Gregor looked grave. He knew the story. How Dracula's older brother, Mircea, had been tortured and killed by the boyars. "God rest his soul."

"Precisely," Dracula said. "He never had a proper Christian burial. I would like his body found and exhumed. And set to rest properly."

"As you wish, lord. It is only fitting."

"Can you tend to it personally, father? Quietly?"

"I can, lord. I will."

"That is very important to me. Quietly. No display. Nothing public."

"I understand, lord. A private service. I will let you know—"

"No, father. I would rather not attend. It would be too painful. Let me remember him as he was."

Again Father Gregor understood. And as Dracula personally escorted him to the door, the priest assured him not only of a Christian burial for Mircea's body, but of many prayers for his soul. Prayers in perpetuity. By the grateful priests and monks in the soon-to-be-endowed chapels.

When Father Gregor was gone, Dracula told Wilk, "Go with him. I want to know—in detail—how my brother's body was found."

But it did not suit him to let certain of his subjects know that he even cared. Not just yet.

2

THE PORTE. In his midyears, Hamza Pasha, lord of the Turks' Bulgar frontier, showed only the barest signs of a paunch on his stocky frame. His hair protruded from under his turbaned helmet in a straight, black fringe. It ran into a thin beard that set off the squarish lines of his ruddy face. His thick moustache drooped at the corners, draping his red lips in what seemed like a steady frown. The frown seemed more pronounced now, and he squirmed in his seat as he gave his first report on the new Wallachian voevode.

It was bad enough that he had to tell the sultan the story, face-to-face, across the small table. It was worse that the *other* Wallachian, in his usual place next to the sultan, had to hear it. But Radu, after all, had become the sultan's...*confidant*. So Hamza had to lay his embarrassment before both.

Some of his men, as they were wont to do—as they had always been wont to do—had roamed into Tirgoviste to "request" some supplies. Dracula gave them a few wagons full. Only a few wagons. It was all he could spare, he said. He would hear nothing of the Turkish commander's protests that more were needed. When the Turks moved to take more, the voevode called his men. They were not much, as the commander told it. A rabble, really. But they were armed. And they far outnumbered the pasha's men.

That was bad enough.

Then, as the voevode sent the Turks on their way—not even offering a night's stay—he gave their commander a chest. A small chest. Two thousand gold ducats. It was his tribute for the sultan, he said. At least, all he could spare.

The commander balked. For one thing, he had not been sent to collect any tribute. For another, the tribute was *ten* thousand ducats, not two. And it was supposed to be delivered by the voevode in person.

But Dracula put the chest on one of the wagons, told the commander he was sure it was in good hands, and gave him a letter to pass to the sultan.

Mohammed had read the letter. In words, at least, the voevode had been humble. He begged the sultan to understand. He could not possibly leave Tirgoviste to deliver the tribute in person; too many enemies still afoot. How would it profit either of them to leave his throne exposed? As for the money, he was giving all he had. His land, as he himself was sad to discover, was indeed a "piss-land." But he would surely pay the sultan what he truly deserved. In time. The voevode begged for time. And in that time, too, he pledged, he would also settle the matter of Wallachia's providing janissary recruits. To force the issue just then would only anger his people, strengthen his enemies. How would that serve either of them? And so on.

Hamza's face burned red just thinking of the episode. What an insult to the Conqueror! What a shameful thing to himself that he had been made part of it! Without thinking, he hawked a wad of phlegm to spit in rage. Then he remembered where he was. He could not spit on the sultan's floor. He had no choice but to swallow.

Yet, through the whole tale, the sultan's face showed nothing. Almost nothing. Only Radu, glancing from close to his friend's side, could see the vein twitching behind the imperial beard. He touched Mohammed's hand, very discreetly, under the table, and gave a squeeze, a simple message: *You are Fatih! The Conqueror! In the end you will win!* He was glad to see the vein quickly calmed.

The sultan, in fact, gave a smile, along with a sigh that spoke of boredom:....*this tedious insect of a voevode.*

He was actually soothing toward Hamza as he bade the pasha to wait to hear yet another report on this Dracula.

The man called to give it had just come, as it were, off the road. He had the same dark hair, eyes, and beard as Hamza, and was about the same age. But his build was lean, and he had the fair skin not uncommon to the Balkan Europeans. He was still dressed in his usual role: merchant; Wallachian. But he was one of the Porte's many "eyes." Mohammed's spy.

He assured His Highness that his report was not only fresh and laden, but true. Particularly so because he had added a new "source" to his network. "He is a Greek, highness. Toma Catavolinos. Volinos, they call him. Recently of Byzantium. *Before* your great victory."

The Greek was perfect for the job. Christian. Orthodox. Seemingly a natural enemy of the Turk. And truly a natural merchant...a man-for-hire.

Through Volinos, the spy had gleaned much on Wallachia: Dracula's partisans sent to help the Moldavian, Stephen; the contingent led by a new face, a boyar, Gales.

With Dracula's help, Stephen was well on his way to reclaiming his throne. The Wallachians—especially this Gales—were serving him well.

And more: Dracula was fortifying places and recruiting men.

The sultan's interest was piqued: "Recruiting? Mercenaries?"

In answer, the spy explained Dracula's plight. Between the concessions he had given the merchants, both the Saxons and his own, the voevode had no money for mercenaries. And still the Saxons were pressing for more. In a phrase, they loved to sell and hated to buy. Especially from Wallachia.

"And that, highness," the spy explained, "is what got our Greek into Tirgoviste rather easily. You see, the voevode tolerates the Saxons. He *welcomes* anyone else who will trade with his people. As long as they trade fairly."

Mohammed pressed, "So who is the voevode recruiting? What kind of soldiers?"

The spy barely suppressed a smile. "They are not really soldiers, highness. They are more like...bazouks. Peasants mostly."

Hamza chimed in, "Aye, highness. That's what my own men saw."

"True, highness," the spy said. "The Greek and I both bore witness. And you know what the voevode calls himself, the offensive name. Well, he calls these men his *draguli*. Dragons. But even his own people laugh at them. At least..."

As the spy paused in reflection, the sultan prompted, "At least what?"

"At least, highness...They laugh at the idea of these 'dragons' being real soldiers. You see, the voevode *has* used them like...constables. They've cleared the roads. Somewhat. Robbers. Highwaymen. In truth, they've done a fair job of it."

And, in truth, they had. In only the few months since he had taken the throne, Dracula had recruited and trained some of his new men and set them to the task of policing his land, just as he had policed Transylvania.

"But that," Hamza said, "is merely like sending one mob against another. It has nothing to do with being soldiers."

The spy agreed heartily, "*Yes!* Exactly, highness. A mob. A rabble. But soldiers? No. Nothing like your own. Nothing!"

But Mohammed only asked, "How many of these 'dragons' does he have?"

"That, highness," the spy said, "is hard to say. He keeps them in the saddle. Always moving. As I said, clearing the roads. But he *is* still recruiting." He ventured a chuckle. "Then again, highness, the voevode has a lot of *bad* roads on his hands."

But Mohammed did not chuckle. He began to slip into thought, his mind drifting behind still-opened eyes. It did not take long before, instead of the room, he saw an image. A familiar, comfortable image: a chessboard. As though laid transparent over a map.

Other images quickly filled in: the pieces. His own—castles and knights—were in good order, though quite a few were still missing: the losses from Belgrade.

Opposite his own pieces, the sultan saw not Dracula, but Hungary. The king. Yes. He was the real enemy. This, Mohammed's "board" reminded him. And it showed more: Hungary's pieces were scattered. Because that is what the king had done with Janos Hunyadi's victory at Belgrade: *wasted* it.

The sultan knew well of the bickering between the king and Hunyadi's sons. He knew it was one-sided. The king had started it. The Hunyadis tried to appease him. More so than their father ever would have. To show their open-handedness, when the king called, they would even go to him alone. Without escort. Right into his lair. But rather than being appeased the king only seemed to grow more suspicious. More jealous. While his advantage from Belgrade slipped away.

As for Dracula, on the sultan's imaginary board, he appeared as a mere single knight. With a few pawns. That was all. Mohammed had to ask himself why? What were his thoughts telling him?

What did he know about this "Dracula"? What did he know really? What did he remember? Not much. Dracula had passed through the Porte as a boy, had been a hostage, when Mohammed himself was still a boy. He was perhaps more storied than most but still insignificant. Even with his proud name that he knew offended the Turk. Even with his latest arrogance in swearing loyalty to the Porte in the same breath that he swore to Hungary. And even with his ridiculous little "dragons." He was a petty prince. Nothing more. And, like all petty princes, it had gone to his head.

So Mohammed's imaginary chessboard had shown him: he must keep his focus on Hungary; Dracula was a mere distraction. And the board had always been right.

Except perhaps once: Belgrade.

But then, as Mohammed thought of it, his strategy at Belgrade had been good. He had lost because of a man: Janos Hunyadi. In a way, in fact, he regretted Hunyadi's death. He had said so publicly. He had proclaimed to the world that he lamented losing the chance to cross swords yet again with the baron—the only Christian who had ever bested "the Conqueror."

But now Mohammed reined in the thought to focus on Dracula. Distraction or no, he had to be dealt with. He told the spy, "Stay close to the voevode."

Mohammed was thinking of Dracula's insults with the tribute and janissaries. And thinking of Dracula's letter, the particular words: *In time.* The petty prince was undoubtedly planning even more insults.

The spy nodded. "I will stay close to him, highness. But better I do it through the Greek, Volinos. You see, the voevode and I once met. At your father's court. It was long ago but—"

Mohammed knew: "But the voevode has a sharp memory. Especially when it comes to his enemies. Or so it is said."

"Yes, highness. Better that I be just another face in the crowd. Better that Volinos approach him. The voevode needs money. Volinos can offer him gifts."

Mohammed approved. "Yes. Let your Greek give him gifts. Cultivate the voevode."

When he sent the spy off he found Hamza already leaning in place, eager for his own orders on Dracula. Mohammed told him, "I am not yet ready for war. Especially a war that might not be needed. Still, do not let the voevode forget who it was he insulted."

The words sent Hamza off with a light step.

When he was gone, Radu asked, "Can you really avoid a war with him?"

"I can try," Mohammed said. "Clearly your brother suffers some delusion. Perhaps I can use that to our advantage."

He had a flash of Belgrade again. Chaos on the field. His wound. And the earth neither knowing nor caring that it was drinking imperial blood.

Since then, despite the bluster about besting all Christians, Mohammed looked at war *differently*. Not that he would shy from it. Hungary, for example. He would surely fight Hungary in time. That was *kismet*: Fate. But now he no longer sought wars that he really did not need.

Radu declared, "If it does come to war, let it be my war."

"Are you so eager to fight him?"

If in different words, Radu had long-since asked himself the same question. Did he hate his brother? He did once. But that was because of shame. His own shame. He had compared himself to Dracula and found himself wanting. He had, after all, *submitted* to the enemy. In all ways. Shame. But he was beyond that now.

He answered Mohammed, "What I am eager to fight is what my brother stands for: the old way. Petty feuds. Lord against overlord. Tear the land apart."

He continued unabashedly, "I once told my brother that I chose to serve the empire—and your father—freely. But I did not. When I first bowed to your father—and took him as my lover—and then took you as my lover—it was in fear. I was a boy. I was alone. I wanted to live. But now I do choose freely. I choose the new way. The inevitable. The empire. Peace under one rule. The *ascent*. I am eager to be voevode to spare my land its agony, to bring it the empire's civilization."

If the declaration pleased Mohammed the sultan, it left Mohammed the man somewhat stiff. He begged his friend's words. "So what you *freely* choose is the empire."

"Yes," Radu said. He took Mohammed's hands and stood with him. "I choose the empire." He gave a low laugh. "And you. Us."

Why did that gladden Mohammed so? He did not understand it himself, except that the affection he shared with Radu went beyond the mere physical. Friendship? Truly. He *liked* this Wallachian prince. He was cultured, a thinker—like a sultan himself. And Radu was adventurous. In all things.

But was it *love* between them? Yes. Love. Not like the love that bound husband and wife, man and woman. It was the love that intertwined two separate lives. Mohammed enjoyed his time with Radu. He wanted to be with him. And now Radu had declared the same in turn.

Mohammed embraced him. A long holding. As it finally loosened, he told Radu, "You must marry. Soon."

Radu understood. His eyes glowed. Marry. Because the sultan was going to remove Dracula. Soon. Radu must be married to be accepted by Wallachia as its voevode. And marriage would bring heirs, Radu's own sons.

As he had often dreamed of it, he would watch his children grow, close with the sultan's own, just as he and his dearest friend would continue to grow closer—as much as their separate lives allowed.

3

TIRGOVISTE. Dracula's eyes spoke for him: "What have you brought me this time?"

Wilk's answer was a rather satisfied smile. He fairly bounced as he led his friend to the courtyard, where the sunshine threw a ragged shadow of a hundred men drawn in ranks over the muddy snow.

Again Dracula's eyes spoke for him; they rolled to heaven. His breath escaped as steam as he muttered something about wishing he could hire mercenaries. Still he began a slow tour of the ranks.

They were much like the other recruits that Wilk had brought before them. Only a few were real soldiers. Mongrel mercenaries mostly. The rest were commoners—peasants and townsmen. Most of the brigade was hungry—in the literal sense. Some bordered on skeletal. Nearly all bounced from one foot to the other, as though trying to shake the cold from the cloth vests that they wore over their tunics as "coats."

Dracula stopped in front of one who looked to be, so to speak, neither fish nor fowl, neither soldier nor commoner. He was armed, but only with bow and sword, an antique broadsword. He was young and fair, almost genteel: wavy brown hair; slight build; smooth features. Yet he was dressed only little better than a peasant.

"Name?" Dracula asked.

"Cirstian, lord."

And, at the voevode's bidding, Cirstian told his tale. He indeed related it like a soldier—and a somewhat hardened one at that—as though recalling a lost battle. His only emotion was an occasional faraway look.

He had lived in a village on the Danube, on the Bulgar frontier. He and his mother had lived alone. They had a few fields and an inn.

For quite a spate, the village had lived in harmony with the Bulgars and Turks—Hamza Pasha's Turks—across the river. Until, that is, late in the past year, near the first Christmas of Dracula's reign. Then the pasha's Turks suddenly swept across the river. They came like a huge net spread wide across the land. They trapped the village, thrashed it, and just as suddenly swept on. Cirstian was one of the very few survivors. His mother…God rest her soul.

And the Turks had moved on through other border villages. Cirstian had slogged through the invaders' wake—carnage and ruin—as he abandoned the wreck of his own village to come to Tirgoviste.

What he did not know—but what Dracula fully did—was that the destruction of the villages was Mohammed's answer to the voevode's recent arrogance.

Dracula asked, "Where was your boyar? Did he fight back?"

He already knew the answer. In the face of the Turkish raiders the boyars had run. Despite the fact that Dracula had expected the sultan's reply, had warned the boyars to be ready, to hold fast at the Danube.

But Dracula would deal with that soon enough. Now he hefted Cirstian's broadsword. "Did you fight the Turk with this?"

"No, lord," Cirstian said. He tapped his bow. "Mostly with this."

Dracula grunted. Good. The man had sense. He was too light for the huge sword. He would do better with his bow—and maybe with saber and lance. Time would tell.

The voevode moved on, stopping to throw a glance at Wilk before he turned to the last rank. Here, typically, Wilk would hide his more *unusual* finds. He indeed had. But his finds this time were even more unusual than usual.

Dracula halted at two who seemed to come as a pair: a legless man propped in a cart; a blind man at the handles. At the voevode's interest in them they grinned. Dracula's assessment to Wilk was terse: "*What* is this?"

Wilk pointed to the blind man. "A physician. We need doctors."

"Aye, lord," the legless said. "And I help him. I find his herbs and mix his cures. As he—" He tapped the cart. "—helps me 'walk.'" He quickly added, "And I can cook. For an army, if I have to."

"Aye, lord," the blind man vouched. "And he's a good cook, too. The best!"

Dracula gave Wilk a stare—a hard stare. In reply, he got reasoning: *They needed doctors and cooks, didn't they? And anyway they'd be behind the lines in the wagons, and good doctors were hard to find and good cooks even harder and…*

But Dracula had already moved on. And stopped again. At a huge man—with one arm. His hair and beard were long and wild. Like his eyes. Like one whose mind was empty. Yet his one arm was as thick as the limb of a stout tree, and he stood tall. So what was he, Dracula wondered, hulk or husk? A strong giant—albeit a cripple—or only a huge, empty husk?

At his side was a club suited to his size. Dracula nudged it with a toe. "What is this?"

The man looked at him dumbly. "A club, lord."

"Are you dim-witted, too? I know it's a club. Is it supposed to be your 'weapon'?"

"Aye, lord."

"You're a farmer."

"I was, lord."

"Was?"

The man explained. His story was like Cirstian's, like so many others in the ragged ranks. His native village had been ravaged by the Turks. He had found a second, but that was razed by brigands. And his third home—in the Bulgar land—had been overrun by the papists on their way to the Last Crusade at Varna. They had raped and murdered his wife—even though she was clearly with child. Then, when they had no further use for her—or perhaps in a twisted rage of pure shame, a sick attempt to hide their guilt—they had murdered her. And, in trying to save her, the giant had only lost even more—his arm.

As the voevode asked, he told his name: Kyril.

Wilk stepped forward and loosened the man's collar. On his neck was a burn—from a noose.

Dracula asked, "Who did that?"

Kyril answered weakly: "I did."

"He hanged himself," Wilk said. "But he's stiff-necked. He was still breathing when they found him."

"So," Dracula said. "Neither heaven nor hell wanted you. So you came to me." He considered, then offered, "You can have a farm again, Kyril. I will give you one. In the safest province I have. You can find another wife."

Kyril shook his head. "No, lord. I want only to lift this sin—" He touched the rope's scar. "—from my soul."

"Ah!" Dracula said. "Sin."

His breath streamed in clouds as he paced the ranks again.

"Any who march with me had better forget *sin*. There are enemies in our midst. Vipers. I have to stamp them out. Fast. And there are enemies all around us who have been trained all their lives for war. *Holy* war—as they see it. Turks. Papists. I have not had you all your lives. So the war I train you to fight—if I accept you—will have to be *unholy*."

He continued, "But take consolation in this. There is no sin in what I do. I am voevode. Shepherd of the flock. By heaven's will. And heaven put *me* here for a purpose. A high purpose. To save the flock."

He finished, "So think on it. Pray on it. Leave freely if you will. But first put some meat on your bones." He pointed to the stables: "Soup."

He did not have to say it twice. The courtyard quickly emptied as the stables filled. Of all the recruits, only one kept his poise. Cirstian. He walked to get his meal.

"Aren't you hungry?" Dracula asked.

"Lord," came the answer, "there are none more hungry."

It made Dracula smile as he strode toward his court. A rare find. A peasant with such pride.

Inside the court, Dracula paused at an anteroom where Prasha was waiting. Her servants held their son. Dracula planted a kiss on his cheek and babbled some father-to-infant gibberish that made the women laugh. As he extended a hand to Prasha she gave him a smile, still just a bit weak. She had taken to sewing lately, always sewing, it seemed. Now she showed her work: a banner. Like the pennant she had once given him in Moldavia, it was emblazoned with the emblem of the Societas Draconis.

"For your men, love," she said. "To raise their spirits in bringing us peace."

Dracula frankly admired the fineness of the work. The blood of the dragon impaled by the cross truly seemed to be flowing in its redness.

Prasha pledged, "And we are going to make tunics. Me and all the ladies of the court. Tunics for all the soldiers. Black. Like your own. To show the penance in our hearts."

Dracula swelled with joy. Slowly, his wife was surfacing from her melancholy. The steady working of her hands was calming her spirit.

He took the hands now and led her into the court, where the throng of the day's audience was waiting. Until then she had actually grown bored with her role of princess on the throne. The business had all been mundane: strengthening forts; shifting the lands of the Danestis' former allies to Dracula's own faction; supplying the new troops...Even endowments to the Church had come to seem rote. But today, Dracula had told her, the real quest for peace—and order—was to begin.

The court murmured at their entrance, and Father Gregor stepped forward to give the couple a blessing. As he did, Dracula noted the boyars grouped at the far wall. They were of the old families, those who had survived through several regimes. Survived by fighting against this side and that. But always *for* themselves. Now, as they made the sign of the cross with the rest, their hands moved only as a matter of form.

On his throne, with Prasha at his side, Dracula opened the audience with two exercises that had also become rote. The first involved villages, those that had suffered in his war of accession, and others that had suffered since from natural disasters. They needed relief for a time, and Dracula gave it: temporary exemption from his taxes. His country's folklore, in fact, would remember him for his compassion for the villages.

The second matter involved a list, a very long scroll of a list. A list of peasants. "These men," he said, "and all of their line, shall henceforth be known as 'free.' By my hand and God's will."

Freed by their service to Dracula—war service, in fighting as his partisans. Now they were no longer bound to any estates, to any boyar.

But, from the group at the wall, a boyar stepped forward. Given leave, he spoke, "Lord, this list of free peasants lately swells. Surely you know how it affects us. This loss of manpower is telling. Especially now."

But Dracula only asked, "Why especially now?"

"Surely you see it, lord. We have lost so many men in wars. We barely have enough now to tend our estates."

"I agree," Dracula said. "Wallachia has lost too many. But...You just saw me sacrifice my taxes. We must all sacrifice. Even the Church. I have also released men from its estates." He looked to Father Gregor. "But they are freely given, are they not, father?"

The priest blushed under the stares of both voevode and boyars. He chose his words carefully—with a twist in tense on the voevode's question. "Yes, lord. They *have* been given freely." Given freely in the past. But in the future?

Turning back to the boyar, Dracula shrugged with open palms. To him, for that day, the matter was closed.

He moved on, "I said before that I take a keen interest in the affairs of my realm. All affairs. None are too small."

As he spoke, his draguli brought a man in chains before him. A young man who kept his eyes averted as Dracula noted his crime: theft. The man looked up only when Dracula told him, "You know what I've done with highwaymen."

The thief showed a twisted smile. "Highwaymen, lord? I'm hardly a bandit. I—"

"I know," Dracula said. "You're going to tell me that the goods you stole were small."

"Aye, lord. And I killed no one."

"True. But you're hardly a mere boy. And no one can recall when you last worked. No village, no estate, claims you. Yet you just heard, as I did—as all here did—that we need hands in the field. Where do you work? Give me the name of just one master—one that I can prove—and you are free."

And the green eyes settled on the thief: *Don't lie.*

The man's tongue was tied.

"As I thought," Dracula said. He posed to Father Gregor, "You've had experience with thieves, father. Thieves in penance."

The priest of course had.

"Father," Dracula asked, "in all of your experience, have you ever known a thief—even a repentant thief—to steal just once?"

The priest was somewhat struck. "No...No, lord. I haven't. Usually—"

"Aye, father," Dracula said. "We can safely assume that, when you catch a thief once, he's stolen before. And when you catch him with something small he's also stolen something large. When his luck was better. Large as...say...a horse."

The thief was quick enough to grasp the meaning. Especially with this voevode, who was fast becoming known for his strange ways. The thief had been caught stealing something small. But this voevode was twisting it into horse-theft. Hanging. Frantically the thief made to argue.

But the voevode raised a hand. "You have logic against you. And the wisdom of the Church."

The thief gasped, "But you can't hang me for—"

"Hang you?" Dracula said. "No. To match those you have surely stolen, I am going to *give* you a horse. Two horses, in fact. All you need do is hold them." He told his draguli, "You know what I mean."

The thief, too, knew. He was screaming and thrashing as he was taken. And the court knew. And stirred. And Eupraxia knew. She gripped her husband's hand and began, "But—"

Dracula answered the grip with his own. One of reassurance. He snapped to the court, "It is my God-given duty to bring order to this land. How many years have thieves plagued us? Thieves and murderers and rapists? Don't they know me yet? Haven't they seen what I've done with bandits? They were warned. I have no time to play with them."

The stirring died.

The voevode called the next case.

The group of peasants—men, women, and children—brought before him were obviously awed by the court—boyars, the bishop's priest...the prince himself. They stood with heads bowed, huddled in the closeness of their group.

"You have nothing to fear," Dracula assured them. He told the court, "They are here at my bidding." He commanded the peasants, "Tell us—tell the world—your story. Speak freely."

An elder stepped forward as the spokesman. The tale was blunt. He and his group were survivors. All that was left of several villages. Like Cirstian, they had lived on the Bulgar frontier. Also like him, they had lost everything in the recent Turkish raids.

"Did you fight back?" Dracula asked.

"We tried, lord," the man said. "But we are only—"

"Aye," Dracula said. "You are only farmers. Do you have a boyar?"

"Yes, lord."

Dracula repeated the "Yes" to the court, noting, "They are not 'free' men."

He quizzed, "Did you pay your taxes?"

"Faithfully, lord."

"Aye," Dracula said. "Faithfully." He addressed the court, "So here, and in so many cases like it, we find some of our worst criminals. How should they be judged?"

The court was puzzled. Father Gregor sought the light of clarification. "Lord, of what criminals do you speak? The Turks?"

"No," Dracula said. "The Turks here are criminals, truly. Preying on our people. But there is a bigger criminal still: their boyar."

The boyars at the wall stirred again. One stepped forward. "How is it construed, lord, that their boyar is the criminal? It was not he who attacked them."

"Nor did he defend them."

"But the Turk—"

"Yes," Dracula said. "The Turk is strong. And stronger still by what he plants in your head: 'Touch one of us, fight us all—our whole empire!'"

The boyar flared, "And who, in truth, can stand against that empire? Can you?"

Dracula warned, "In my court, address me as 'lord.'" He asked Father Gregor, "If a man takes a fee for a service and does not deliver that service, what is he, father?"

The priest knew how Dracula would construe the obvious answer. He resisted—because voevodes came and went while boyars remained.

But Dracula insisted, "What is such a man, father?"

The priest wavered, "Well, lord, ordinarily—"

Dracula cut to the quick. "He is a thief. No less. He acts in bad faith. As the boyar did here. He took taxes but abandoned his people in their need."

Now another boyar stepped forward. "Lord, such a charge has never been made by peasants against a boyar. Not in our whole land. Not in our whole history. It runs counter to the law."

Dracula declared, "No peasants make this charge. I simply called them as witnesses. *I* made the charge. *I* heard the case. And *I* pass sentence. I am taking the boyar's lands."

The boyars fairly bolted from the wall: *But the law—!*

Dracula's fist struck the throne. "Law!? Justice! I will take the lands. And I will also take the burden of defending them. *Or*—will any of you take that burden?"

No answer.

Dracula closed, "I thought not. Not against the Turk. The matter is ended."

The boyars glared. But they began backing off.

Father Gregor came to their side. "Lord, we understand your purpose, but—"

"Father," Dracula said. "This is not a Church matter."

The priest persisted, "But—"

The green eyes stopped him. "Remember, father. Govern your souls. Leave the flesh to me."

A dead silence fell on the court. But it was suddenly shredded by a cracking of whips—and brays and screams. They came from the courtyard, where a newly condemned thief had been tied between two horses sent flying in opposite directions against the feeble hold of his arms.

4

AS THE CHILL of the stream numbed him again, the man left his two sons at the work and sloshed onto the bank. He leaned on his spade and gazed across the field, across the Danube, to the gray horizon in the Bulgar land. The "Mud Month," as some called it—March—was well on its course. It would not be long before the dank days passed and the earth would bloom and breathe of lush growth.

For a peasant, the man had already seen his fair share of seasons. His dark hair and beard were more than frosted with silver, but he joked that it was only a sign of wisdom. His body was lean and nimble, molded by its work. And, if the years had sapped a bit of his own strength, his sons were young and strong. When the time—his time—came, they could easily run the farm alone, just as their two sisters, like the blossoming women they were, already ran the cottage under their mother's guiding eye.

Leaving his spade planted in the dirt, the man turned back to the boys and watched with satisfaction as they steadily kept to their task of clearing the stream. It was a man-made stream, dug by the long-forgotten families who had tended this land, boyar's land, before the peasant's own family took the tenancy. The stream ran almost straight from the river, across the field leading to where he stood, and skirted the pasture of the low hill behind him. It ended in a broad pool at the end of the pasture.

Like the tenants before him, the man and his sons were clearing the stream, from river to pond, of the winter's debris. With the renewed flow would come the river's fruit—fish—lured on by scrap meal generously peppered into the water. Over the warm months, the fish would grow and fatten. In autumn the stream would be dammed at the river. The fish would be driven into the pond and netted in droves to be smoked and salted for the next long winter.

Wading into the work again, the father made his sons laugh as he cursed at the chilled water gripping his groin. But the laughs were stopped dead by the shrieks that suddenly pierced the air. The man dropped to the mud and flattened. His sons crawled to his sides. Even before they peered over the bank they heard the hoofbeats. Turks. In turbaned helmets. Akinjis. A small party of raiders. They had come from along the Danube and—save for one who trailed at a sulking trot—were already sweeping toward the cottage.

The man shook as he pushed his sons: "Go!"

He did not have to say where. They scampered on all fours into the pasture, for the hill.

For a flash, the peasant thought of the spade. But only for a flash. He left the spade as he ran for the cottage, which the raiders had noosed in a shouting, swirling circle. What good would a spade do against them? The peasant cursed himself. He had heard the news of the others…the farms…whole villages…Surely his sin was pride. He had thought that somehow he would be different, that the suffering of the Turkish raids would pass him by. And so he had stayed on the farm. Now his prayer gushed: *Christ Jesus! Have mercy!*

A rider peeled from the circle and bore down on him, sword drawn. It was only then that the akinji who had trailed the rest set spur. As the peasant saw, he was clearly not Osmanli. He was swarthy—African. He hurtled across the field and jolted to a stop in front of the peasant so that the attacker could only pull rein and swear. And he was still swearing at the African as they led the peasant between them to where the rest of the raiders had dismounted and pulled the women from the cottage.

The raiders' leader, a petty officer, came forward. "Don't worry, old man. I'm in a mood to be generous. You can live past this day. To rebuild." He gave an aside that brought a howl from his troop. "What the hell. We can't plunder empty land."

But in the next breath he turned on the African, mocking, "Still trying to play the saint?"

The African simply grimaced, as though at a foul taste. "I told you when you picked me for this. I have no stomach for it. It does not serve Islam."

"It serves the pasha," the leader said. "So do I."

As though to punctuate his words, he was already loosening his belt and walking toward the women. He had his orders: *Make the Wallachians suffer.* The old peasant started but was held. His face was also held, to his wife and daughters, with the officer's admonition: "Shut your eyes even to blink and I'll pluck them out myself."

The peasant would have to witness his hell.

The officer made a pass of the women, who, like the old man, had crumpled in a fit of shaking and sobbing. The raider shoved the mother aside. "Old. Toothless. Worthless."

Again his troop howled—except for the African, whose hand went to his sword. But could he strike his misguided brethren? Did he have the right? Did he have the courage? His head dropped. He turned his back. He could only utter prayers in a steady stream.

The officer barked through the daughters' tears, "If you strip nicely you'll have something to wear later—when we take you to the pasha."

This was the hard lesson that the empire was teaching Wallachia. Land razed. Women degraded. And taken. To be degraded again and again. Only old men were left to tell of it. If they were lucky. They would babble it in crazed grief to let the people know what Dracula's defiance of the sultan had cost them.

As the women only went on sobbing, the officer grabbed one. He held her dress so that it tore away as he flung her to the ground.

From the hill across the field came galloping hoofbeats. A small troop. Smaller than the raiders'. In black tunics.

The peasants were forgotten as the raiders turned in amusement at the intrusion. At the foot of the hill the riders stopped to discharge a boy—one of the peasant's sons. He was sent back up the hill to safety as the troop came on. It stopped a sword's length from the raiders. Its leader was Cirstian. He had been weighing his situation since the farmer's sons had stumbled on him: How could he do what he needed to do here?

He opened with deference, "Your master rules the other side of the river."

For an instant the raiders were stunned. Then they guffawed. Their leader mocked, "Pardon me, *lord*. Perhaps we should just go back."

Cirstian played into it. "I think it would be best."

"Well, *dunghole*," the raider retorted, "you think wrong." He turned to his men, jerking a finger toward Cirstian. "Do you know what he is? He's one of the 'dragons' we've heard so much about." He turned back to Cirstian. "Well, dragon, what you really are is a glorified peasant. A real heap of dung. Apparently you can't even count."

His point was clear. His men outnumbered Cirstian's thrice over.

He declared, "So I'm going to rape that woman. Then that one. And then maybe the hag. Just so you can see it."

Now Cirstian goaded, "I can't let you do that."

"How will you stop me?"

"Maybe I can't. Maybe I'll die trying."

"You *will* die trying."

Cirstian dismounted and drew his saber. The raiders stirred. All of them.

Cirstian challenged, "Are you afraid to fight me alone?"

The leader smirked. "What honor is there in fighting *you*? A peasant? I'd just as soon slaughter you, be done with you."

Ah!, Cirstian thought, the disdain of chivalry. He should have expected that. To a soldier, an officer, a peasant was almost less than human. So he lied, "I am not a peasant, sir. Surely you've heard that some of us are soldiers. Mercenaries. And, in my own province, I am a lord. So are you afraid of me or what?"

The leader was not afraid. He drew sword. "When I'm through with you I'm going to skin your 'dragons'—your peasants. Skin them alive."

Cirstian backed his men off. He wanted the room. He needed it—as he had expected. The akinji's blade matched his bluster; it took him only a short time of parrying to sense that he clearly had the upper hand. Cirstian's moves were basic. Primitive. Mostly in retreat. And still, as Cirstian had hoped, the raider suspected deceit. It was in his eyes: *Surely this mercenary lord has better moves than he shows.*

It was only slowly, wisely, that the akinji came on. And Cirstian's mask, as it were, came off. The akinji flew at him. Once. Twice. And Cirstian's fumbling defenses were telling. Fortunately for him, his opponent decided to toy with him, to savor the time for the kill to make the story of his prowess even better for the barracks.

But the raider's time suddenly ran out. From over the hill came hooves at a gallop, a dark mass of riders with Dracula himself at their head. Sharing his saddle was his guide—the peasant's second son. Wilk was at their side.

Cirstian had played his gamble well. Now he stepped a bit farther from his opponent to pronounce: "Fool."

The raider leader was furious. But he was also desperate. He had no time for revenge. He led his men in a leap for the saddle. That far, they got. But not much farther. Dracula peeled from his troops, sending them on with the order, "Alive! I want them alive if you can!"

Most were brought back alive. Only a few were belly-down across their saddles. Dracula raised one of the lifeless heads. It was bashed to the proverbial pulp. He turned to the dragul holding the corpse's reins: one-armed Kyril. In place of the shield he could not carry, he was protected by a harness of armor. His lance was red—on the butt.

Dracula chided, "You know, there's a reason for that point on the other end. In a real battle you won't have time to swing a club."

He did not wait to hear Kyril's excuses. He wanted Cirstian's report: how the farmer's sons had found him; how he had sent one on with a rider to fetch the main column; how he had the other son lead his small troop straight to the farm. Cirstian also told of his dilemma: how to hold the raiders until the column arrived. Which had been the whole point of his challenging their leader.

Dracula snapped, "Why didn't you just wait for us?"

Cirstian gestured to the peasants, locked in one another's arms now but still sobbing in shock. "Because, lord, I've seen too much of that."

Dracula sighed. "You're lucky to be alive."

Cirstian acknowledged, "Aye, lord." He looked to the raiders' leader. "He was very good with the sword."

"They all are," Dracula said. He spoke for all of his men to hear. "Which is why I tell you: train. *Train.*" His next words came in a breath, to Cirstian. "If I make you boyar here, will you defend this land as you did today?"

It took a moment for Cirstian to realize, to drop to his knees and bow. "I will, lord. To the death."

And so Dracula began a new pattern to his reign. The record of his time as voevode, in fact, would show many worthy peasants raised to boyar.

He now had the raiders brought before him. On their knees. His eye rested on the one, the African. They had met before. But it meant nothing to Dracula now. His accusation carried the raiders' sentence. "Murderers. Rapists. Thieves."

Their leader only glared. "We are soldiers of Hamza Pasha."

"Then I'll do the pasha a favor: clean his ranks of scum."

"What we did we did on his orders."

Dracula pronounced, "Then he has commended your fate to me." He told his men, "Bind them. Tightly." As it was being done, he called to the peasant, "You seem to have enough trees. And we have the rope."

The peasant came barreling to him, his mouth literally frothing in rage. "Let *me*, lord! Please! I'll hang them with my own hands!"

But Dracula counselled, "No. You are a farmer. A man of peace. As God made you. For you, mortal revenge is mortal sin." His voice rose again to teach his men. "But for me—and mine—it is our duty."

The raider leader warned, "Go ahead. Hang us. And see what Hamza Pasha does to you. To all of you!"

But the words did not strike Dracula with the threat intended. In his mind, they merely resurrected a realization: *Terror.* The Osmanlis' best weapon. And, unlike other weapons, terror was cheap. As cheap as a prisoner's life.

Dracula's realization developed into a mutter: "No rope. Impalement."

As the prisoners' eyes bulged, Cirstian repeated to their leader, "You *are* a fool."

Dracula asked Wilk, "Do you know the method? Impalement?"

Wilk shrugged. "You mean...?" He raised a forefinger like a tiny stake. "I've never seen one. But I could try."

Dracula waved him off and turned to the rest. "Do any of you know how to do it?"

Their shrugs, too, belied their ignorance.

He heaved a sigh. "All right. I'll do the first myself. But pay attention."

As the reality became undeniable, the prisoners bolted in their bonds and pleaded, begged, until they were kicked and gagged into silence.

It was then that the peasant's wife came forward. She had her own plea for the voevode—for the one akinji who had shunned the atrocity to her family. When she finished the tale, Dracula addressed the man: "Ibrahim."

The African answered almost in shame, "Yes, lord."

"Ibrahim," Dracula said. "What did I tell you the last time we met?"

The akinji was frankly amazed. "You remember that, lord?"

It had been almost ten years. When Dracula was just seventeen. On his first attempt to take the throne in Tirgoviste.

But Dracula remembered, as he repeated his words now: "You ride with the wrong company." He declared, "I remember many things. It is a gift of God."

"Yes, lord," Ibrahim acknowledged, "it seems so. And I, too, remembered your words. I kept them in my heart."

"But still kept the wrong company."

"Yes, lord. Kept it well past its time—for me. I am a soldier. And a good one. In battle. But not in tormenting peasants. And that is what war has become. I have witnessed too many atrocities."

"Then at the least," Dracula said, "I should pluck out your eyes, the eyes that mutely watched these atrocities."

Ibrahim muttered as though in inward acceptance, "If it be the will of Allah…"

Dracula quizzed, "Are you so casual about losing your eyes?"

"No, lord," Ibrahim said. "Nor about being impaled. Believe me. But…I think I knew for a long time: I am not a soldier for this time and place. I think my heart—God in my heart!—told me. Even as you told me. But my pride…" His eyes dropped. "So how can I complain now of God's judgment?"

"And what if," Dracula asked, "God moves me to set you free?"

"Lord, I will devote myself to Him. No more sword. No more wealth. Only Allah—greatest and best!"

"Well," Dracula said. "Your faith—and this woman—have saved you. Because God has moved me to set you free. To live the rest of your days as you just spoke. And to take a message to Hamza. Agreed?"

Ibrahim nodded.

"Tell him what you witnessed," Dracula said. "And tell him I know how he and the empire think. That we are barbarians. That we need your 'civilization' to save us. But we are not barbarians—as this woman's compassion—and my mercy to you—show. We have our own civilization. We need only to be left alone."

Ibrahim replied with his own compassion, a word of caution, "Lord, you know that you will not be left alone."

"Of course," Dracula said. "But just tell the pasha—and the empire…"

When Ibrahim was sent on his way, Dracula called for what he needed: stakes, mallets, grease…

And the rest of the raiders were impaled. On the Bulgar frontier. On the bank of the Danube. On Hamza Pasha's side of the river.

5

TIRGOVISTE. The boyar Gales was slightly older than his voevode. He was also a bit taller and thinner, almost angu-lar. He had the very dark hair of some of the

Balkan peoples, with trim beard and moustache. His skin was smooth, but like the Turk's or Tartar's: smooth, light honey. He approached Dracula now with mud still on his boots. Foreign mud. Moldavian. His service to Dracula there was done; Stephen had reclaimed his throne.

Wilk, too, entered the court with mud on his boots. He, too, had been hastily called from his service to the voevode. The mud on his boots was from a grave.

They were barely seated when Dracula began: *News.* News from everywhere, it seemed. But all springing from Hungary.

Janos Hunyadi's oldest son was dead. Executed. Or murdered, as some said. By his king. Or, at least, on his order; the timid king would never have struck the blow himself. The elder Hunyadi had been seized on a trumped up charge of treason. Within a day he had his "trial." He was promptly taken to the block in a public square.

If he had not been much like his father in life, in the wariness of politics, he had certainly matched his prowess in facing death. As told by the many witnesses, the episode would be etched in Hungary's history.

Once, twice, *three times* the executioner's sword fell on Laszlo Hunyadi's neck. Yet three times it failed to bring death. The victim, in fact, finally leaped to his feet, literally holding his half-severed head to his neck. He bolted from the block drenched in his own blood and screaming that he had suffered enough. He had to be dragged back for the final blow.

And after it had fallen the king took his next step. A rather uncertain step. He took Hunyadi's younger son, Matthias, as hostage.

Wilk was incredulous. "Hostage?"

Dracula threw up his hands. "I can't believe it myself. But apparently he was suddenly afraid of Hunyadi's old faction. He thinks to keep Matthias as insurance—on his own life."

Wilk chuckled. "Then he's made two mistakes. He should have been ready for all-out war. And—"

"Aye," Dracula finished. "He never should have left one son alive to take revenge. He'll have his problems now."

Gales squirmed in his place. "Damn *his* problems! What about the rest of us now? Doesn't he realize what he's done?"

"Oh, yes," Dracula said. "I think he does—now. You see, while he was up to his nonsense, the Turk swallowed Serbia."

It was a bit of an overstatement. The Turk had already had a firm grip on Serbia. The only thing that had kept the land from being annexed outright—especially after Belgrade—was Hungary. But now that Hungary was adrift in its king's folly…So Serbia really had not been swallowed. Only digested.

As Gales made to flare again, Dracula stopped him. "There's more. Much more. This mess in Hungary has spilled right to our door. It certainly didn't take long. Already the boyars were here to see me. The old families. And the Church. It seems they've suddenly taken a liking for the Turk. They want me to appease the sultan, make amends."

Again Wilk was incredulous. "Including paying the child-tribute?"

Dracula affirmed, "Including paying the child-tribute. As the Church sees it— as the bishop himself put it—'better to lose a few lambs than the whole flock.'"

Wilk commented only, "Heady. Very heady."

"Ah," Dracula said. "But the headiest of all is yet to come. The Hungarian merchants. The Saxons. With their king preoccupied, they began harassing our own merchants again. When I warned them to stop, they took to harboring a claimant to my throne. So what next? Maybe they'll hire mercenaries. March on me outright."

Gales's skin had gone sallow. "Don't make light of it, lord. Maybe they will. Maybe the boyars are right. And the Church. Maybe we should appease the sultan. Maybe we need him. At least for now."

Dracula posed, "You mean, like Serbia tried to appease him? Or like so many others? The Bulgars. The Greeks. Where are they now? In turbans. Or graves."

The voevode counselled further, "On the other hand, look at the Albanian, Skanderbeg, and even Janos Hunyadi. Their lands, at least, are still free."

"But for how long?" Gales said. "The Albanians barely hold their mountains. And Hungary…" He heaved a sigh. "Forgive me, lord. You know I am a soldier. I am not afraid to fight. But I've been at war so long. And this news…As you said, Hungary's *mess* has become our own."

"There's nothing to forgive you for," Dracula said. "In truth, at first, my own thoughts were like yours. *Damn that king!* But then…Perhaps there's Providence in all this."

Gales laughed. "Please show it to me, lord."

But what Dracula showed was a cup. A gold cup. A goblet. Heavy. He set it on the table. "A gift. From a merchant."

"From the Greek?" Wilk asked. "Volinos? Another gift? And another handsome one."

"Handsome, yes," Dracula said. "But not from Volinos. It's from an Italian. A Florentine. He wants to trade in my land. And after showing me such respect—"

He tapped the cup. "—how could I refuse? And he thought my sole condition—*honesty*—most fair. In fact, he was a bit surprised that I even mentioned it."

Wilk noted, "Hardly like the Saxons."

"Exactly," Dracula said. He peered into the mirror of the goblet. "And that set me to thinking. About the Saxons. They look for profit now in our world's confusion. We should learn by their example. Their *bold* example. We should take the profit ourselves."

"I don't follow," Gales said.

"The Turk has taken Serbia," Dracula explained. "But the Saxons aren't running for the hills. Why not? Because—turmoil in Hungary or no—the Turk is still wounded from Belgrade. And he has, as it were, just gorged himself. On Serbia. He was still weak. And now he's stuffed. Clearly he's not ready for war. Or he would be in Hungary even now. That, I think, is what the Saxons see. And they do roam far and wide."

He continued, "And what do the Saxons see at their own backs, in their own land? Their king on edge now. The king, the counts and barons. Old factions. All on edge. Frozen. And so the Saxons become emboldened. Against a man who was at peace with their king. With all of Hungary. A man who simply refuses to bow to their arrogance: me."

"But are they right?" Gales asked. "About the Turk?"

"I think so," Dracula said. "At least for now. But, of course, if things are not settled in Hungary soon the Turk himself will become emboldened. In the meantime...But that brings me to you, my friend. You've done me a great service. Twice. I would give you some reward. An estate. A rather large one. In the south. Next to the new boyar, Cirstian."

Gales smiled wryly. "On the frontier. I dare say, lord, I would settle for a rather small estate. Farther north."

Dracula answered wryly, "But that you already have. It's what you started with, eh?"

"It is in fact, lord. Of course I accept what you offer. And graciously."

"And graciously," Dracula said, "I will remember it as yet another service. Because the Turk, wounded as he is, will not simply lie still. He will begin preparing the way for his next step. Here. Against me. He will seek to sow even more confusion. In the south. More raids. Feints. So Cirstian will need help. A skilled sword. *Your* skilled sword."

Gales pledged, "And he will have it, lord."

"Then go now," Dracula said. "Teach Cirstian how to fight. And let him teach you how we're dealing with raiders."

When he was gone, Wilk noted, "I don't think he was jesting. I think he'd rather be riding north."

"Aye," Dracula agreed. "He was born a boyar. So he seeks the easy path. And yet, in many ways, he's like Cirstian. He still has things to learn. And he will. Soon enough. I wish you could have heard the bishop and boyars. One after the other...singing the same song: Make amends with the sultan. So I asked in turn: Will the sultan make amends with me? To a man, they assured me he would."

Wilk observed, "As though the sultan himself were telling you."

"Quite. The metropolitan even extolled the Turk's tolerance. It seems that the 'Conqueror' has suddenly restored the Church in Constantinople."

"So they've been talking to the Turk. Boyars and Church both."

"There is no doubt in my mind. And whether I offer amends or not—and whether Mohammed accepts them or not—he has other plans for me."

"Rebellion."

"Aye," Dracula said. "For all of his schemes, the Turk is getting predictable. He dangles peace in front of my eyes while he plots to set the boyars at my back. Soon enough he will try to put Radu on my throne."

"While the Church looks the other way."

"As usual. What does it care who's voevode?"

Wilk asked, "So how shall we begin?"

Dracula answered, "With you telling me about my brother."

Mircea. The mud on Wilk's boots was from his grave.

"Then," Dracula said, "we'll recall the draguli from the roads. Quietly."

Wilk gestured to the goblet. "That could also buy us mercenaries. Quite a few, I think."

Dracula chuckled. "I have something else in mind for it. As quickly as things will happen now, this land needs what the Turk would call 'an object lesson.'"

6

FOR ALL OF HIS TROUBLES, Dracula, on this day, was a fairly happy man. It was not the precious goblet in the velvet sack he car-ried. Nor the purpose he had in mind for it. Nor was it the first breath of the first spring of his reign...the trill of birds...the breeze laden with the perfume of forest, field, and garden...

It had been Prasha's wish that they take the leisurely ride in the carriage. Prasha's wish. To leave the sheltering walls of the palace and ride through Tirgo-viste. It was the first time in so long that her smile seemed as warm as the sun-shine itself.

As their excursion began, the prince was content to hold his formal place opposite the princess. They were every bit the royal couple, marked fore and aft by their mounted escort, on an outing amidst their subjects. In their path, the city awakened to the spring like a body awakening from a long hibernation. Its "lifeblood" coursed through its veins: merchants with loaded wagons…tradesmen laden with tools and materials…idle gentlemen on horseback…

Shopkeepers waited in doorways and windows. An occasional priest mingled with his flock at the market stalls—a good time for pious reminders on morality. Beggars leeched onto the traffic as it passed. And all bowed to the voevode's carriage.

As Prasha took it all in, Dracula, in turn, was rapt in her. Her pallor was finally giving way to her complexion's natural cream color. A blush had returned to her lips. Her hair had been curled softly so that it fell in waving tresses that straddled her shoulders front and back. It was held in place by a simple dressing, a thin headband of braided gold dappled with the points of gems that glittered red, blue, and green as they caught the sunlight. On one arm she wore a similar braid, its head circling her forefinger like a ring, its body coiled about her wrist and running under her sleeve, like a mythical vine tracing its roots to the very essence of mystery.

She was startled as Dracula sprung to sit next to her and lock her in an embrace. The passersby who had seen his advance clucked in good-natured teasing. It rose to laughter and catcalls as the young princess squirmed and giggled in resistance. When she finally relented to give the prince a single kiss, they gave him a mock cheer.

Settling next to her, he pledged, "I would give my entire realm just to keep you like this. Damn the melancholia!"

"That's the beauty—the mercy—of it, love. You don't have to give your realm. Just keep to this new good work that you are about."

Dracula was puzzled. "New good work?" As though for a clue, he glanced to the sack. But it could not be that. He had told no one what he intended for the goblet.

Prasha persisted, "You can't keep the secret, love. I already know. Father Gregor told me."

"Told you what, love?"

She answered in a word: "Peace."

"Peace?"

"With the Turk. He told me about how you will make overtures to the sultan. And how the boyars support it. What with Hungary in turmoil again…"

But Dracula no longer heard her. He understood. The Church, as it were, had crept into his bedroom—between himself and his own wife under his own sheets. Father Gregor had seduced her with the sweet word: peace. All the sweeter because she longed for it so. And who to know that better than the priest who lingered so close to her? And she, in turn, was to innocently seduce her husband, the voevode. Meld him to what the Church had lately sought of him.

Had the seducer here been a boyar—even the highest in the land—Dracula's reply would have been swift and terrible. But the Church…Even the voevode could not challenge it outright. But Dracula would answer. He would tell the Church. But not in words, mere words. As he had already told the bishop's representative, his actions would speak for him. And thank God soon.

But the fury showing on his face had brought Prasha to silence. Now she continued timidly, "He wouldn't lie. Not a priest. You will make peace?"

And, to assuage her fear, Dracula lied. "Perhaps Father Gregor misunderstood."

Prasha concluded grimly, "Then there will be no peace."

Dracula took her hands. "But there will, love," he insisted. *"In time."* He groped to explain. "Remember Uncle Bogdan. Killed on a ride like this—a peaceful ride—in his own capital. And remember *how* they killed him. And our families…how they were murdered. Are our boyars now so different?"

"I thought they were," Prasha answered. "Your enemies fled when you took your throne."

"Aye," Dracula said. "The guiltiest did. Or perhaps they were just the most honest. They at least admitted their treachery by running. But those who remain—save for the very few—have hands just as red."

As though to punctuate, he flipped a panel under the seat to show a compartment filled with weapons. "Like my uncle…I can't even ride in peace in my own capital. Wolves, love. Wolves all around us."

Aside from showing her the weapons, he could have also told her of the other precaution he had felt compelled to take. He had spaced men all along their route, draguli out of uniform to blend with the populace. But already she was upset by his words, and he still had more to tell.

"Look, love. Look around you. Right here in our streets. Even if we didn't have wolves to plague us, we have jackals."

What he meant was obvious enough. "The beggars?"

"The beggars. Look how they cling to honest men…to the merchants' wagons."

It was as he said it that his eye caught one of the merchants. Caught and darted on. Quickly. Deliberately. Just as the merchant's eye also darted from the voevode.

But Prasha's next words about the beggars recaptured her husband's attention. "They are the poor and unfortunate, love."

"Poor?" he challenged. "Look. Look how many are whole. Whole and able. Yet they beg. While our farms need hands. And when the time comes that I ride—as I must, love—these jackals themselves will puff up into wolves: robbers...looters...and worse—if they get the chance. Wallachia simply can't afford them."

But Prasha singled one out in passing: old, shrivelled, crippled. "And what of him? Is he a jackal?"

"No," Dracula said. "He is unfortunate indeed."

As the carriage left the streets and cleared the city, he appealed, "Do you understand, love?"

"All too well," she answered. Her eyes had misted over—as they often did with the melancholia. "Our troubles have just begun."

Dracula urged, "No, my love. It is our *work* that has just begun."

But she only mocked the word: "'Work.' Boyars...Saxons...And now even beggars."

"Yes," he said. "And all the rest. Turks. Hungarians. Highwaymen and thieves. Bear with it, love. When it is done you will see. And be proud. We will not leave this land as we found it. We will raise it. By the grace of God."

But the route he had chosen for the ride was nearing its end: a fountain. It was in a lonely clearing by the road. As the carriage reined in, he took the goblet from the velvet sack. He dipped it in the fountain and gave his wife to drink. Then he soaked his own sleeve and wiped the sweat that had beaded on her brow.

Leaving her in the carriage, he called Wilk aside to show the goblet. "I am going to leave this here."

Wilk was puzzled.

"My gift," Dracula said. "For the people. Our own and foreigners alike. When they come to this fountain they can use it to drink. *Use* it. And put it back. For the good of all."

Now Wilk understood. An object lesson. A test. Of sorts. Of a whole people's honesty.

"Of course," Dracula said, "if it does get stolen..."

Wilk assured him, "It won't."

Dracula agreed, "No. It won't. But our 'eyes' can't be obvious."

The draguli left to watch the cup would be hidden.

"Also," Dracula said. "In the city…there is a merchant. I will describe him and his wagon. He couldn't have gotten far. I want him watched."

"What if he tries to leave?"

"Let him," Dracula said. "For now."

When he rejoined Prasha for the ride back, he assured her, "Even if our work has just begun, love, we are at least finally about it."

7

EASTER DAY. TIRGOVISTE. For all of their differences, the Christian sects, Roman and Orthodox, have always agreed on one liturgical principle: The highest of their holy days is Easter. Even though Christmas marks the birth of Christ, and hence of the Christian Faith itself, it is Easter that marks the pinnacle of the holy days.

On the first Easter of Dracula's reign, Wallachia celebrated as always. Even in the meekest of villages, the people dressed in their finest clothes to gather for the long, solemn Mass, the traditional spiritual ritual of the occasion. Afterward, they spread the last of the winter's special stores—smoked meats and fish, dried fruits, nut-laced honey-breads—for the temporal celebration of feasting and dancing.

In Wallachia's capital, scores of boyars and their families also celebrated on a scale befitting their station. Following custom, they attended Mass in the prince's own chapel, then carried their festivity into his palace.

To accommodate the throng, the voevode's court was converted to its second function as a dining hall. It was tended by no less than a small army of menservants.

The head table was as sedate as it was small. It was set before the thrones of the voevode and his wife. At the side of the princess was their son tended by a nursemaid. At the side of the prince was the single guard—by custom, a mere token, standing off to the side—in this case, Wilk. As was the princely couple's due, they were offered the first and choicest ladles of each serving. Though Dracula passed them straight to his wife's lips, she ate only as much as she smiled: sparingly.

From the head table down, the boyars were seated in rank order, from the oldest, highest families to the lesser—like Gales and the new boyar, Cirstian—seated in deference near the walls. As the ranking cleric, Father Gregor held a place at the first boyar table.

It was at the point when bellies were full and the wine was flowing that music suddenly blared from the courtyard. A raucous piece. A dance. Flutes, fiddles, drums, cymbals…Like the piper's mythical tune, it drew all heads, but especially those of the ladies and children. Graciously, Dracula rose and took Prasha's hand. He bade her to take their son and lead the boyar families to the new festivity outside while he kept the men to himself.

It was to the first waves of the laughing and clapping of the women and children outside that Dracula turned to their husbands and fathers. "On this day, I would like to create a new tradition for our humble land to remember. I would like to tell you a few riddles."

From a voice half in the cup came the comment, "Like a jester!"

Other voices, also in their cups, laughed: the voevode as jester.

And Dracula laughed.

"First," he said, "I would offer a riddle of Easter: If Christmas marks the very birth of Christ, why is this day the holiest of our days?"

But that was no mystery. The answer came from many voices in many words: *Easter was when the Lamb of God died for man's sins. Yet it marked Jesus' triumph over death. It gave man salvation.*

"But can you tell me in a word?" Dracula said.

It was Father Gregor, also a bit in his cup, who gave the answer: "Resurrection."

"Aye," Dracula said. "Resurrection. And so I ask further…If we rejoice at this miracle achieved by God-Become-Man, should we not rejoice when mere mortals also achieve it?"

It was the priest again who gave voice to the puzzled silence of the hall. "No mortal ever has."

"But some have," Dracula said. "In a way. But hold that. Let me pose another riddle. Call it a riddle of numbers." He asked a boyar—and not a particularly old man, "How many voevodes have you known?"

"In my lifetime?"

"Of course."

The man shrugged with a smirk. "Twenty?"

Another voice instantly bellowed to top that number by five. Twenty-five voevodes. And it was on like a game: twenty-six, twenty-seven, twenty-eight…give or take a few. The laughter rolled with each number called, until a gray-beard stood—a bit unsteadily—and thumped a table: "Thirty! I've seen thirty come and go!"

The throng hooted and cheered until yet another of its members, with barely the trace of a beard yet, also stood unsteadily and thumped: "Well I've seen seven already! So imagine how many more I'll see before I'm as old as you!"

The hall erupted again and Dracula spread his hands for silence. But he had to wait for it. Wait. And, even then, as it was falling, someone demanded, "So what's the riddle here?"

"I will tell you," Dracula said. "But not just yet. For I have a third. A riddle of death. On this Easter, think of how our Christ Jesus died. Scourging. Crown of thorns. Crucifixion. Can you imagine a more horrible death?"

Father Gregor was first to respond. "Surely not."

Dracula challenged, "'Surely not,' father? *You* can say that? Think, father. Think of another death. One that you witnessed. In a way. A man buried. Alive. Face down."

The priest and many of the boyars blanched. They knew of the death of which Dracula spoke. Knew well. His brother's. Mircea's. People still spoke of it—in whispers. The recent investigation had confirmed the horrible details. And Father Gregor himself had opened the coffin.

Dracula repeated, still calmly, "Buried face down. So that—as his tormenters shouted to him—even as he was lowered into the ground—if he dug his way out he would only dig his way to hell."

Now he had the hall's attention, wine or no.

He asked again, "Can you imagine a more horrible death?"

Father Gregor was quick to speak not only to break the silence, but the mood. "But why dwell on death, lord? We should turn to other things. To this very day."

"Aye," Dracula said. "Let us turn to this very day. Let us turn back to my first riddle. Resurrection. What mere mortals have achieved it? Of whom was I speaking? I will tell you. I was not speaking of a single man, but of families. Two families. My own. And my wife's. They were tortured, raped, and murdered. Almost stamped out. Almost. And yet..." He spread his hands as though to indicate himself: "Resurrection."

Again the priest tried to deflect the voevode's meaning. "I see, lord. You speak of your son. The preservation of your line. By God's good grace."

"Yes," Dracula said. "By God's good grace. Two families marked for murder, for extinction. Two families resurrected. Which leads to my second riddle. Numbers. It was not so long ago that some of you stood in this very room and complained of my making free peasants. We have too few men already, you said. Too many lost in war. And I agree. Wallachia has lost too many men to war. Why?"

He gave the answer himself. "For the same reason you have seen so many voevodes. Intrigue. Treachery. By you. *You.* You plot to keep the voevode weak.

His weakness breeds war. War kills our men. Then you complain of it. To the voevode."

One of the boyars sprung to his feet. "So your 'riddles' are really threats."

"Threats?" Dracula pondered. "No. They are more like reasons."

"Reasons?"

"Yes," Dracula declared. "For what I am about to do. Do to the men—you!—who are as guilty as any for my brother's cruel death."

Another boyar rose. "You forget, *voevode*—our men outnumber yours."

"That's very true," Dracula said. "But yours are outside the gates and mine are within. And the gates have been locked."

He turned to the young boyar who had boasted of already having known seven voevodes. "You, sir," Dracula told him, "were wrong. Dead wrong. You marvelled at how many voevodes you will live to see. But you will not see even one more voevode. Nor will any of my enemies here. You know who you are."

And they did. For his *friends* had risen along the wall and—with the small army of servants—drawn daggers.

Father Gregor jumped to his feet. "You cannot—!"

The green eyes speared him. "I will not tell you again. Leave my realm to me."

The priest was brushed aside as the boyars were bound. As though in question, Wilk threw them a glance and raised a finger to Dracula. The forefinger. Impalement?

Dracula gave a nod with a missive: "Can you imagine a more horrible death?"

As the first of the prisoners were led into the courtyard, the sound of music and gaiety appropriately enough died.

Dracula asked Wilk, "You know what to do with the rest?"

With the boyar families. Wilk knew. The able-bodied had a purpose.

Dracula asked, "The castle's ready?"

The castle. The fortress that would soon be known—and known forever—as Castle Dracula.

"Aye," Wilk said. "All's ready."

As he left, Prasha entered, holding the young Vlad close. She was not just pale. She was white.

Dracula tried to assure her, "It *must* be done, love."

And so, on the first Easter Sunday of his reign, Dracula did as he had said: He created a tradition—a legend—that his land would never forget.

8

SUMMER. TRANSYLVANIA. The training had served the troops well. They were used to the regimen now: Sleep by day, ride by night. So, on this day, as the sun fell, the men rose with barely a prod from the sergeants.

They were well served, too—particularly the draguli—by what they had been in their past lives. In the highland woods that they now found themselves, as the heat of the day turned to mist in the night's chill, the insects swarmed to the very hint of the warmth of a body. Especially the gnats. They stuck to the skin even as they were squashed. They crawled into hair, ears, nostrils...even the sockets of eyes. But if soldiers were used to such hardships, what peasant was not?

Like the more experienced soldiers of the boyar allies who rode with them, the draguli ignored the insects and the dampness and the chill. They ate, according to plan, in silence and without fire: grain chewed like cud...bread...water. They brushed the horses to keep the beasts calm. They sharpened swords. They waited. As peasants always waited: in silence.

They watched as heaven sent what they could only take as a blessing: clouds. High clouds drifting toward the moon. Dracula had brought his men to this spot Tartar-style: creeping, sneaking, to their target. All the way from Tirgoviste. Move by night. Move to the very edge of the target. Like the Tartars. Then charge. All-out. Even if the victims suspected an attack—even if they had scouts and pickets—the attack would overwhelm them before an alarm would do any good.

Now the woods' veritable symphony—the crickets—covered the rustling of the brush as Dracula ordered the ranks forward. Not that the cover was needed. The town was still a bit up the road.

Before stepping onto the road, Dracula called his commanders: Wilk, Cirstian, Gales. The final leg of the plan was simple: Ring the town, close in. They would wait for the clouds to shroud the moon.

There were no questions. But Gales noted, "Once we take this step..."

He had raised the point before. As Dracula had also raised it with himself. Once the night's business was finished, Hungary would be furious.

But Hungary was still led by its weak king, secreted away in his palace with his hostage, Matthias Hunyadi. The king had become so timid, in fact, that it was hard to say which of them was the prisoner. So Hungary would be in no position to act on its fury. By the time it was, as Dracula gambled, other things would outweigh the fury. And further, as Dracula pointedly told Gales, "There are some things that I will not tolerate. From anyone. Whatever the consequences."

Cirstian and Gales were sent back to the rear, with the other boyars and their banderia. When Dracula rode they would follow.

With the troops set, Dracula and Wilk waited in the van. They were watching the clouds when a word was hissed at their backs: *"Strigoica!"*

They turned to the dragul who had voiced it and followed his finger pointing to the road. The silhouette was small but clear in the silver light. A woman. Old. Bent. Hobbling toward the town.

Dracula saw no point in running her down in the upcoming attack. And she just might provide some information. He ordered, "Fetch her."

It took a second for him to realize that no one had moved.

"Fetch her."

But he saw the look on the men's faces: fright. As they variously began making the Sign of the Cross, Dracula only frowned and passed the order to Wilk, "Fetch her, will you?"

Wilk had already started when he thought to ask, "What's strigoica?"

"Witch," Dracula explained.

Wilk stopped. "Witch? You mean...?" He threw a nod to the old woman.

Dracula snapped, "That's what they think."

A dragul amended, "Or she might be the Woman in White, lord."

The Woman in White. Death. Everyone knew her. She was part of the lore of all Europe. Meet her face-to-face and your days were ended. Wilk was frozen now.

Dracula heaved a sigh. "Not you, too? You can't believe in witches?"

Wilk groped. "*You* believe in comets."

"That's different," Dracula said. "That is astrology. This is superstition."

But as Wilk still hesitated Dracula gave a disgusted swipe of the hand. "Worthless! The lot of you!" He started for the road himself, swearing audibly about hiring mercenaries.

The woman stopped when she saw him, but the meeting was calm. He was patient in leading her back, offering an arm to help her. As he returned to the woods, his men recoiled. The woman was holding a cat. It caused more signing of the Cross. A dragul whispered to Wilk, whose eyes widened as he whispered to Dracula in turn. "It could be her familiar."

"Her what?"

"Familiar. The cat. It could be her link with the devil."

Dracula just shook his head as he turned back to the woman. "Grandmother, what are you doing here at this time of night?"

She stroked the cat. "Looking for this little devil."

The last word made the men nearly jump. As she looked at them curiously, Dracula said, "Pay them no mind. They are *addled*."

"Who are they?" she asked. "Who are you?"

Dracula gave a non-answer: "Soldiers. Tell me, grandmother, have our comrades reached the town?"

"Comrades?"

"Other soldiers."

"No. No soldiers."

"I see," Dracula said. It was as he thought: The town had no garrison. Why should it? The Saxons had always been under the kings' special protection. Who would dare defy them?

"Well, grandmother," Dracula said, "you really should not be out here at night."

"What do I have to fear?" she said. "I'm already threescore years. I couldn't leave this little one lost."

"Of course not," Dracula said. "Still, stay here until we ride. We will take you back to the town."

He barked an order—a firm order—*no more superstitious nonsense*—to escort the woman to the rear.

When the clouds touched the moon, he mounted and led the troops onto the road. Canter. Trot. Full gallop. They followed the road right through the town, fanned out, and closed in. The first of the people roused from sleep had time only to run to their doors to see the riders swarming. They and the rest were rooted from the houses and herded into the main square in a stunned silence.

Dracula's troops dismounted. They worked their way through the mass of prisoners, separating the men from the rest. Then they separated the burghers— and the claimant to Dracula's own throne whom this Saxon town had harbored—from the other men.

Dracula called the claimant forward. "By what right do you claim my throne?"

"I am your brother," the man said. "Your half-brother."

It was as Dracula had heard. The man claimed to be the bastard son of Dracula's own father. The voevode smiled wryly. The man seemed to believe what he claimed. And who could say…Most noblemen kept mistresses. It was almost *de rigueur*. And Vlad Dracul had been no different than most.

"Well, brother," Dracula told him, "I suppose I should show you mercy." He called a priest from among the townspeople. "Bring a book of the Rites."

The Last Rites.

The book was brought. Dracula gave it to the claimant to read. To read his own Last Rites. When he finished, Dracula himself took a sword and carried out the sentence. No discussion. No pleas. Quick death. Mercy. Beheading.

Dracula then had the burghers marched into the woods. To do some cutting. While they were at it, he chose a spot on a rise at the edge of town. There, he ordered a table set by the townspeople. A banquet. It was ready by the time the burghers were marched back. Each with his own stake.

The people were made to sit in the dirt and watch. To bear witness as Dracula and his officers sat and ate while the burghers were impaled.

Both the executions and the feast took hours. When they were finally done, Dracula strode to the massed people. He spoke to the priest, but loudly enough for all to hear. "I did not start this feud. It can end here. Or get worse. Much worse. The choice is yours. Tell the other towns."

He was mounting with his troops when an old woman hobbled from among the people, even as the priest tried to hold her back. Hours before—in another lifetime—she had met the voevode in the woods. She had asked then who he was. Now she was not asking. She would tell him who he was.

She snarled, "'Dragon?' Great warrior?" She spat a single word in his own Romanian language.

It sounded like *Tseh'-pesh*. It was written *Tepes*: "Impaler."

9

AUTUMN. TIRGOVISTE. As Dracula approached the court hall, Wilk was already waiting by the great doors. He reported to the voevode, "They're taking the clothes."

"Good," Dracula said. "Then maybe they'll come for the rest."

"I think they will. I also popped a few kegs. Just enough to give them a whiff."

"What did you tell them?"

"That it's a celebration. Of your victories over your enemies."

"Indeed it is," Dracula said. But before the "celebration" there was other business at hand: "How many cases?"

"Five."

Dracula was pleased. "Only five. For the whole week. This land is learning. Good. We can finish them. Then finish with the other."

He entered the court and called the cases. Five separate cases. Theft. All caught "red-handed."

The first: *For trying to steal the people's cup—the golden goblet that the prince had left at the fountain. Guilty.*

The second: *For trying to steal the people's cup. Guilty.*

The third, fourth, and fifth. The cup. The cup. The cup. Guilty. Guilty. Guilty. No discussion. No pleas for mercy. Dracula was not interested in excuses. Not interested in hardship, deprivation…or even, as some of the culprits out-landishly claimed, the good works they had intended with the gold they would have gotten from selling the cup.

At each verdict, Wilk raised the finger: *Impalement?* Dracula gave five nods.

When the cases were done, Dracula went to his quarters. Prasha, as usual lately, was in bed, rapt in her sewing. The baby Vlad slept in a crib nearby.

Dracula asked quietly, "Will you come with me today, love?"

Her eyes remained fixed on cloth and needle. "No, I will not." She offered without rancor, "In truth I *cannot*. I simply cannot."

And, in truth, he loved her the more for it. Her tenderness. Her compassion. And yet that compassion ran counter to what he had to do.

He offered in turn, "Please, love. Understand." As he had told her before. "I could not leave things as they were. I cannot leave this land as I found it—in its *insanity*. The boyars killed our families. They killed one another. And they killed our people with their intrigues. They would have gone on killing. Unless I did what I did."

"Unless you cut them out. Completely. To the roots."

"Aye," he said. "To the roots. If I left their families alive, it would have only begun over. With our son and their sons. And over. Long after we are dead."

She did not see the longing glance he threw to their son.

He continued, "And the same it is with the Saxons…and all the rest. And what I do, love, I do not do lightly. I pray on it. As I have prayed ever since the time we spent with Stephen. When he urged me to find God again. And I did. So I pray. You know that, love. And always the same answer comes to me: I was made—molded in my own hardships—for this land in these times. Clearly, this is what heaven intends. That I finish what I started. And when it is done—"

She injected the fact, "I might not live to see it."

It was true. He knew it only too well. She had too much compassion for the brutal business he was about. The business, as he saw it, that he *had* to be about—even though it drove her to her spells of melancholia. He could only hope…But this business took time. Wallachia had been sick for a long, long time.

So he left her to her bed, but her image stayed with him as he left the palace and rode to the appointed place. It was a hall. A large hall. It stood alone at the edge of the city. He had found it in ruins and restored it for this single occasion.

The beggars streaming toward it cheered him as he waded through their mass. In fact, in the new clothes he had given them that day, they hardly looked like beggars at all. He had even opened a makeshift public bath for them. They were clean. Dressed. Some even primped. They seemed very much like the everyday folk they had once been, except perhaps for the heavy smell of wine now hanging on their breath.

With their prince to lead them on, their step was light as they entered the hall. It was already set for the banquet: food, wine, music. And, though there were hundreds of beggars, there was room at the tables for them all and still more.

The sun went down with the first courses. As fast as the food disappeared into mouths—and sometimes into pockets—the trays were heaped afresh. From his solitary place at their head, Dracula kept the feast lively. When one band of musicians tired, another was brought to stoke the festive mood. And, as casks were emptied, they were promptly rolled out, and full ones were rolled in.

It was well into the night when one of the beggars rose at the prompting of those around him. They laughed when he teetered and nearly fell. Yet when he spread his hands they joined him in calling for silence. And, considering the condition of the audience, it fell silent rather quickly. All except for one poor fellow who was among the true cripples. Epilepsy. He rocked in spasms until, at the speaker's gesture and amidst laughs, his hands and feet were held to keep him still.

Before the speaker could begin, Dracula noted, "I am impressed. You seem to be a man of some standing here."

The crowd bellowed that he was indeed. One shouted that he was, in fact, like their own prince. The beggar prince. As the rest began hailing him as such, the man merely bowed graciously to the voevode.

Even Dracula had to laugh. He invited, "Then speak. As from one prince to another."

The man gathered himself against his teetering. He said sincerely, "I am honored, lord." He began, "First, lord, please accept our gratitude for your kind hospitality. For everything. These clothes. This feast."

The others murmured in approval.

"But, second, lord," the man said, "why? Why are we honored like this? Us? The beggars?" He chuckled. "Even our fellow citizens ask. The shopkeepers. The peasants. Even priests. 'Why are you scum being invited to this banquet? Why not us in your place?'"

At that Dracula laughed, replying, "Fortunately I don't have to answer to them."

"But, lord," the beggar persisted, "there's much reason in what they say. It's not just that we're beggars and they're 'respectable.'"

At the word his comrades grumbled and sneered.

"The fact is, lord," the man went on, "you were vexed with us beggars. You sent your men to chase us from the streets."

"Aye, I did," Dracula said. "And yet, like waves on the shore, you receded before my men, but always you came back."

A man rose and jerked a thumb to his back. "Well I, for one, lord, didn't recede so good. I got the lash marks to prove it."

The others shared his guffaws as they hauled him back into his seat.

Dracula pressed the spokesman, "But tell me...I urged you all to work, yet so few of you did. Why?"

"Lord, I can only speak for myself. Work for what? I was a farmer once. Sun to moon, I worked, on all but Sundays and holy days. But what I grew was taken by taxes. By the prince—with all respect. And by the Church and my boyar. If it wasn't taken by taxes, it was a flood. If not a flood, a drought. If not a drought, the Turks and brigands. Lord, I live better now on the streets—and with no boyar on my back."

"What if the whole land thought that way?"

"I said, lord, I can speak only for myself. And I admit, lord...even the life I live is not easy. Not easy for the spirit."

Dracula chided, "And you set an ill example. Of sloth."

"For who, lord? I couldn't blame a common man tempted to my life."

"And when foreigners come here, you give the wrong impression of our people."

"How so, lord?"

"They think us lazy. And dull."

"Or perhaps, lord," the man said with a wink, "they think us clever. Too clever to work like animals."

Dracula chuckled. "In truth, my fellow prince, I've often heard men marvel at you beggars' cleverness. They wonder why they work so hard when you seem to live almost as well. But let me ask further...What if war comes to our land? Will you fight?"

"In truth, lord, what could I offer? I know nothing of fighting."

"What if the enemy comes to take you?"

"For what, lord? What would I fetch even as a slave?"

Dracula made to conclude, "Then you have nothing to offer anyone?"

The beggar took mock offense. "Please, lord. Of course I have something to offer. I offer the chance for better men to practice charity."

And again Dracula had to laugh as the man and his "subjects" howled.

When the din died, Dracula rose and paced among the tables. "Tell me. Any of you. What do you think of heaven? What is it?"

"Bliss," someone answered.

Dracula asked, "But what is bliss?"

Some flung mock answers: Bliss was a full cup, a maiden's loins...Then a real answer came. "Bliss is seeing God. That's what the priests say." Another voice called, "Bliss is the end of worldly troubles."

To that voice, Dracula turned. "Aye. The end of worldly troubles. That surely is bliss!" He snatched a cup and toasted: *To the end of worldly troubles!*

As the beggars cheered and drank, the band was struck up again, and soon there was dancing in the aisles. Dracula called to his servants and led them among the tables in a sudden attack. An attack on all empty cups. He himself worked with the servants urging his guests to drink...drink...

At one point, a man clutched the voevode's sleeve. "Thank you, lord! Thank you! On this night, even a beggar like me feasts like a boyar!"

"Aye," Dracula assured him. "*Just* like a boyar."

The end of the day stretched into the beginning of the next and crept into twilight before the hall was finally quiet. Quiet except for snoring. And for the rocking of one man. The epileptic. Dracula held the man's nose and filled his mouth with wine, until he, too, was slumped over.

Then Dracula called for Wilk. With him was Father Gregor, bleary-eyed and agitated, disgusted at the bacchanal sight.

"Who is it, lord?" the priest asked. "Which of them needs the rites?"

Dracula answered, "All of them. Except—" He pointed Wilk to the beggar prince. "There's hope for him yet," Dracula said. "His mind's alive. When he wakes, give him a purse. Send him back into life."

Father Gregor's eyes were clear now. Wide. "But the rest...Lord, you can't...Please..."

Dracula was patient. With a foot, he nudged the epileptic. "This one, father, has no mind." He pointed to a woman. "She lifts her skirts for copper coins. She is poxed." And he pointed to another and another: hopelessly crippled—in body, mind, or spirit. All of them. As the voevode saw it.

But the priest was compelled to beg, "Please, lord. Show them mercy."

Dracula spread his hands to the hall. "I already have, father. Look. *In vino miserciordia.*"

In the wine, on that night, there was mercy.

10

1458. THE PORTE. The merchant-spy did not know where to begin. Hungary or Wallachia? The *new* king or Dracula? And he was not sure how the sultan would take some of this news. Did it bode ill or good?

Mohammed, sitting across the low table with Radu at his side, prompted, "Hungary."

The spy began. Hungary had a new king: Matthias. Matthias *Hunyadi.* The former king was dead.

It seemed a mystery how he had died so suddenly. It *seemed.* One morning, he simply did not awake. But the whispers claimed to know: the "quiet cup." Poison. All of the factions, they said, had grown tired of the king. Weak. Ineffective. Since the execution of Hunyadi's older son, he had become a recluse, secreted away with his prisoner, Matthias, behind castle walls.

After his death, the factions offered the crown to Matthias.

The spy waited to gauge the sultan's reaction, even as Radu also waited. Mohammed took a long breath. His head rose. He smiled. He slid his own plate of sweetmeats to the spy, who hoped this good mood of the sultan's would hold as he proceeded to tell of Dracula.

The sultan, of course, was already abreast of certain events: the boyar massacre, the raid on the Saxon town, and the mass murder of the beggars.

He knew that Dracula had feasted among the impaled in the Saxon town. And he knew why: a message to the sultan himself. Dracula knew of the Turks' own gesture of feasting among the corpses at the long-ago battle of Kossovo. And he had seen the Turks feast as they watched an impalement—the first that Dracula himself had ever witnessed. So he was telling Mohammed now that he could be just as coldly brutal.

Mohammed knew, too, of the details of the beggars' murder. After the voevode let them drink themselves into a stupor in a great hall, he had the hall boarded up and burned to the ground.

Now the spy said, "Highness, if I may…Let me add some detail to what you already know. But let me save the greater news for last."

Given leave, he continued, "Highness, above the Danube, this 'Dracula' is now called *Tepes*. And the name has carried to your own lands. Your own people now call him *Kaziglu*."

Kaziglu. Turkish: the Impaler.

The spy explained, "He is considered something of a jin. A devil. A bogeymen. Mothers cow mischievous children with the threat: 'Kaziglu will get you.' And your soldiers on patrol tease the new recruits: 'Beware of Kaziglu!'"

Mohammed and Radu chuckled. Was this the image that the "Son of The Dragon" had intended?

Radu scoffed, "Well it's no mystery how he got the name."

Mohammed darkened just a bit. Amused by the name or not, he was also reminded of all the recent complaints from Hamza Pasha. No matter how many raiders the pasha sent at Wallachia, Kaziglu, or his new frontier boyars—the lethal pair, Cirstian and Gales—seemed to be waiting. The Danube was dotted with raiders rotting on stakes. Hamza was clamoring for all-out war.

"No," the spy agreed. "There is no mystery about the name. But there were other mysteries about the man himself. Two in particular. One solved. One yet unsolved. The first is that of the boyar families."

He elaborated. When Dracula impaled the boyars, he had their families—the able-bodied at least—herded into a column and marched from Tirgoviste.

The spy himself posed for emphasis, "Marched to where? I followed as close as I could. And our Greek, Volinos, also followed on a different tack. But the time came when we had to turn back to avoid suspicion. And the boyar families never returned."

Mohammed asked, "But you solved this mystery?"

"Yes, highness. And learned something else by it. You remember early in Kaziglu's reign when I wrote that he was fortifying certain places. Well he kept one secret. On the Transylvanian border. A fortress. A wreck. He used the boyar families to rebuild it."

Castle Dracula. As the spy had learned...Dracula had prepared the site in advance of the fatal Easter Day. Tools for cutting rock. Kilns for drying brick. Makeshift huts. Huts. Nothing more.

He had his victims—women and children—marched to the spot and worked—to death—still in their Easter finery. As the months passed and the victims dropped and rotted in the dirt, the castle rose stone by stone.

Radu was appalled. "Gruesome."

"Yes, lord," the spy agreed. "But the second mystery is even more so. Kaziglu. Impaler. But where are his impaled victims? They seem to disappear."

Mohammed grunted, "Disappear?"

"Yes, highness," the spy said. "He impales them in public places to…" He gave a cough at the upcoming pun. "…make a point. But after some days they disappear. Stake and all."

Radu suggested, "Maybe the people take them down."

"I think not, lord. Kaziglu has a law: Take one down and you hang in its place. On the same stake. And his laws are obeyed. In fact, that is where he finds most of his victims. Lawbreakers. Thieves, murderers, and the like. Hundreds of them. Maybe even a thousand—or two—by now. He holds his own courts. His sentence is always the same. For everything. And then the bodies disappear."

"Gruesome indeed," Radu said. "Surely his madness grows worse."

Mohammed agreed, "A berserker."

"Yes, highness," the spy said eagerly. "A berserker. For hear now the last of the news." The news that he knew would please the sultan. "Kaziglu's raid on the Saxons has fanned to a near-war. If it is let to go on…" He raised an eyebrow.

The sultan, too, raised an eyebrow. As did Radu. Their look begged the rest of the story.

Dracula's raid on the single town the summer before had the exact opposite effect of what he had intended. The Saxons were hardly like mischievous children. They were not so easily cowed, even by the Impaler. Why should they be? Their service to Hungary's kings was *special*—money—so they enjoyed special protection. And they of course had money for a war of their own.

After the raid they hired garrisons and fortified their towns. They also found more claimants to Dracula's throne and began hiring men for them as well.

But neither was Dracula cowed by the Saxons, money or no. Like a dagger, he thrust into Transylvania again and again. He overran the garrisons and burned the towns. He exterminated the claimants. In his wake he left the land, like the Danubian border, dotted with the pale. He made war against the whole Saxon race. Even women and children went on the stake.

"Surely, highness," the spy finished, "if this is let to go on…"

But Mohammed and Radu were already grinning. With his own hand, the sultan began pouring wine for his spy, who blurted, "Highness, no. Please. I am not worthy—"

Mohammed waved it off and also poured for himself and Radu. "A toast," he told the spy. "To your usual good work. You will go back and finish it for me. But first…you will be smothered in my favor. And in pleasure." He gestured to his hair. "Gold. Fire. Onyx."

Gold, fire, onyx. The spy's skin tingled at the very thought. Smothered in *pleasure*. By the women the sultan kept for his special guests. Golden-haired women. And those with hair like fire. And like onyx. Two kinds of onyx. The long, silky blackness of the women of the east. And the tight, brushed curls of those of Africa. All women of rare beauty. And technique. And taste.

And more, the spy thought…smothered in the sultan's *favor*. That meant gold. Real gold. And jewels and who knew what else? The sultan could be a generous man.

Even as they drank and he was given leave, the spy was thanking heaven for his fortune. For Kaziglu. For it was Kaziglu—truly—who had brought him the sultan's favor. And with these favors, perhaps—when his work with Kaziglu was done—he would ask the sultan's permission to retire. Surely it would be granted. He had served long and hard. And he had sharpened many "eyes"—men like Volinos—to take his place in the sultan's service. So he would have his own estates and his own rare maidens and…He could already see it.

When he was gone, Mohammed asked Radu, "My friend, can you yet be a bit patient?"

Could Radu wait just a little longer to be voevode?

Radu was beaming. "Of course."

He fairly leaped at his friend, sending them both to the floor laughing. Of course they would wait. Because their enemy, Dracula, had made a *colossal* mistake. One that could easily lead to his complete and utter undoing. And the undoing of Hungary as well. Especially if this new king, Matthias, proved as petty and hapless as the king he had just replaced.

11

HUNGARY. Over the past weeks, King Matthias had spent more time in the small room on the plain wooden chair than he had in the court on the throne. He was piecing together his faction and the beginnings of his reign.

If his eyes were still tired from his recent ordeals—his brother's execution, his own imprisonment—it was the tiredness of awakening. Each day the eyes were more alert. His twenty-year-old face with its slightly heavy jaw had already all but shed the lines of his grief.

For the work at hand, he was dressed simply. His tunic, leggings, and short cap were gray—plain, if soft. His only adornments were a thick gold chain that showed the royal seal and a weighty gold ring that had no significance other than the fact that he liked it.

He nodded to the steward to summon his last caller of the day: a former enemy of his father's. A mercenary. His name was Jan Jiskraz. Matthias was somewhat surprised when they finally met face to face. Jiskraz had begun his career so long before, in the old Hussite wars, as one of the Protestant reformers fighting against the papists, against the chivalry of Hungary itself. After that, he had taken sides in Hungary's own civil war, fighting on behalf of a bold queen against Janos Hunyadi's faction of barons. It was from that war that he now held a province near the country's northern border.

But that war, or the bold queen's name, would not be even mentioned in this meeting. Jiskraz had been summoned for business. New business. Not for old sentiment or hard feeling.

What surprised Matthias was the mercenary's appearance. His bowl-shaped hair was white, his face well creased. But he was still built like a dagger, and his accoutrement only strengthened the image: heavy, bark-colored leather, studded and polished; vest slightly winged at the shoulders, belted tight at the waist; snug chaps; boots to the thighs. And Jiskraz's eyes still showed a very dark blue.

Matthias addressed him frankly, "We can be of use to each other."

The frankness struck Jiskraz. Was this new boy-king a fool, admitting so easily to a need? Or was he just...practical? Eminently so—stating the obvious rather than haggle about it.

Jiskraz waited for him to go on, but Matthias also waited, and he was the king. It was left to Jiskraz to respond. "I would keep my northern province, sire. With peace between us."

Matthias gave a nod: *reasonable.* He stated his own price: "I need you to stand by. Maybe to fight. Soon."

Jiskraz was not surprised when the king elaborated: the south. Transylvania. Wallachia. Dracula and the Saxons.

Jiskraz started to offer, "Sire, the sultan—"

"Pardon," Matthias said. "But I know. The sultan's 'eyes.' He is watching this feud and gloating. Hoping that we and Wallachia tear each other apart. Which is why it must end."

Jiskraz wondered: *But why me?* The king had other men.

As though reading the thoughts, Matthias was again frank. Not baiting. Without guile. "Are you afraid of Vlad Dracula?"

Jiskraz answered without guile. "The only man I ever feared—and yet yearned to fight—was your own father. My men would make mincemeat of Dracula's."

Matthias prompted, "And yet..."

Jiskraz gave the answer, "Dracula himself is...relentless."

And his thoughts followed. The man who attacked Dracula would have an enemy for life. So this is what Matthias would have: Jiskraz against Dracula. Let Dracula's vengeance fall on the mercenary, not on the king himself. Like playing a pawn against a pawn.

But these thoughts, too, Matthias seemed to read. He assured Jiskraz, "I will not use you lightly. I would rather it not come to war. I would bargain for Vlad Dracula's peace. To a point."

Aye, Jiskraz thought. *To a point.* Because even if Dracula accepted the king's peace he would have to face a reckoning. It was inevitable. Because in attacking the Saxons the voevode had, as it were, slashed the king's own purse. Sooner or later the king himself would have to make good the loss.

12

1460. THE PORTE. The spy was grave in giving the news: "High-ness, Kaziglu's feud with the Saxons has ended."

Even as he uttered the words, he thought of the sultan's disappointment. On this trip, there would be no rewards of women and gold. And the spy's retirement from the service would undoubtedly have to wait.

But Mohammed's frown was only slight. He looked to Radu and shrugged: *So what if the feud had ended? The prospect of Hungary fighting Wallachia, tearing each other apart, had simply been too much to pray for.*

And, peace with the Saxons or no, Kaziglu still had his problem. His attack on the king's merchants could not be erased. Or forgotten.

But the sultan's frown arched a bit when he heard how the peace had been effected. The king. Matthias. He had been patient. Two years patient. He had talked to one side and the other. Over and again. Even as they persisted in their killing. "And," the spy noted, "he talked quietly. No bluster. No tantrums. It was only when he brought them close on their own terms that he imposed his. And in no *uncertain* terms. They could accept the peace or face his wrath."

So Matthias, Mohammed now knew, was not at all like his predecessor. Not rash. Nor petty. Nor afraid.

A worthy opponent.

And his terms to Dracula and the Saxons had been blunt. Essentially everything reverted to pre-feud status: *Honor the trade agreements. No harboring of each other's enemies.* Further, the Saxons were to pay Dracula a sum toward their own future defense. Against whom? The king could only have one enemy in mind: the

Osmanli empire. But Dracula also had to pay the Saxons reparations. For the destruction he had caused. And he had caused so much destruction that the scales of payments weighed against him. Heavily.

The sultan asked, "Didn't the king give Kaziglu anything else?"

"Only a vague promise, highness. Nothing written. More of…an assurance. A military alliance."

Mohammed grunted. In effect, the king had made Dracula the Saxons' protector. Or at least their first line of defense. Against the sultan himself. At Dracula's own expense.

As for the promised alliance, would the king honor it? *Could* he? Really? Would the Saxons let him?

Matthias had given Dracula only words. But even words set on paper were only as thin as the paper. And the king had not even set his "alliance" on paper.

How much of all this, Mohammed wondered, did Kaziglu understand? Did he really believe that his slate with Hungary had been wiped clean? Or was he even now, as it were, looking north over his shoulder, waiting for the king to exact the Saxons' retribution? It all came down to one thing.

So Mohammed decided, "We know Kaziglu is mad. We must see *how* mad."

He would send his spy yet again to Wallachia.

13

MONTHS LATER. CASTLE DRACULA. The castle had its first guest. A reluctant guest. He had been taken crossing the border into Wallachia after his latest meeting with his master, the sultan.

He was naked now. Stripped of his merchant's disguise. He sat in the only chair in the small, dank, windowless room. It was set in the center of the floor. His host stood before him. Wilk, Cirstian, and Gales completed a circle around him.

"Do not tell me a second time that I am mistaken," Dracula said. "I remember the first time I saw you. When I was a boy, a hostage in the sultan's court. I remember when. You were giving the sultan information. It was so long ago, but I even remember what you were wearing and what the sultan was wearing and the color of the floor tiles and…You see. It's a gift of God, my memory. And the second time I saw you was in my own capital. As the princess and I rode through the streets."

The spy hung his head. He avoided the stare of the green eyes and tried to hide his trembling.

"You are a rodent," Dracula said. "A rat. An old rat. A cunning rat. But a mere rat nonetheless. And it's a poor rat that has only one hole, eh? Think of the gold you've packed away. And how you might not live to spend it."

The spy caught the word. He clung to it: "'Might,' lord? 'Might?' Then might I still li—?"

Dracula dismissed the thought. "You see," he told the others. "Like all the Osmanli, this one is used to using the mind as a weapon. But now the weapon is turned on him. He thinks of all the men that he's lured into the spot he himself is in now. Caught. Trapped."

To the spy's own surprise, even in the cold room, he felt the sweat running under his arms. With an effort he kept his head. "You said 'might,' lord. Is there still a chance—?"

He flinched at a sudden movement from Wilk. But Wilk was simply showing a ring, taken from the spy's own finger. He slid the gem on its face aside to reveal a hollow. Filled with powder. Poison. He noted, "I think he'd prefer this just now."

"Aye," Dracula said. "So would I in his place."

And Cirstian and Gales agreed around, *Aye* and *Aye*.

Dracula continued, "I am going to spare you the usual epitaph for a spy: *Coward. Gutless. Sells men's souls—for thirty pieces of silver.*"

Thirty pieces of silver. Like Judas in the Christian scripture betraying the Lord Jesus.

Dracula noted to his men, "Look at the vein throbbing in his neck."

The spy went hot then cold. His trembling rose to an outright shiver.

Dracula pronounced, "You have offended me with your feet—when you first trod my soil."

Wilk began an imaginary list: "Feet. So we'll need pins. Barbed pins."

"Aye," Cirstian said. "And a hammer."

Gales finished, "And a brand. With coals."

The spy swooned. But the mercy of fainting did not take him. He heard Dracula go on.

"And you have offended me with your hands—when you wrote your secret messages to your pig sultan."

"Hands," Wilk said. "We'll need a vise."

"And a saw," Cirstian added.

"And tongs," Gales said.

The word bounced from the spy's rumination: "Tongs?"

Wilk explained with a gesture. "To wrench—no…to pry—your fingers from their joints. Before we saw them off."

The spy slid from the chair to his knees, head pressed to the floor. "I am an old man."

"Perhaps," Dracula said. "But you'll be much older after the first hour of torture."

The spy pleaded, "But I can help you, lord. I can—"

"You can what—offer what a spy always has to offer? Information?"

"Yes, lord. Yes. I know much. Very much."

"You will tell me anyway," Dracula said. "Trust me."

"Yes, lord. I won't deny it, lord. You can pull what I know from me. I'm an old man. Weak. But…But I can serve you much better. I can."

He took Dracula's silence for hope and pressed on. "The sultan still expects to hear from me. If he doesn't he'll know something's gone afoul. But I can tell him whatever you want. Anything. Lull him. Gull him. Anything."

Dracula paced a bit. "It might be worth it to me. Serve me to save yourself from torture."

The spy seized on it. As he had traded like a merchant before, he made to trade now. "And what if I do more, lord? Much more? Might I save myself from death? I can—"

"Serve me *very* well," Dracula offered, "and I promise that you will not fear even death."

The spy lifted his eyes. "But…"

As he hesitated, Dracula stated the obvious. "But how do you know I'll keep my word?" He forced a laugh. "Aye, with the likes of you, how do I know myself?" But he placed a hand on his breast, on his dragon emblem. "I swear it. It will be as I said. You will not fear even death. *If* you serve me *very* well."

The spy's words flowed even as he took his seat and huddled in his nakedness. He spilled the sultan's plans. As though his life depended on it. Verily. "Pardon, lord, but the sultan thinks you mad. He thinks to use it against you. He wonders if you realize the mistake you made with the Saxons. The king will be their vengeance. Sooner or later. They will force him. The sultan wonders if you realize this."

Because, as the sultan saw it, if Dracula realized that, he might be tempted to renew his ties with the Porte. Of course, there could be no real reconciliation. Not after Dracula's insolence to the sultan. But if the voevode were mad enough—and fearful enough of the king now—he might be tempted.

The spy explained, "He is going to try to trap you. He will send a delegation. They will be haughty. Accusing. They will remind you that you owe tribute and janissary recruits. And that you have killed Hamza Pasha's men. But they will hold out the hope of your making amends. *If* you come to the Porte."

Dracula laughed. "He thinks I'm that mad?"

The spy shrugged. "He thinks it worth a try, lord. It's cheaper than war, eh? And that's where I come in. He waits to hear from me now, to know your state of mind. Do you fear Hungary? Might you be tempted to come to the Porte?"

"And if I don't come?"

"Ah, lord. Then, you see, he'll only try another ruse. Another trap. He will send, as it were, the 'roundabout word. He will say that he still wants to parlay. To settle your differences. He will offer that you meet in a mutually agreed place. Not with him, of course, but his man. Hamza Pasha."

Dracula was weighing, "Meet where?"

"On your own border. Under terms that will make you feel safe. Even more than safe. But, lord...The one who brings his offer to you will help seal your fate."

"Who is it?"

"A 'neutral.' A merchant. One who has given you many gifts."

Dracula guessed, "The Greek."

The spy nodded. "Volinos."

Wilk injected, "He seems a fop. Nothing but a fop."

The spy laughed. "It is only part of his disguise. Give gifts. Play the fop. What harm could there be in such a man?"

Wilk shook his head. "Diabolical."

"Truly," Dracula agreed. "And I suppose if the sultan can't trap me..." He looked to the spy.

"Yes, lord. Then war. Even now, the sultan is assembling troops. He would rather avoid the war, but...He is fairly recovered from Belgrade. And he wants Wallachia settled before King Matthias grows any stronger."

Dracula considered. "He plays chess, this sultan. Always with the board. Always. So now he plays Wallachia to the edge."

The spy breathed easier. "Yes, lord. And I can help you. Surely you see it."

Dracula agreed, "Surely. In fact, we can make it all quite a farce. A jest. If you play me true."

His eyes sought the spy's. And in the entire room the spy saw nothing but the eyes as Dracula spoke. "But if you play me false—if I even think you play me false...Your mind will be asking your soul how it is that your body is still alive."

It needed no elucidation.

Dracula took his men aside. "I learned one thing from Janos Hunyadi. If war is inevitable, start it. Choose the time and place and everything else you possibly can."

"But what of the king?" Gales asked. "The 'rat' just said it. The king won't join us."

"Aye," Dracula said. "The rat said it. And the sultan—and common wisdom—believe it: *The Saxons are sacrosanct.* They are money itself. The king's money. Cross them, and the king has no choice but to be your enemy."

Gales advised, "And what chance will we have without Hungary?"

"What chance indeed?" Dracula said. "And the common wisdom might be right. Unless...Unless we start the war and do well. Very well."

"Yes," Cirstian said. "How can the king turn his back on a victory over the Turk?"

Gales noted, "But we have no cannon. None to speak of."

"But I think we can find some," Dracula said. "In a 'mutually agreed place.'"

Wilk added, "And Moldavia should join us."

"Yes," Dracula said. "It's time I sent to my cousin. Let him know what we are about. Tell him to send what he can."

14

TIRGOVISTE. Vlad III, princeling of Wallachia, was unaware that his father was watching. The boy was rapt in his own fan-tasy, playing "horsey." His mount was the carved head of a pony set on a stick that he straddled to "ride." As Dracula watched, as fast as the boy was scooting along the halls, it seemed that he might, in fact, have hooves—or even wheels—instead of mere four-year-old feet.

Reining his pony to a turn, Vlad saw his father. They both grinned and extended their arms. Vlad flew into his father's embrace and clung as he was lifted from the floor. He beamed at being asked—and beamed even more at knowing—where his mother might be found: "Mommy sewing."

But, of course, Dracula thought. Sewing. As always. In the room she had taken for her quarters. Her own, separate quarters.

But the door to the room was open, as it always was when the boy was playing outside. Prasha had not, at least, shut out their son.

Dracula sent the boy to his game again and stepped into the doorway. In the windowless room, his wife sat at a small table, working by the glow of a single lamp. She faced a side wall, half turned from the door, but Dracula knew that she

saw him. Yet she did not turn even when he entered the room and sat on the bed
behind her.

He asked quietly, "Do you hate me so much?"

Her hands were working...working...Spinning minute detail into her cloth.
The design was striking. But faceless. No dragon now. No banner for her husband. Just a splash of color. Intricate. Demanding a fine, steady touch. But when
her hands stopped they were trembling. "I do not hate you."

As though ashamed of the trembling, the fingers sprang back into their work.
Her words came evenly. "I don't hate anyone really. What is just is. The way of
the world. Our world. Wars. Feuds. Family against family. I was naive to think it
could be any other way."

His hand stroked her shoulder. She did not recoil. But neither did she warm
to him.

She continued, "You are right in what you said. If you did not kill our enemies, we ourselves would be dead. And if you do not tame this land it is lost. To
the Turk. Or Hungary. Or its own lust. For blood."

"And if you see that, love," he began, "can't you—"

Her answer cut, "No. I cannot accept what you...what has been done. I
should have gone into a cloister. Or..."

His answer cut back. "No, love." The very thought of her shut away from the
world revolted him. But he could think of nothing else to say...until the tiny feet
scurrying in the hall prompted him: "What of our son?"

But her head remained bowed in the silence of her work.

He rose. There was no point in asking her to join him at court. That, too, had
ended. As he left the room, he indeed felt as though he were leaving a cloistered
cell. The thought stayed with him as he wound his way through the shadowy
halls to the threshold of the court.

As he entered and took his throne, the throng assembled for that day fell
silent. Among them were the leading citizens of Tirgoviste. The city "fathers."
And the fathers of towns and villages across the land. And a grand delegation
from the sultan himself.

Just as the spy had predicted, the sultan had sent his ambassadors to make
demands. They were conspicuous now in their dress; rich, as though to boast of
their empire's grandeur compared to poor Wallachia. They were also conspicuous
in their numbers; fully a dozen, like a reminder of the masses they represented.
And they were conspicuous in their attitude. They stood apart, as though dis-
dainful of rubbing elbows with even the greater of the natives; they stood almost
on their toes, as though expecting the voevode not to keep them waiting.

But Dracula's eyes passed over them. He knew how the sultans used their court like a stage. A stage to show the world what they were about. So on this day he had set his own court like a stage.

He began by calling a case, that of a merchant, the same Florentine who had given him the gift of the gold goblet. As the merchant approached, Dracula addressed the court—letting his eyes linger a bit on the Turks.

"Some time ago, this gentleman asked permission to trade in my realm. He asked with respect. I gave the permission. On certain conditions. I promised that, as long as he kept those conditions, he and his goods would be under my protection.

"He kept his part of the bargain. But, as you know by now—to the shame of this whole nation—his coach was robbed just yesterday of one hundred and sixty gold ducats."

Dracula called forward the city fathers of Tirgoviste. He continued, "The theft occurred here, in your city, my capital. You know what I said. If the money was not returned by this very hour, I would blot this city from the earth. Burn it down."

Already his land was following the tale and would etch it in its folklore. *Burn it down.* The entire capital. Did the people believe that their voevode really meant it?

He asked the merchant, "Sir, was the money returned?"

"Yes, lord."

"In the same purse?"

"Yes, lord."

"In the same spot—the exact same spot in your coach—from which it was taken?"

"Yes, lord," the merchant said. "The exact spot. The very spot on the seat where the cushion dips—" He tapped his rump. "—from all the sitting."

Dracula quizzed, "Then all is well?"

The merchant gave a shrug, a half shrug, as though considering his final assent. But the green eyes gave him pause. "Well, lord…Very strange. But I think the purse now has a hundred and sixty-*one* ducats."

"I see," Dracula said. "You *think* it has." He turned to the city fathers. "Did you play any chicanery? Did you perhaps not catch the real thief, only repaid this man with your own money—and too much at that?"

The city fathers assured him. They had played no chicanery. They had merely spread Dracula's threat, and the whole city, as it were, had turned its eyes on itself. All of its eyes. In every mansion and hut, every cellar and alley…And the thief—the real thief—had been caught. With the purse. With the ducats. One hundred and *sixty*. Exactly. The city fathers could look the voevode in the eye and swear it.

"Then we have a mystery," Dracula said. He advised the merchant, "You had better check your count. Perhaps there is no extra ducat."

As the man was led off, Dracula turned to Wilk. "Are there any other cases? Any thefts? Rapes? Murders? Any at all?"

There were none. Dracula nodded. He had often considered a lesson that he had learned long ago, a lesson from classical history taught to the sons of nobility.

It concerned ancient Greece, in a town where the men were free, where they had no king, where they governed themselves. By democracy. And loved their freedom. Too much so, it seemed. Too many took freedom for license. The town was plagued by crime.

To remedy the situation, the town decided to give itself over to a lawgiver, a despot. He would codify the law and, for a time, have absolute power in enforcing it. When he "civilized" the town again, he would step down. And eventually he did.

But when he first wrote his laws the people were shocked. He had one penalty: death. For murder—death. For theft—death. Even for vagrancy—death. The people complained that, the harshness of it aside, it just did not seem fair. Why should a murderer and a mere vagrant share the same fate? And the despot answered: He would gladly give murderers a worse punishment than death—but he could not contrive one.

To Dracula, the Greek despot simply had not tried. Of course men feared death. But they feared it even more so when it came in an ugly form.

So Dracula could tell the assembled fathers of his land, "Our people, too, are now civilized."

Then he beckoned the Turks. They came forward eagerly, heads held high. Some wore a slight smirk, as though bemused by what they had just witnessed. At the throne, they grouped behind their leader in a crescent and barely gave the voevode a proper bow.

Yet Dracula was polite enough: "I hope your stay here has been pleasant."

"Pleasant enough, lord," the leader said. "But, as you know, we are not here for our pleasure."

"Then state your business."

"It is simple enough, lord. His Highness has sent us to tell you that you have reneged on your oath of loyalty. You have not paid your tribute. You have given no janissary recruits. And our men have been murdered on your border."

As the court murmured, the man pressed on with a slight smile. "His Highness orders that you come to the Divine Porte to answer to him directly. You are to bring the tribute. And the recruits. And, as our custom demands, kneel and kiss the sultan's hem. Further, you are to bring your wife and child..."

The court grumbled. The green eyes flashed. But the man proceeded, very secure in whom and what he represented.

"...as well as your 'associate,' the Pole, Wilkowski. And certain of your boyars. Including the two, Cirstian and Gales. And His Highness also directs that your answer be immediate...as it were, lord, 'short and to the point.' They are his own words."

There was a slight stirring at the door as the Florentine merchant returned. But he was quickly forgotten as Dracula replied to the ambassador. "Is that all 'His Highness' *orders?*"

The man's smile widened. "Yes, lord. That is all."

Dracula began, "When you approached me today, did I mock you?"

The man was perplexed. "Mock me, lord?"

"Mock you. Did I have jesters lead you to my throne, insulting you at every step? Did I call your land a piss-land? Did I incite my people to laugh at you?"

The ambassador understood. He knew the devices employed by sultans at court to demoralize and humiliate certain of their "guests." And he knew that these devices had once been used on Dracula and his father. But the ambassador evaded, "That is not the issue, lord. We only come to—"

"Aye," Dracula said. "To demand our gold. And children. And my own *wife!* To give me orders about my men. And to preach of your customs: 'kiss his coat.' Yet, in my own court, you breach *our* customs."

The man was puzzled and vexed. "Which custom, lord? I am not aware—"

"You saw men approach me," Dracula said. "Did any wear a hat? No. They bare their heads in respect. As our custom demands. Yet you—all of you—come with heads covered."

The ambassadors' turbans.

The leader rejoined, "Lord, you know well why we wear the turban. It is hardly a 'hat.' We remove it for no man. Our Faith forbids it. Even the sultan does not demand—"

"You are not in the sultan's court," Dracula said. "You are in my court. But I will leave this matter for the moment. Let me first address your master. He wants my answer to be immediate. So be it. Tell him this."

Dracula looked now to the men he had called to court that day. To his people. "No one comes into my court—or even steps on my own soil—to give me orders. And no one demands Wallachia's money. Or children."

The court itself seemed to draw a breath. A long breath. To raise its chest. Wallachia's chest. In pride.

The ambassador began, "You realize, lord—"

"Yes," Dracula said. His eyes remained on his people. "I realize."

As his people also realized. He would *surrender* nothing.

The ambassador gave a nod and made to turn.

"Wait," Dracula said. There are still two matters at hand here." He beckoned to the crowd, to the Florentine merchant. "Have you counted the ducats again?"

"I have, lord. There is an extra ducat. As I thought."

"As I *know*," Dracula said. "I put it there. Now go to the window and tell me what you see."

As the merchant did, he gave an audible gulp. "There is a man impaled, lord."

"Not a man," Dracula said. "But a thief. The thief who stole your money. And if you had not told me of the extra ducat you would be planted next to him even now. Go in peace, sir. You, at least, respect the ways of this land."

He turned to the ambassador. "Which brings me back to you. To the matter of our respective customs. Of your 'hats.' In your arrogance today, you also told me that your master demands my answer short and to the point. His own words. So be it. I will answer just that way. And, in so doing, I will also help you keep your precious customs."

15

FIVE YEARS in Dracula's realm had served well for Toma Catavolinos. He had arrived as seemingly nothing more than a refugee from Byzantium, a merchant half-ruined by Osmanli conquest, a man who, despite a natural good nature, often cursed the sultan by name.

Over the months in Wallachia, he had grown steadily, if slowly, prosperous, ostensibly from nothing more than his trade. Rings sprouted on his fingers. Gold grew around his neck. His clothes of common cloth gave way to felt, silk, and satin.

Even before he had arrived in the land, a dash of gray had touched his temples—as he often lamented himself, from the trauma of what he had lost at Constantinople. But in Wallachia the gray had not spread. His trim hair and beard had kept their youthful darkness, so that the flecks of gray only made him seem somewhat distinguished. And every hair on his head was set in place, carefully tended each day by his personal groom.

Toma Catavolinos. Prosperous merchant. His fellow traders listened when he spoke. Yet with Dracula he was content to be just Volinos, the grateful merchant who brought gifts and tales of his travels—a friendly diversion from the voevode's world of intrigue and war.

Now, as Volinos's master, the captured spy, had predicted, the Greek had sought Dracula for a meeting of great import. Only he, the voevode, and Wilk sat in the court. As usual, he wore a smile. Also as usual, he brought a gift. A gem. Modest. But sparkling. For the princess. He spent a few moments telling of how he had acquired it, and a few more praising its qualities. It was only then that his brow wrinkled and his voice dropped.

"Forgive me, lord," he said, fumbling with his hands. "You know I am not used to your world...politics. But I was asked to give you a message. I would have preferred that it come by someone else. But the Turk passed it to me—to one of my men—in the Bulgar land."

He told the story. He had a concession in the Bulgar land. The Turks knew his men. They knew they were based in Tirgoviste. Almost casually, Hamza Pasha himself had approached one of the men and asked him to carry a message. A message for Volinos, in turn, to carry to Dracula. Nothing in writing. Just words. An overture.

Volinos added, "I myself never travel in the Turk's land. After what they did to my city..."

"Aye," Dracula agreed. "And to your poor emperor. That gallant man. Constantine. I suppose if he'd had more like you..."

Volinos lamented, "Yes, lord. But we all did what we could." He moved on to the message, speaking slowly as though to recall the exact words. "It is not Hamza Pasha, but the sultan himself, who bids you. He would still like to settle your differences. He would like to parlay."

Dracula questioned, "Even after what I did to his ambassadors?"

Volinos raised an eyebrow. "In truth, lord, I thought the same thing. After all...*nailing* the turbans to their heads..."

That is what Dracula had done to the sultan's ambassadors. Right there in his court. On the stage he had set.

"Then again, lord," Volinos said, "you didn't kill them. Or even hurt them seriously." He chuckled. "Except for their pride."

Dracula had ordered that *short* nails be used. Very short. Tacks really. Just enough, as it were, to answer the sultan as he had demanded: "short and to the point." And just enough to etch yet another story in his land's memory.

He said now for Volinos to note, "But it's certainly not something the Turk takes lightly. Which is why I must doubt this offer."

Volinos said evenly, "The meeting would be in a mutually agreed place. Even in your own land. Near your border. The sultan, of course, will not be there himself. He will send Hamza Pasha. And each of you can bring a small escort. But only a small escort. Each with the same number of men."

Dracula looked to Wilk. Having expected Volinos, they had already decided to play the farce to the hilt. Wilk shook his head suspiciously.

"I agree," Dracula said. "I smell a trap."

Volinos made as if to ponder before offering, "Lord, perhaps I can help you."

"You?" Dracula said. "You never even think of politics anymore. You just said so yourself."

"True, lord. And I say it again. After losing what I did...our brave emperor...But I am a merchant. And I would urge you to weigh this offer like a merchant."

"How so?"

"First, lord, consider. Does a parlay—a real parlay—have any value to you?"

"Regrettably," Dracula said, "yes." He spoke words he knew the sultan would want to hear. "I could use the Turk's friendship now. I fear Hungary. Because of my troubles with the Saxons." He added for measure, "In truth, sometimes I...my mind...my temper. It gets the best of me."

Volinos assuaged, "That is understandable, lord. The burden of your office. Perhaps, in fact, that is what the sultan sees. After all, he has his own burden. No doubt it drives him to anger sometimes. Anger he later regrets. Perhaps that is why he makes this offer. To see if the two of you can come to terms with cooler heads." He pressed, "So the Turk offers something you want. It's just the price— the fear of a trap—that holds you back. So why not 'hedge' against the price?"

Dracula listened and Volinos explained. "*If* you agree to meet, lord, what spot will you choose?"

Dracula made as if to consider the question for the first time. He finally concluded, "Near Giurgiu, I think."

Though Volinos tried to hide it, Dracula saw the flicker in his eyes. Giurgiu was a Turkish fortress on the Danube river. If Hamza could snatch the voevode there...

Dracula continued, "Near Giurgiu, a short ride inland, are flats. You can see the land all around. To the horizon."

More importantly, in this spot that Dracula pictured, the fortress itself was beyond the horizon. Out of sight.

Volinos said, "So there is nowhere to hide men. So you see, lord. You have it."

"I do? Have what?"

Volinos grinned. "Your parlay. If you want it. With nothing to fear. In fact, my lord…I think I can help you even more."

He waited for Dracula, as it were, to bite: "Help me how?"

Volinos leaned forward and, for effect, whispered. "You will have a small escort. He will have a small escort. And I will have a small escort."

"You? But—"

"Pardon, lord. As I said, the Turk knows my men. Knows their faces. Knows them as merchants—harmless. He would suspect nothing of them. So when I carry the message back that you accept the parlay, I will also ask permission to attach a caravan to your party. For my protection. Yes. My own protection. Because I, for once, will ride with the caravan. I don't think the Turk will object to harmless merchants tagging along."

"But how does that help me?"

"Because, lord, whether the Turk believes it or not, my men can fight. If they have to."

And Dracula seemed to realize, "Ah! So I, in effect, would have more men than Hamza."

Volinos beamed. "Exactly! Your back would be well guarded, my lord. By your men and my own. You can have your parlay in peace. Or, if Hamza seems insincere…you can simply turn and ride away."

Dracula looked to Wilk, who shrugged. But the voevode only dangled the bait a bit longer before the sultan's "eyes": "It sounds good. But I will have to think on it."

16

AUTUMN 1461. CASTLE DRACULA. The sound of Prasha's steps pad-ding across the stone floor of her bedroom made Dracula hesi-tate outside the door. He stood in the darkness of the tower stairs and listened. She seemed to be moving about, walking, stopping, walking again, as though busy at some task. It did him good to hear it. And did him good to see the light slicing into the darkness from the crack of the threshold.

Was she adding a touch to the room, hanging a tapestry perhaps? Or was she simply stoking the small hearth, or just pacing as she read a verse? Whatever, it was good to imagine her at something that took her out of her dark thoughts, or out of her incessant make-work sewing. And good to imagine her room bathed in warm, bright light.

But other sounds muffled her movement: the echoes of the celebration on the small field below the castle walls. There, the draguli had been assembled with whatever dependents the maverick band had: wives, lovers, old folk, children…On this, the last day of their stay, they feasted and simply played, as their voevode had bade them. From their camp came the crackling of the huge bonfires that staved off the chill of the late afternoon. Through the crackling came singing and laughing and the low drone of the chatter of the massed voices.

Dracula rapped on the door and called Prasha by the word he especially felt for her now: "Love?"

Her steps came promptly, the bolt clicked, and the door opened to flood him in light. Prasha was smiling, and her dark eyes readily met his. She wore only a white linen gown that showed the silhouette of her form underneath. Her dark hair hung loose. Her lips wore a blush. Her skin seemed coated with the soft hue of the light. As Dracula extended a hand, she took it and walked with him to sit on the bed.

He stroked her hair and made to kiss her. She accepted the advance. But, as he could feel, only *accepted*. Her hold was firm but not hungry. Not grasping. Her kiss was merely like the kiss of a friend.

He kept his sigh of disappointment low, silent. He reminded himself that it was all only natural. She seemed to have risen from her melancholia and seemed to be rising still. But that, he knew from experience, came slowly. As things were, he would be content with it.

And he was content, too, as he looked around the room. It was as small as any in that compact fortress, especially since it was perched at the pinnacle of a tower. But here, at least, the austerity of the castle had been softened: quilted bed; table and chair; tapestries; hearth…

The tower itself rose like a cylinder on a far corner of the castle walls. It had, as it were, two "eyes," two low, broad windows. Inside, they had the luxury of panes of real glass that opened fully like small doors. Outside were metal shutters that could be closed in times of trouble.

Each of the windows showed its own panorama. One angled toward the field far below where the draguli were now encamped. The other overlooked a sheer drop, down the castle walls, down a ravine, to the banks of a river, the Arges. On a map, the river seemed to point straight from the edge of Wallachia up into the cusp of Transylvania.

Dracula took Prasha's hands, hoping that his words would not melt her smile. "It has come, love. The time."

As the words did not seem to sting her, he continued even more frankly, "War, love. With the Turk. I will have to go. But I will return to you. As fast as God permits."

Again she showed only acceptance, a slight nodding of the head, like resignation behind her cheerful front. It made Dracula begin pouring out reasons and promises: *He had not sought the war...He wanted only for their land to be left alone...When the war was over...*

But even behind his own words his thoughts tugged at him. Wallachia's wars would never end. Certainly not in their lifetime. So perhaps he could keep her here. Away from the turmoil. Safe. Content. And warm to him again. Perhaps he could. When the worst, at least, was over.

But even as he was speaking Prasha rose and went to the windows. She raised a finger to her lips to stem his words and whispered, "Listen. It sounds almost like voices."

His eyes misted. Was she still so out of touch as to not know what she was hearing? He explained, "They *are* voices, love. Our troops. They are singing and—"

She giggled. "Not them. I hear them, of course. But listen. The water. The river. Its babbling sounds like their voices."

"Whose voices, love?"

"The children. The mothers. But they're laughing again. As when they were alive and happy."

Dracula knew. The children and mothers of the boyar families. Those who had perished building the castle.

Again Prasha giggled. "I think their souls went into the river. At least, it sounds like it. Sometimes."

Dracula felt no malice, no mocking, in her words. She was simply telling him. Telling him what she heard. Sometimes.

He went to her and knelt. His arms wrapped around her waist and he buried his face in her softness. Her hands enfolded him, fingers stroking his hair, as he had seen them stroke their son's. His arms clung to her and he told her, "I love you dearly."

He rose and kissed her and backed to the door, so as to leave her with his longing look.

Back on the tower stairs, he drew a long breath. He squared his shoulders. The time had come and was taking him. He reminded himself that he could no more resist than—he had to ask:...*than a moth could resist the flame?* He forced a cynical laugh inside. So be it.

In the bowels of the castle, a pair of servants were already waiting for him. Near the door where they stood, the only light was a thin grayness that spilled from the high recesses of an adjoining corridor. The light died well before it reached the stairway where Dracula descended. So the servants heard his steps before they saw him emerge like an embodiment of the darkness itself.

He looked at the cart they had brought. Food. Wine. He gave a nod.

When he led them into the room, the spy rose from a chair in the corner. He was not naked now but dressed in his usual merchant garb. A flash of fear crossed his face but dissolved as he saw Dracula smiling, and saw the food. As the voevode beckoned, he came to the table in the center of the room. From under the cart, Dracula took a small chest. He flipped the lid to show the spy's belongings: rings, gold...all that had been taken from him.

The voevode assured him, "You served me as you promised: very well indeed."

Dracula himself set the table with a tray of food. From another tray he took two goblets, face down. Dracula righted them and poured wine—for both of them, the spy noted, from the same pitcher. When the voevode toasted, the spy drank. And within seconds collapsed.

Poison. His own. The powder from the hollow of his ring. Dracula had laced it onto the bowl of one of the goblets with a coating of honey.

He told the corpse, "I kept my word. You didn't fear death. It came to you unperceived." He told the servants, "You know the part I want. And you know where to take the rest of it."

One grunted a laugh. "He'll be ripe by the time we get there."

"Yes," Dracula agreed. "But that's the point, isn't it?"

He left the castle for the field. Dusk was already falling. As his troops saw him, they began to grow silent and rise. He waved them back to their festivity. He had some words first for Wilk, Cirstian, and Gales. As he sent for them and waited at the head of the field, he scanned the mass before him. There were no skeletons among them now—no one starving. Only lean muscle. And full, red cheeks. And smiles as they shared meat at the spit and danced to the roving musicians.

At one fire, children sat in a close circle as an old woman strode among them. In the flickering of the flames the children's shadows were frozen, while hers moved with her words, sometimes gesturing abruptly, sometimes creeping in slow, dirge-like sweeps. Dracula mused at the sight. What better place than this outcast ridge for the old to pass Wallachia's lore to the young? It seemed to fall to the grandmothers to warn the generations of the spirits, werewolves, and even vampires that everyone knew stalked the land. And the crone would swear on her soul to the truth of her tales, just as Dracula remembered an old woman swearing to him as he sat at just such a fire in what seemed like another lifetime.

When his commanders arrived he told them, "We'll send riders again to Hungary and Moldavia."

"And hope they'll come," Gales said.

"Hungary should come," Dracula said. "The pope has sent money."

Money for a crusade. Against the Osmanli. And King Matthias had taken the money.

Dracula added, "And both Hungary and my cousin will have time to gather men. Because I am going to 'drag my feet.' I will not start the war until winter."

The three nodded. They understood. Winter. When the Turk would find it hard to move. By spring, with luck, Dracula would have caused enough destruction—have at least the one major victory—to draw Hungary to his side. And with Hungary—or without it—would come Moldavia. How could Stephen fail to support his cousin?

Still Gales laughed nervously. "This war...I never knew I was such a gambler."

Dracula spoke past the comment, "Remember that the sword alone is not our hope. Not our main weapon. We cannot defeat the Turk with just the sword. So no matter what, *we must see this through to the end.*"

It was Wilk who extended a hand. And Cirstian who took hold of it. Dracula and Gales added theirs to lock the pledge.

As they turned to the field, the festivity was fading as the people were pressing around a flatbed wagon. They came in silence as though in procession to a shrine. On the wagon, in the light of the campfires arched against the blackening sky, stood a young woman, almost still a girl. Her hands rested in the fold of her lap. Her eyes were distant. She began a lilting ballad in her high, delicate voice.

She sang of the land, the native land, of its mountains, forests, and plains...as one would perhaps sing of a mother, a wellspring of life, a spring made the sweeter by her children, by the people.

All lands had such songs. They were sung often in times of strife—and sung always in the face of war. The last lines formed an image, more in the voice itself than in the words. An image of a woman. A young mother perhaps. Looking off to where her men had gone to battle.

It was only when the song ended and the woman rejoined the crowd in its silence that Dracula himself mounted the wagon. His troops pressed closer to hear his address.

But he simply pointed...south...to the battles yet to be fought. His words were neither shouted nor whispered. He told them only, "Make your mark."

And, within moments, the farthest man in the farthest rank had heard the words.

17

FEBRUARY 1462. GIURGIU. On the sand-and-scrub flats a few leagues from the fortress, the sun shone brilliantly but gave no warmth. At the head of his caravan ambling next to Dracula's column, Volinos sank deeper into his thick, fur cape, so that, with the bulk of his fur hat, his face was covered save for the eyes.

He gave an exaggerated shiver. But it was more from his excitement than from the cold. The trap that he had helped set over so many months was about to spring shut. The Impaler, Kaziglu, seemed secure in the fact that he was riding with the caravan. Fifty extra men. His edge over Hamza Pasha two-to-one. But, when Hamza appeared, Volinos would show his true colors. The dreaded Kaziglu would not leave the "parlay." He would be taken. Dead or alive. But hopefully alive. For then, Volinos knew, the sultan would really show his gratitude.

To mask his excitement Volinos exclaimed, "Damn it's cold!"

Dracula only answered with the old peasants' jest: "That's because of the weather."

In truth, the frigid air, even as it gusted the patches of dusty snow, warmed Dracula's heart. Giurgiu was alone. Locked in the ice of the Danube and of the Bulgar land behind it.

Volinos's fur-muffled voice spoke again, again as though damning the weather. "I almost look forward to sharing the Turk's hearth."

"No doubt," Dracula said. He brought the dual column to a halt. He further played his part in the farce by sending scouts forward, saying for Volinos to hear, "If I even see a bird flying crooked I am turning back."

Volinos's eyes crinkled over his masked smile. Kaziglu, he knew, would see nothing to make him turn back. Even if Hamza had needed to hide men, there was nowhere on these flats to do it. And Hamza did not need to hide men who, as it were, were already hidden—right next to Kaziglu.

On the horizon, the galloping scouts shrunk into tiny dots, then specks. The specks disappeared and reappeared, leading a cluster of other specks. They grew into a column as long as Dracula's own: Hamza Pasha leading fifty sipahis. He came only at a canter, but, when he halted before Dracula, promptly drew his sword. "You would do best to surrender."

He was a bit surprised when Dracula answered calmly, "Treachery, aye? And why should I surrender?"

Hamza grinned. "The numbers are against you."

On the cue, Volinos signalled to his men, who also drew swords.

But even as they did Dracula took a sack from his saddle and handed it to Volinos, who, smirking and somewhat puzzled, opened it. And screamed and flung it away. So that the head of his former master—the spy who had been poisoned at Castle Dracula—went rolling over the flats.

Dracula said, "Now I give you the same advice. Surrender. For the same reason. You see. Your scream seems to have conjured a lair of dragons."

And already the land was backing his words. Volinos, Hamza, and the men with them began blinking as the far flats began to disgorge dots all around. Black dots. Waves of them. Coming not from on the earth, but from *under* it, inside it, where they had been dug in and hidden. Now they were spreading in a thick circle quickly closing in.

Dracula shot to Volinos, "Your swords are already drawn. Do you prefer a gallant death here, or…do you think your sultan might ransom you?"

His look asked the same question of Hamza, even as Volinos shouted to his men to drop their weapons.

Hamza hesitated but also decided not to die there, on a nameless flat, at the hands of this petty voevode. Of course the sultan would ransom him. So he surrendered. With a grimace.

The black circle converged, led by Wilk and Cirstian. The prisoners were made to dismount and tethered in a long line, while Dracula sent riders back inland, where Gales had been dogging his tracks with the boyars' banderia and the rest of the draguli.

Dracula offered Wilk, "How would you like to play the role of pasha?"

Wilk gave a mock gesture of the Muslim *Salaam*, touching his fingers to heart and lips. The draguli laughed and hooted as he dressed in Hamza's clothes, adding a little stuffing for authenticity. Dracula himself also changed costume to assume the role of a sipahi. His men took the identities of Hamza's and Volinos's men.

A short while later the Turkish garrison in Giurgiu saw a curious sight. A single rider, a sipahi, flew toward the fortress just a half-league ahead of a small band, which, in turn, flew a half-league in front of a swarm. The swarm was dressed in black: no doubt Kaziglu's men. The small band seemed to be led by Hamza Pasha and...*and a black-caped rider.* Black cape: Kaziglu himself? Bound in the saddle? Captured? Could it be? The sultan would be elated. And very generous.

The single sipahi drove to the fortress walls and confirmed it all in flawless Turkish: *Kaziglu! We have him! Kaziglu!*

Over and over he shouted it. He did not even have to cry to open the gates. The commander was quick not to lose such a prize.

What followed on that day was recorded by history in Dracula's own words. Written words. Preserved in a letter from him to King Matthias of Hungary. A letter dated from Giurgiu:

> "By the Grace of God...I found out about their trickery and slyness, and I was the one who captured Hamza Bey in the Turkish district and land, close to the fortress called Giurgiu...our men, mixing with theirs, entered and destroyed the fortress, which I immediately burned."

18

MAY 1462. THE DANUBE. Dracula's February letter from Giurgiu was not the only one he sent. He sent others—and envoys, too—to King Matthias, to Skanderbeg in Albania, and to his cousin in Moldavia. He sent to the west, the east, the north...to Christian and Muslim—rebel Turks...to anyone who he thought might join him against the empire.

He reminded them of the Porte's oppression and pointed out the myth of Osmanli invincibility. From Giurgiu, he told them, he had swept all along the Danube and into the Bulgar land. He had destroyed the sultan's ports on the river, as well as his cities and towns inland. In one two-week spate he had driven his cavalry over *eight hundred kilometers.* To many of the sultan's subjects—particularly the Bulgar Christians—he had come as a liberator. To the rest he had fallen like the Sword of Vengeance.

In his dispatches he meticulously listed the number of those he had killed. Killed in battle or massacred outright. Listed them by their cities, towns, and villages. Soldiers and civilians. Women and children.

Almost everywhere he had been he had left nothing—nothing—that could be of use to the sultan.

He also told of the first Osmanli army sent against him, of how it had torn into Wallachia to repay him "eye for eye," and of how he had met it head-on and eradicated *half* of its *eighteen thousand* men.

As Janos Hunyadi had once done, he even proclaimed one of his victories by sending the Hungarian king sacks of severed enemy heads.

But the best he received from any potential allies were promises. Skanderbeg refused him outright. A matter of honor. The Porte had offered the weary Albanians a three-year truce. And they had accepted. But the worst that Dracula received—as from Hungary—and his own cousin in Moldavia—was an ominous silence.

No help had come.

But Mohammed had come. In the name of Holy War, *Jihad!* In this month of May. The same month in which he had conquered Constantinople. His lucky month, as his astrologers advised.

The Conqueror had come. With *ninety thousand* men. Sipahis. Akinjis. Janissaries. Bazouks. A massive artillery brigade. And four thousand Wallachians—those who had fled Kaziglu's reign—led by Radu.

In his numbers and fortune Mohammed felt secure. Yet there were things about this war that already made him feel quite something else: vexed. Disturbed.

Months before, when war with Kaziglu had seemed more and more inevitable, he had envisioned a classic campaign of retribution. He would lead his army en masse. He would bring them up the Danube on a fleet as long and broad as a mythical sea serpent, a force that could strangle the land itself. Or he would lead them across the Bulgar land. Not in a single column. No track of land could support such a monster of an army with its appetite for food and fodder. He would lead his troops in, say, three columns or four. Each again like a mythical serpent, each on its own track, moving close and parallel, fed by the requisition from his Bulgar subjects. The columns would converge on a spot near the Danube, melding into a single mammoth body ready to leap at Kaziglu.

But Kaziglu's own campaign had confounded any such visions. Every port on the Danube had been razed or at least crippled. Every port except one, called Braila, which Kaziglu—for not-so-subtle reasons, as Mohammed saw it—had left virtually unscathed. None of the other ports could now dock a large fleet or shield ninety thousand troops. As for the Bulgar land, Dracula had left a huge swath along the river like a desert. There, no army could expect to feed off the land.

So Mohammed had divided his troops, and divided them again. He himself had taken a division on a flotilla up the Danube. A flotilla impressive enough of itself: one hundred and fifty vessels—warships, transports, barges, skiffs...

The other division was broken into small columns. They had made their way on far-flung tracks through the Bulgar land, drawing on the requisition where they could, but, like the fleet, forced to haul the bulk of their own provisions.

The army had managed to converge, with the columns now massed and tramping along the Bulgar shore in the shadow of the fleet. But Mohammed's progress had been hampered. And his horde of ninety thousand was forced, as it were, to feed off itself—at least until, as he hoped, it could feed off the pillage of Wallachia.

But where would he land in Wallachia? He would have to make a beachhead. And ferry his men across. Was the Dragon waiting? For once, Mohammed did not know. His "eyes" were failing him.

At about the same time as Giurgiu had fallen, the sultan's spies—or what was left of them—began swarming across the Danube. They had hit the Bulgar shore running, afraid even to glance back, lest a "dragon" were on their heels. And all babbling. About a terror in Wallachia: draguli swooping down, suddenly aware of who the sultan's spies were.

So now, where the Conqueror usually had answers, he had only questions. How in heaven's name had he been "blinded" in Wallachia? How had this Dracula taken Giurgiu? Was it Volinos? Had he been a double-spy? Where *was* Volinos? And Hamza? Some of the surviving eyes had claimed that both had been killed at Giurgiu. But, no, others said, they were made prisoners. Both. And yet Dracula had made no overtures for ransom. A ransom for a pasha. Hamza Pasha. A huge ransom indeed!

But more to the problem at hand, Mohammed knew that Dracula now had artillery. From Giurgiu. Not a massive brigade like his own. But enough to savage a landing. If Dracula were hiding. And waiting.

But again, some of the surviving spies had claimed that Dracula had moved inland, holed up behind the "walls" he had built before: Bucharest, Snagov, his castle. But, no, others warned. He was waiting. This Kaziglu *Bey.*

The *Lord* Impaler.

That is what the Turks now called Dracula. Bey. Lord.

That alone made the sultan spit as he peered from his ship to the Wallachian shore.

If he had any consolation in this campaign so far it was that he had thrown one of Dracula's traps back into his face. The port. Braila. Why had Dracula left it unscathed? It was so obvious as to be childish.

The sultan had simply cruised past Braila. After razing it with cannon and raiders. And now he laughed aloud at the thought.

At the same time, in a camp not very far away, Dracula, too, suddenly laughed. To his three commanders' curious looks, he said only, "Braila."

And they all laughed.

For them Braila had served a dual purpose. Just as some people had flocked to Dracula as a liberator when he started his war, others had fled in his path. They were the sultan's "quiet" allies, his sympathizers, who had hoped to endure the Impaler's reign until Mohammed put his own voevode on the throne. But when the war started they were finally forced to declare their loyalty; they took refuge in the fortified towns on the Turkish border. Braila had been one of those towns.

But Mohammed had been rightfully suspicious of Braila. Surely Dracula had left the single port to tempt a landing. Where he was waiting. *If* he was waiting. The sultan had decided not even to take the chance. Which is why he had simply razed the place. That the people cried out to the raiders that they were the sultan's allies made no difference. Who, after all, would not swear loyalty at the point of a sword?

So unbeknownst to the sultan he had destroyed his own allies. And, in so doing, he had narrowed his options for a place to land. Narrowed them to somewhere up river, where Dracula's camp was now hidden.

But when the laughing over Braila subsided Dracula noted Cirstian and Gales looking toward the unseen river as though brooding. It was Gales who spoke first, almost to himself. "We are alone."

No help. Not even from Dracula's own cousin.

The voevode's voice was low but hard. "Alone perhaps. For now." He still had hope, the fact that Hungary had accepted the pope's money for a crusade—Dracula's "crusade." But help or no, Dracula reminded his commanders, "We are in it. To the end."

Gales suggested in a question, "What of Bucharest and Snagov? Tirgoviste?" Might not the army be better off behind the walls?

Dracula looked to Wilk. "What did we learn in Moldavia?"

"Aye," Wilk said. "Our best fortress is the land. Who knows this land better than we?"

"And," Dracula said, "I'd wager that the sultan, too, wonders about Bucharest and Snagov. He wonders if we are there—else why would we have built them? Or are we here, waiting for him? Let him wonder. Until he sets foot on the land."

Cirstian asked, "Can we stop him here?"

"No," Dracula said. "He outnumbers us three-to-one."

But, if not pleased with the numbers, Dracula was pleased with what they meant. He had thirty thousand men. Only eight thousand were his and his boyars'. The rest were "the people." Dracula had called. And they had come. Even against the Conqueror. Or perhaps *especially* against the Conqueror. Because, for all of the hard lessons that their Dragon voevode had taught them— for all of the impalements…his swift, hard justice—he had indeed raised them. In spirit.

No longer were they plagued by thieves. Even thieves who hid behind noble birth. No longer did the Saxons—or even the dreaded Osmanli—put their heel on Wallachia's neck with impunity. The people's "fathers" had heard Dracula declare it to the sultan's own ambassadors: *No one took Wallachia's tribute. Or children.* Not without a fight.

And with a voevode so eager to lead the fight the people were eager to follow. They had heard what he told his army: *Make your mark!* And so they had come. Peasants. Townsmen. Guilds. In twos, threes, small bands, and whole columns. They had come. Twenty-two thousand. To make *their* mark. To fight even the dreaded Osmanli. They had come, even though, in making his call, their voevode had fairly warned them, as the lore of the land had inscribed his words in history: "It would be better that those who think of death should not follow me."

Dracula repeated to Cirstian, "No. We can't stop him here. But we can make him *pay* for landing. And for every step he takes." He told Gales, "We can make the 'Conqueror' wish that he never even heard of Wallachia."

As though conjured by the words, a man came running from the edge of camp. A peasant. He was armed and dressed lightly so that he could fly unburdened. He carried only a bow and a few arrows. He wore only tunic and breeches, not even the "armor," the padded clothing, of the other peasants. And his feet were bare. And muddied now. From the silt along the river.

Through his sweat and heaving breath he gave the news: "Lord, the Turk lands."

Dracula turned to Gales: "Do us the honor."

A short while later, Dracula and his commanders were watching the landing. From the thickets near the bank. Mohammed had chosen one of the spots that Dracula, in effect, had chosen for him—one of the few spots on that stretch of the river where the thickets receded to leave a long, broad flat for a landing.

Behind the thickets, waves of Dracula's men were dug in. In trenches. And the rest of the army was being called at the double from its far-flung perimeter on the river. All converging on the one spot—with the cavalry dismounted, lest a stray snort from a mount ruin the surprise.

As for God's most intelligent animals, Dracula did not have to warn them of the penalty for a stray cough or sneeze.

As the defenders watched, the invaders began spreading along the shore. Bazouks first. In the smaller boats. Their eyes were wide and darting. Darting in grim silence. Into the thickets and the unseen Wallachian terrain, the unknown stretches beyond the shore. And darting even behind them, as though Kaziglu Bey might rise from the very river at their backs.

But as their human waves steadily swept ashore the bazouks dared their first whispers and nervous smiles. From their boats they hauled their cargo: weapons and stores. And whips, chains, and shackles—for the slaves they were already counting. Soon they were joking and waving back to the fleet to send the first of the cavalry.

It was when the first barge touched the shore and discharged the first akinjis, already mounted, that Gales turned to Dracula. But Dracula only shrugged. He had given the command to Gales; the boyar could make his own decisions.

So Gales did. He waved the army from the trenches into the thickets and mucked an arrow with pitch and sulfur. His eyes studied the bank. The akinjis had set spur. Heading for the thickets. To give the Conqueror new eyes. To guide the rest of the landing.

At Gales's gesture a peasant came to his side, knelt, and struck flint to oiled straw. A flame leapt. Gales took a bow and lit his arrow. He aimed, letting the shaft rise and fall with his measured breath. The breath stopped. The arrow flew. An akinji took the strike in full stride and pitched backward out of the saddle. The thickets shrieked a war cry and the air hummed with a veritable rain of arrows.

But the rain had barely fallen when, according to plan, the defenders, to the man, dropped back into their trenches. As expected, from the ships and the opposite bank came a thunder like the falling of God's own hammer. Mohammed had used his guns exactly as Dracula would have—had their roles been reversed. The cannon had been trained on the thickets. Just in case. And, as the case had been proved by the arrows, the guns had tried to annihilate the defenders, blow them to hell with one massed volley.

But the balls and chain-shot blew over the trenches, and the defenders emerged, secure in the fact that they had earned a respite of several minutes before the guns could be reloaded. So another squall of arrows hit the beach. Pitch and sulfur…hissing shafts…

The scene played over. Gales called cease-fire and dropped his men to the trenches. The cannons roared. The arrows flew again.

And, even safely away near the far shore on his well-armed flagship, Mohammed had a flash of Belgrade: screams of agony...cries of victory...burning powder...burning wood...burning flesh.

On Kaziglu Bey's shore the sultan now had only corpses. In mid-channel his boats backwatered—away from Kaziglu Bey's land. He could stop the retreat, force the landing. By swarming the shore. But the Dragon, too, had cannon—the guns of Giurgiu.

Even then Gales looked back to the guns, hidden away from the thickets. He told Dracula, "They are ready."

But Dracula shook his head. "He's not that stupid. He'll have to show something. For his men's spirits. So he'll lay off the land and throw a few volleys. Nothing more. He'll look elsewhere to land."

There was no point in the defenders wasting precious powder and shot in a duel for mere show.

"Then let him shoot at trees," Gales said. With Dracula's nod, he waved the army back inland.

As they went, Dracula assured him and Cirstian, "So now you see. Our enemy is neither infallible nor invincible."

19

THE CONQUEROR decided to let his "lucky" month pass. It was the moonless night of the fourth of June when the Wallachian scout crawled to the river's bank. He would not dare show a silhouette to the water or the opposite shore, a silhouette that would show black as mortal sin on the night's own dark soul.

He himself was looking for just such silhouettes. He froze in place. His eyes strained. His ears perked to the rippling waves and the hum of the crickets. His nostrils flared to the breeze. His breath flowed as slowly as that of a monk's at prayer.

The night told him nothing. Inside, he swore. He would have to go into the water. No one would know if he did not. But the bank was high enough that something drifting low on the river might slip—might have been slipping even then—under his view. He would not let that happen. He slid over the bank and into the water. His feet found bottom, he stood submerged up to the neck, and, as he had expected, his thoughts began to run.

Even as he scanned from the rippling murkiness to the paler shades of the Bulgar shore the inner voice nagged—almost cried: *Were there really creatures in the river, as the old crones swore? Were there really spirits, the souls of those who had drowned? Would he suddenly feel the grip that would pull him under? Who really knew how a man died on a dark river?*

He swore again inside. He was no child cringing at a campfire with some grandmom spinning tales. No superstitious bumpkin. Not anymore. He was a soldier of the voevode, the Dragon himself. There were no creatures in the water or monsters on the—

Something brushed his leg and his heart almost stopped.

He was beside himself now. He thanked his guardian angel and patron saint that he had corked the scream in his throat. What the Dragon would have done to him if he had alerted the Turk!

No creatures, he reminded himself. No monsters. Just the river. The Bulgar shore. He locked on them and waited. Waited. Marvelling at how he could still feel his sweat when he was up to his neck—

He saw it. A log? No. Too long. But low. Very low. It had passed all too quickly. No point in following it on. Up river, the opposite shore rose in a bank that would shroud anything passing. But another object came. Slowly. It was squarish. Square top and sides. Drifting. No. There was noise. Muffled. Cloth on oars. Barely pulling.

Even the sharp rocks on the shore did not distract him as he pulled his feet from the cursed water.

In the darkened camp, Dracula's troops saw a blink on the far river and heard the rumble of cannon. In the darkened tent, Cirstian and Gales jumped to their feet. But seeing Dracula and Wilk still sitting, listening, they stopped.

"Downstream," Wilk noted.

"Aye," Dracula agreed. "Where his ships are."

His brow wrinkled. It was too obvious—to land where the ships had been riding in plain sight. Unless Mohammed was playing the *too* obvious.

Dracula was still pondering when the riders came. From upstream. They came in a string, one after the other, all with the same report. All along the bank, the scouts were slogging from the river with the news: *Barges.* **Upstream.**

Cannon downstream. Barges up. Mohammed was staging a diversion with the cannon on his ships. So Dracula answered with a diversion. He sent Gales toward the ships with a few regiments, a few cannon, and the order: "Make noise. Make him think you're the whole damn army."

Dracula took the rest of the *whole damn army* upstream, where he found his scouts still scurrying back and forth carrying more bits of Mohammed's plan. Barges, skiffs, all of the sultan's transports were landing. Led not by bazouks but janissaries. Janissaries! With cannon. Huge batteries.

Dracula had to wonder how many guns the Conqueror had brought. But he wondered while he worked, deploying his troops. Wilk already knew his place, behind the rest of the army with the artillery. He spaced the guns far apart so as not to make an easy target, but he reminded the gunners, "Shoot where I shoot!" Concentrated fire. He also reminded them, "By the numbers!"

The numbers. He himself was no real gunner. He had learned the rudiments. But teaching other men…? Moreover, powder and shot were so precious to the defenders that they had spared only a few live rounds in practice. For the rest of their training they had simply gone through the motions. To make their learning easier Wilk had broken the drill into numbered steps: *One—swab the bore. And swab it good. Two—load the powder.* And so on.

At the van of the army Dracula gave Cirstian the cavalry. He himself dismounted and took the infantry. He would try to keep the invaders facing front, while Cirstian split his force and sent them walking their mounts—walking…no hoofbeats—to the flanks.

Word quickly spread in the darkness among the infantry: The Dragon himself would lead them! Dracula fired a flaming arrow with the cry, "By the Grace of God!" The words thundered in chorus from his troops and the sky was suddenly streaked with a hail of flame.

As fast as the volley flew and the first screams rose from the Turkish lines the Wallachians dropped and hugged the earth. Dracula waited. There was no fire from the enemy cannon. He stole another few steps and triggered another volley—with unlit arrows now, to keep his ranks obscured. But the janissaries hurled their own flaming volleys so that the ground on both sides was dotted by pitch-and-sulfur torches, making the battle seem like one between two armies of shadows.

Dracula began leading his troops in crawling and firing from a crouch. He was stealing a few paces of ground when the entire shore flashed and roared. The ground heaved. He felt his back stung as though by a cat-o-nine-tails, heard the screams from all around, and felt the warm ooze under his armor.

Wilk froze the flash of the enemy cannon in his mind's eye. He adjusted the barrel of his gun and fired. The shot exploded just short of the janissary ranks. Moments passed. The rest of the Wallachian battery began firing at the target. Not a barrage but staggered shots as each gunner found his bearing.

While they took their turns Wilk guided his crew in reloading: *One. Two…*The Turks fired. At the infantry. Still. And with less of a bang, it seemed. So, Wilk thought, the enemy was ignoring his gunners to stave off the infantry. And his own first shots had apparently taken their toll of the Turkish cannon, paring the batteries down just a bit. Perhaps so. Because he had a slight advantage. His own men could focus on the giant flash of the enemy battery. But the enemy saw only "blinks" of Wilk's battery. Scattered blinks. Dark, flash, dark. Like trying to spot fireflies.

He fired his second round. Another of his guns followed. Then a third. But the fourth exploded. No Turkish gun had fired and Wilk swore. *Number one. Swab the bore good.* Lest a stray spark left in the barrel ignited your own powder as you reloaded. So many gunners—even the best—died that way.

On the field Dracula saw that his guns were giving him some relief from the enemy artillery. Under his armor the wounds had stopped oozing. Bites of shrapnel. Only bites. The blood had matted on his shirt. He began crawling again and shooting. The ranks were refilling at his sides. The janissary guns still pounded them. But that was to be expected. Hoped for. Because that meant that those guns were ignoring his own artillery.

The earth began grumbling. Not a volley of cannon. A subtler rumbling. Swelling. Hoofbeats. From the flanks, the shore. A thin cry: "By the Grace of God!" Then it echoed in chorus. With shrieks. Cirstian's cavalry had fanned wide and was crashing on the enemy's sides.

Wilk fired his third round. The enemy guns flashed and, in the instant, Wilk knew that something was wrong. Something in the angle of the flash…in the very sound of the volley…He was ripped from the ground and into the air and slashed, punched, kicked…

The enemy guns fired again. Into the flanks. At Cirstian. And fired again. At the infantry on the field. Dracula was numbed by the concussion. His ears seemed clogged. His eyes and nostrils burned from the smoke. His mind cried, *How many guns? How many guns had Fatih brought? How many to fire at all sides at once?*

A hundred and twenty guns. A massive brigade. Enough for both a diversion and to cover the landing front and flanks. To get them, Mohammed had even repeated what he had done at Belgrade: melted down Christian church bells from his beloved Constantinople. And he was using his guns. With the janissaries. He had learned from his first foiled landing. Now, as it were, his spear was tipped with his heaviest, sharpest point.

Dracula stood. He flung his bow aside, drew sword, and bellowed to the Grace of God to let his men know that he was charging.

They had regrouped around him yet again when he hit the janissary ranks. He focused only on the cannon—the cannon, with the gunners scrambling to reload. He cut his way through their infantry guards and began hacking, hammering, flying along the line of the guns. But a wall of flesh met him, a wall barbed with mace, sword, and axe. From the shore came the cry, *Allahu Akbar! God is great!* It roared and roared again from the far flanks, where barges and boats were hitting the shore, disgorging men both mounted and on foot, and pushing back into the waves to fetch the men still waiting on the Bulgar shore.

Then the cry rose in Turkish: *The ships!* The Conqueror himself was coming. Despite the diversion staged by Gales, it was clear now to the invaders where Dracula's main forces were.

Dracula watched his men around him throwing themselves, hurling themselves, on the enemy "wall." But they only chipped at it and paid in blood for the fragments they took. Padded clothing and great heart simply could not match armor and superb training and great heart.

Dracula called his men back before retreating into the darkness. He pushed them on, away from the shore. Pushed them to crawl on their bellies to dodge the last enemy shots. Pushed them ahead of him, driving them on—a good shepherd to his flock of dragons.

When he reached the line of his own guns, he looked for Wilk. He found the first gun—or where it had stood. He found Wilk fairly far off. Head down. Streaked in blood. But sitting nonetheless.

When Dracula shook him Wilk looked up. Then he looked at his hands. Both there. Ten fingers. He saw his legs and wiggled his toes inside his boots. He managed a smile and a question: "Did we win?"

Dracula gave him a hand to rise and the answer: "Does it sound like it's over?"

20

ON THE DAWN of the second day after its baptism on the Danube, Dracula led his army from a thick stand of woods onto yet another stretch of Wallachia's plains. Like the plains they had already drawn the invaders across, this one seemed endless—a sea of knee-high grass, running from east to west on the flanks, on to the north toward far-off Tirgoviste.

This particular stretch suited Dracula's purpose. At a rise about a mile from the woods he reined in and deployed his advance guard in what would soon become the center of his line. He looked back south, to his army. For all the fury of its first battle, it was virtually intact, still almost thirty thousand strong, making its way in a broad column. At the very front were the wounded in wagons. Behind them came the precious artillery led by Wilk. The guns were typical of the field artillery of the time; wheeled gun carriages had yet to be perfected. The cannons, on fixed wooden frames, were hauled in wagons.

Then came the infantry, just emerging from the woods now, led by Gales. Farther back, still out of sight, Cirstian and the cavalry formed the rear guard.

The column was dogged by two other lines clinging to its sides. Ragged lines. Refugees—the luckless peasants who had found themselves smack in the path of the war. They herded their larger livestock along with them. Their old and young, their smaller animals, and their other worldly possessions they hauled in wagons and carts and on their backs, hugging the army as best they could. The truly luckless, they knew, would be those who fell behind…into the path of the bazouks.

For all of their mass the columns—soldiers and civilians alike—were remarkably quiet. Save for the bleat and snort of the animals, and the occasional wail of a babe, the only sound was the hissing of feet slogging through the dewy grass.

As the artillery reached the rise and began deploying on the far flanks, Wilk settled next to Dracula. He looked past the rest of the army, above the trees, to where smoke marred the blue of the sky in the distance. "The bazouks are it early today."

Burning the villages in their wake.

Dracula answered almost to himself: "Yes. It seems they like to play with fire." He nodded to himself as though to mark the thought. He told Wilk, "Keep those people moving straight ahead. Along with the wounded. The flanks here are marsh. Tell them that. Marsh all around. But about an hour out they'll find dry ground. Tell them to take it. To the flanks."

To the flanks. Out of the path of the armies, of the war.

Dracula added, "And tell them not to waste time looking back."

As Wilk went about it, Dracula himself rode to the wounded. In the first wagon were the army's physicians. Chief among them was the blind man who had joined him long ago, his legless companion propped at his side at the reins. Slacking the reins he threw a look to the other wagons and proudly told his voevode, "We did what we could for them, lord. They should all live."

But this, he knew, was only part of what his voevode wanted to hear. So he had his blind "feet" carry him from the wagon to lead Dracula down the line, to a wagon laden with barrels. "There it is, lord," he proclaimed. He gestured to his blind companion. "And he's never made better."

"It's true, lord," the blind man vouched. "Just half a tick and…" He shook his head in finality.

The other went on a bit sadly, "We even tested it, lord. Some of the badly wounded...Rather than linger they preferred..." He shrugged.

Dracula uttered, "May they rest in peace." He then ordered, "I want a barrel set by each well, by each pool. But for God's sake don't dump it until we pass."

Legless nodded. He ordered his "feet" on to the last of the wagons. They were set apart from the rest—far apart—and kept apart by guards spaced at a distance around them.

"Plague," Legless said. "Don't go any nearer, lord. God forbid."

Dracula looked at the wagons. Most of the passengers were prone. To the few still upright, he nodded, as a salute. A few smiled to him. Grimly. And knowingly.

Past them was another group on foot. They needed no guards to fend traffic off. They were wrapped in rags and carried bells—the age-old warning of lepers.

Of them Legless said, "They'll change to their good clothes. They'll look like any other peasants. Easy prey."

He—and his "feet"—chuckled.

And farther, past the lepers, was a bevy of women, also on foot. Pretty. Dressed like peasants. But also dressed to be comely. These, Dracula approached and looked down to from the saddle. He addressed their leader, "Alma, you know what you are about?"

In the glance they exchanged they could read each other's thoughts. Dracula was bitter. Bitter at the path she had been set on so long ago in Tirgoviste—when he had first tried to take the throne and the Turks had raped her. And Alma was bitter. Sent back to her family but stained. Stained physically. Ruined. Beyond any compassion of the voevode or her family.

Now her lips were painted to be full. And she licked her lips. "Oh, we know what we are about, lord." She led the others in a laugh and said as though with a vengeance, "We are only going to give what was given to us."

Dracula could only say, "Bless you."

But that only made Alma lead the others in a louder laugh. "Bless us? Oh, lord...is the time ever past for that."

Even Dracula was glad to be done with the "inspection." He watched them move into the plain—physicians with their barrels of poison...the plague-stricken...lepers...poxed women...

He wondered at these strange "weapons" that God had placed in his hands. But they had been placed nonetheless. And he would use them. History would bear witness: He would use them. Just as nations long after would use weapons of chemicals and "germs."

As he rode back to the rise he had to cross the line of refugees. Among them, he saw one—an old man—with his family. The family had grown from just a wife and two daughters. One of the girls had taken a husband and been blessed with an infant. Long ago, on the Danube, the voevode and his draguli had saved this family from raiders. Even so, they barely acknowledged him now. As Dracula stepped into their path, only the old man glanced up, his eyes speaking for him. They were wild—like a stalked animal that could neither run nor fight. They seemed to ask: *What good did it do to save us then?*

The old man stepped around the voevode's horse and herded his brood on.

By mid-morning Dracula and his commanders were waiting on the rise with the army formed behind them. They held the center of the line with the infantry at their backs, cavalry on the near flanks, and artillery farther out. Behind the army itself, the last refugees were safely away, mere dots on the far plain. The first of the sultan's scouts were already visible in the woods. The spirals of smoke in the southern sky had taken giant steps closer, marking the invaders' approach.

"When the battle starts," Dracula counselled, "they're going to try a ruse. It's their way."

"A feint?" Gales asked.

"Exactly. By the akinjis and bazouks. They'll come on and give way…And we're supposed to follow. As his light troops collapse in the center, his heavy will close on our sides." He confided, "But we are going to turn the tables. With their own scheme."

"How?" Gales asked.

"By offering something irresistible," Dracula said, and he explained what he had in mind.

But, even as he finished, the echo of shouting carried from the deep woods like the distant roar of the sea. As it swelled, the brush and foliage of the entire forest seemed to be moving. Soon the movement showed its true nature: bazouks. Swarming through the woods. They poured onto the field, came on a short way, and stopped—but still shouting, and jumping in place, and jeering at Dracula's line, like a rabble of madmen.

In sharp contrast—which held the eyes that saw it—the Turkish cavalry followed from the woods. In even, ordered lines. Ready formation. Akinjis first. Sipahis next. All silent. All focused on Dracula's rise. They held their reins taut so that their mounts stepped high, as though prancing on parade.

They were formed in separate regiments, but for most there was only a nuance that set them off—different color pennants, slightly different weapons…But one regiment, on the enemy left—facing Dracula's right—was very distinct.

Cirstian, the former peasant, had only heard of such soldiers. Heard of them in vague tales that carried across the continents like legend. He asked, "Moors?"

Gales answered, "Numidians."

Their exploits laced classical literature as examples for all of Europe's hereditary nobility.

"The best horsemen in Africa," Dracula added. "As good as any light horse in the world. Both Rome and Carthage sought them as allies."

"But that was centuries ago," Cirstian said.

Gales spat, as though cursing his own luck. "Aye. Centuries ago. *Before* their hearts were inflamed by Islam."

"You see there," Wilk pointed. "The 'tunics' over their tunics. The 'cloth' on their saddles."

Cirstian peered. "Like fur."

"Fur indeed," Wilk said. "Skins. From their land's big cats. Big as our bears. Each of their warriors, it is said, has to kill his own—with only spear and dagger."

"Worse," Gales said. "You know that this regiment came as a 'gift' from their sultan to the Grand Turk."

Cirstian understood: "Handpicked."

"And all ready—eager—to reach Paradise," Gales said. "He's even put them on our right."

The place of honor in pitched battle. Facing the enemy's strongest arm.

Dracula noted Gales's frown and chided, "I said they were *as good* as any light horse. They bleed. They die. They serve now as akinjis. And we are no strangers to akinjis, aye?" He turned to Cirstian to change the subject. "The other night, at the river, you cursed the janissaries, how they stopped your charge from the flanks."

The infantry janissaries had ways to stop cavalry: fireworks thrown at the horses' feet; walls of spears; the ground studded with holes to break the horses' legs.

Dracula told Cirstian, "Why not get even?"

Cirstian tapped his sword. "I intend to."

"That's not what I mean," Dracula said. "I mean pay them in kind. When we leave this field we will march straight across the plain. They will follow."

The rest of the picture, Cirstian painted for himself—and for the men he promptly sent to the plain with shovels, axes, and poles.

Across the field the bazouks began going even wilder as the rest of their army came on. The huge batteries of cannon...the janissaries...Then the Osmanlis' "voices" of war—huge drums—started to pound to hail the sultan himself. As at Constantinople his entire army shouted over and again: "Fatih!" The Conqueror!

A platform appeared and the sultan appeared on it. He extended a hand. His army fell silent.

Wilk sat up in the saddle and farted. As Dracula and Cirstian and the men around them laughed, he explained, "It seemed appropriate."

The enemy tightened ranks, matching their lines to Dracula's. But their lines were thicker and longer. The janissary block anchored the center—fronting, guarding, the sultan. And fronting them were the bazouks. On the flanks, the cavalry wings were wide: akinjis closer in, sipahis out. Then the clusters of guns.

Dracula's brother, Radu, and his Wallachians could be seen near the sultan's pavilion: reserves.

Behind Dracula, among the peasants, the sergeants barked: "Hold your bowels now! They've only come to take your daughters to a party! They want to visit your churches!"

Then came the more sober order from Dracula himself: *Heed the trumpets. The trumpets. The signals.*

On his platform, Mohammed knelt. His infantry knelt. His cavalry bowed their heads. When the sultan finished his prayer and rose the army gave the shout: *Allahu Akbar!* Then at once they fell silent so that only the thin voices of the *ulamas*, the holy men, stirring them to the holy war, carried from their ranks.

And the armies faced. Only faced. No movement. Until the grass gave up its dew. A full hour.

Gales twisted in his saddle. "What's he doing?"

"Waiting," Dracula said. "To see how reckless we are. And as far as I am concerned he can wait until hell freezes over. He's the 'Conqueror.' Let him conquer."

He dismounted and had his men stand at ease.

It was only minutes later when the Turkish ranks began to part, to open gaps from which platforms—scaffolds—were brought forward all along the front. The bazouks burst into a cheer, a massed jeer. Into their swarm, from behind the lines, bound men were pushed under the lash. Some were peasants. Some wore black: draguli. The prisoners of the first battle. They were kicked and spat upon and lifted onto the scaffolds.

As nooses were placed around their necks, Dracula's army rose and raised weapons to the field. He called them to order—back into silent ranks. He would not have them goaded into a rash charge. He called for a priest. As one hustled forward, he pointed across the field: "Last Rites. Quickly!"

If he could not save his captured men's lives, he could at least save their souls.

The priest was uttering the words as the bodies began to drop on the gallows, a batch at a time, one batch after the other, until the invaders had no more prisoners and casually removed the scaffolds from the stage of the field.

Dracula could feel every eye on the field holding him. Perhaps, he thought, he should have saved a few of his own prisoners—like Volinos or Hamza Pasha—to goad the invaders in turn. Then again, he thought, his prisoners would serve their purpose soon enough.

So he simply called for a pole. A plain pole. He mounted. Rode out a space. And with a dagger sharpened the end of the pole. Sharpened it in full view of the enemy. And planted it. A single stake.

He rode back to his ranks and called for another pole of sorts. A furled banner. Carried by one of his black-shirted riders. At Dracula's nod the banner was loosed: The Dragon. His men hailed it with their own name: *Draguli!*

Now the sultan saw no gain in waiting. He signalled the war drums to sound. The akinjis burst from the flanks. The bazouks ran after them in the center. It was a head-to-head challenge.

Dracula accepted. He raised his sword: "By the Grace of God!" His army surged behind him.

Before the sides closed, the guns on both sides collected their toll for crossing the field. Dracula's few cannon raked through the akinjis. They killed almost as many as the larger Turkish batteries, which had focused on one target alone. And though the troops around Dracula fell, he came on with the dragon banner still flying at his side, while his men still vied for the dangerous place of honor immediately at his flanks.

In later years, veterans on both sides would carry the tale of how the "Dragon's Son" fought on that day. Like a god. Perhaps a demigod of ancient India. A *kshatriya*. Did he sprout four arms? Did each wield a sword? He drove into the enemy ranks like a scythe.

It surprised no one, then, when the invaders began giving way. The akinji horses capered and turned tail. They conceded a few strides, stopped, and tried to make a stand, only to give way again. The bazouks, too, gave way to the mad rush of Wallachia's peasants.

Behind the janissaries, the Conqueror smiled. His mind called to his soldiers on the field: *Bait them! Bait them! Bring them on! Very good!* Not only were his troops falling back, they were slowly funneling the battle to the center of the field, clearing the way for the heavy cavalry to come sweeping in from the flanks.

But the dragon banner suddenly stopped. Black-shirted riders swarmed around it. Like a wall. They began pulling back. In their midst, through the commotion, a rider could be seen slumped in the saddle. The word flew: *Kaziglu! Kaziglu was wounded maybe killed!*

Trumpets sounded. All across the line the Wallachians backed from the battle and began running for their rise.

The akinjis and bazouks watched as the ground between them and the enemy widened. Should they stand? Should they chase? Of course they should chase if Kaziglu were down. But they needed orders.

Could it be? Mohammed thought. *So easy?* Of course it could. The fortunes of battle—Heaven's blessing—had swung his way. Kaziglu had been reckless. And he had paid.

The drums passed the sultan's order. The akinjis and bazouks were unleashed. The sipahis dashed from the flanks. The artillery threw shot far afield into the running Wallachian rabble. *Allahu Akbar!* The janissaries stepped out, keeping a tight formation, but at the double.

Radu rode to Mohammed's side. Through a broad grin he pleaded: "Let me go!"

His friend only laughed. "No need." Why should he risk losing the prince—ally, friend…?

He was hurt when Radu spat and cursed. But the prince would understand when the heat of the battle passed. They would live…both…as they had planned. The war would not have stolen it from them.

The dragon banner had reached the far rise. Its little "dragons" were running after it, and the peasants after them. As the banner disappeared over the rise the Wallachian gunners, too, fled, abandoning their cannon even fully charged.

It was a mad dash by the invaders now. How many slaves could they take? Who would get Wilk and Cirstian and Gales—get the sultan's great reward for them—*if* they were still alive? And, Oh!, the reward if Kaziglu were still ali—

The dragon banner reappeared on the rise. It stopped just enough to show: Kaziglu. Very much alive. Levelling his lance. Shouting. Charging. His entire army was massing around him, as though the blades of grass of the plain had become men to move with him. On the flanks the Wallachian gunners appeared with nothing more to do than set fuse to already charged cannon.

The shout. The explosion. The smoke. The fire. A blast of the Dragon's breath. Point-blank.

The invaders reeled. They stumbled back in a daze. The Wallachians pounced on them.

The Conqueror shook in a rage. Again he heard Radu call to him. He waved it off. He signalled the drums. The janissaries spread in a solid line—a breakwater to steady the army's retreat.

On the field the dragon banner stopped. Trumpets sounded. The Wallachians backed onto their rise, seemingly scouring the field as they went—wounded, corpses, swords, shields...They formed again into tight ranks, poised and simply waiting on the rise, their banner flying above them. All behind the solitary figure of Dracula.

21

IT WAS DAYS LATER, at the peak of the afternoon, when the scout came galloping back to the sultan. The sun was so hot, in fact, as it was destined to be all that summer, that it had burned the clouds from the sky and left the grass of the plain limp.

Kaziglu, the scout reported, was waiting on a distant rise. The man swore to it on all that was holy. This time, Kaziglu was waiting. To make sure, the rest of the sultan's scouts were keeping the voevode under eye. If he tried any tricks, the sultan would know at once.

The day before, the scouts had come flying back to the army, shouting the news that Kaziglu was on their heels. Chasing. Charging. With his whole army. Tartar style. He was running the scouts right back into the main column on the point of his own attack.

Mohammed had frantically shouted orders. The drums had pounded. The army had deployed.

But Kaziglu did not come.

Mohammed had no choice but to have the scouts flogged. He knew they were telling the truth: They had seen Kaziglu coming. But the entire incident unnerved the army, made it feel uncertain and foolish. To restore its confidence, the mistake had to be laid on *someone*: the scouts.

So today the scout was as careful in giving his report as the sultan was in acting on it. Kaziglu's army, the scout said, was drawn in formation. Waiting to offer battle. And it seemed like no ruse. His artillery was set on the flanks. And more, though the plain was broad, he had made the proposed field of battle narrow; he had diverted some nearby streams to turn the far flanks into marsh.

Diverted streams, Mohammed thought. Another trick. Like all the rest. In truth, Kaziglu's schemes were working on the mind. The invasion was a week into Wallachia. But it seemed like a year. And, at that, the week itself had produced little. The grand army should have been halfway—at least—to Tirgoviste. Yet it had made only little more than half that distance. Because Kaziglu was setting the pace.

After the first pitched battle, the armies had stared each other off to finish the day. Though hardly satisfied with the situation, Mohammed had accepted it. He had been tricked in his first encounter. His troops could use the day to regroup. They would fight again the next day. And they would win. All the commanders, in fact, came to the sultan—on their own—to swear it.

But on the day after that first battle Kaziglu was gone. Vanished into the night, into the plain, with his whole army.

It both encouraged and yet discouraged the invaders. Kaziglu was running, admitting that his army was no match in stand-up combat. Yet he had gone so quietly. Like a ghost, the men whispered. Like a jin. With his whole army. The rabble had slipped away like the most cunning of skilled troops.

But Mohammed knew how to quiet such whispers. He gave chase. Kaziglu could hide his men, but not their tracks. The Wallachians would be caught and shown to be all-too-human.

Then came the pits. Kaziglu had left them in his tracks. Deep pits. Lined with stakes. Covered with fresh sod so as to blend in with the plain. A few scouts were the first to disappear—men and mounts swallowed whole. After that the army was careful stepping in Kaziglu's tracks.

But the next pits were not in his tracks. A few bazouks were lost scrambling to scavenge an abandoned wagon. A few akinjis died approaching a stream to water their horses.

The scouts studied the traps and thought they detected a telltale sign: a slight furrow where the sod covered the pits. But at the next such furrow there was no pit, nor at the next or the next…Though there was a pit at the fourth. Not at the furrow itself, but slightly before it—so that the scout going to investigate was taken unawares. And the stakes in that pit were small, like daggers—half-daggers.

It would have been better for both the scout and the whole army if he had died outright. But he had to be silenced. "Put down." Right in the pit. Like a wounded animal.

After that, Mohammed had his scouts run spare mounts ahead of them. As though the dumb beasts were blessed by heaven, the trick of the pits ceased.

Then came the wagons. The "refugees."

The scouts saw them far out on the plain, like marooned sailors drifting on the sea. Clearly Kaziglu was nowhere in sight. The bazouks were eager to claim the prize.

They of course went cautiously. And en masse. It did not surprise them that the stranded refugees made no attempt to run. Run where? They would be caught. And the chase would have only inflamed the fury of the captors.

Mohammed halted the army to let them watch. The bazouks' antics would raise their spirits. And so they did for a time. In the first wagons were women. All women. The bazouks shouted it back to the rest of the troops, who went into a frenzy of cheering as the raping began.

Even as it did the other wagons were taken. Swarmed. Picked clean—bazouks fighting over goods, over captives who might make good slaves.

Then came the word: *Leper!* Somehow it shot clean through the mayhem so that everyone heard it. Another word followed: *Plague!* And the women being raped started to laugh, and to shout: *Pox! Pox!* They were all poxed! Venereal disease.

The bazouks tried to flee back to the army. They did not even think to punish the women, to murder them on the way. They did not want *poxed* blood on their hands. They wanted only refuge. Haven. But how could Mohammed let them back? They had touched leprosy and plague. They had rolled in the pox. They had to be staved off with threats. Abandoned. As the rest of the army skirted the cursed spot.

Then, that very night, came the hooves. As it was, the army, understandably, was not really sleeping. The sound of the hooves brought them to their feet, dazed at first, then scrambling for weapons and into huddled ranks.

The hooves were Kaziglu's whole cavalry. They had to be. They came on like a distant, rolling thunder, from the blackness of the plain toward the sultan's camp.

Then they stopped. Stopped. The camp braced. Nothing. Minutes mounted into an hour. The hooves came again. Again from a distance. A rolling, swelling echo. From the *opposite* end of the plain.

Again they stopped. Again time passed. Again they came from another direction.

It was the janissaries who salvaged spirits then. The janissaries with their arquebuses and cannon. At their own request, Mohammed let them line the guns on the perimeter of the camp and cut loose with a massed volley. For an instant the flash turned night into day as though to remind the troops and enemy alike of the hard power wielded by the Osmanli army. But the flash showed nothing. No Kaziglu. And later that night a hail of arrows as ghostly as the hooves suddenly fell on the sultan's camp. It was the janissaries again who kept their heads, who sprang into ranks to unleash their own arrows and bolts and bring the enemy fire to an abrupt halt.

And so the past few days had gone. Kaziglu's tricks: traps, feints, false alarms. They had slowed the army and rattled its nerves. But the sultan had the janissaries and cannon—and a trick of his own now, if Kaziglu indeed gave battle.

Mohammed gave his order in a single calmly spoken word: *Deploy.* He hoped that the army was as impressed as he was with its own machinelike motion. The artillery wagons spread to the far flanks. The cavalry spread. The center formed. It was like watching a great bird of prey flexing its wings and raising its head.

From where they waited, Dracula and his commanders saw the "great bird" approach like a giant cloud shadow drifting over the plain toward their very feet. The far wings of the invaders' formation began pitching forward, farther ahead even than the cavalry.

Gales noted with concern, "They're coming within range."

"Aye," Dracula said. "He wants to force a battle. A clash. All-out."

"Why oblige him?" Gales asked. "As you said, he's the 'Conqueror.' Let him conquer. Let him chase us."

"That works as a tactic," Dracula said. "But not as a strategy. I can't concede the ground all the way to Tirgoviste."

Gales's eyes fixed on the enemy horde. "But we can't beat him in a pitched battle."

"Not yet," Dracula agreed. "We're still like a wolf against a bear. We'll have to wound him. Bleed him. Wear him down and run. Without getting our own ass chewed."

He watched the sultan's strategy unfolding. The enemy cannon indeed came within range and began to deploy on the farthest flanks. Even with the sipahis and akinjis standing close behind them, the batteries dangled like bait.

Dracula told Wilk, "He wants a duel. His guns to ours."

"Why not?" Gales said. "It makes sense for him. He can afford to lose one-for-one."

"Exactly," Dracula said. "He's playing chess again. He means to trade us piece for piece because he has more pieces."

Wilk injected, "As it is, we don't have much powder and shot. Not enough for a long war. So why not trade him gun for gun? Take what toll we can."

"Aye," Dracula said. "You trade him, shot for shot." He told Cirstian and Gales, "And we, too, will swipe at his guns. He will move his other 'pieces' up soon enough. His cavalry to ours. Infantry to infantry. They will come straight on. We will meet them straight on. But then I want you to turn to the flanks, to the guns. Storm them. Destroy them. And run."

He sent the commanders off, and, in short order, Wilk began firing, taking what enemy guns he could while they were still digging in. But that advantage passed in short order as the janissaries set their batteries in place and returned fire.

For a time it seemed like the rest of the armies did not exist. On both sides, explosions crept along the far flanks of the plain like the terrible footsteps of some invisible giants lumbering their way toward the respective batteries. The shots began finding their range, their mark, as the gunners found just the measure of powder that would carry their volleys right into the enemy emplacements. Wilk had fired first; he found his mark first. An enemy gun exploded. The Wallachians cheered. But the janissaries were quick to find their mark. Quick to give their own side cause to cheer.

The duel was only minutes old when the Osmanli drums sounded to the cry: *Allahu Akbar!* The Turkish infantry began a slow, deliberate walk up the center of the field, picking up the cavalry wings along the way, until the entire formation was aligned in a phalanx, a thick, solid line sweeping steadily on.

On the Wallachian side, the Dragon banner unfurled, *By The Grace of God!*, and the army advanced behind the voevode.

It had been days since Mohammed had been in such high spirits. The guns' roar. The cries. The tramp of feet. Even the screams of wounded and dying men only made it seem more like a pageant. When the two armies closed and finally sprang at each other, he decided to add a touch. From his pavilion, set at the rear high above his ranks, he ordered his ulamas to rush out into the ranks to shout their inspirations in a frenzy. And he ordered a military band to begin blaring martial airs.

He watched the Dragon banner in the center of the field. He did not care that it neither wavered nor faltered. Let it stand, he thought. It made no difference if Dracula died that day. Oh, he admitted, of course it would make a difference. But it was not essential. He had other plans for Kaziglu that day.

The Dragon banner stood. Dracula and his infantry were holding their own against the janissaries and bazouks. Exactly as Mohammed wanted. The Osmanli cavalry began inching back on the flanks, just inching, just a bit farther back from the artillery. Soon, Mohammed thought, Kaziglu would do what he would do in his place: have his cavalry flanks spring for the exposed guns.

From his place with the artillery, Wilk stepped forward. He no longer recoiled at the roar of the guns, or at the enemy shot tearing the turf around him. Fate was fate. Under such fire, all a man could do was endure. And fire back.

He knelt and peered through the smoke. There were no visible surprises. No cause for alarm—no *undue* cause, what with the enemy three-to-one against. In fact, there was reason to hope. The enemy cavalry was being pried back. Pried. Slowly. But surely. Soon the enemy guns would be exposed. Cirstian and Gales would bolt for them. Then all would be in flux. With luck, they would "give" the enemy much more then they "took."

He saw a ripple move through the Osmanli ranks along both flanks. A ripple as though a small crowd were trying to push through a larger crowd. Push up, toward the guns. Sure enough, a separate contingent of janissaries appeared on each flank. Just at the edge of the cannon. They could not be seen by the Wallachians on the field. And on both flanks they were hauling something. Something long, like a cannon, or a log—a ram? It was all a bit obscure. But what good would a ram or another cannon do on the field?

On their respective flanks, Cirstian and Gales felt fortunate. Plain lucky. Each hoped the other was doing as well. Not only were their ranks holding fast in the grind of the static battle, they had actually pushed the enemy back. Not enough to alarm Mohammed obviously. He probably was not thinking much of the few feet of ground. He was still rapt in his set-piece battle. And the Wallachian cavalry was drawing abreast of his exposed artillery.

Across the mass of his reserves, Mohammed's eyes met Radu's. Radu raised his lance. He was ready. Eager. All he needed was the order. But the sultan had to give no order. He needed no reserves. All he needed was to wait.

On the field, at almost the same instant, Cirstian and Gales saw their chance. The enemy guns were fairly exposed. The two boyars charged them.

The Wallachian ranks swirled. Those locked at center field with the enemy stayed locked, dug heels to hold the line behind Dracula. The rest bolted after their boyars, to the flanks, to the enemy guns, which were still focused on Wilk's emplacements as though oblivious to any danger from the field.

Cirstian and Gales saw the gunners suddenly try to turn the cannon. It seemed that some would make it and fire, stem the charge, but not enough. Then the air itself around each boyar seemed to explode.

Wilk saw: Greek Fire. What the janissaries had hauled along the flanks were huge tubes and bladders. Bladders of skins gorged with the incendiary liquid. The janissaries squeezed the bladders like a bellows—to shoot the liquid, holding a torch to it as it went. It had its own roar. Low. Hoarse. The roar of an inferno. It turned the air to flame, a shiny green, blue, and yellow. Huge balls of flame that seemed to just hang in space.

But around the balls the fire spread, flowed. For a moment it thinned, as though catching its breath, and in the thinness could be seen whole figures, man and horse, charred and crumbling, and others aflame, thrashing and screaming.

The bellows roared again. The Osmanli cannon joined them, turned now to the field.

Dracula was still at the center of the field. But he had *felt* it all. The shudder of the very air. The heat. Followed by the massed volley of the cannon—as though in an orchestrated triumph. He heard the screams and choked on the billowing smoke. He smelled the unmistakable smell of burning flesh. Human flesh. Even before Wilk had the trumpets sound retreat, Dracula was pulling his men back.

Mohammed laughed aloud while his mind screamed: *Dragon! Ha! Here is your "dragon"!* He grabbed his crotch to make the point.

While his army chased the Wallachians he surveyed the entire scene. The enemy cannon were still firing, but the batteries were thinner than before. His own batteries, too, were thinner, but their roar was still enough, still deep. The Dragon banner was escaping. The Wallachian peasants behind it were showing impressively quick feet. The Wallachian cavalry, on either flank, was a mere rabble, a running rabble. It had left much of its bulk still roasting on the field.

Radu galloped to the sultan's side, sword drawn. "Now! I can take him!"

But Mohammed only grinned and shook his head. "Why rush? He's ours for the taking now!"

He raised a hand for the drums to slow his army's pursuit. When the last of the enemy disappeared over the far rise he called a halt.

He had not had much of the Greek Fire. He had captured the precious bit when he took Constantinople. He had never duplicated the formula. The Greeks he had taken alive obviously did not know it; the cruelest tortures proved that. But Mohammed was glad he had saved the Fire for this occasion.

What did Kaziglu and all his peasants and little "dragons" think now?

The sultan was still gloating when a wave of smoke carried from over the far rise.

22

MOHAMMED had pitched his camp in the style of the ancient Romans. It was surrounded by a deep trench and dirt walls. The dirt had been scooped back from the trench and shored with wooden palisades.

Behind the trench and walls, the sultan's pavilion was set in the midst of the janissary encampment, which itself was set in the midst of the other contingents. Not even a bug could approach the sultan without being challenged.

His tent sat like an oasis, a safe, pleasant haven. It had several rooms whose fine cloth made a cool shade under the blistering sun. Throughout the rooms were gold vessels of fruits, wine, and water, all within easy reach. At the sultan's command, silk had been spread on the floor so that he did not even have to tread the soil that to him seemed so cursed.

If he had wanted, he could have had concubines fanning the air day and night and smothering him in pleasure in bed. But he had chosen only one bed-mate, one tent-mate: Radu.

It had been so long since they had been together like this. Since long before the campaign. Because as soon as the army had begun to assemble Radu had been consumed with preparing his troops. He had one thing on his mind: his throne. It was not so much that he had shunned pleasure. He simply did not have time for it. Not even with his sultan and dear friend.

But that drought had finally been broken the night before, and now Mohammed lay contentedly, propped on an arm in the pool of soft pillows and sheets, just watching Radu's naked form stretched facedown in the inner twilight of their "oasis." His hand merely touched the auburn hair and slid to the smooth skin when Radu wakened and sat up. His words were soft but about business: "We've been here two days already." As Mohammed said nothing, he pressed, "The men are rested. We should move on."

Mohammed sneered. "Rested? Really?"

Radu reminded, "This *is* war."

Mohammed heard himself snap, "And I *am* Fatih!"

Radu only parried, "Yes. This is war. And you are the Conqueror."

Yet the army had been standing—stagnant—for two days.

And there, in his own tent, with his friend at his side and his army all around him, Mohammed suddenly felt alone.

It was not the troops themselves, nor Radu, who had ordered the halt in the march. It was not any of them who could give the order to move on. The power was his. Fatih's. The Conqueror. But he was not of a mind to issue any orders.

He offered as an excuse, "It has been a long time since my last campaign. A long time since I actually had sword in hand."

A long time since Belgrade. At the thought of the place, he saw the familiar image: the chaos of the battle...his own wound and blood...

Radu offered in turn, "No, my friend. It is not your last war that haunts you. It is this one. You expected an easy campaign."

As he let the rest of the thought go unspoken, Mohammed's head dropped. And this sultan, the Conqueror, who prided himself in hiding his feelings even from his own beard, finally admitted: "This Kaziglu...this *Dracula*...has gotten into my head."

Gotten into his head. Turned the best weapon of a long line of sultans against a sultan himself. Terror. Fear.

Radu himself felt the pain of it. Outraged by the spell suddenly fallen on his friend, he snarled, *"You are Fatih!"*

"Yes," Mohammed said. "And we won the last battle."

Burned Dracula's men in Greek Fire. *Shredded* them with chain-shot. Showed them hell as near as a man could see it on earth.

Mohammed lamented, "Yet what did they do? Did they crumble? Lose heart? Did they quit the war? Scatter to the winds?"

Radu of course knew the answer. As though inspired by the example of the Greek Fire—as though they suddenly found that they revelled in hell themselves—Dracula and his men had scorched the earth. Even as they had retreated over the rise from the last battle, they had set fire to the plain. Then the villages beyond it. And the forests beyond them.

"Are we *chasing* them?" Mohammed said. "No. We are *following*. Just following."

"Yes," Radu declared. "And we'll follow all the way to Tirgoviste."

Mohammed asked himself: To Tirgoviste? He no longer saw this war in terms of time and place. He had still only been in this land a matter of days. But they seemed as long now as the days of Creation. Or *Damnation*. And Tirgoviste? It seemed like a legend. A figment. At the gates of Hell itself.

Radu counselled, "Now that you know what he's done—gotten into your mind—you should be able to shed it. Shake it. Do not let him play on your fear."

But fear, Mohammed knew, was a feeling. A feeling not so easily shed. It had to be undone with the mind, with thought. Like chisels and picks, thoughts had to strike the fear, pull it apart and show its flaws. Show that it was not real or so overwhelming.

His army still outnumbered Dracula's *three-to-one!*

But Mohammed muttered, "First I hanged his men in front of his eyes. Then I burned them. *His* men. He who always repays at least 'eye for eye.' And he has prisoners. My men. At each turn I look for his revenge...look to find my men butchered or...But we find nothing. Nothing. So what has he done with his prisoners? This not knowing is worse than finding them butchered. It is not like this *Dracula*."

Radu came behind him and began kneading his shoulders. Their tightness told him what he already knew: "You are thinking too much." He soothed, "If he has gotten into your head, *you* should get out of it. *Do* something!"

"Do what?"

"Keep following him."

To where? Mohammed thought. He had already followed through battles, over the hidden pits, and through pox and plague. He had followed after the flames, until the entire army—men, beasts…and even he, the sultan, were all scarred by soot—until Dracula's fire, combined with heaven's summer sun, made Wallachia indeed seem like hell. Until the men joked—surely with gallows humor—that they could roast meat simply by holding it in the air.

As though that had not been enough, Dracula had sprung yet another trick: poisoned water. Wells. Whole streams. Laced with lethal mixtures. Parched men and beasts scrambled for a drink only to die. So now the army had to send back even for its water.

Scorched earth. Poisoned water. Would the land ever recover?

Did this Dracula care?

No. Clearly he did not. And this, Mohammed knew, is what gave Dracula's terror its frightful power. The Tartar, the Mongol—even he, the Turk—unleashed terror on others. Burn *their* villages. Kill *them* to strike fear into their hearts. This Dracula—and all those who followed him—would kill *themselves* rather than give in.

Radu was right. The Conqueror had expected an easy campaign. He knew the Wallachians were stiff-necked. Yes. That they were. But not even the Albanians had shown such…fanaticism.

So follow Dracula to where? Long ago, Mohammed's own great-grandfather, the sultan Bayazid, had followed an enemy: the dreaded Tartar, Timur "The Lame"—Tamerlane. And Bayazid had died in a Tartar cage. A cage. Drawn across Asia to display Bayazid like an animal.

Yet one slip, Mohammed knew…one mistake with this *Dracula*…and he might find himself praying for death in a cage.

Radu urged again, "Follow him."

The sultan did not know how to answer. In the simplest terms, all of Wallachia was just not worth it to him. Not Dracula's Wallachia.

Radu understood the meaning of the silence. And he understood more: Mohammed regretted this war. He would have retreated. But the world was watching. How could he run and save face?

Radu gave his friend's shoulders a gentle shake. "You have done enough. It is I who would be prince. You have brought me this far. Me and the army. This magnificent army. Let *me* lead from here. Who could say then that you haven't done enough? You have your empire to rule."

Mohammed turned to him. Behind his beard his lips trembled. He took Radu's face in his hands. "Do you know what he'll do to you if he takes you?"

Now it was Radu who snapped. "Am I your wife, a frail woman to be protected? I am a man! I would be prince! Let me go!"

Mohammed knew that he was right. If nothing else, they simply could not remain frozen. Still he shook his head.

"Then let us take a smaller step," Radu said. "Send to Stephen, my cousin. Or do you forget that he hasn't joined my brother?"

It seemed so far afield that Mohammed laughed. "Do you really think Stephen would join *us*?"

"Directly? No. But he has not joined my brother. I think he is a very practical man. I will send to him."

As Mohammed shrugged to grant it, Radu pushed on. "And we should send scouts ahead. At least see where my brother is now. See what he is about."

Mohammed's laugh now was cynical. "What scouts? Who would dare such a thing?"

He knew. Sultan or no, whippings or no, it would take a rare man to stalk Dracula—truly stalk him—now. Scouts could be sent. They would go. But their hearts would not be in it. Who could trust what they said they saw? And who could say that they had lied, that they had not even dared approach Dracula's camp?

But Radu was prepared for this: "Your Wallachian janissaries. I know my people. My brother's defiance of you is their disgrace. To erase the shame they will brave anything. I am sure of it."

Again Mohammed simply shrugged. The Wallachians had been taken into the corps during the reign of Dracula's father. Forced recruits. Stubborn. Some had even revelled at first at Dracula's defiance of the Porte. But Mohammed had "culled" their ranks. Purged them. They served humbly now. And it made no difference to him if a few were lost scouting their Kaziglu-Bey.

23

THE WALLACHIAN JANISSARY, Ali Hamed, had willingly volun-teered for this mission. Four others—native countrymen, fel-low janissaries—had joined him.

Why not? It was their native prince, Dracula, who disgraced their very blood by defying the sultan. And even on this most dangerous of missions they had the honor of following the great Ali Hamed. Great, even though, like them, he was still a very young man. Great, but not from any particular physical prowess. He was only slightly taller than average. With his brown hair, beard, and eyes, he easily blended into any band of common recruits. It was his bravery that set him apart. And his renowned loyalty to the sultan.

Ali now returned to the spot where he had left the last of his men hidden. His shadow made the man jump. The wide eyes spoke: *Kaziglu! I thought you were Kaziglu!* Ali merely smiled and shook his head: *No Kaziglu.* It was just as the man breathed easy again that Ali slit his throat. Waited till his back was turned, seized the head, cut the throat. So quick, so quiet. Ali could even hear himself think: *I do unto you as I would have you do unto me. I would rather be dead than betray my land and religion.*

Severing the head was a bit bloody. It stained the janissary uniform. But that, Ali knew, was good. It would only make him the greater when he returned to the sultan; it would be proof that Ali had been in a skirmish. A skirmish where he lost his four comrades.

He put the head in a sack with the other three. He changed from his uniform to Wallachian clothes. Simple clothes. Like those of the peasant he had once been. And he again felt like that peasant: Giorgi. The Turks could call him Ali Hamed. He was still Giorgi.

He simply walked until Dracula's own scouts found him. The heads lent his story a bit of credibility. When he was taken into the camp, he was at once proud and distressed by what he saw. The army of his native countrymen was indeed a most improbable band. Even the draguli had been mostly peasants, like him. And most of the rest were still peasants in fact. Yet this was the army that gave *the Conqueror* so much trouble!

The camp was set in a foothill forest which, if it did not exactly cool the air, at least blocked the worst of the sun. The Wallachians sat in the shade in small clusters, quietly idling like peasants in a respite from their toil. To Giorgi, they could have been woodcutters or farmhands or hunters at rest. They looked every bit the part except…

So many of them had been scarred by the Greek Fire. Men and beasts both. Their eyes were distant, frightened. Even those who had not been scarred wore the look of fright, mixed with disgust. It could have been them lying so horribly wounded. Yet there was little they could do to ease the particular brand of pain left by the Fire.

In Dracula's tent, Giorgi also had the mixed feelings: pride and pain. The voevode he knew easily enough; and the green eyes were as boldly penetrating as men swore. Wilk, Cirstian, and Gales were also easy enough to distinguish; they had been described often—as special targets—in the Turkish camp. Now, as Giorgi saw, the two boyars had also been burned by the Fire.

If the wounds were not critical, they were ugly. Cirstian's cheek was marred right up into his hairline, as though a lash had been laid with a vengeance on his fair looks. Yet he seemed none too upset as he dabbed the scar with a cool compress. Gales was scarred from chest to cheek. His wound, like Cirstian's, was a puckered, pale white. He hung his head and winced with each touch of his own compress.

As Giorgi knelt to Dracula, he was bid to rise, to face the voevode directly, to tell his story. He did not flinch under the emerald stare. He explained that the Osmanli called him Ali Hamed. He had been with the enemy a long time. With them but not *of* them. He had gained their trust and their hearts. But each time their backs were turned…He made a motion like the swipe of a dagger. He was let to show what he had brought in the sack, telling Dracula, "I led them. I took them one by one. Traitors."

But Gales posed outright, "How can we trust him?"

Dracula's eyes were still on Giorgi's: "We can trust him."

Giorgi spoke as though to console the wounded boyars, "My lords, you are both lucky." He had seen them in the battle, on the very point of the conflagration. But sometimes the Fire did that, blew over the first ranks to fall worse in the rear.

Gales retorted bitterly, "Lucky? My horse was fried alive right under me."

As he trembled at the memory, Dracula laid a hand on his shoulder to calm him.

Still Gales flashed back to the battle. "Those men…" He closed his eyes and shook his head.

Giorgi spoke, "That is why I have come here, my lords. You suffered much in the last battle. But the great 'Fatih' is the one losing heart."

As Gales looked at him with clear suspicion, Giorgi willingly sought Dracula's stare. "I swear it, lord. It is why I was so eager to come here. To tell you. The sultan is losing heart. The janissaries try to spur him on. And your own brother spurs him on. I heard it myself when they sent me here." He felt compelled to add, "Your brother seems well enough, lord."

As Dracula ignored it, Giorgi continued, "But the great 'Fatih' will not move. The best he would do is send me to scout."

Dracula gave a slow nod. Truly it was as he suspected. Why else would the sultan have holed up in camp? Holed up after a victory in battle? Still he asked, "Giorgi, are you sure that he isn't simply waiting? For more troops? For whatever?"

Giorgi shook his head. "I can only say…I see no sign of new troops. I hear no whispers. I know only what I do see and what the men say. The 'Conqueror' is losing heart. You can see it in his face—when he shows his face. I saw it myself. I heard it in his voice. So I tell you, lord: Strike him now and he might break."

Gales was incredulous. "Strike *him*? He can still swallow us whole!"

Dracula raised a hand for silence. He gave a nod and Giorgi understood. The commanders would discuss things in private. Yet before Giorgi made to leave Dracula offered, "Stay here with us now, your own kind. You have done me a great service."

Giorgi demurred with a smile: "I must go back, lord. For two reasons. First, I can still be of service to you. I am your 'eyes'—and 'hands'—in Fatih's own camp. Once again he will think me a hero. *His* hero. I, the only one who lived through this very mission. I burrow deeper into his trust each day. But more...I hate them so. They stole me from my family and land. From my life. It is not yet time to leave my work behind. At least, lord, not as long as you fight them."

But when he was gone Gales began, "My men are drained. The Fire burned more than their flesh."

Dracula did not argue. "Which is why we need a victory."

Gales posed, "Can I be frank?"

Dracula agreed, "You have earned it."

Gales declared simply, "We cannot win. Not by fighting him head-on. Not by meeting him on the field."

Again Dracula did not argue. "I will not meet him on the field. Not this time."

"Aye," Wilk agreed. "Better to catch him in a 'box.'"

Cirstian guessed, "In his camp?"

"Exactly," Dracula said. "In his camp. At night. By surprise."

Gales muttered as though to himself, "This *is* too bold."

"We either fight," Dracula said, "or we simply let him push us across the country."

Gales countered, "Or we can fight like the Albanians, like Skanderbeg."

Dracula answered bluntly. "Skanderbeg will lose in the end. And fighting the way he does he will live like a rat in the meantime. The mountains are his nest now but the Turk will ferret him out."

Gales persisted, "But this...attacking *him*—in his *own camp!* We stake all on one throw!"

"Yes," Dracula said. "*All.* We will hold nothing back."

"The trick," Wilk noted, "will be to make him think that we attack from one side. Only one side."

Cirstian saw the possibilities. "His whole camp will rally around him."

Dracula prompted Gales, "Can't you see it? If we can draw them all to one side of the camp...Think, man. Think. We *can* win."

Gales sighed. "And if we don't?"

"That's the best of it," Dracula said. "We don't have to kill him. Just weaken him even more. Kill him if we can. But just weaken him. He still has to face the 'Forest.'"

The Forest. Wilk and Cirstian smirked at the thought.

Gales only hung his head. He said resignedly, "You are determined to do this thing."

Dracula answered, "I am. I said from the first...we will see this war through to the end."

"You think we can feint him to one side of the camp?"

"Yes."

"Then let me lead the attack on the other. Let me put the knife to his heart."

Dracula hesitated. "Are you up to it? Are your men?"

"My men," Gales said, "are like yours. They will do whatever I tell them."

And Dracula considered. It made good sense. If he himself led an attack on one side of the camp, the sultan would surely be drawn in. So a bold thrust on the other side by a good man—a man like Gales...

24

FOR DRACULA'S PURPOSE, the night of June 17th was near per-fect: moonless; a damp wind threatened to kick up a storm. It would blow hard, fade, blow again...The invaders, huddled in their camp, were grateful that they needed blankets to sleep. The chill lulled them. The swaying of trees and swishing of debris tossed by the wind masked any other sounds of the night. Like the sounds of Dracula's men.

They were still covered by the woods when they dropped to their stomachs and crawled. To an eye from the camp's palisades, there was nothing to see in the forest save for a barely darkening shadow on the ground. A shadow that spread so slowly as to be just another shade of the murky night. Out of the woods and onto the plain...

If the sultan had been afraid to move for days, his troops at least felt lucky that he had found this spot for their camp. It was a league or so beyond where Dracula's scorched earth had ended—as though past the point where Kaziglu had finally run out of evil. And it was poised near the forest. A good place to rest and yet be ready to push on. But now the grass of the plain hid the slithering shadow almost to the foot of the camp trench. There the shadow stopped while the men in the front rolled onto their backs and began hauling on ropes. A small party on each line, each line dragging a log or a ramp or a ladder.

Giorgi knew the approximate time: about three hours after sunset—the first thick of the night. He walked across the camp and faded into a good spot. He tucked himself among bundles of supplies next to a corral about an arrow's half-flight from the walls. And he had arrows enough. And a bow and pitch and a small bundle.

He was so used to this sort of thing. On similar nights in similar places he had waited. Sometimes his ambush was on orders, to surprise the sultan's enemies. Sometimes it was on his own—his own war against those whom he still considered to be his captors: the sultan's men. He did not even worry about being caught any more. His hand—his whole being—was steady.

He saw the silhouette of a sentry on the wall suddenly straighten as though leaning on the palisades. Leaning. Looking out toward the forest. For just a second. But by the time it backed away his bow was ready. Before the sentry could shout the alarm he was dead. Yet the others on the wall began stirring. Scrambling. Pointing out over the walls into the night. Then the shout: *Kaziglu!*

Giorgi struck flint to an oiled cloth and let flaming arrows fly in all directions. Fire in the camp. Confusion. Then he stamped the cloth out, rolled into the corral, popped the gate, and stampeded the horses. He rolled back into his place to see the shadows pouring over the walls. Dracula's men. As yet they were not shouting; they were leaving that to the defenders. Giorgi could picture the waves of Wallachians yet to come, dropping their logs into the trench, then the ramps over the logs, then the ladders onto the walls. They had to get over...over...in just a spot or two at first—clusters of men to gain a hold against the thin line of Turks on the inner wall. They had already done that and were clearing the wall. Giorgi helped with a few more arrows.

But he felt the time to stop firing. Felt it. From his long experience. Turks were streaming all around him to the walls. Many of the officers led their brigades with torches. Giorgi readied his bundle. This, too, would take timing. For his own sake.

He was glad to see Dracula's men gain solid footholds. They dropped from the walls and formed their own brigades, ragged groups, like small mobs. As they pushed out from the walls, most stayed close to one another to ready for a massed melee. But some scattered into the camp—to knowing suicide—to add to the general confusion.

Their sacrifice was not in vain. As they spread, the defenders saw enemies on all sides. But which was the main attack? The question froze the Turks in place.

As they regrouped in orderly contingents at the heart of the camp, the attackers claimed the space below the palisades.

The last of the Turks deserting the wall ran into Giorgi's position. They were glad to find a janissary but they were also frantic: *Kaziglu! Kaziglu himself!* They had seen him.

"The sultan must know!" Giorgi told them, pushing them on into the camp. "Tell him! 'Kaziglu!' 'Kaziglu!' And tell him that Ali Hamed will stand this ground."

As they ran on he loosed his bundle: Wallachian clothes. He changed, wrapped his janissary whites, and stashed them near the corral. He waited for Dracula's men to overtake him then slid along their lines till he saw the thickest ranks: the voevode's own guard. Giorgi shouted until Dracula heard him and called him to his side.

Giorgi had only to give a firm nod. All was going as planned. Even better. In the camp now, the ground between Turk and Wallachian was a no-man's land. But the space was filled with Turkish tents, corralled horses, and supplies. More, the Turkish cannon were near-useless—unless Mohammed was willing to ravage his own camp to bombard Dracula's men.

Dracula let his men run on, to lay insult on the camp. Scattered horses, burning tents and supplies soon drew the first Turkish contingents out. Their panic faded as their trained bodies and minds settled into formation and went about their work. Had Kaziglu really come in force? Or was this just a raid? It was the task of the first contingents to find out.

Moving out into the camp, they groped in the darkness for what seemed like an eternity, slowly fanning into a line as though to sweep the camp. But part of the line found a hail of arrows, part found the enemy in the flesh—in thick bands—and part found nothing to block its path. So gradually the line was shaken and scattered. It was past midnight when the survivors of that first line fell back from their skirmishing to tell the sultan: It was indeed a full-scale attack— led by Dracula himself.

Behind a wall of janissary shields, Mohammed was oblivious to the wind still whipping, still threatening a storm. Oblivious to the acrid odor of burning tents and supplies. Oblivious to the cries of his commanders looking to him for the order to save the camp, to drive the enemy out. Better that, they cried, than bear the insult any longer. They still had the overwhelming odds.

But it was Radu who literally shook the sultan: "Let us go!"

Mohammed gave a nod to the rest but locked a hand on Radu's arm.

The Turks charged with the battle-cry: *Allahu Akbar!* It was made the more terrible by their desperate resignation that many would see Paradise instead of the next dawn.

In the light of the burning camp, Dracula saw them coming. He called to his men to form the line and hold firm. Hold. He sent the order to close his planned trap: to call Gales over the walls at the opposite side of the camp at the sultan's back.

Arrows and bolts flew, arquebuses fired, and the lines lunged at each other. Dracula's line staggered at the sheer weight of the Turkish charge but his men dug in their heels and lashed back. It was as though the darkness gave them strength, the strength of anonymity and confusion. There were no janissaries here. No sipahis or peasants. No ranks. No clever tactics. Just souls fighting hand-to-hand with whatever was at hand. And all his men had to do, Dracula knew, was hold.

But many were suddenly possessed to do much more. They tore their way through the enemy ranks or dashed far around them to run on—for the sultan himself. The enemy chased. The melee spread. Dracula waited. Gales! Gales! Where the hell was he? Or was he already in the camp, his charge drowned out by the greater battle? So much time had already passed that it had to be so.

It was Giorgi's hand that caught Dracula's shoulder. Cirstian had come from the flank bearing the news: No Gales. Beyond the wall, from where he was supposed to have come, there was nothing. Nothing. Not even the hint of a skirmish. He was gone with all his men. Clearly *deserted.*

There was nothing for Dracula to look to now but the battle in front of his eyes. His men were giving punishment. But they were also getting. And the janissaries were returning to their senses. They were pulling from the melee and gelling into disciplined ranks, forming into small companies like roving bands of butchers. And Dracula simply did not have the men to stop them.

He spread the word to retreat. Passed it from rank to rank so as not to inflame the enemy with a general show of submission. Before pulling back he made a last lunge forward to stagger the enemy line, to give as many of his men as possible a chance to make their escape. His ranks lashed out then withdrew, step by step, under the fire of their short bows. Behind them their rear-guard had long-since erased a section of the camp wall and ditch. As the army receded toward the spot Dracula grasped Giorgi's arm: "Come with us."

But Giorgi refused, "No, lord. Let me go. And God go with you."

In separate directions, they both disappeared into the night.

There were still two hours before dawn when Giorgi emerged near the sultan's tent. He was Ali Hamed again. Janissary. Tattered. Smudged. Bloodstained.

Bloody sword in his hand. Pleading for his commanders and the sultan to hear: "Chase! Chase! The bastard's on the run! I can lead to his camp!"

His comrades took up the shout. Radu added his voice. If not totally swept away, Mohammed could not help feeling a bit like the Conqueror again. "Tomorrow," he counselled. "Rest now. We will chase him tomorrow."

25

ALI HAMED had been given the honor of leading the army in pursuing Dracula. He returned to the main column now, past the sipahis and akinjis and his own janissary brethren. Straight to the open wagon of the Conqueror himself. He dropped from the saddle and bowed, stomach to bare earth.

Mohammed called him closer. He was amazed at this Ali. In truth. Where did the man find such courage?

Ali leaned forward to speak in confidence and considered: Could he draw his dagger and kill this *pig* now? No chance. Not really. The sipahis would draw as quickly as he. And the sultan wore armor under his robes. Thick armor, lately. So Ali simply reported, "Highness. In the woods ahead…"

"What?"

"The answer to a mystery, highness. Kaziglu's poor victims. I left my scouts to mark the place. At least…the beginning of the place."

The sultan asked for no more details. He was flushed as he looked ahead toward the unseen place. But he was compelled. He told Ali to lead on and Ali looked grave as he proceeded. But behind the gravity he was laughing. He had led the Grand Turk to where Dracula had told him. But Dracula had warned Ali to brace for what he would find. The Conqueror had no such warning.

Dracula had chosen a spot—chosen it *years* before for just this day—a spot where this road to Tirgoviste ran broadly through the woods. Broad enough so that the sultan would not shy from it simply for fear of a trap. Still, Mohammed sent the bazouks far ahead on the flanks. If there was a trap, the screams of these dreg-and-dross wretches would alert the rest of the army.

Ahead and behind, the sultan's wagon was surrounded by his commanders, themselves surrounded by sipahis and akinjis and janissaries. The head of the procession had just reached the woods when the first bazouks came stumbling back to the road. To a man they were blanched. Some had fresh stains on their tunics…from their own retch. They were moaning, wailing: *The dead!* And the first of the smell seemed to follow them. The smell of the dead indeed. Dead *men*. Human beings. The smell went not only into the nostrils, but the throat. It churned the stomach and flooded the mouth with spit. It threatened to seep into clothes, into hair…into the skin itself. It made the dumber animals rear and snort.

At the head of the column, behind his grave look, Giorgi smiled inside. He was particularly amused at the sight of the scouts he had left at the place. They, too, were pale and had fresh stains on their shirts. Some were still doubled over. They looked at him now with more than the common hatred of the rank-and-file trooper for the strict officer. *How could he have made them wait there?* And yet they had to admire him. Ali Hamed, the Brave. Even as he dismounted and waited for the sultan, he held his head high, as though immune to the very miasma of the place.

The van of the army parted and the imperial wagon ambled forward. Already the sultan held a cloth to his face in a vain attempt to ward off the smell. He looked around at the forest. *The Forest.* It straddled the road for perhaps a mile square. This was what Dracula had done—had been doing—methodically—with his victims: *The Forest of the Impaled.*

As Mohammed looked from his rolling wagon, the bodies seemed to be coming to him, rather than he to them. He pressed a hand to his brow to dissolve the illusion. He found the presence to give the order: "Stop."

Again he beheld the Forest. Thousands. *Twenty* thousand, some would later say. *Thirty. Forty.* But who would take census on such a macabre thing?

Men, women, and children, they were impaled in all states. From all angles of the stake: through stomach, anus, back…In various stages of decay. From as far back as the first year of Dracula's reign. Some were only bones. Some wore scant swaths of flesh. And some—Dracula's prisoners from the past few days—seemed almost alive.

They had been raised on their stakes at varying heights. And highest of all—and closest to the sultan's approach—were two in particular. He knew them not from their faces, which were rotted away, but from their dress, which had been kept impeccably intact—just for this occasion.

Toma Catavolinos. Hamza Pasha.

As they had been men of rank in life, Dracula had also raised them, as it were, in death. On the highest of the stakes.

Nearest them was a third man. On a very low stake. The sultan's spy. Headless. His poisoned corpse had been hauled all the way from Castle Dracula.

Strangely, the sun was soothingly warm on Mohammed's face. He heard the forest birds singing, chirping away. Even as the flies and maggots crawled over the corpses.

Then a movement on one of the stakes caught the sultan's eye. Movement. Life. The man was alive—or at least not yet dead. He was a prisoner from one of the recent battles. He moaned as though to speak.

Even as Mohammed recoiled, the air zipped: an arrow. Mercy. The impaled man was now dead. That fast, a carrion bird lighted on the arrow. Its eye, too, caught the sultan's. The curve of its beak seemed like a natural smile. It tore at the bleeding flesh. The air zipped again: an arrow for the defiling bird. But the bird had barely dropped when another swooped to feed on it, and yet another took the empty perch at the corpse.

"Highness. We should move on."

It was the janissary commander. In an order that Mohammed had not even heard, the commander had already set his troopers to two grim tasks: burying the remains of Hamza; doling arrows in the name of mercy to any of the impaled who looked too "fresh."

Mohammed gaped at these simple soldiers going about the work as though it were any other. And he gaped at Radu, whose face, while twisted in disgust, was also twisted in a rage that spoke clearly: *How could his brother have done such a thing? His own people!* The impalements themselves were bad enough. But this...*Monstrosity!* The Forest.

The commander began again, "Highness..."

Radu finished the sentence with a resolve: "We should move on."

What kind of men were they? Mohammed thought. Even Radu. They were supposed to be *small* men, compared to him—*Fatih!* Yet they made *him* feel small. They saw what Dracula had done—the awesome terror of the Forest—and yet they would just..."move on."

And those around the sultan heard his thoughts of that moment escape in words. Words that in fact were later written into history: "How can you defeat a man who would do such a thing?"

26

THE SULTAN did move on. But only far enough from the Forest to dig another trench and build more walls, where he again stagnated for days. Behind the trench and walls and all of his army, he stood in the middle of the night in the middle of the innermost room of his tent, pacing to the flicker of a single small lamp. He wrung his hands. He had not touched strong drink, but still he felt a lightness in his head. He bent over Radu and wanted to scream: *How can you just sleep!?* He wanted to scream to the whole camp: *How can any of you sleep!?*

A slight rush of air behind him made him jump and almost fall. As he whirled toward it, a curse caught in his throat. There was a shadow. A man. And somehow Mohammed knew: *Osman!* Leg Breaker. Founder of their tribe.

Mohammed blurted, "I must be dreaming."

Osman spoke in a voice that was deep—and gravelly, when he wanted it to be for effect. "Of course you are dreaming. I am long-dead to this world."

He was not the towering figure that Mohammed had thought him. If he showed a wiry strength, his height was just average. And he was bandy-legged—no doubt from a life in the saddle. His skin was a swarthy caramel. His eyes were dark but reflected even the dim light of the lamp like a sparkle. His dark hair ran into sideburns that themselves ran into a thick moustache. He wore not silk but plain cloth. But impeccable. Pure white. He wore it as a tribesman would wear his best suit: grateful to have the luxury.

He looked up at Mohammed's height and grunted. In contempt.

Mohammed ignored it, as there was something that he would ask of the great Osman: "Leg Breaker, have you come to give me guidance?"

"Guidance? I am not aware that you prayed for any. Then again, you don't pray for much of anything any more. Not the great *Fatih*."

Mohammed bucked up. "I am *Fatih*. I took Constantinople."

Osman spat, "*Gunpowder* took Constantinople. Gunpowder and janissaries. And even at that they took only a shell, an 'empire' already dead."

He looked at the sleeping Radu. "In the other world, his father is very proud of him."

Mohammed fished, "And what of *my* father?"

Osman ignored it. "And his father is proud of his other son: Dracula."

Mohammed fumed a sigh. "So you have come to mock me. Degrade me. I. Who *did* conquer Constantinople."

Osman retorted, "I fought the Greeks when they still had an empire."

Mohammed countered, "I fought Janos Hunyadi."

"Aye," Osman said. "And he beat you. At Belgrade. With a crazy priest and a handful of peasants."

"I fought—and defeated—treacherous rebels."

"And your great-grandfather, Bayazid, fought Tamerlane."

"And lost," Mohammed said. "He died in a cage."

"Yes," Osman answered. "As your laments so often remind me. You would think that *you* died in that cage. But your great-grandfather did fight Tamerlane. You, your bowels would give way if you even saw Tamerlane."

"I face *Dracula*. You don't know him. He is a madman."

Osman gave a low, long—and gravelly—laugh. "Yes. You face Dracula. And crumble. You are only *Fatih* when the numbers are great in your favor and the enemy is weak of will. Then you strut on a high horse. You play at war as you play at your game of chess. You cling to your lover, this Radu, so afraid to lose him in a fight that must be. To his credit, *he* understands. He yearns to ride and fight—even against his own brother. Against Dracula. But you, you cringe and cling."

Cling. Mohammed hung his head. "My love for him—a man—is against the Word, the Law. Does it shame me in heaven?"

Osman sneered. "Do you think love is your problem? When your 'chess squares' run with real blood—and, heaven forbid, your own blood—you lose heart. When you see men impaled—as you yourself impaled men—your tongue turns to dust. Your father told you long ago: Do not let yourself grow soft. But you curled your lip at your father. And his words."

"My father once set himself above the Law."

"And you do not?"

Mohammed kept his head low. "Leg Breaker—great one—give me guidance. Please."

Osman spoke, "A man—especially one who would call himself *Sultan*, 'Authority'—must look into his own heart for guidance."

Mohammed confessed, "There is too much clutter around my heart."

"Yes," Osman agreed. "Clutter: gold...silk...lovers...You are afraid to lose any of it. And unless a sultan is willing to lose *all* of it he is not really a sultan. So now you see only one of the ways that success can ruin you. No wonder this Dracula has gotten into your head."

Mohammed confessed again, this time to a fear. "He almost killed me in that night attack. I would have died in this wretched land. Great Osman, give me guidance."

"Guidance. Hear then: A man—especially a sultan—must be able to live by the Law he claims to profess...oh, you, who think yourself higher than the Law."

"I hear," Mohammed acknowledged. "Still...I need guidance further. About this war...this Dracula." He knelt and set his brow to the ground. "I pray for it."

Osman grunted. Approvingly. He spoke a parable. "You are a man in a duel. Both you and your opponent have drawn blood. Yours runs under your armor. You can feel it. Do you yield?"

Mohammed held his humble position but answered boldly: "No."

"But he's drawn blood."

"But he, too, is wounded. How badly? Do I know? Can you tell me? Why should I yield when I might be winning?"

"So," Osman said, "you at least still *think* like a Turk." He shot a question: "How many men marched with you to this war?"

"Ninety thousand."

"*Ninety* thousand. You lost only six thousand in your first battles. You took about the same from Kaziglu. But he started with only thirty thousand. How many dead were counted from last night?"

Mohammed blushed in shame. "Ten thousand of ours. Five thousand of his." He complained, "But many of ours are also wounded."

Hearing Leg Breaker sigh in disgust, he quickly added, "But many of his, too, must be wounded. Yes. I lost sixteen thousand. But I had ninety. He lost eleven thousand. But he had only thirty. And I have artillery. How many guns can he have left? Or powder or shot? He didn't steal all that much from Giurgiu. And I have the janissaries and sipahis. And Radu. Radu! I can—"

Hands took his hands and he looked up, expecting to see Osman finally reaching to accept him, to give his approval.

But it was Radu. "What? You called my name." He noted Mohammed's pose. "Are you praying...sleeping? What?"

The Conqueror gripped the hands and stood. Yes. He had been dreaming. But he remembered what a wise man once told him about his dreams: They were his own thoughts. Thoughts. Schemes. So his mind was working again. Thinking. Scheming. About the war. About Dracula. How to beat him. So the dross—the fear—must be falling from his thoughts. Indeed he did feel lighter. Looser. And his lightened thoughts were running: *Outside there were so many good men. God-fearing men. Brave soldiers. All looking to him. All he need do was...be their sultan.*

But his thoughts were stemmed by a call from outside. A sharp whisper. A pasha. "Highness!"

Mohammed himself went to draw back the flap. He was surprised that the light of day flooded his eyes. Had he been so long in his dream with Leg Breaker?

The pasha hurried inside, away from the ears of the guards. "Pardon, highness. But soon the whole camp will know: *Plague!*"

Radu shot, "The Pestilence?"

"Heaven forbid," the pasha said. "But bad enough."

Not the Great Pestilence, the Black Plague, which could have taken the whole camp...the whole country. But bad enough: Cholera.

The pasha declared, "I swear, it must have come from the foul vapors of that *place*. The dead."

Mohammed felt heavy again. Stiff. Tight. But he caught himself. He could not give way to fear again. He *would* not. He refused. He *was* Fatih!

And with that declaration came a glimmer. Plague. If it was a curse it was also a sign. Guidance. Yes. It opened his eyes further and put words on his tongue.

He sent the pasha off and told Radu, "I cannot stay here. I am sultan! I cannot stay where there is plague. I must put my common sense above pride. And I must put it above pride in another way as well. *I* am delaying the defeat of your brother. Your stiff-necked people fear me. Hate me. 'The Turk.' So *you* will lead the army from here on."

It took a moment, but Radu beamed at the realization and brightened even more as Mohammed continued. The sultan would depart that same day. But he would leave Radu with the strength of the army, including whole regiments of sipahis and janissaries.

He told Radu, "Win. For the 'Light.' For the empire."

"I will win," Radu pledged. "For the empire. And us."

The sultan echoed, "For the empire."

Radu began, "But I must have your permis—"

Mohammed cut to the quick: "Do whatever you must. With my blessing."

Radu repeated, "Then I will win. I know just what to do. It is just the right time to change tack against my brother."

They were embracing tightly for the long farewell when the pasha called again from outside. "Highness. Riders. Our messengers from Moldavia!"

Mohammed swore under his breath. *What now?* Had he only conjured Osman for more trouble? Well, he thought, whatever the news, whatever fortune it brought, good or ill, it was no longer his. It all belonged now to his Wallachian vassal.

27

NOVEMBER 1462. The war was over. What was left of Dracula's army was strung along the last league of the road that climbed to the Castle. Their horses were all-out: heads twisted to suck wind…coats lathered with sweat—white, frothy sweat that bubbled in swaths on the neck and in the crotch of the hind legs—the sweat of beasts in distress. Where the sweat met the air of the falling mountain dusk, steam rose from the riders, as though they had just emerged from Purgatory itself.

Dracula was at the head of the column a half-league from the castle. He knew where he was but did not know. Just as he saw and did not see the castle garrison riding out to meet him, to bring him a fresh mount to hurry him into the safety of the walls. He took the mount, but not to ride to safety. He also took a trooper's lance and wordlessly led the garrison back down the road…past the trailing troops all the way back to the rear-guard, who, struggling themselves, had still refused to abandon any stragglers.

Dracula's mind was absorbed just as it had been on every stride of this last ride from the war: Hungary...Matthias; Moldavia...*Stephen.*

Stephen. Dear cousin. Comrade-in-arms. Sworn ally.

And in the last days of the war he had joined the other side.

He had joined the Turks in attacking Chilia, the fortress that Dracula had strengthened as the secure "swinging door" protecting both his and Stephen's border. Stephen's "arrangement" with Radu and the sultan was simple: When they took the fortress, it would go to Stephen.

Why? Why had he done it? Common sense, he would say. Practicality: *Need makes strange allies.* And Stephen's plain fear of the Turk. How could Dracula have even thought to defeat *the Conqueror?* Chilia was going to fall anyway. To the Turks. Better, Stephen concluded, that he take the valuable "door" instead.

But to Dracula there was no excuse. How could there be from his *dear* cousin? If there was any justice in it, it was that Stephen had been carried from the siege of Chilia with a bad wound of the leg. And the fortress had not fallen.

And Hungary...Matthias. It was bad enough that he had refused to join Dracula, to even answer him. Worse, he, too, had turned in the final days of the war. Even while Dracula still fought, the king acknowledged Radu—the sultan's ally!—as the new voevode of Wallachia.

Dracula now knew the mistake he had made with Hungary. Oh, the king, too, would argue that it was all common sense. Pure politics. Dracula was losing. Why not appease Mohammed, acknowledge Radu? No, it certainly would not make Hungary and the empire allies. But it might at least delay the inevitable war between them, give Matthias more time to prepare.

That is what the king would say. But Dracula knew the real reason: Money. The Saxons. He had underestimated their hatred. And their power. Even over the king.

Dracula had hoped that a quick victory would force Matthias to join him. But the Saxons would have none of it. And the king could not afford to anger his richest merchants.

With the cost of the new warfare—gunpowder and cannon—what king could? Dracula understood fully now. Too late. The rules of politics had changed. A common merchant with gold was more valuable to a king than a prince with a sword.

Stephen's defection. The king's declaration. The war had wound down quickly, if bitterly. But it was Radu—and Dracula gave him his due—who sped it on its course. It was not so much his action with the sword—bold enough in itself; the brothers went for each other's throat. It was really what Radu had done with the pen: *Amnesty!* He offered it in his own name and the sultan's. Any Wallachian who would lay down his arms—save, of course, for Dracula and his commanders—would be forgiven. Even the draguli would be forgiven.

For Dracula's troops, it was the last chance for survival. They had fought the sultan and were still fighting Radu. And Stephen. But they had lost a third dead, a third wounded. They had no hope of succor, and each battle only pared them down. How could Dracula deny them this last chance? So he let them accept the amnesty. His draguli and some of Cirstian's men refused to leave him. Theirs was the only refusal he would accept.

So it was they whom Radu and his Turks now chased. Chased blindly. Heady with the scent of final victory. Even though they, too, were exhausted from the pursuit.

Now the pursuers found Dracula waiting around a bend in the road. Wilk and Cirstian had also taken lances and fresh mounts and joined him. The castle garrison was spread full and thick across the road. Radu's men rounded the bend and saw them and tried to pull rein. Dracula and his men leveled lances and set spur.

Radu's van was erased. Even the corpses were hacked to bits as Dracula led his men in dismounting and leaving a grim warning straight in Radu's path.

The empty mounts of Radu's men careened back down the road to the rest of their army. A cannon boomed from Castle Dracula's walls. A single shot. But precise—from months of gauging the range of the road. It hit Radu's column where a bend of the road showed through the woods. No other message, no other shot, was needed. The pursuers pulled rein, halting the chase at least until nightfall. Dracula remounted and slowly led his troops back to the castle.

As he entered, there were two things for which he yearned. One of them waited with a matron at the gates: his son, Vlad. Dracula was barely out of the saddle when the boy was wrapped around him. Somehow the very sight made the troops stand taller. Tears trickled from the boy's eyes: "Mommy's sick."

The matron whispered, "The melancholia, lord. But a bit worse than before."

Dracula swept his son up and hurried into the fortress, to the tower, to Prasha's rooms. To his quiet rap on the door, she bade him enter in a voice that seemed calm and strong enough. Inside he found her kneeling to the opened windows. And she looked as she did when he first met her: shimmering dark hair; smooth, porcelain skin; full, red lips. All of it was set off strikingly by her white dressing gown. She smiled to see her husband: "You are alive."

He helped her rise and locked her in the embrace with their son. The full of his yearning was sated now. His lips tasted her eyes, her cheeks, and mouth. Her own kisses smothered him and Vlad. The boy giggled and spread his arms to hold the family together. When he was planted on the floor again he asked, "Mother, will you get well now?"

Dracula answered for her: "Yes. Mother will be well. She is already on the way." He lifted his son again. "I've been away so long. Can I have mother to myself?"

Graciously the princeling agreed. But as he was carried to the door he turned to his mother again with a simple request: "Kiss."

She gave it, and he was going to the door again when he asked his father, "Is mommy crying because she's sick or because the Turks chased you here?"

"Neither," Dracula assured him. "It's because mommy is well and is happy to see us."

"She's crying because she's happy?"

"Aye. Mothers do that sometimes."

The boy made a sour face and they both laughed. But his mirth quickly gave way. "Papa, will the Turks get us?"

"No," Dracula said. He gave his son a squeeze and sent him along.

Alone with Prasha he said, "Thank God, love. I expected to find you…They said…"

"I am *not* well," she said.

He saw it in her eyes. If her hair and complexion had been tended, no cosmetic could disguise the sadness and the hollows. He insisted, "You will be well now."

"I wish it were so, love. But there are too many…things."

"What things?"

"The voices. From the river." The boyar families slain so long ago. "They've come back. Always back. Almost always. And their shadows. They follow me along the walls even in broad daylight. They kept whispering that you would be killed."

"So you see," Dracula said. "They cannot be real. I am not dead."

She seemed not to hear. "The bishop even sent Father Gregor to exorcise the place. But the voices stay. And the shadows. They said you would not find rest. Even in death. They said you would walk…"

She could not finish. She wept. Between sobs she confessed, "It is my fault, love. I wanted them to leave me in peace. I told them that I was innocent. That it was you…Their death…And the beggars and cripples…I blamed you."

Gently he shook her. "They are not real."

Her eyes tried to reach into his, as though to seize the reassurance. She even affirmed, "I know they are not real. They cannot be." But she wept.

He lit a candle against the fading dusk and laid her on the bed and just held her. He filled his mind with her, not in the words of thoughts, but in the feel of her and the image before him—a soft figure in white, breath silently rising and falling. He wondered if he could save her—how he *would* save her. The melancholia was like a ghost. There but not there…nothing to take hold of…haunting. If only it *would* take form, he thought. Even as a demon who defied exorcism. Then—*By God!*—with his bare hands he would…

Like a whip, something cracked on the wall and skittered across the floor. Dracula bolted from the bed, sweeping Prasha with him, and they saw it: an arrow. Its point had been blunted. Its shaft was wrapped with a scroll.

Dracula made to shutter the windows but Prasha stopped him. "No, love. No."

With windows closed, she would feel the closeness of the room. Like a tomb.

He backed her from the windows and spread the scroll:

My lord they bring the cannons up tonight
No slow siege All-out attack Tomorrow No quarter
Fly if you can G

"G." Giorgi.

The folklore of the land would capture the rebel janissary's last exploit of the war: how he had gauged the light in the tower as the best place to send his warning—*All-out attack*. Radu would fall on the castle with his artillery and Turks—to kill his brother outright. No quarter!

Even as Dracula was thanking God again for Giorgi, Prasha lamented, "The voices said this. I will die here. Or worse."

Worse. Die like the other women in her family.

Dracula was adamant: "No!"

Even as she babbled her doubts and fears he explained his plan. They would run. All run. The castle was built for just such a contingency. A secret passage. By the next dawn…

But she was convinced. "No, love. With me you would never escape. Not you. Not our son. The voices will not be cheated."

It was pointless to argue. Instead he went to the door and called for the guards to rouse Wilk.

When he turned back, she was at the window again. The side overlooking the river, the Arges. She was facing him, so that the night framed her. Beautifully. White skin. White gown. Dark hair. Moist ruby lips.

She was smiling. "I know how to save you. Save you both."

She blew him a kiss and stepped into the night.

Into the night. From the window. To the Arges hundreds of feet below.

All in a second. One motion. No time even for Dracula to shout.

Though he was frozen, his heart raced. Tears welled and poured from his eyes. Tears without sound. His arm rose. His hand opened to the night.

He heard the knock and Wilk call. He felt no time pass, but Wilk was suddenly with him. What was Wilk asking and what was he answering? Dracula felt his friend squeeze his arm and hurry to the window.

But what was left to see?

Wilk shuttered the windows. He, too, had tears in his eyes as he took Dracula's arms. "Think of the boy. If you can, think of the boy."

Dracula felt the scroll still in his hand. Wordlessly he gave it to Wilk, who read and asked, "Do you want us to fight?"

Dracula shook his head. "The well."

Wilk understood. But as he went to pass the order he would not leave his friend alone. Soon they were both under the moon in the courtyard with the troops and the castle household gathering silently around them. A groggy Vlad was brought to Dracula wrapped in a blanket. Wilk himself put the boy into his friend's arms. The very touch seemed to restore Dracula's voice. He began giving quiet orders.

Castle Dracula had many secret passages, but one was crafted specially: the well. Above the water line, when the bricks were pulled away, a passage opened to steps that descended all the way down to the banks of the Arges.

Soldiers were sent down first, then the servants, then more soldiers. As they went, the last troops in the castle stripped the rooms and piled everything of value in the courtyard. What Dracula would not take would be burned.

He was sending everyone else ahead, but Wilk and Cirstian refused to leave him, and some troops refused to leave at all. They preferred to mask his escape by staying to hold the enemy at bay. It was the one-armed Kyril among them who pleaded their case: "Lord, if the bastards find the walls bare, they'll only run you down."

Dracula took Kyril's hand. "Then do as you will. But only for one day. A single day, Kyril. Do you understand? A day. Then you run."

As Dracula finally descended into the well he turned back. Not for a last look, but to tell Kyril, "Don't let them get my guns."

"They'll get nothing, lord."

But Dracula said, "They can have the horses. The beasts served well. Let them live."

Then he blotted the castle from his mind.

At the banks of the river he lingered over the water. A body in the rushing flow would wash away like a twig. He began to tremble but felt the bundle in his arms. He still had his son.

From nearby villages, his troops brought horses. It was said that Dracula tied his son to the saddle for the trek into Transylvania's Carpathians. It was near dawn when he led his party into a clearing and called his two commanders aside.

"We part here. No arguments."

He and a few draguli would go to the only place he could: Hungary. There, at least, Radu could not yet follow. Perhaps, Dracula thought, the king would at least give him refuge. Or—if the Saxons protested even that—he could gather himself and move on.

"When I am safe," he said, "I will call you."

He made final dispositions. The Dragon had more than one lair. To all appearances, the last of his army would simply melt away.

He told Wilk, "You will take my son."

Cirstian offered, "If I can, I will find our lady's body."

They all embraced and Dracula went to his son. The boy was standing but barely awake. He asked, "Mamma?"

Dracula knelt and simply asked his own question: "Who are you?"

The answer had long-since been planted over and again in young Vlad's mind: "I am Vlad, son of Dracula, who is prince and son of a prince."

"Yes," Dracula said. His arms enfolded his son. "And I love you."

The son knew: "You are leaving again."

"I am going to the king. You will go with Wilk. I will call for you."

"Is mommy going with you?"

As Dracula's eyes dropped, the boy's instinct triggered again: "Is mommy...is she an angel now, papa?"

"Yes," Dracula said. "Think of her that way."

Vlad gave a nod then asked, "I would rather stay with you, father."

"Of course you would," Dracula said. But he saw an image of himself, long ago, taken by the Turkish sultan as a hostage, a pawn. And, strangely, he saw Radu.

As he hefted his son into the saddle behind Wilk, he asked, "Can a prince spare a kiss for a prince?"

The boy leaned to him. They kissed. And hugged.

As Wilk started off, Vlad turned back. "Father, you won't become an angel, too, will you?"

To himself, Dracula laughed bitterly. "No. I will not become an angel."

His own first steps in the parting were marked by the faint echo of cannon. Radu's men at the castle.

Above him, the Transylvanian peaks rose greater than three thousand feet, slick with ice and snow. Generations later, the local peasants would still boast that it was their ancestors who helped the Dragon make the climb.

Prasha's body was never found. And—also through generations—the peasants would still call that stretch of the Arges *Riul Doamnei*: "The Princess's River."

PRISONER

1

DECEMBER 1462. **THE HUNGARIAN BORDER.** Of the thousand men facing him across the snow-crusted field, Dracula could see that only a few were the king's regular troops. Only a token contingent. The rest were mercenaries—and special ones at that.

The dragul closest to him advised, "Maybe you should just turn back, lord. We'll buy you enough time."

"No," Dracula said. "It seems that the king wants me. Indeed. But not dead."

"Pardon, lord, but how can you be sure?"

"I have my reasons," Dracula said. "And the most telling right now is this...Do you see the crest on those mercenaries? It belongs to Jan Jiskraz. And I'd say that's him at the fore with one of the king's own captains. So if the king wanted me dead we'd be fighting for our lives even now."

As the dragul only spat, Dracula smiled. Spat, his man had. At the thought of fighting Jiskraz himself. Not bad for a "dragon" who only months before had been a mere peasant. Not bad at all.

But Dracula waved for his men to wait as he rode ahead. He would brook no objection. He was probably right that King Matthias wanted him alive. But the same charm might not extend to his mere handful of draguli. Not with Jan Jiskraz. Not on some nameless winter field.

Yet Jiskraz met him with a hint of a gleam in his cold blue eyes. Like the look of one predator to another. He even gave a slight nod.

The man with him was indeed a captain of the king. But a captain without pedigree, no coat-of-arms. He was of early middle age. Tall. Somewhat burly. Powerfully muscled once. But the muscles had gone a tad soft. They were now what a peasant might mock as mere "beer muscles." The captain's brown hair hung long under the helmet. He wore a beard, through which now showed, clearly, a sneer.

It was as though, Dracula thought, the king were here but not here. Represented but not represented by this nondescript officer who had probably climbed the ranks from the status of mere commoner. So this captain was no more than the king's "eye," a witness to ensure that Jiskraz did the king's bidding. But what was that bidding? Over the past weeks, Dracula had sent riders ahead asking the king for asylum. The king had directed him to this field.

It was Jiskraz who spoke first, quietly: "Is this all to your party, Vlad Dracula?"

Dracula merely replied with his own question: "Are you here to take me to the king?"

The captain laughed. "Take you to him? You are under arrest. You and everyone with you: the boyars—Cirstian and Gales...the Pole, Wilkowski...and your family. All. Under arrest." He flicked a finger across the field. "Even those *vermin*."

Jiskraz ignored the man. He ameliorated, "Those are the king's orders, Vlad Dracula. But perhaps we should discuss them in more privacy. And comfort."

"What discussion?" the captain barked. "They are orders!"

This, too, Jiskraz ignored as he led the way to a tent. Inside, he had a servant bring the three of them cups of hot, spiced wine.

He offered a seat, but Dracula declined, proceeding to the question, "What charge is laid against me?"

Jiskraz merely gave him a packet. "They are letters. Copies actually. Of letters given the king by the Saxons."

Dracula scanned one, then another, then laughed. "Are they all the same?"

Jiskraz answered, "More or less."

They would be passed on to history as the "Rothel Letters." Supposedly written by Dracula after his war against Mohammed. Letters allegedly written to Mohammed. In which Dracula begged His Highness's forgiveness and begged further for a chance to renew his Turkish alliance—by the incredible offer of helping to deliver King Matthias himself into the sultan's hands.

Dracula's own conclusion on seeing them would also be adopted by history: "No one will believe this."

Even Jiskraz smiled some. "Well, they are the evidence against you. Will you come with us? There's really nothing to fear. At least as long as you are in my charge. Beyond that..." He shrugged.

"Beyond that," the captain blustered, "you deal with the king."

Dracula answered Jiskraz, "If I feared the king I wouldn't have come this far."

Jiskraz mused, "You seem rather sure of yourself."

"I am," Dracula said. "For three reasons. First, the king—like the 'Conqueror'—wants Wallachia. I am his best available candidate."

"He can find others," Jiskraz cautioned.

Dracula repeated, "I am his *best* available candidate. I don't take the king to be a fool."

As the captain bristled at even hearing such a judgment, Jiskraz affirmed to Dracula, "He is no fool."

"Second," Dracula said, "the Turk fears me: 'Kaziglu.' Certainly this no-fool king can use that to his advantage."

Jiskraz acknowledged, "The Turk fears you. The king can use that."

"Well, then," Dracula said, "why should I fear the king? If he is truly as astute as we think, I gave you two good reasons why he should keep me alive."

The captain challenged, "You said you had three reasons."

Dracula finally spoke to him. "Well, the third, you see, is a bit unpleasant. It has to do with the pope."

"The pope?" the captain sneered. "What does an Orthodox heretic like you know of His Holiness?"

"I know," Dracula said, "that His Holiness gave your liege money. Money to join a 'crusade.' *My* crusade. Against 'Fatih.' Your sire took the money. But he did not join, aye?"

The captain snarled and actually raised a fist. How could this "Impaler" so insult the king!?

But he suddenly stopped short. What stayed his hand? What kept him from striking Dracula? Was it the shocked gasp of Jan Jiskraz? Or the Dragon's green eyes? Such hatred in them. Like a roar in itself.

For the rest of his days, the captain would wonder which it actually was that had stopped his fist.

He heard Jiskraz fume, "The king gave orders. But he did not want this!" The captain did not argue as Jiskraz "suggested" that he leave. When he was gone, Jiskraz offered, "He is a bit zealous."

"Yes," Dracula said. "Zealous. He's come far, no doubt. I suppose he would go further still." He asked, "And you, Jan Jiskraz, would you go further still? Why have *you* come to arrest me?"

"I tell you frankly," Jiskraz said. "It is what the king wished. I follow his orders, no more." He moved on, "And where are Cirstian and Gales? And your man, Wilk?"

Dracula added, "And my son...and wife?"

"I do not ask about your son and wife. But the others..."

Dracula began, "My wife..." He shook his head.

"I am sorry," Jiskraz said. And he waited a respectful moment. "But I must ask...as the king bids me...the boyars and Wilk?"

"You would take them?"

"If I could. As the king bids."

"To the block?" Dracula asked.

Jiskraz gave a slow nod. "The king wants *you* alive. Not them."

"Then go find Gales," Dracula said. "He is still about. Somewhere. Hiding. He deserted me in battle. The rest..." He shrugged. He repeated, "Why are *you* here to arrest me? Why do you suppose the king wanted that?"

"Yes," Jiskraz answered. "Why did the king want you and me to meet as enemies? It's no mystery there, aye? The king is a smart young man."

Matthias would have Jiskraz arrest Dracula, take the brunt of Dracula's resentment.

Jiskraz continued, "But I am a smart *old* man. I intend to fade away quietly— on the estates I worked so hard to earn. So I want no trouble with you, Vlad Dracula. As far as I am concerned, you can leave here now if you wish."

"And go where?"

"Aye," Jiskraz said. "And go where? Whatever future you have is with the king. I thought you would see that." Yet he offered, "Your draguli can go. I will even help them on their way. I tell you again, Vlad Dracula, unabashedly: I want no trouble with you."

"You have none," Dracula said. "Just let me bid farewell—and some of this hot wine—to my men."

"Done," Jiskraz said. But as Dracula made to leave Jiskraz added, "You almost beat him. Alone. You, Vlad Dracula. You almost beat the Conqueror."

"Yes," Dracula said. "Almost. This time. Perhaps our young, 'smart' king should have joined me."

He was gone, and the old mercenary was still chuckling, when the captain returned. Jiskraz gave him a piece of advice: "You are trying to build your reputation on the wrong man."

2

FEBRUARY 1463. HUNGARY. The room was like an eye at the brim of the world. It topped a tower on a fortress on a hill overlooking the Danube just outside the capital city of Buda. It was a stone room—ceiling, floor, walls. It had only the barest furniture: cot, table, chair…The thick door was bolted from the outside. The single window above the river was barred, though it did have the amenity of a clear pane of glass.

Dracula sat at the table staring through the window. Under a gray sky, the river was crusted with ice. Hills, fields, and forests were all draped in snow. Far away on the opposite bank, a horse-drawn sleigh looked like a speck on a canvas. A canvas. The river would move artists to verse and great melodies. It moved common folk to sentimental reflection. It moved Dracula to none of these things. He was barely aware of the cup in his hand.

The bolt snapped on the door and he frowned: *The captain? Again?* The man had become like a shadow, his own personal haunt. But as Dracula caught two figures, not one, from the corner of his eye, he turned. With the captain was a priest. Papist—as Hungary was papist. He wore a black cassock and a crimson cap that barely covered his trim, white hair. He was thin and of average height, but a slight stoop made him seem shorter. Still, his complexion was clear and ruddy, and his blue-gray eyes were bright and alert.

The captain, as usual, barked in speaking to Dracula. "Stand!"

The priest quickly countered, "Sit, sit, sit."

The captain blustered, "You should give father your chair."

The priest told the captain, "Just get me another. Please."

"But father…how can I leave you alone with the likes of him?"

"Just bring the chair," the priest said. When the captain left, he complained to Dracula, "I will never understand a soldier's temperament."

Dracula scoffed, "Him, father? A soldier?"

The captain heard it. As he brought the priest's chair, he mimicked Dracula, "Him, father? A voevode? He's a common sot now."

The priest chided, "This bickering does neither of you honor." He had the captain leave and asked Dracula, "What is it between you?"

"It is not my doing," Dracula answered. "He is a small man looking to grow larger—at my expense. But enough of him, father. What of you?"

"I am here at the king's bidding, Vlad Dracula. But, in truth, I am not sure where this bidding leads. In his own words, he wants me to 'cultivate' you. For what…?" He shrugged. "But I am not a spy. I will not play you false or betray your confidence. I made that clear."

Dracula raised an eyebrow. "Made it clear to the *king*?"

The priest gave a nod.

"Rather a bold thing for a mere priest to tell a king."

The priest smiled. "My standing is special, I suppose. My own father, you see, was a cardinal of the Church."

Dracula began, "But a cardinal…"

"Yes," the priest acknowledged. "A cardinal is certainly a cleric. And clerics are certainly sworn to celibacy. But my father never denied me, his 'bastard.' Quite the contrary. His influence once gave me a place as soldiers' chaplain. I dare say it still keeps me at court."

The priest gave his name: Father Elemar. He continued, "And you, Vlad Dracula. Everyone now knows something of you." He knew the open chapters of Dracula's life: Fugitive, Prince…husband and father…and now the king's Prisoner. "In truth, Vlad Dracula, I am thrilled that the king chose me for this. If I may say, I would very much like to know you for my own curiosity. You seem a rare man. At once both famous and infamous."

"And which do you consider me, father?"

"I do not know. But I hope to. That is…if I do not offend you."

"Ask what you will, father. Ask freely. Perhaps there are things I will ask of you."

The priest grinned and nodded. A fair bargain. "I will answer if I can."

Dracula filled his cup and offered it. As Father Elemar declined, he drained it himself and refilled it. "Begin where you will, father."

The priest nearly tittered—the scholar hurtling into his research. "You are a remarkable man, Vlad Dracula. Whatever else you prove to be, you are certainly Christendom's crusader." He whispered as though in confidence, "Which our Holy Father will not forget. Nor let the king forget."

"No matter what the Saxons say?"

Father Elemar affirmed, "No matter what the Saxons say. The Church has an interest in you. More than perhaps you thought. More than you told Jan Jiskraz when you surrendered. Bear that in mind. Let it sustain you. You were right in what you said then. The king took Church money to join your crusade. He reneged. But your case is more than a matter of money. The pope will not let you, our sole crusader, be delivered to your enemies."

He continued, again as though in confidence, "But the king has no intention of delivering you to anyone. You were right about that, too. You are too valuable a soldier." He reflected, "I dare say that's it. That's why he sent me. To learn more about you. To figure how best to use you."

Dracula echoed, "'Use' me." Again he drained his cup. Again he refilled it. "This is how he uses me, father: cup, window, cell…In fact, just before you came,

I was wondering if it is real. Any of it. Including the past. To come to a state like this. It is like a dream. A bad dream."

"And so it might seem, Lord Prince. So it must often seem to men like you. You gave so much and yet…"

Dracula noted, "'Lord Prince.' And not spoken in jest. And, yes, father, I did give much. I gave all. And yet…" He spread his hands. "This is now my reality." He pushed past it. "But what news from the outside?"

The priest frowned. "There has been a second blow to Christendom. The Albanian, Skanderbeg, is beset by plots. Not from the Turk. But from fellow Christians. They would take his land even before he wrests it back from the Turk."

"Such things can't surprise you."

"No. Sadly they do not. Not in our world."

"I feel for Skanderbeg," Dracula said. "I often wondered…I thought it inevitable that we join forces. Else why were we placed in the same time and place? Against the same foe?"

Father Elemar agreed, "Yes. Like destiny."

"But history is the Master Story Teller, aye, father? It spun its own tale. It kept us apart. At least so far."

The two seemed lost in the thought for a moment—Skanderbeg and Dracula united in the same cause—before Dracula posed, "But, father, you said a *second* blow to Christendom. What was the first?"

"Why, your own defeat, of course. I said—all the west says it: You were our sole crusader."

"Aye," Dracula said. "I was." But his eyes looked past it, to the window. "My wife was a suicide. She died in the Arges. Staring from this window—though I know it is impossible—I saw her body in the river below. More than once."

Father Elemar held an appropriate silence before proceeding. "You fought for the Cross. For the faith. Do you still have your faith?"

"You mean, do I still believe in God? Let me just say that I am tired of playing the biblical Job. If there is a God, He has doomed me to suffering. And I don't much care for it. But you—a priest—must condemn me for saying such a thing."

"Condemn? To do so would only be glib. I have not suffered what you suffered. And I do not presume—as Job's friends presumed—to know the will of God."

Dracula laughed. "Now it is I who find *you* remarkable, father. A priest who admits ignorance of God's ways. While so many lesser men—like the captain— do presume to know them."

Father Elemar was amused. "He claims to know God's will?"

"In my case he does. He claims that God is punishing me. In fact, I think the captain believes that he is helping in the effort."

"Helping?"

"In his own 'subtle' ways. He often spits in my food. Once he even mixed urine with my wine."

Father Elemar went red. "Does the king know this?"

"I am not privy to what the king knows. Or intends. Perhaps the captain acts on the king's orders."

The priest shook his head. "I doubt it. And I think I can help with this. But…I would move to other things, Vlad Dracula. That is, if I do not offend…"

"Ask what you will, father."

"They say that you killed forty—fifty thousand. Of your *own* people."

"I didn't count," Dracula said. "I didn't have quotas, father. But I'd say the figure is good…forty, fifty thousand. Not counting those I killed in war."

"That's a *tenth* of your native race."

"Aye, father. Wallachia was quite rotten. It needed a good 'pruning'…thieves, murderers, and the like."

"And then there were whole Saxon towns. Women and children."

"They were my sworn enemies and the families of my enemies. You know how we civilized people make war, father. If I let the children live they would have feuded with my descendants. Down through the generations. The land would never know peace."

"But your methods…the stake."

"That was a message to the Turk. He taught me impalement. Terror. I wanted to let him know that I could—I would—be just as terrible."

"But your beggars and cripples. You…you…"

"I exterminated them, father. Wallachia could no longer afford such a burden. Not with the Turkish war cloud hanging over our heads."

"*You* made such a decision?"

"Who else would? I was voevode."

"But such a harsh judgment."

"Harsh, father? Let me ask. Which is more important, body or soul?"

"The soul, of course."

"Yes. And what is a cardinal sin? Is it venial or mortal?"

Venial sin: as the Church propounded, a minor stain on the soul. But mortal sin condemned the soul to hell.

The priest replied, "A cardinal sin is a mortal sin."

"Aye," Dracula said. "And sloth—chronic sloth—like that of the beggars—is a cardinal sin. Cardinal. Mortal. As the Church preaches. So the Church condemned the beggars' souls. I only condemned the bodies."

"But the Church gives man a chance to repent."

"So did I, father. So did I. In everything I did."

Father Elemar was a bit flustered. "Even if such logic held, the Church does not condemn cripples for merely being crippled."

"Nor do I, father. But I was the shepherd. The single shepherd. All of Wallachia was the flock. I had to shed the burden of carrying the few so I could save the rest."

The priest gave a pronounced frown. "Where, Vlad Dracula, did you get such *desperate* ideas."

Dracula in turn frowned. "You wouldn't believe me if I told you."

"Tell me. Please."

"As you will, father. My 'desperate' ideas came from prayer."

Father Elemar actually flinched. "Prayer?"

"Yes," Dracula declared. "Long ago, I had given up on prayer...on faith...on God. It was my cousin—my *dear* cousin, Stephen—who guided me back: 'Pray. Pray, and see the rhyme and reason of your life.' So I did. The rest you know."

Father Elemar argued, "Did you really believe that such things flowed from prayer? The Saxons? The beggars? Impalement?"

"Why not?" Dracula said. "Surely you know your Bible, father. Midian: the entire city destroyed at God's command, except 'the girls who have not known man intimately.' Or Jericho: 'And they utterly destroyed everything in the city, both man and woman, young and old, ox and sheep and donkey...' I never killed ox and sheep and donkeys, father. But need we go so far back? Basil, father. The Byzantine Emperor. Just a few hundred years ago. Basil the 'Bulgar Slayer.'"

The priest knew the infamous tale. Basil the Bulgar Slayer. His empire was plagued by the Bulgar tribes. In 1014 A.D., after capturing 15,000 of them, he blinded nine out of ten and left the tenth man in each rank with only one eye. So they could lead their brethren back to their king, Samuel, who, it was said, died on the spot at the sight—or, so to speak, the lack thereof.

Dracula reminded Father Elemar, "They say that Basil was one of the first warrior-monks. He spent half the time in the saddle and half on his knees. Praying. So where did he get his ideas, father?"

For a long while the priest was stumped in thought. He finally asked, "Vlad Dracula, what did you pray *for*?"

"I prayed as a voevode prays: 'Teach me to smite my enemies.'"

Father Elemar gave a slow nod. "Yes. As the ancient Hebrews prayed: 'Teach me to smite…' As Basil prayed: 'Teach me to smite…' As devout people pray all over the world. As I prayed: 'Teach me to spread the Word. The Word. What *I* believe. *My* religion. And so we have our crusades, our jihads. Holy War. Can you believe it? *Holy* War?"

"So you are saying, father, that my prayers were 'skewed.' All of my prayers were skewed. I prayed for the wrong thing. So my actions were also skewed."

"Something like that."

"Then perhaps, father," Dracula said, "we are only here for the amusement of the angels."

"No," Father Elemar answered. "We are not here for any such amusement. I once spoke to a man a hundred years old. He marvelled that even then he was still learning something new every day. That, I believe, Vlad Dracula, is what we are here for. To learn. To grow. To the very end of this life. Into the next."

He followed, "You said before that you wondered if any of this was real. Yes, it is real. Painfully real. Real death. Real suffering. Real Black Nights of The Soul. Otherwise, there would be no learning. No growth. No real growth."

They sat in silence as though both weighing the words. Finally the priest chuckled. "I am pontificating." He rose. "I must go."

Dracula offered, "You are more than welcome to stay, father."

"I wish I could," Father Elemar said. "I have other duties. But I will return."

He was approaching the door when Dracula asked, "Father…My wife. Her death. Do you believe…?"

Father Elemar read his eyes. "Her suicide? Do I think she is in hell because of it? No, Vlad Dracula. I do not believe in hell. I said, I believe in growth. Only growth."

As he rapped on the door to call the captain he turned back. "Vlad Dracula, try not to drink so much." When the captain appeared, he told him, "Henceforth, one of our priests will serve the Prince's meals."

3

1466. IT PLEASED FATHER ELEMAR that Dracula had been moved to new quarters shortly after their first meeting. He liked to think that his own recommendation had something to do with it. Perhaps the king accepted at least part of his counsel.

The new quarters were in another tower, but a more elaborate tower in a more elaborate fortress—the king's own summer palace. All of its rooms—including

Dracula's—were finely appointed. The palace was the king's showcase for what he wanted the world to see as his enlightened, Renaissance spirit. He would dazzle his guests with art, music, the very architecture of the place...and certain exhibits.

Father Elemar was somewhat less happy about the captain. He had recommended that he be replaced, but to no avail. Could it be that the king wanted just such a man in the position? Someone to remind Dracula that he was not quite sacrosanct? In any event, the captain seemed to have been reined in some. His surliness with Dracula had been reduced to a mute look. And, when Father Elemar was present, he had the sense to at least act polite.

But on this particular day the priest could manage to ignore even the captain. And as he sat with Dracula he accepted a cup of wine. A single, cordial cup; there was no keeping up with Dracula when it came to wine.

The green eyes easily discerned, "You have good news, father."

Father Elemar responded with a question: "Are you content here, Vlad Dracula?"

The answer was laced with sarcasm. "Content? What's not to be content, father? I don't lack for diversion. I have so many visitors."

Visitors. Of all the king's "exhibits," Dracula was surely the most popular.

He grumbled, "I don't know what they expect to see. Half think I'm a devil. I swear they look for a tail and cloven hooves. And the things they ask me...Do I impale birds and mice in my little jail here?"

"Ah," the priest consoled. "Those tales come from the Saxons. They won't let your reputation rest."

"Yet to others," Dracula said, "I am an angel. The Terrible Sword of God's vengeance on the heathen."

"It must make you wonder sometimes. Who are you really?"

"No," Dracula said. "I am well past that. I know who I am: Dracula, Voevode."

"So you still pray like a voevode?"

"Pray, father? I *think* like a voevode. I always will. Because that is what I am. If I was wrong in what I did—any of it—then let my sin stand to Wallachia's good. Let it keep criminals and invaders and scheming boyars at bay. As it will—if Fate grants that I ever sit my throne again."

Father Elemar seemed to speak past it. "Vlad Dracula, the king's plans for you are finally starting to unfold. That is the good news that I bear. He is considering a marriage for you. *Considering.*"

"To whom?"

"Her name is Ilona. A distant cousin to the king. Only a few years shy of your own age. Never married."

Both the priest and prospective bridegroom saw the wisdom in it. A political marriage. An alliance. By blood. A clear statement to the Saxons—and the Turk and all the rest—that Matthias would use Dracula. But that he would also, as it were, keep him on a leash. A royal leash.

Father Elemar asked, "Would you consider it? Would you marry again?"

Dracula answered, "Not for love." But he admitted, "This marriage could suit me. The only door opened to me." He mused, "What does the girl look like?"

Father Elemar muttered to himself. "Yes. 'Girl.'" He gestured to the door. "Why not see for yourself?"

As Dracula grinned and nodded, the priest called to the captain, who escorted the lady into the room with a bark at Dracula: "Stand!"

Already rising, Dracula bristled, "Quiet, oaf. I know my manners."

Ilona was just about his height. Her dress was simple but touched with lace. Her bosom seemed to fill its ample folds—an effect accentuated by her perfectly erect posture. Her skin was fair, her lips full. Her eyes were hazel. Her honey-brown hair was gathered at the crown but let to fall back freely almost to her waist.

Her face was squarish. Was it beautiful? Just pretty? Only soft? It was enough to hold Dracula's smile. And she wore very little cosmetic.

Father Elemar introduced them, prefacing Dracula's name with "Prince."

It was then that Dracula drew her first frown. In trying to give a gracious bow, he teetered. The wine. Clearly.

She seemed to consider what to say. She chose: "You are right, captain. He seems decorated for winter: green eyes shot with red."

The captain guffawed—until the priest shot him a look: *Out!*

As he closed the door behind him, Ilona asked, "Are you always like this, Vlad Dracula?"

Father Elemar blushed.

Dracula groped to retort: "Well, my lady…Are you calling me a drunkard? Then I tell you in turn: You are fat." He took a long pull of his cup.

Father Elemar took a long pull of his own cup. He started to speak but Ilona stemmed his words by simply pacing slowly around Dracula. Once. Then twice. And, in the second pass, Dracula noticed that her dress indeed hugged her waist. A cinched waist. Slender. She caught Dracula staring. Had he glimpsed a smile?

She ended the encounter with a terse, "Thank you, father." She went straight for the door.

Dracula dropped back into his chair muttering: "Shrew…"

Father Elemar said curtly, "But hardly fat!"

Dracula frowned. He took another long pull of his wine and lamented, "The only door opened to me." He raised his cup and resolved, "I will take it. I will marry her."

Father Elemar gave a cough that checked the declaration.

"What?" Dracula asked.

"I said. The king was *considering* this marriage. It was offered on two conditions. The second seems moot now."

"What is the first?"

"The obvious," the priest answered. "In order to marry in Hungary—"

"I would have to be papist. Convert."

"Yes. I don't much like it myself. You should know that. A man should be let to believe what he believes."

"It makes no difference to me," Dracula said. "But it will make a difference to Wallachia—if I am ever again to be voevode."

Father Elemar advised, "I think you might. In time. Just now, the king has another candidate. One Laiota."

"Laiota?" Dracula mused. He knew of the man. Until then, Laiota had been only a petty player in Wallachia's politics. Dracula summed it, "Laiota blows with the wind. The king would be better with me as his candidate. Now. A loyal ally. But I would have to remain Orthodox—for my stiff-necked people."

"In truth, Vlad Dracula, I don't think the king cares what religion you profess—theologically. But practically…Hungary would frown on a member of the royal family marrying anyone but a Catholic. And then there's the matter of the Saxons. Conversion would give you the Church's stamp of approval. With that, even the Saxons would have to stand at bay."

Dracula said easily, "No matter. I will convert."

Convert. And bide time. The conversion need not be permanent—if things worked out.

He asked, "So what is the second condition?"

"Yes," Father Elemar reflected. "Well, that might be more difficult—now. You see, Ilona must also give *her* consent."

Dracula smirked. "To a political marriage? Since when does the bride have a say in such things?"

Father Elemar chuckled. "Since the bridegroom is Dracula."

The green eyes peered. "I am not sure I appreciate the jest."

"Pardon," Father Elemar said. "I meant no offense. Not really."

"Then none taken," Dracula said. "Not really. But why didn't you tell me the conditions before she came?"

The priest shook a finger at him. "Because I promised not to. The lady wanted to meet you as you are."

Dracula hung his head. "And she did. And now there will be no marriage. On the same day I saw the 'door'—finally—I also saw it close."

He went for the wine but the priest stayed his hand. "You don't know what you saw, Vlad Dracula. You don't know that 'girl.'"

"Why was she so rude? The first meeting?"

"Rude?" Father Elemar answered. "I believe she was just frank. I also believe she smiled."

"You saw it, too? Strange woman."

Father Elemar corrected, "Good woman." He counselled, "Which is why I asked you before if you still pray like a voevode. This, Vlad Dracula, could be a crossroads for you. One of those choices that we humans are let to make. A God-given choice." His voice softened. "So I would tell you as a friend. If Ilona accepts you, take the high road. Leave the past behind. All of it."

"All of it?"

"All of it. Start a new life with this new woman. This gift of God. And forgive. Forget. All of it. Right up to this moment. Even the petty things...like...like the captain and his boorishness."

But Dracula shook his head. "I can't do that, father. For two reasons. First, to renounce my past would be to renounce myself. It would surely leave me condemned to hell—if there is such a place. All the dead...those I killed...I did what I did with open eyes and open heart. With purpose. To free Wallachia. How can I renounce that now? Then all the dead would be in vain."

A thought struck the priest: "Your life has been something like the sacrifice of Cain. And, like Cain, your efforts seem to have been flung back in your face. But learn, Vlad Dracula. Heed the lesson of Cain and Abel."

He quoted from the Biblical story: 'If you do well, will not your countenance be lifted up? And if you do not do well, sin is crouching at the door; and its desire is for you, but you must master it.'

Father Elemar commented, "A man is not merely what he does. He is much more. He can take all of his losses and failures and set them aside. He can choose. A new life."

"Perhaps," Dracula said. "But there is also my second reason."

The priest asked, "Which is?"

And now it was he who heard a chuckle. "Father, you ask me to forgive and forget. But it is you who forget: You are speaking to *Dracula*."

4

ILONA AGREED TO THE MARRIAGE. It was effected that same year, and fairly quietly—particularly in regard to Dracula's conversion to the Latin Church.

They lived in the city of Pest now, just across the Danube from the capital city of Buda. In later times, in fact, it would be the joining of the two cities that would give Hungary a new capital: Buda-Pest—Budapest.

Their house was modest: two-story masonry with unelaborate rooms. Though, like most real estate, its value lay in location. It was not the fact that it was in the wealthier quarter with the merchants and nobility. Their houses, too, were small. But they were all within the precious protection of the city walls and the king and his army.

The couple sat now, both with needles and cloth in hand, in chairs obliquely facing near a second story window. The mild breeze of the day freshened the room. The sunlight made their close work easier. Still, Dracula had cause for complaint: "Each day they spin a new tale about me. A new lie. Now they have it that I wanted to murder my whole country."

Ilona said only, "Did you?"

Dracula frowned. "They say that I sold my soul to the devil."

She repeated: "Did you?"

He retorted: "For what? This?"

She pricked herself with her needle and swore.

He continued, "They say that I killed my own men. Supposedly, after each battle, I beheaded those who were wounded in the back, on the grounds that they had run from the enemy. And before you ask—*No! I did not.* Which is why my men stayed with me to the end."

"Yes," she said. "They say that when you were captured you had at least ten with you."

"I had a hundred, at least. I could have had thousands."

"Then why didn't you?"

"For what? To see them slaughtered by your cousin?"

As his hands quickened in their work, she leaned toward it. "What is that?"

"A banner."

"Of what? A dog?"

He snarled, "A dragon!"

A dragon. Like the banner he had flown before. The dragon of the Societas Draconis. But without the Cross.

He went on, "It was bad enough when it was just the Saxons spreading lies. Now it's the Russians. And my own people. They hate me because I converted from their Church. So they make me out to be a butchering berserker."

"Well, then," Ilona said, "you are assured a place in posterity. Like the bogeyman."

Dracula flung his sewing aside. "I need wine."

"A cup a day is all you get—and that at night."

"I'll have it now."

"You'll have it tonight and no sooner. It helps you sleep. Otherwise your sleep is vexed. No doubt from nightmares about what you have done."

He mumbled, "Nightmares—from what I'm doing now." He rose to fetch the wine.

"Go," she said. "And I will have this marriage annulled."

He stopped, sighed, and resumed his seat and sewing.

She chuckled. "If only they knew the truth. Their 'butchering berserker' spends his days sewing." Her voice softened. "But I know why you sew. You told me of how Prasha sewed. Her memory must weigh heavy on you."

A silence passed between them.

"In truth," Dracula said. "I would gladly put this aside. I could do your cousin much more good than I do him now. Albania is very quiet. Some say because Skanderbeg is dead. And your cousin, it seems, will soon be at war with my own cousin. My *dear* cousin, Stephen. Yet here I sit—"

"Yes," Ilona said. "Craving wine."

He hurled his sewing against the wall. She did not so much as flinch. He rose and went to the window. "Why did you consent to this marriage? Why did I?"

"Marriage?" she said. "There is no marriage without consummation. You spent our wedding night in the cup. The weeks since, you have spent brooding."

From the window, Dracula saw his guard. The captain. Still keeping his vigil. Not at all inconspicuous.

"Perhaps," he said, "I brood because I'm a prisoner. Even in my own house."

Ilona answered, "I haven't chained you. Leave. Go back to the tower."

The green eyes could only roll to the sky. "Woman, why do you plague me? Why did you hate me from the first?"

She asserted, "I did not—and do not—hate you."

"But not once have you smiled for me. Not once!"

"Yes I did. Once."

It struck him. "On the first day we met."

She was surprised. "You remember?"

He grunted. "It was a fleeting smile indeed. A glimpse. I wasn't even sure I saw it."

"But it was there for you to see. And you did."

"Then why haven't you smiled since? Why such a shrew?"

She set her sewing aside and stood to face him. "Vlad Dracula, you were offered to me as a last chance. My family was eager for me to marry. As so many women's families are. So they gave me a 'woman's' chance. I could marry you or be sent to a nunnery. A nunnery does not suit my purpose."

"Which is?"

She ignored the question. "I thought long and hard about you. Not another woman in a thousand would have considered a marriage to a man called such a beast. Even under the threat of a convent. I wondered: *Were you really a maniac?* If so I would have shunned you—convent or no. But I trusted Father Elemar. He assured me that you were no maniac."

Dracula reflected, "'Remarkable,' he once called me."

She agreed. "Remarkable. And famous. And infamous. And I, quite frankly, consider you troubled. Yet...If I were a younger woman...or one of singular beauty...I would look elsewhere for a husband. But marriage, you see, has evaded me. Or I it. And that no longer suited me. Yet I had one other question about you. Were you really still alive? Or had you truly lost *all*? You drank, they said. You brooded. You seemed content to sit in your tower."

"But consider my circumstance."

"I did. You have lost so much. Too much. So you had a right to drink—for a time. And to brood—for a time. But for how long? I was offered your hand long before our first meeting. I was told of your drinking, so I waited. When I heard of no change in your ways, I decided to draw conclusions for myself."

"But you attacked me on our first meeting. You were rude. You were—"

"You were drunk. What better way for me to see if you were also alive? And, though numb with drink, when I challenged, you answered. It wasn't much of an answer, but—"

"But you agreed to marry me."

"I have gambled."

Again Dracula reflected. He asked, "After I called you fat, did you deliberately cinch your dress?"

"You mean," she answered, "like this." She cinched her dress. "So you did notice."

"You know that I did, woman. What man wouldn't. In truth, you cut a...a *splendid* figure."

"Thank you, Vlad Dracula," she said. She raised a finger to hold him where he was. She left and returned with wine. And *two* goblets. They sat. She poured, noting, "This wine, I saved from our wedding night."

As they sipped, she said, "They say you have a son." She saw the suspicion in his eyes and assured him, "You can tell me the truth. I am not my cousin's spy. I am your wife. Is your son still alive?"

"Yes."

"So you lost Prasha. Your dear Prasha. But your boy is still alive."

"His name is Vlad. He is ten years old now."

"Is he safe?"

"He was the last time I saw him."

She took his hand. "Your burden is indeed great."

He acknowledged, "It is. But I accepted it—in whatever form it would come—when I first sought my throne."

"And you would seek your throne still."

"Aye."

"Then I fear that some day I will lose you to your quest."

"Would you keep me from it?"

Quietly, she laughed. "You, Vlad Dracula? *Could* I keep you from it? No. Not you. Nor would I. I would not keep you from your chosen purpose. And so I must think...What will I be left with?"

Dracula opened his hands, as though to indicate his poverty. "What would you have me give you?"

Her hazel eyes locked onto the green. "Give me what I have chosen as my purpose: children."

5

1467. THE PORTE. The sultan was in high spirits. High because of the baggage trains streaming into the courtyard below his veranda. They carried his tribute. *Part* of his tribute. Trains had been arriving almost every week from all corners of the empire. On this day, like the rest, they were crowded into the courtyard.

He was exultant, too, because of the news of the past months. Overwhelmingly fortuitous. It raised him even higher at the pinnacle of his world.

But on this day his spirits were highest of all because of the last train rolling into the yard. It was led by the man who held two special places in his life: Radu.

Radu indeed sat the saddle like a prince. It was hard to believe that he had once been described by court chroniclers as no larger than "a bouquet of flowers." He was tall in the saddle. Erect. Naturally and easily. His auburn hair was rich dressing enough for the crown of his head. He was draped loosely in a cape the color of the deepest fringe of the night sky. Auburn hair. Midnight blue cape. Like a prince from mythology. The cape was spread behind his saddle like a fringe on his mount.

He reined to the side to let his train amble among the others into its appointed space. As he dismounted and started for the palace, Mohammed left the veranda to hasten their meeting. Their broad smiles were like magnets. Radu knelt and planted his forehead in the dust. As Mohammed personally lifted him and gave him an embrace, the leaders of the other trains stared in envy of "Wallachia."

The two walked back to Radu's train as though nothing existed around them. Strolling. Gripping each other's arm. Eager to get past the pleasantries—Radu's journey, the state of their respective households—to the news.

But where to begin? Albania of course. Skanderbeg was dead. Even as he had persisted in his guerilla warfare against the Turk, petty nobles had begun picking at the land around him. His thin resources were spread even thinner in constant skirmishing. As the resources were drained, so was his spirit.

The sultan could be dispassionate as he considered it all now. Both he and Radu could almost feel sorry for the dead rebel. Skanderbeg had tried to reconquer his land to rule it, rebuild it, see it grow. His enemies, almost literally, only wanted to get a foot in his door. Like common politicians. Just a foot. Just enough to snatch what they could for their personal fortune. Grab-and-run. Let Skanderbeg fight the Turk. To his enemies, his was a hopeless cause anyway.

Radu noted darkly, "As though he had been pecked to death."

Mohammed agreed, "Yes. And we all have carrion birds at our backs."

He let it go unspoken that it was the lesser rulers—like Radu—who had much more to fear from "carrion birds." By nature such predators fed on the weak.

Skanderbeg. Dead. The rock of Albania's gates split asunder—in a way that seemed to the sultan like Heaven's hand itself. And yet there was news to rival it. On Radu's own border. Hungary had invaded Moldavia. And lost.

What had possessed Matthias? Apparently the smell of easy prey. His logic was simple. It was a roundabout way of fighting the inevitable fight: against the Turk. Hungary could absorb Moldavia and become that much stronger.

Logic dictated, too, that the victory should be quick. The king had Hungary's chivalry—the heavy knights. Stephen had an army like Wallachia's: mostly peasants.

But lately Stephen had made his army even more like Wallachia's. He had adopted Dracula's device of granting "free" status liberally to the peasants who distinguished themselves in his service. War service.

And Stephen of course still had his "fortress." The forest. The Vaslui. Where long ago he and Dracula had routed Poland's chivalry.

He used the same tactic against Matthias as he had on the Poles: ambush. The king fled Moldavia with a "souvenir": a wound—in his back.

Mohammed and Radu could not help sharing a laugh as they pictured it. The sultan sneered, "A pox on them both and better for me."

Let Hungary and Moldavia tear each other apart. All the better for him if his enemies never learned.

His eyes lighted on the tribute from Wallachia. Two men wrestled to unload a chest and hurry it into the palace. But it was another part of the tribute that had caught the sultan's eye. A boy. A janissary recruit. For once, with Radu as its voevode, Wallachia gladly paid the child-tribute.

The boy was small, even compared to his small companions. Like a "bouquet" himself. His skin was fair, his hair and eyes dark, and the eyes were wide like those of a cornered doe. As the sultan approached, the boy dropped to the proper bow. All the boys had been taught as much on their long trek from home. Given leave to rise, he pulled himself up stiffly and craned his neck to stare at the two great lords.

Mohammed spoke softly, in the boy's own language: "Why are you afraid?"

The boy had also been taught already to answer superiors promptly. But now he could not speak. He only blushed, as though caught in a sin.

To his surprise, the sultan only smiled. "You have nothing to fear. Look. Your own prince, Lord Radu, is with me. He is going to make sure that you are comfortable here."

"Of course," Radu said. He knelt to the boy's level and took his hand. "His Highness and I both want you to like it here. We are going to see to it."

The boy's eyes were still wide. To the sultan's asking, he managed to give his village and name: *Piotr*. Peter.

"I know why you are worried, Peter," Mohammed said. "You miss home. Sometimes, when I was a boy, new places made me miss home, too."

Peter heard himself say, "Highness, I miss mamma and papa. And my brothers and sisters and friends."

His heart leapt. Had he said that? Why? They had told him never to speak to a superior unless spoken to first. And this...The Grand Turk! He expected nothing less than a cuff on the ear.

But Mohammed said only, "Peter, to miss your family is only natural."

Radu ruffled the boy's dark hair and threw a glance to the courtyard. "Look, Peter. You are not alone. And I'll wager that most of these boys feel the same as you."

It did give Peter some relief. And he was also suddenly proud of the looks of the other boys and even the Turkish soldiers; envy at his being singled out by the sultan. He ventured, though quietly, "Highness, will I ever see mamma and papa again?"

"Of course. But first you must learn many things. And you have to learn well."

So Peter knew. Home was far away not only in distance, but also in time. The sultan and prince talked nice, but they were not going to let him go home any time soon.

And in his mind he saw his home. On the day they took him. Nobody knew they were coming. There were not a lot of them, just a few Turks and Prince Radu's soldiers and the new boyar's men. But mamma and papa and all the grown-ups looked scared. All of the soldiers talked nice—like the sultan and prince now. But they said that some of the boys would have to go with them.

When they picked Peter, mamma and papa both cried—but not in front of the soldiers. Papa looked up to God and asked Him to send back Prince Dracula. He used to be afraid of Prince Dracula. But when the Turks came he wanted God to send him back.

"See these men?"

The sultan's words brought Peter's mind back to the yard. He was pointing to the soldiers in white. "They came here just as you came here. Do they look sad?"

Peter had to say that they did not.

The sultan gently shook a finger. "And as soon as you get used to it here you won't be sad either."

Not be sad? Peter thought. Away from mamma and papa and his village? And as young as he was he was also sorely worried about something else. He had to know—even if it made the sultan and prince mad. "Highness, will you make me give up Jesus?"

On the day he was taken, his mother had whispered to him never to give up Jesus. It was far from the village, when the Turks finally told the women to stop following the train. The women had been weeping and begging at every step, hoping that God or persistence or a chink in the soldiers' hearts would give them back their sons. The Turks were polite but firm. They stopped the train and gave the women a moment for a last farewell.

In that moment, Peter's mother's eyes suddenly went dry. That is when she whispered about Jesus. Tell the Turks what they want to hear, she said. But never give up Jesus. *Never.* From his own mother.

Now the sultan was saying, still softly, "With us, Peter, you will learn to see Jesus in a new way. You will also learn about another great man: The Prophet—praise his name! And new things—wonderful things!—about God. We would never—never!—try to take you from God."

Prince Radu added, "Peter, His Highness and his people are our friends."

But that was not what papa had said. Still, Peter knew to smile.

And that made the sultan smile. "Peter, do not trouble yourself with so many questions now. In time you will learn the answers. While you are here, I will be like your father, and your teachers will be like uncles. And all these other boys—like brothers. A whole new family here until you see your own again. But for now…are you hungry? Would you like some sesame and honey?"

On that, Peter had no hesitation. Nor did the other boys as the sultan called the same question to each group in its own language.

Like magic, servants appeared from the palace with laden trays. They, too, spoke to the boys in their various tongues, giving the same invitation like a chant: 'Take all you want. But eat all you take.'

To Peter, they gave the biggest, stickiest pieces.

As the boys gorged, the sultan walked among them telling them of their prospects: new clothes, the best food…Most would become soldiers—brave and famous. Some would become important ministers—like the lords in their own lands. They would build bridges and mills and roads and…But to do this they would have to become men. And to become men they would have to give up childish things. What man cried on leaving home to live on his own?

In the end, the sultan returned to Peter and beckoned to a nearby janissary. The man came and bowed smartly, full to the ground. The sultan said proudly, "Peter, this man was once like you. He is from your own land. He is now a hero. Rise, Ali Hamed. You will be this boy's teacher. You know how to guide him."

And Ali Hamed—Giorgi—answered: "Most assuredly, Highness."

Walking with Radu toward the palace, Mohammed moved quickly to other business: "Wilk and Cirstian?"

Radu frowned. "Gone. Like phantoms."

Mohammed stifled his own frown. Phantoms? Then why was he losing patrols in Wallachia—especially near the ruins of Castle Dracula? Men rode out and disappeared. How could Radu just accept that the two henchmen were gone?

The sultan got the same answer on Prasha and young Vlad. Gone. To where, Radu had no clue.

And it was the same with Gales. With that one, the sultan did not know which side of the ledger he should read from: *Punishment* or *Reward?* Was it true what was whispered, that Gales had betrayed Dracula in the end? The sultan would have liked to have Gales to get to the truth. But Gales, like the others of Dracula's inner circle, remained a mystery.

A few steps more and it was Radu who asked, "And what of..." He almost said 'my brother.' "What of Kaziglu?"

Here, at least, Mohammed thought, the picture was a bit clearer. Because here he had looked with his own "eyes," not through those of a mere voevode. Kaziglu was still in Pest with his new wife. She had just given birth to a child, a son. So perhaps it was true what was also whispered: Prasha was dead. At any rate, Kaziglu's new family was watched closely—at once guarded and confined, it seemed—by a particular captain and his men. There was no getting to Kaziglu. Not with the knife or "quiet cup." Not yet.

"But," Mohammed noted, "we can still strike him. He has become a papist."

But that, of course, Radu and his countrymen already knew. He assured the sultan, "Believe me, I will not let them forget it."

And there was still one person of import to discuss. But Mohammed waited for Radu to raise the name: "Laiota?"

Hungary's new candidate in Wallachia—at least as long as Dracula was kept on the king's leash.

Mohammed turned the question. "What do you know of him?"

"His star was never very high," Radu said. "It is even lower now."

Lower because Laiota's patron, King Matthias, could not even defeat Moldavia's peasants. So what Wallachian would support Laiota now against Radu, against the sultan?

Mohammed was content to let the subject drop. He could have told Radu much more of Laiota. That he was no fool. That he knew he had lost prestige along with his king. That he had made quiet overtures to the Porte; Laiota was "available."

But Mohammed let it all drop. What had the battle of Belgrade taught him...and the war with Dracula—the terrible Forest? Yes, of course Radu was still very special to him. But he was sultan. And sultans, even more than other men, often found themselves suddenly alone.

But, inside the palace, the door of his private quarters was barely closed behind them when he turned. Their embrace now was sealed with groping hands, eager to tangibly feel what had haunted their thoughts during their long separation. Their clothes were half undraped when Mohammed stopped to caress Radu's face: the fair, fine lines…the blue eyes lilting now…Radu's lips were raised to him and he drank…a long, thirsty kiss. It was only broken as Radu turned his head for a low laugh. "Today I saw you a bit out of character."

Mohammed was piqued. "How so?"

"With our young recruits."

"They are children," Mohammed said. "Is it wrong to show them a little softness?"

Radu agreed, "Not at all."

No, Mohammed thought. *Not at all.* But his actions with the new recruits had more purpose than just sympathy. Show the boys a little softness. Let them learn to love him—or at least not fear him—from the first. Plant the seed.

One Skanderbeg was dead. Mohammed would do everything reasonable—bend a bit—not to breed another.

He was leading Radu to the inner rooms when they saw the chest that had been brought from the Wallachian train. It was already placed singularly on a table. As Mohammed reached for it, Radu stopped him. "Let me. Please."

At Mohammed's nod, he raised the lid. Gold. Wallachia's tribute. Eight thousand ducats.

Eight thousand.

It had always been two thousand more, but Mohammed was content now with the eight. Show Wallachia a little softness. Plant the seed.

One Dracula was gone. Mohammed would do everything reasonable—bend a bit—not to breed another.

Radu said, "Tomorrow you will have this chest from my own hands. Before your entire court. Before the world." He added teasingly, "As I kneel and 'kiss your hem.'"

Mohammed answered teasingly, "Why wait for tomorrow? Kneel and 'kiss my hem' now."

6

1474. PEST. The way he hugged the roof, one might have thought that he was married to it. Both his heart and mind raced like those of a thief when the law is closing in. He listened to the orders shouted on the street below: *This way! That way!* He breathed just a mite easier as the running steps faded into the darkness.

A floor below, Dracula was already up and dressed at his bedroom window. He told Ilona, "Our friend, the captain. He's chasing something. A thief maybe." Or was it an old enemy stalking Dracula himself? "Stay with the children. Lock the door."

She went to the children's room. He heard the lock click. He opened the window and listened. *Quiet. Very quiet.* Then: *"Psst! Psst!"*

He drew a dagger and cautiously glanced up at the sound, at the roof. It took a second for the face to register: *Wilk!* The past decade had taken most of his hair. Dracula beamed and gave a hand as Wilk swung from the eaves feet-first into the window. Dracula caught him in midair to muffle the landing. The catch turned into a hug then a little jig. *After so many years!*

They checked themselves. Quiet. Quiet. Dracula closed the window and they stifled their laughs as he patted Wilk's bald pate while Wilk, in turn, poked the paunch at Dracula's middle.

From downstairs came a sharp rap at the door.

Wilk lamented, "I'm afraid that's for me."

Ilona called. Dracula bade her to stay where she was. Stay with the children. He was hustling down the stairs when the rap turned into a pounding and command: "Open!"

The captain.

Ilona called again. Dracula staved her off: "Just stay with the children, dear!" He jiggled the lock on the door to hold the captain for a another moment. He peered through the door's peep. The captain's sword was bared. But he was alone. Dracula gestured to Wilk, who padded down the stairs and faded into the dark near the landing.

Dracula opened the door. The captain barreled his way in. Dracula was quick to raise a finger to quiet their words. He warned, "Don't wake my family!"

The captain grimaced. But Ilona was, after all, the king's cousin. He would be sure of his "mission" before he disturbed her. Still, he laid the point of his sword on Dracula's chest. "A man came this way. I am going to find him."

"What man?"

The captain leered. "A thief, maybe. Or...or is it one of your vermin?"

Dracula scoffed, "You're dreaming. But knowing you, you probably chased your own shadow."

The sword poked.

Dracula smirked, "So where are your men?"

The captain grinned. "Just a call away. No one will slip through our 'noose.'"

Ignorant man, Dracula thought. A fool to the end. In the captain's grin he saw the hunger—for glory: *Brave captain. Set his trap. Went in alone. Alone. Captured Dracula's man.* What would the king say about that?

The captain prodded with the sword again. He saw Dracula's dagger and took it, flung it aside. "I will search the entire house. Stay in front of me."

Dracula was pliant. "Where do you wish to start?"

It made no difference to Dracula. Any way they went, they would have to pass the landing. Dracula was already in stride.

Something flew from the dark and hit the captain square in the face. Wilk sprung and seized his hands. One of Dracula's hands stifled his mouth. The other made a quick swipe across his throat. The captain buckled and sagged. He was lowered to the floor.

Still it was not without some noise. Ilona called. Dracula answered: "Just stay with the children!"

Wilk had retrieved the object that he had thrown at the captain: his boot. He was slipping it back on. "You keep saying 'children.' We heard of only one."

Dracula said proudly, "Two!" The shard of blade in his hand was bloody. He wiped it on the captain's shirt and slid it back into its secret place: in his hair. The same blade in the same place for so long—since the old sultan, Murad, had tried to rape him in the harem. It was shortly after the attempt that Dracula had hidden the blade, swearing to himself that he would never again be without one.

He continued, "Two boys. And good ones." He chuckled. "She's afraid they take after me."

Wilk answered the next question before it was asked. "Vlad is fine. A good boy. A good *young man.*"

Dracula's eyes misted. He had been in Hungary for what…twelve years! His son was a man. "Does he know me?"

"He both remembers and is proud of you. He trains well. He will make a good prince."

"And the rest?" Dracula asked. "Cirstian?"

Cirstian was well, Wilk said. As were all the rest. Even Kyril. Big, one-armed Kyril. And they had all kept their swords honed on the sultan's patrols in Wallachia.

Dracula shot, "And Gales?"

At that, Wilk shrugged. He told Dracula what history would tell the world. Gales was gone. Gone. Dead? No one knew. Pure mystery. Surely Gales had been sought. Surely no one had found him. He had apparently run far to escape Dracula's inevitable wrath. The name Gales just dropped from the chronicles of Wallachia's boyars after Dracula's war.

But time was short.

"So many times," Wilk said, "we tried to reach you."

Dracula noted wryly, "As did the sultan and Saxons."

With their assassins.

Wilk gave a nod to the captain. "Give him his due. He was a good watchdog."

Dracula eulogized only, "A dead dog now."

"Aye," Wilk said. "And finally I reach you. And what better time. Do you know what's afoot?"

He was surprised that Dracula knew only of Skanderbeg's death. That was very old news. But lately the king was keeping Dracula ignorant. Because he would not have Dracula know that his worth was growing.

In the past year especially...The pope had been urging a new crusade against the Turk. He had brought Hungary and Moldavia—the recent enemies— together in an alliance. Perhaps not a fast alliance. But an alliance nonetheless. And together they had made a lightning raid on Wallachia and put Laiota on the throne. Radu had been forced to run to the sultan.

"Then there will be war," Dracula said. "Mohammed will send him back with an army."

"No," Wilk said.

Dracula was baffled. "*No?* But why would the Turk just—?"

It struck him. Why would the Turk let the allies just put Laiota on the throne? Why would the sultan not fight back? Unless...

"Yes," Wilk said. "Laiota has declared his new alliance—with the sultan!"

A grin exploded on their faces.

But Ilona called again and again Dracula had to stave her off. He muttered to Wilk, "Just wait till she sees these stains." The captain's blood. "I'll never hear the end of it!"

But his thoughts were drawn back to the news: "Laiota the sultan's man..."

He wrapped Wilk in a hug and urged, "Go now." He threw a finger to the captain. "His men will come snooping soon enough." He pointed Wilk back to the stairs. "Wait by the window."

As Wilk stole up the steps, Dracula kicked the captain's corpse. He told the deaf ears, "What he just told me makes you irrelevant."

Surely. The king would be furious about his captain. But he needed a new candidate in Wallachia.

Dracula waited a moment for Wilk to ready himself by the bedroom window. Then he went to the door, flung it open, and rushed into the streets with a cry: "Help! Thief! Help!"

7

THE CAPTAIN HAD BEEN the king's man, so the king held the hear-ing. Quietly. Only Father Elemar sat with him as the Church's representative, a most credible witness to the proceedings.

Dracula wore an air of appropriate gravity. His story was simple: *It was dark. There was a commotion outside. He went to investigate. A man with a drawn sword barged through the cracked door. There was a scuffle. The man was killed. Dracula ran for help. Only then did he see that the man was the captain.*

Who could refute it? Not even the king's own cousin, Ilona. Darkness. Confusion. She really had not been sure what she had heard.

So the king heard Dracula's testimony and pronounced: "And so it will be written. A case of mistaken identity. Seemingly self-defense."

Having said that, Matthias settled back in his chair and told Dracula, "But I don't believe it."

For some moments he just stared at Dracula. The voevode was what, ten...twelve years his senior? Was he trying to make a fool of him, the king? And, if Dracula would do this now, what would he dare when he was finally off his leash?

The captain's men had assured Matthias that they had indeed been chasing someone. Someone who the captain thought had gone into Dracula's house.

That the captain went in alone did not surprise the king. The captain was surely a "hungry" man, and pompous. Like so many of his class. He wanted the glory of the "catch" for himself.

But who was it who had "visited" Dracula? Matthias had given it much thought. One of Dracula's men. It had to be. In and out in a furtive rush. The hapless captain left behind.

Matthias continued, "It is fortunate for you that this happened when it did. But that you already know, of course. That is why your man came in the first place. To tell you." He did not wait for Dracula to deny it. He merely finished with a word: "Laiota."

Dracula mounted no denial. Nor did he admit anything. He answered only, "Laiota, sire, is what I always said he is: two-faced."

Matthias confirmed, "And now he holds your throne for the sultan."

And Radu? For now, he was only a pawn in reserve. Laiota was on the throne. It was easier for Mohammed if he just stayed there.

"So you," Matthias concluded, "are my candidate. But not by choice."

"Your father and I were once allies," Dracula said. "Not by choice. But it worked well for us both, sire."

Matthias spoke past it. "This alliance comes with conditions."

But of course it did, Dracula knew. And he knew the very first before the king voiced it: religion. Dracula would have to keep his adopted religion; he would have to rule Wallachia as a Roman Catholic prince.

He made the appeal that he knew would be futile: "Sire, I could serve much better as a member of my native faith. Wallachia will never accept a papist prince."

The king reiterated, "No reconversion." He looked to Father Elemar.

"Vlad Dracula," the priest explained, "this is the will of the Holy Father."

"Then advise him, father," Dracula said. "Urge him to relent. For all of our sakes."

Father Elemar assured him that the appeal would be carried to the pope. And Dracula knew that it would. And that it would do no good. So he would return to Wallachia as a papist. For a time. Bide time.

The second concession he had also expected. After the Church, he would have to appease the Saxons—as far as that was possible. And men of money were appeased with money: more concessions in Wallachia's trade than they had ever had before. Again Dracula agreed. Because again—as always—it was a matter of biding time.

"Finally," the king said, "you must accept the other member of our alliance."

He gave Dracula a letter. It bore the seal of Moldavia: Stephen.

Dracula read. Stephen gave no apologies for having joined the sultan in Dracula's war. Yet he did have regrets that it had to be so. Had to be. Because Dracula's war, as Stephen had seen it, was folly. What country alone—especially a Wallachia—or even his own Moldavia—could defeat the Osmanli empire?

He had joined the sultan when asked so that he could salvage what he could: Chilia. The fortress. The "door" between him and Wallachia. What should he have done? Let the sultan take it?

No, he had no apologies. But he did have regrets. But they could be put in the past now as he and Dracula renewed their alliance in arms. Because this war would be different. They would have Hungary with them. They could win.

Dracula read and smirked. Especially at the end of the letter, where Stephen offered him a token: troops. Only two hundred. But specially trained. A corps around which Dracula could rebuild his army.

The king cut to the quick. "Moldavia, too, is a necessary condition. If I can accept Stephen, you can. For the cause."

"Aye," Dracula said. "For the cause. So be it. But the two hundred—"

The king preempted, "But nothing. You will accept them. Because I have precious few of my own men to spare."

Dracula acquiesced. In fact, the issue gave him a lever. Because he, too, had a condition. Just one: "A full pardon. For my draguli, sire. No trouble with you or the Saxons."

Now it was Matthias who smirked. "But all this time you swore that your 'dragons' were dead."

Dracula shrugged.

Matthias agreed to the pardon.

Dracula qualified, "In writing, sire."

Matthias rose. "In writing." He started for the door. "Frankly, I wonder if you are more trouble than you are worth. My captain notwithstanding—*my* captain—I still have to explain you to the Saxons."

"Pardon," Dracula said. "But may I also be frank, sire?"

Matthias stopped. He turned. Of course he would let Dracula speak, if for no other reason than to show that he was not afraid of his words.

"*Frankly*, sire," Dracula said, "I often think of your father. He would have joined me in my war. The Turk would be gone from Wallachia now. Maybe from all of Europe. And the Saxons would be in their place. Their proper place."

A blush began to rise on the king's face. But he caught it. He answered as he continued to the door. "My father was a man of another time, Vlad Dracula. As are you."

When he was gone, Father Elemar judged, "Neither of you are men to be trifled with."

"Well then," Dracula said. "So much the worse for the Turk."

And the priest had to ask a final question. "Vlad Dracula, was the captain's death really an accident?"

Dracula answered, "Father, it was an accident that the captain and I ever crossed paths."

8

ONLY MONTHS LATER. THE PORTE. This was not the meeting that Radu had expected. Or requested so many times over the past months. Why could it not be that he and his friend just settled the matter in private? A shared supper...a cup of wine...old bonds renewed. In truth, to Radu, it had been too long since they had been together like that.

But Mohammed faced him now across a small table. A formal meeting. Sultan to voevode. A minister held a third place, as though between them, at one end of the table. They sat cross-legged—in the style of the old Osmanli steppe tribe.

So be it, Radu thought. He would make his case formally. He spoke quietly but in earnest. "Highness, how long will you let Laiota keep my throne?"

Mohammed answered evenly. "This is not the time for a change."

Certainly a sultan owed no explanation. But he deigned to grant one. Why? Old feelings? Or just the echo, the memory of old feelings? He had to admit that it was awkward facing Radu like this. But things had indeed changed.

He would make no move in Wallachia, he told Radu, because of the Christian alliance: Hungary and Moldavia..."And now your own brother." *Kaziglu*. Resurrected. As though from the grave. "They are already on the march. Not in Wallachia. Not yet. First they are clearing their Serbian flank."

And none "clearing" it more efficiently than Dracula. The sultan had literally winced when he first heard the reports.

The minister injected to Radu, "Surely, lord, you understand our position."

Surely Radu did. He understood the cold politics. The Porte had its new Wallachian candidate; it needed no trouble with Laiota now. Not in the face of invasion.

But Radu also understood...Whoever fought for the sultan now in Wallachia would earn the right to keep the throne after the war. The unwritten law: War service earned the throne.

So Radu appealed beyond politics. He laid an open hand on the table. A gesture to his friend. His special friend. But Mohammed did not take hold of the hand. Radu had no choice but to slowly withdraw it.

When the minister spoke again, prattling on about the politics of the situation, Radu understood even more. The minister was only parroting what the sultan had decided long before. There was no meeting here. The decision was already final.

Radu blushed. The blush of the loyal vassal—and so much more than just a vassal—betrayed. He heard himself stammer, "Is this the empire I serve?"

He heard the sultan answer: "It is the empire that we all serve." Yet Mohammed offered, "But you, my friend, more than most, know how broad the empire is. You know the work to be done. And the rewards to be had. What can I grant you?"

Radu's blush only deepened. He had served. In all ways. With his heart. And he had dreamed. From so long ago. But now…

The minister was prattling again. Words:…*the empire's position…the difficult Wallachian situation…but things could change in time…*The breath of words to warm the face of a cold betrayal.

In the time that the words bought, Radu gathered his own face. He even managed a smile when the sultan repeated, "What can I grant?"

"My Highness," Radu said. "If you were in my place, what would you say? You would be sultan. I would be voevode. So I am going to presume on our friendship. I am going to keep my sword sharp and my men ready." He told the minister, "As you said, things could change."

But, when he was gone, the sultan only sighed. Change? It was a critical time for the empire: *Hungary. Moldavia. Kaziglu. Laiota. And Radu.*

In truth, as he saw it, the time for voevodes in Wallachia had passed. It was time for the empire to step all the way to the Danube. To stand on Wallachia's stiff neck. To face Hungary squarely.

This, he had decided long before the meeting.

And, as he thought of it now, he saw an image: an infant. Dead. Murdered. His own brother.

He had done that for the empire. Just as he now did things not as Mohammed—a man with feelings—but as *the Conqueror. Authority.* For the empire.

9

1476. TRANSYLVANIA. It was late summer. The best time for the quick campaign: *Strike fast. Reach the objective. Hold until the snows…until the enemy was bogged down.*

Dracula had moved to Hungary's southern province months before just to prepare. He sat on the edge of the bed now and listened to the bustle from the nearby fields: troops being readied—wagons loaded, horses snorting, the rattle of arms and armor…And through it all, through his open window, the busy chirping of birds.

As he finished dressing, he toyed with the birds, mimicking their whistles, then slightly changing their calls to drive them into a confused silence. He went on with the game as he checked his weapons. Saber—sharp as ever. One dagger. Two. Three. All ready. All honed nicely. All slipped into different places on his person.

And the last blade: the shard that went into his hair.

Donning his armor, he was surprised that he still had to squeeze into his breastplate. He had lost most of his paunch in the past year's Serbian campaign. He had worked to keep it off: training, light food…wine only sparingly. But a layer of fat still clung to his waist. It occurred to him to see the armorer for a larger breastplate. But he squeezed into the one he had. He would just make it a point to shed the extra pounds. Surely.

He heard Ilona downstairs erupt angrily at the children. He chuckled. Her short temper had nothing to do with the children really. It was the same as before Serbia: the anguish of the soldier's wife.

Outside, solitary hooves trotted to the house. Dracula stamped his feet on the floor to make his boots snug and hurried downstairs. Ilona's hands were indeed filled with the boys. Toddlers both. She was trying to feed and dress them both at once—and with only two hands. Dracula himself went to see to the rider.

It was Father Elemar. For his age, he dismounted smoothly, if slowly; he had never forgotten the skills of his long-past days as itinerant chaplain. Dracula invited him inside, but he balked. He would see Dracula alone. News. The kind of news that Father Elemar had never learned to break easily. He began, "Your brother."

He waited for Dracula to acknowledge, "Radu?"

The priest nodded. "Yes, my friend. He is dead."

He continued quietly as Dracula listened. The news had come from the Porte itself. Radu had died at the turn of the year from a malady. With the official report came an "official whisper": the malady was the pox—syphilis.

As Dracula gave only a quiet smirk, the priest made to console him. "I suppose you are confused, my friend. Should you mourn or not? He was your enemy. But he was also your brother."

"In truth, father," Dracula said, "I mourned for him long ago." The news had only pricked the painful memory.

Dracula went on, "Tell me, father. Does this 'pox' story make sense to you?"

In truth, the priest had wondered about it. "It raises so many questions."

"Aye. My brother had his famous lover. Does *he* have the pox? Apparently not. He also had a wife. Does she have it? Apparently not. So why such a fanciful story? We know only that Radu rode to the Porte. He never rode out. But it wasn't enough for them to kill him. They have to dance on his grave. Sully his name."

"But why? He was their ally."

"Why indeed? To know that, father, you have to know the sultan's mind. He is trying to plant a thought in my country's head: *Your voevode died of the pox. He was a degenerate. Finally cursed by God Himself.* It sullies the entire land's name. It is the first step in planting the broader thought: *You are not fit to rule yourselves.*"

"But the sultan already rules Wallachia. Through Laiota now."

"A pawn. As Radu was a pawn. You play chess, father. When do you discard a pawn? When you have bigger prey in mind. I would say that the sultan wants Wallachia outright."

"And Laiota? Where would he fit in?"

"The sultan will tolerate him for a while. At least long enough to help in this war."

The priest pronounced, "Devious. Treacherous."

"Aye, father," Dracula said. "Which is why I mourned my brother so long ago. He chose to serve the devious and treacherous."

The first rumbling hooves were leaving the nearby camps. And the first among the first were Dracula's Hungarian allies. Not the king's men, but those of a nobleman. They passed Dracula's house flying the banner of their lord's notable family: Bathory. Their commander for the expedition, Stephen Bathory, had mustered a grand army of twenty-five thousand. He would come to a bit of fame for it. But the real fame for his family—if a somewhat dubious fame—would come generations later from a countess. Elizabeth. She would show an appetite for blood—quite literally—rivalling that of Dracula himself.

Watching the troops pass now, Father Elemar was prompted, "Is it true what they say you did in Serbia?"

In the last year's campaign. Dracula acknowledged, "Yes, father. I impaled all my prisoners."

It had been witnessed by no less than the pope's own ambassador.

Father Elemar continued, "But they say you also—"

"Yes, father," Dracula confirmed. "I even impaled the dead. First I quartered them myself." He made the slicing motions with a hand. Quartered: cut in four. "Then I put the separate pieces on the stake."

This, too, the pope's ambassador had witnessed and passed on in his letters for history.

Dracula offered, "Understand, father…As the sultan sows seeds in Wallachia's mind, so do I sow in his own: '*Kaziglu* is back. Kaziglu-*Bey!*'"

The second columns wheeled from the fields. More Hungarians. Serbs. Finally the black-clad regiments.

Waiting for them, Dracula also had a question. "Tell me, father. Is it true what they say of my cousin?"

Stephen. Months before, Mohammed had chosen Moldavia for his first counterattack on the new Christian alliance. He had sent an army a *hundred thousand* strong. Stephen, with some Polish allies, had only half that number. But his free-peasant soldiers proved as ardent as ever. And he had his "fortress": the thick forest—the Vaslui. He proclaimed his victory in a letter to Christendom and history:

> When we saw this great army, we rose valiantly,
> with our bodies and weapons, and opposed their onslaught;
> and, Almighty God coming to our aid,
> we conquered the enemy—
> our enemy and the enemy of all Christendom.
> We destroyed him, and trod him under foot.

And now Father Elemar confirmed: For so "trodding" the enemy, Stephen was dubbed by the pope himself with the official title, *Athleta Christi.* "Athlete of Christ." Champion.

It had Dracula chuckling as the draguli reined in at his house. He, a papist prince. And Stephen, *Athleta Christi.*

At the head of the draguli, as ever, were Wilk and Cirstian, leading Dracula's own horse. Directly behind them was Kyril. Big, one-armed Kyril. A sergeant now. In place of his lance, he carried two long stakes. Already sharpened. One longer than the other.

All of the men in the column, from the oldest veterans to the newest recruits, wore versions of the same smile. The smile of men who had seen Death and the Devil, and who knew that Death—and probably the Devil—would take them soon enough. But men who—Death and the Devil be damned!—still clung to their lord's first command: *Make your mark!*

Dracula pointed to Kyril's stakes. "What's this? New issue?"

The giant grinned. "Aye, lord. This one—" He shook the longer. "—is for the Grand Pig himself. The other here's for Laiota."

It sent up a laugh, even from Father Elemar. But the priest felt compelled to intervene: "Kneel! All of you! For a blessing!"

There were a few stray laughs, and even Dracula looked perplexed.

But the priest insisted: "I did not ask. I told you. Kneel!"

As Dracula knelt, the rest dismounted and followed his lead.

Father Elemar's blessing was silent and simple. Complete in itself: *Guide them, Lord. And give them the grace—the wisdom—to follow that guidance. Please.* To the troops, as he made the Sign of the Cross, he said only, "Dominus vobiscum!" *The Lord go with you.*

As the troops remounted, Ilona appeared with the children. Father Elemar offered yet another silent service, taking the boys under his arm so that husband and wife could part in peace.

Dracula walked his wife a few steps off. Her eyes were dry, but they were telling—as the eyes are always telling. Dracula tried to comfort her. "We have already been through this."

The past year. Before he left for Serbia.

She told him unabashedly, "I was afraid then. I am afraid now."

He tried to make light. "Afraid of what?"

"You are going to *war*, man."

He lied, "This will be even easier than Serbia. I doubt that Laiota will even try to hold Tirgoviste."

"Good. Then as soon as you get there I will join you."

"No."

No. The lies and making light were done. He was going back to Wallachia. As a papist. It would be a long time before it was safe enough for his family to join him. Even there, in fact, in Transylvania, as the king's own ally, he had yet to reunite with his first son, Vlad. He had kept the boy from the king. Just as he would keep his new family from the Wallachians. Until he was secure on the throne.

He hugged Ilona. They swayed in the hug. He whispered, "I am sorry for any grief that I have caused you. My lady."

She whispered in reply, "We have already been through this, too." Before Serbia. "I told you then. You have apologized enough. God knows."

"Aye," he said. "God knows." His arms tightened on her. "Tell me, woman. Has this marriage given you what you wanted?"

"I told you that already as well. Yes. It gave me all that. And more."

His troops respected the privacy of their first parting kiss. Heads turned away as though there was nothing to see. But, as he took her for a second—even deeper—a howl rose and spread over the entire column.

The couple strolled back to their children. Dracula knelt. He asked the older boy first: "Who are you?"

"Son of Vlad Dracula, Prince of Wallachia."

He asked the younger and got the same.

Both boys got their hugs and kisses.

Dracula went to mount. Ilona stopped him. With a gift: a thick, folded bundle of cloth. She coaxed, "Open it."

A banner. A dragon. Like the dragon he had always worn. But changed now as he had tried to change it once himself: no cross.

She laughed. "I still say…yours looked like a dog."

He passed it to Wilk, and it passed from him to be raised on a lance. As it was unfurled, a single voice was moved from somewhere in the column: *"Dracula!"* The cry echoed immediately in full chorus. Dracula.

He mounted. Ilona blew him a kiss. He sent one in return. He called the banner to the very fore. He set the column to a trot. He suddenly called a halt.

He reined his horse about. For Ilona. From the saddle, he lifted her off the ground for this last kiss. He set her down.

A dagger appeared in his hand. With hardly a motion, it took a lock of her long hair.

Spurring back to the column, he tied the honey-brown pendant around his neck.

10

NOVEMBER. TIRGOVISTE. It had almost been like a gift for Dracula's forty-fifth birthday. He had reentered his land with no real resistance. Laiota had withdrawn south, near Bucharest, closer to the Danube, to his Turkish allies. He had conceded the north, Tirgoviste, to Dracula, who could now claim to have begun his third reign as voevode.

Stalemate. At least until the next spring. And both sides seemed content with it. The Christian allies returned to their own lands. Dracula, they reasoned, was on the official throne. His draguli—some five thousand—were enough to hold it. There would be no counterattack in the winter snows. They would take up the war again with the first thaw.

On the other side, the sultan likewise positioned his candidate for the future. Laiota had his own five thousand, plus about an equal number of Turkish auxiliaries. Enough to dissuade even the bold Kaziglu from any thoughts of fighting on his own.

As to the future, the next spring…Mohammed gave the Christian alliance something to ponder. He called on the northern Tartars for a favor. *Noblesse oblige*. Even as the allies withdrew north, they were greeted with the news of Tartar raids on their eastern borders. Through the long winter, the allies would think... *Would the Tartars return in the spring? Could the allies afford to fight both them and the war in Wallachia?*

Stalemate. Tenuous. But it gave Dracula time to face his first real resistance in Wallachia.

The bishop of the land, the metropolitan himself, came to the court for the meeting. His body had wasted with age; not just thin—brittle. The arch in his back gave him a staggering gait. His eyes were gray as the winter sky and lighted on the people and things around him only in spurts, as though he were attached to only one thing in his last years: himself—his role in his Church. With his black garb and grizzled beard, not only his eyes, but his entire face seemed borne on a storm cloud.

He hobbled into the court propped on the arm of his subordinate: Father Gregor—still the Church's representative at court. The priest had weathered the changes in voevodes as he had weathered his own creeping mortality: virtually untouched—mere streaks of gray in his dark hair...an extra ripple under the chin...And the large silver cross that he wore on his breast had turned to gold.

Dracula began with an amenity: He was grateful that the Church had come to the meeting. To make the point, even as he spoke, his own two hands, as it were—Wilk and Cirstian—served the clerics food and wine.

But the metropolitan, too, made a point: He ignored the amenities. No bread broken, no cup shared with heretics. He said only, "If you had not called this meeting, I would have. This situation is intolerable. We have never had a papist prince. Not even for one day."

Dracula sought to maneuver through agreement: "Precisely, Holiness."

The bishop merely seized on it: "Then you wish to reconvert?"

Dracula did not flinch: "Yes, Holiness."

Nor did the bishop flinch: "Good, my son. Then we will do it forthwith." He knew what Dracula must answer.

"Holiness, I need the Church's patience."

"You are asking what I cannot give—what I *will not* give. I will not set this precedent. *A papist on our throne.* Already in my lifetime I have seen our Church forced to cross the line. *Papist monasteries. Child-tribute.*"

"Holiness," Dracula argued, "there are those in the Church who know me, who keep faith in me even now. People and priests both."

The metropolitan knew that it was true. There were those—people and priests both—who swore by only one voevode. They had witnessed. Dracula was *their* voevode to the bone. No matter what religion he ostensibly professed.

"Perhaps," Dracula tempted, "they remember my many endowments to our Church."

He looked to Father Gregor to perhaps add a word. But the priest's eyes were averted. Clearly he was there—and content—in the shadow of his bishop.

And the bishop sneered. "Vlad Dracula, you know as well as I do: Your endowments served us both. Shall I give you a name?"

As he did he gave a glance to Father Gregor. "Snagov. Our monastery. But *your* stronghold. And how many more of these two-edged gifts did you give?"

"Many," Dracula retorted. "And as you say, Holiness, they did serve us both. And I never paid the heathen the child-tribute. I never will. Can Laiota make the same pledge? Not when he's already pledged to the sultan."

The bishop countered, "And the sultan has already pledged to me. We can keep our Church. No mosques. And we can also keep our prince in the True Faith. Will your king match that offer?"

The answer was plain: The king was bound to the pope.

Dracula questioned, "Holiness...in truth...how long will the sultan keep that pledge?"

The bishop replied with practicality: "At least he offers something. It is the only offer we have."

Dracula seized on it. "No, Holiness. I, too, make an offer. No mosques. No papists. I only ask for time."

The metropolitan posed the rhetorical: "How much time, Vlad Dracula? Can you tell me?" He repeated, "We have never had a papist prince. Not even for one day."

Dracula changed tack. "Holiness, understand...I had no choice but to convert. For now. I have a God-given duty."

To rule. To take back the throne.

But the metropolitan countered, "Are you asking me to justify your conversion?"

Clearly the bishop could not. Not with his own God-given duty.

But his voice softened. "Vlad Dracula, perhaps it is you who should be patient. Renounce the papacy now. Wait on the Lord."

The words leapt from Dracula's throat. "Wait on the Lord? Holiness, I was a prisoner for *thirteen years!* And I am still a prisoner now—to the pope!"

As the bishop said nothing, he continued, "Holiness, understand. I know you understand. I need the king. For now. I need his troops. I need his cannon. His cannon. You know how many guns the Turks have. Enough to take Constantinople!"

The bishop only shook his head. "I understand *this*, Vlad Dracula: You are choosing as you see fit. But the Church must do the same. The Church cannot be at peace with a papist prince."

Beside him, Father Gregor was frozen. Eyes still averted. Face blood-red. Mind racing through the memories of Dracula's past reign. How far could the bishop push?

But Dracula's voice replied calmly. "Holiness, we have more in common with Hungary than we will ever have with the heathen. At least the king, like us, is Christian."

The bishop retorted, "You should know better. *We* are Orthodox. How many times have the Papists themselves reminded us?" He fairly spat, "And now they would set the pope's tiara over our prince's own crown."

Dracula was thinking—*Was there no moving this old man?*—when the "old man" pressed. "I told you, Vlad Dracula. If you had not called this meeting, I would have. This situation is intolerable. It is my duty to ask you now...Will you renounce the Darkness and return to the Light?"

Dracula answered as expected. "How can I do that, Holiness?"

The bishop warned, "Then you leave me no choice. The Church prescribes clearly what I must do in this situation."

Father Gregor almost spoke—almost shouted to object. His mind raced: *The bishop or Dracula? Who did he fear more?* But he feared both and could not choose. In truth, even if he could have chosen, the fear had seized his tongue as it had his whole body.

He heard the bishop pronounce the curse of the Church itself: excommunication. And he heard the actual words of the curse prescribed in the Orthodox tradition, as they were laid on Dracula: "*...and after thy death thy body shall remain incorrupt and entire...*"

To the Church, Dracula was now anathema. Unholy. By the bishop's passing the sentence, the faithful were banned from supporting him in this world. Heaven was called to reject him in the next. And even the earth was commanded not to receive his dead body, but to leave it "entire."

Father Gregor was bathed in sweat. But there was no sweat on the old bishop. He knew only too well: No voevode—not even the Impaler—would dare fight the Church.

Having pronounced the curse, he was also politic. "I understand, Vlad Dracula, that things in this world change. Sometimes quickly. As though by a flick of God's finger. So the Church's door is always open to you."

The bishop was confident. But not mad. He would at least leave the voevode an option.

He went straight for the door with Father Gregor nearly stumbling on behind him.

When they were gone, Wilk suggested, "It would be easier if we could just make them 'disappear.'"

"No," Dracula said. He also knew what the bishop knew: "Kill a priest, create a martyr." He gave a sigh. "In truth, I expected as much. But at least the old bastard knows that I'm a reluctant papist."

Cirstian began, "Laiota. If only—"

"Yes," Dracula said. "If only we could make *him* 'disappear.' A quick victory. Before spring."

Before spring. Before even his allies deserted him to watch their own borders for the sultan's friends: the Tartars.

Wilk noted the obvious: "To take Bucharest we need guns."

"And we have no money," Cirstian said. "Except..." He brought a small chest. Inside was a purse. A small purse. And a goblet. A golden goblet. The same once given to Dracula by an Italian merchant.

Cirstian explained how they had come by the small treasure. "We caught one of Laiota's boyars. One, I would say, of dubious loyalty and 'sticky fingers.' Alas, he is no more." He suggested, "The cup, at least, would buy a few guns."

"Which would do us no good," Dracula said.

To lay siege to Laiota, they needed more than a few guns.

"We will need something else," Dracula said. "Some 'door' to open."

An opportunity. A ruse.

Cirstian was closing the chest when Dracula stopped him. "Put the cup where it belongs."

Back at the fountain. From where so many had tried to steal it. Against Dracula's will.

"It served us before," he said. "Let it serve us now. Let it remind my people who sits on their throne again."

11

BUCHAREST. IT WAS THE NEW YEAR, January 1477, when Laiota came to a meeting with a string of boyars at each hand. He was a head taller than all of them—in fact, taller than any man at the table. His thinning brown hair was just beginning to go gray. His oval face seemed the longer, weighted as it was by a short moustache running into a trim beard at his chin.

The men with him were his *chief* boyars. An exclusive group. They were so closely tied to him now that his fate was their own. The realization showed on their faces: taut lips, wrinkled brows...And even before they were seated it peppered their anxious words with the name of the main threat to their life and limb: *Tepes.* Dracula. *Only scant months until spring—until he came for them.* Laiota ignored them. He brought them to silence by leaning across the table to the small cadre of Osmanli officers, to the bey, their commander, at their center. The commander looked somewhat younger than his fifty years. His dark olive skin was almost completely unwrinkled. His body was combat-lean. He had only one streak of gray—of white—in his dark hair. He liked to joke that it was a souvenir from the war against Kaziglu.

Laiota began, "I have given it much thought. He has far more to worry about than we do."

He gave his reasons. Dracula was alone in Tirgoviste. Would his allies return in the spring? Or would they be frozen at home, checked by the Tartar threat? If they did not come, Dracula could not hold out. Even if he had the stores to withstand a siege—which he did not—he had only a few cannon. But Laiota—his Osmanli allies—had cannon. Cannon and stores enough for a siege of wooden-walled Tirgoviste.

And more: Dracula had his problem with the Church. His motives—his very name—would be stained with doubt from every pulpit in the land. So come spring, he might be very alone indeed.

The commander nodded. Laiota's reasoning was good. In the short time that the commander had known him, he gave Laiota his due: Laiota—a thinker. Somewhat.

From the end of the table came another voice. A third party. The Church. Its representative: Father Gregor. "It is all true. As I witnessed myself. Tepes worries about his lack of cannon. And about his problem with us."

The commander had also come to know this priest as a "thinker." Somewhat.

Laiota continued, "Tepes, too, has to realize where he stands. He can wait—and worry—to see what spring brings. Or he can do something. A victory over me now would surely tempt him."

The commander agreed, "Surely. But how to convince him that such a victory is at hand?"

Dracula would have to be thoroughly gulled to march through the winter against a force twice his own.

"I think I know a way." Father Gregor again. "But you will have to be bold to try it."

Bold, the commander thought. Of course with Kaziglu you had to be bold. Truth be told, the commander's joke about the streak of white in his hair was only a half-joke. The streak had in fact appeared after the war of '62. Of all these provincials, these "thinkers," only Kaziglu understood his country's one chance for freedom: terror—make the empire fear him. All he needed behind him was a solid ally or two and his own people.

Yet now his allies were in doubt, afraid of a Tartar invasion.

And his own people—Laiota and this priest with the big gold cross—were scheming against him. The commander had to wonder: How much did either of them really think?

Laiota…Did he look past this war? Did he see the Porte absorbing his land? Would he have the sense to bow and say, *Yes, Highness, take what is already yours?* Then he might at least keep a title and some estates. But, no, he would not be content with that. He would go on scheming his way to an early grave.

And the priest…his Church…They cared no more for Laiota than for Kaziglu—or any voevode. Yet did they really think to survive on their own? Even if the sultan let them keep their religion, the people would soon see that, under the Porte, it was a religion for the second-class. Those of the True Faith—Islam—would be more "equal" than all the rest under the law. So "hungrier" men—as most men were—would convert to Islam. The Wallachian Church would be left with only the poor of spirit. The poor of ambition. The dregs.

But the priest was saying in earnest now, "Tepes still has his supporters. Even in the Church. Even among the 'shepherds.'"

There were still those priests who saw Dracula as their only hope.

Father Gregor explained, "Despite what the metropolitan has decreed, they quietly let it be known that they want Tepes on the throne. And some, it seems, have gone even further. When Tepes was in Hungary, they helped his draguli. They even gave them information to ambush the sultan's patrols."

The commander noted, "Kaziglu's own 'eyes.'"

Laiota flared, "Perhaps we should pluck them out!"

Father Gregor gave a nod. "We should. But not yet. Not until we use them to deceive Tepes himself."

12

DAYS LATER. TIRGOVISTE. The old priest's coarse robe was still stained with mud and dripping with melting snow. As he entered the court, he withdrew the hood to show a balding, gray pate. His withered frame seemed lost in the robe's ample folds. Though his back was bent, his hurried pace prompted the guards to lead to the table near the throne where Dracula waited. The priest bowed and accepted the chair that the voevode offered. He also accepted a hot brandy, shivering off a chill at the first sip.

He had one "stone" ear, as he called it. So he craned his head when listening and raised his voice when he spoke. "Lord, I hope what I have to tell you does a service."

He would do almost any service for Vlad Dracula. Because long ago, in 1448, he had met the voevode. He had stormed into the young Dracula's court to damn him for the destruction being done to Tirgoviste by Dracula's Osmanli "allies." Dracula had given Father Tibor his word then: a pledge to some day defend Wallachia from its enemies. All of its enemies. He had asked Father Tibor to bear witness. And, through the years, Dracula had proved as good as his word.

Father Tibor now had only one visible tooth, a front upper; so he tended to chew his gums between sentences. He glanced to Wilk and Cirstian standing next to Dracula, as though to share with them all what he had to say.

Only a few days before—three?...four?—his memory wasn't so good anymore—but it was four—four days ago...Some men came into his small village church. They wore swords. At first he thought they were robbers. Or Turks. His eyes weren't so good anymore either.

But the men were soldiers. Wallachian. Laiota's. They asked him to come with them. Right away. They wouldn't say where but they had to go quick. He had to ride a horse.

He chewed his gums and continued, "We went into the woods. Far. They wouldn't take the roads." He grimaced at remembering bouncing in the saddle. He laid out his next words like a revelation: "We went to Laiota's camp."

Dracula asked, "In Bucharest?"

"Outside," the priest explained. "In the marshes."

Dracula looked to Wilk and Cirstian. *Marshes? What was Laiota doing in the marshes?*

The priest went on, "I can show you the way. I think. They took a twisted way. But I remember. Yes. I remember."

Laiota's men had come for him because a man—an officer—needed the Rites. He was sick. Dying. Then, after the priest gave the Rites, some others wanted a blessing. He gave that, too. He had to be fast, though. They were all in a hurry. Laiota, it seemed, did not have much time.

Dracula prompted, "Time for what, father?"

"A retreat, I'd say. I think he's leaving. It looked like it. His Turks were riding off. Their wagons were full: tents, food…They were taking it all. And Laiota's men were getting ready to follow. They had everything stacked up."

"They struck camp?"

"Not yet, lord. At least, not then. They needed more wagons. I heard them curse: 'Where the hell are the wagons?' They wanted to leave with the Turks."

"The Turks left?"

"Yes, lord, they did. I saw it. South."

Wilk asked, "Did you see any guns? Cannons?"

The priest nodded. The Turks had taken some. All they could carry on their wagons. But Laiota still had some, too. Thirty. More than thirty, the priest had counted. Lined up with barrels of powder and shot. Ready to go. Waiting, he expected, for more wagons.

"Big guns?" Wilk asked.

The priest thought. He looked at the long table. "Half as long as this. With mouths like—" He made a circle of his fingers.

"Field artillery," Cirstian said.

He, Dracula, and Wilk had the same thought. *Thirty guns. With powder and shot. Crawling south on wagons.*

The priest repeated, "I think Laiota is running away. I thought you should know, Vlad Dracula."

Dracula pressed, "Father. How many men did they have?"

The gums chewed as the priest calculated. But an afterthought intruded: "They made me swear not to say—not to tell anything I saw." He chuckled. "But an oath to a heathen—or his allies—is no good."

His thoughts went back to numbers. "I counted men in a single pack and tried to guess the number of packs in their camp."

He had guessed well, according to what Dracula already knew. He had seen four, five thousand each, for Laiota and the Turks.

Dracula and his commanders left the priest at the table, where a meal was promptly set for him. He dug into it, remembering after only a few bites to bless himself first.

Dracula and his commanders paced and talked. Was Laiota really leaving? Why? Because the Turks were leaving. If they really were. And if they were...The question again: why? Trouble in the east?

Questions. Call a priest to give Last Rites? Yes. A devout dying man would want to save his soul. Laiota would grant it. Especially since he knew that the Church loathed Dracula. No priest—especially this harmless old man—would betray Laiota, the voevode supported by the bishop. Or so Laiota would reasonably think.

Cirstian vouched, "This priest has helped us before. When you were in Hungary. He has always been reliable."

"Aye," Wilk agreed. "He knows what he sees—bad eyes and all."

Dracula had one last doubt. "Could Laiota know the priest helps us?"

The others shrugged. Not likely. It had been months—almost two years—since Dracula's release from Hungary—since the priest had last actively helped them. If Laiota had suspected Father Tibor, the priest would have been gone long ago. Surely. But here he was—head now bent over his plate.

And the news that he had brought was something that Dracula sorely needed. Laiota running. For whatever reason. Wagons crawling through snow. It would take days for Laiota to reach the Danube, the Turk. His Osmanli allies had gone on ahead. Dracula could catch him. Catch him alone. If he struck fast.

He went to the priest. The stone ear missed the voevode's first words. The priest jumped to Dracula's touch. "Oh. Lord. I didn't hear you. This bread is good. It chews easy."

"Father, did you come here alone?"

Alone and straightaway.

"I want you to stay here. Just tell me where Laiota is. Wait here till this business is done."

"No, lord. Let me go with you. I will show you."

Too slow, an old man on a horse on a winter's sprint. Dracula squeezed the priest's shoulder. "No, father. You have already done very well." He pressed a purse into the priest's palm.

The priest pressed it back. "No. I don't want it. Just beat them."

He looked up from his plate, straight into the green eyes. "They tell us, Vlad Dracula, that you are a papist now. They think we're fools. That bishop...When the Turk comes, he'll run. But I can't run—run and leave my people. And that Laiota...He'll give our children to the heathen."

13

FEBRUARY 1477. THE BUCHAREST MARSHES. It seemed like a real stroke of luck. It was just a slow day's ride south of Bucharest where Dracula found the tracks. Fresh tracks. Wagons and horses. A path had been beaten across the snow on the marshes. And those who had struggled to make the path—Laiota's column—had apparently been slowed in the process.

The late afternoon sky was an anomaly. It hung over the checkerboard of marsh and forest like a cauldron of molten iron, complete with its own vapor of gray clouds. But the steaming cauldron froze the land and drew the breath of men and beasts in thick white puffs. It also raised a white mist from the sweat of the scouts' horses as they reined in from a gallop at Dracula's side.

Just ahead, they reported. That's where Laiota lay. In camp. Where the marsh finally gave way to thicker woods. His retreat had been slow indeed. Crawling. And he apparently needed a night's breather before dragging his wagons on into the forest. In fact, he had not even bothered to unload them. He had formed them into a loose makeshift wall, a half-circle with its ends touching the woods. His men were already huddled around fires for the night.

Dracula had to ask: *The wagons still loaded?* The scouts affirmed: the guns still on the wagons, still wrapped in cloth against the weather.

Dracula believed: Laiota did not think he was being followed. He asked further, "No sign of Turks?"

No sign. Only marsh all around and woods behind.

Dracula turned to his commanders.

Cirstian looked at the firmament of the sky. "We could have more snow tonight."

Then no chance of a battle tomorrow. Not in drifts.

Wilk agreed, "And Laiota could keep crawling away."

Dracula had a final question for the scouts. "Can we get men into the woods behind him?"

First one, then the others, shook their heads. Men would have to cross open ground to get into the woods. Laiota would see them. Unless they took hours to swing far around or wait till the dead of night.

There would be no wait. Dracula told Cirstian, "Hold five hundred."

A reserve. Hopefully for no more than catching stragglers.

As Cirstian rode, Dracula looked back to Wilk, to one of the stakes that he had taken from Kyril. "Wouldn't you rather have a lance?"

"This is just as good," Wilk said. "For sticking pigs."

The dragon banner was unfurled. The wind accommodated. It spread the banner full. Dracula set the column moving, gathering speed as it went. Across a frozen marsh. Through a stand of trees. Another marsh, more trees...then the marsh where Laiota waited.

His wagons were on the far side fronting the woods. The wide open semicircle that the wagons framed contained Laiota's men. They began shouting and scrambling as Dracula came on. The men at the wagons pulled at the cannons, at the cloth wrapping. Dracula could almost see the panic in their faces: *Too late! Tepes was on them!* They ran from the wagons to where the rest of their men were mounting. Dracula's men fanned out at the gallop. He took the right, Wilk the left. They streamed through the line of Laiota's wagons. The draguli raised the cry: *Dracula!* Get Laiota. Get his men. Don't let them slip into the woods.

It was almost imperceptible how Laiota's men were formed: clusters...separated by gaps. Through all of the shouting Dracula thought that he actually heard the single word: *Fire!* From between the gaps in Laiota's lines, Hell itself roared.

With the thunder of the guns the ears were filled by other strange sounds: zip and zing. Like Heaven's own whip. A barbed whip. Tearing the very air. The sounds of canister and chain-shot.

Dracula's horse buckled and threw him. The beast's legs were mangled. He squealed pitifully, his eyes wild with fatal realization. He was bathed in blood. Dracula's legs, too, were bleeding. They seemed peppered with fire. The shredded shot had perforated his armor. Yet he rose.

Through the smoke of the volley from the woods he could see shadows flying. With the shout: *Allahu Akbar!* Turks. Flying right along the line of wagons, from the flanks across the center of the field. Behind Dracula.

Who would stop them? Dracula's entire line had been raked by the shot. Raked and ripped. Shattered. Stunned. And now it was beset by akinji and sipahi with the scent of the crippled prey in their nostrils.

The dragon banner still flew. It came to Dracula's side, drawing stragglers with it. Among them was a regiment still fairly intact: Moldavians. The two hundred given by Stephen.

At the edge of the woods, Laiota was cheering, shouting, laughing. Urging his men on. He had dragged his feet, as it were, to lure the madman Tepes on. And now he had him. There were no guns in the wagons. Only props hidden by cloth. The cannon had been waiting all along. With the Turks. In the woods.

Beside him, the Turkish commander's joy took a different form. Near bliss. Silence. A glow. *How generous would the sultan be?* He would find out soon enough. He—the man who would bring the head of Kaziglu. Kaziglu-Bey. Or…Could he possibly hope? Could he take Dracula alive?

Far across the field, Cirstian needed no orders. His reserves shot like an arrow onto the marsh, to the wagons, to the Turks' backs. But the Turks could afford to split their troops, to turn and meet him while still closing their noose on Dracula. They had the numbers. They had them even before the barrage. And now the odds were much more in their favor. And they, too, were desperate. As were Laiota's men. This had to be the fight to the death. How could they find the courage to face the Impaler again if he escaped them now?

Dracula looked behind. The mass of Turks. A solid wall. Surely Cirstian was battering that wall. But there was no sign of even a crack. Ahead…Laiota's men. And the cursed guns. Cannon. Always his nemesis, it seemed. And banners: Laiota and the Turkish command. And of course the woods themselves.

Dracula pointed his sword ahead. There lay whatever revenge he could take. And whatever chance for escape he might win. Kill a few bastard gunners. Maybe Laiota. And a bey or two. Maybe make the forest.

Cirstian saw the banner move, saw it pushing through Laiota's men. Even as he looked, it fell. But it rose again. He lowered his head and charged, hammering with his sword, heaving into the ranks of the enemy.

There was no earth. No sky. Perhaps not even the flesh that formed men and horses. In battles like this, it was the souls that fought. A tempest of spirits. Searing to one another's very touch.

The heat of Cirstian's charge took him to open ground. Open ground—but with the enemy still clinging, swarming, scorching him as he passed.

He saw the banner. It had not made the woods. It was at bay on a low rise. But lunging. Lunging. Thrown back. Falling. And yet rising still.

He was driving to the rise when he heard the shout. A cheer. It spread. All around him. The way before him seemed to clear. The enemy was parting around him. Scattering. For the woods. He was shouting himself, and at full gallop, with his men flowing easily behind him, when he reached the rise.

The snow was red. The banner was planted on the rise. The crest, the slopes, and all around were strewn with dead. Only a few men still staggered and crawled, or knelt propped on their swords with the last of their life spilling into the ground.

In their midst one corpse stood out from all the rest. Headless. From its neck Cirstian took a "pendant": a lock of honey-brown hair.

Of Dracula's last earthly battle it would be written...The fighting had been fierce. So fierce that, of the two hundred Moldavians that Stephen had given to Dracula—and who in truth served him well—only ten left the frozen field.

LEGEND

CONSTANTINOPLE. The gray-bearded commander beamed with pride as he watched Ali Hamed walk back across the barracks. The janissaries, the old man thought, were blessed with such men. And blessed by the younger man whom Ali Hamed was going to fetch: Ali Sherif. For Ali Sherif was Ali Hamed's protege—placed under his wing years before by the sultan himself. With such a tutor the young man was sure to make his own name as a hero of the corps.

In truth, he was already on the way to it. A fine soldier. And not yet twenty. He had grown tall for one who had been so small. Tall, lean, and hard. Like a young oak blossoming in the light shed by his teacher.

Where the teacher went, the student also went. On the morrow that bond would take them east. To rebel lands. As eyes of the sultan. Roam the country, not as janissaries, but as two non-descript travellers. Look. Learn. Glean valuable information. They had been eager to volunteer for it.

And their last request before going had amused the commander. Amused him in a way that evoked his smile of pride. The two had asked the honor of standing guard over Kaziglu. On this, the eve of their dangerous mission. Stand guard. How could the old man refuse? Surely these two deserved the honor of some day saying that they had stood guard over the dreaded Kaziglu-Bey.

As always, few words passed between Ali Hamed and his student. They readied their gear for the next day's ride. They napped. They awoke just before the midnight watch, took sabers and lances, and went soundlessly to the palace courtyard. There, under the sultan's many balconies, just beyond the gates, in the public streets, where the people could stop and see, was Kaziglu. Kaziglu-Bey. Dracula. His head on a high stake.

The head had been preserved in honey and spice. But it had hung for weeks now, and the preservation was beginning to fade; the visage was "melting."

But by now, too, the novelty of Kaziglu was even beginning to fade. Not gone. Not with the infamous Impaler. Crowds still gathered and stared each day; they could boast in later years that they had seen *him*. But none came in the dead of night now, staggering and bemused from a secret "sin," a jug of wine. Not even the sultan came to his balconies on restless nights anymore to just gaze.

A boring post. The guards were glad when Ali Hamed and his protege relieved them. They stretched and yawned and jokingly bid good night to Kaziglu before hurrying off.

Master and student took their places, one on each side of the stake. They stood in abject silence. Straight. Not even glancing at each other. One hour...two...

Then Ali Hamed did give a glance and Sherif was on his way. Gone for only a minute. He returned with a sack. From it he took a head. A mannequin. But made to look real enough. Carved like Kaziglu, down to the newly "melted" features. Smeared with fat. Coated with the residue of honey and spice.

Ali Sherif used the end of his lance to reach and retrieve Dracula's head. And to put the mannequin in its place. Dracula's remains went into the sack, which was returned to its place of hiding. The student returned and joined his master at the post. Straight. Silent. Barely breathing.

On the morrow, at the end of their watch, still before dawn, they would leave. With their true lord's remains. They would start east but swing north and west: Wallachia. They would find Cirstian. Or, more likely, he would find them—in the mountain shadows near Castle Dracula—where the sultan's patrols were already mysteriously disappearing again.

Then there would be no more Ali Hamed or Ali Sherif. They would be dead to the corps that thought it owned them. They would shed the cursed names and become who they always—always—had been: Giorgi and his young protege, Peter.

Just a few weeks later, in the receding storm of an early summer night, they waited with Cirstian and big one-armed Kyril and their draguli on the lake banks across from Snagov. A silent staccato of lightning showed the monastery on its island, showed the water finally calming; it was long seconds before thunder trailed the lightning. They left the shore thickly guarded and pushed off in two boats: a coffin, a small box, a few men...

There was no procession to meet them on the island. Just a lone monk whose brethren remained cloistered in their monastery for the night. Perhaps they were even praying for Dracula, for the repose of his soul. Regardless of what their bishop had said, they remembered Vlad Dracula. His endowments. And the way he fought for their poor land. If no ceremony, they would at least give him a grave.

The monk was silent, as though rapt in a prayer that he would not violate with speech. With gestures he led the way to a chapel, to a freshly dug grave inside. Near the altar. A shallow grave. Anonymous. The dirt and then the floor stones would be replaced. *Requiescat in pace*. Rest in peace.

The coffin was set in the hole and opened. Dracula's body—what was left of it—had been preserved like the head and dressed in black cloth—as though in his dragon uniform. A black cape was its shroud.

The monk knelt, took the wrapped head from the smaller box, and laid it in place at the corpse's neck. He lowered his eyes. No prayer had been requested. But he would offer one. Silently. As he made the sign of the Cross to begin, the corpse's head rolled to the side and had to be laid in place again. By the prayer's end, a trickle of blood oozed from the wrapping at the corpse's neck. Curious. But hardly alarming. The primitive preservation had not sealed the body. The trip to the grave had jostled the corpse, obviously stirring its lingering fluids.

The prayer ended. The lid was placed on the coffin. The monk left. Only the four—Cirstian and Kyril, Giorgi and Peter—remained. Staring. The finality of it all...

Then they saw the...vapor...mist...

It poured from a breach in the coffin lid. It pooled on the floor and began swirling slowly. Spiraling. Rising.

Cirstian tried to explain it: "A miasma."

A gas. From the corpse.

But the "miasma" grew, a spiraling pillar, to the height of a man.

Kyril blessed himself with the sign of the cross. "An apparition."

The "apparition" took the vague form of a man.

"A ghost," Giorgi said. "*His* ghost. It must be."

But the "ghost" took solid form. In a black shroud-like cape. With Dracula's visage. And green eyes.

Peter recoiled. "A demon!"

The green eyes began a slow sweep from one face to the next.

Cirstian insisted, "A miasma. We just buried him. He is on our minds. The gas plays with our thoughts." He looked to the door. "Fresh air."

In fresh air the miasma and its hallucination would dissolve. Cirstian led the way backing to the door. The figure followed. Almost floating, then walking, like a man. As it passed the altar—the cross—it visibly flinched. And in the flinch Peter saw: curled lip...long, sharp tooth...When they cleared the doorway and the figure was still with them he knew—knew from the lore that was gospel in his world. He hissed the word: *"Vampire!"*

Dracula answered: "Indeed."

"Impossible!" Cirstian said. "Our minds are playing tricks."

Kyril posed, "But the same trick? All of us? We all see him!"

"Of course you do," Dracula said. "Because I am here. And real."

And Peter repeated: "Vampire."

Dracula considered the word. "Yes. I believe that is what men would call me."

Cirstian spoke as though to himself, "But how...?"

"The Church's curse," Dracula said. "You were there. Neither the earth nor heaven will accept my body. It seems so."

"But how, lord?" Kyril asked.

Dracula shook his head. He no more understood his "resurrection" than men understood their birth. But still seeing fear and confusion in the four faces he began giving reassurance...reciting things about the past...about the draguli and the war...about Cirstian and Kyril and Giorgi...

Still Cirstian refused to believe. Until the green eyes held him. And he *felt*: Dracula.

Dracula asked about Peter: "And who is this?" And Giorgi was drawn into an explanation...speaking...with this improbable image of his lord.

As Dracula spoke on, they were all drawn into acceptance. He remembered, he told them, the last battle with Laiota. They asked: *Where had he "been" after that—heaven or hell? Had he seen God...or...?* But where he had been, he told them, had been like sleep. In truth, that was all he could say. His eyes had closed on the battlefield. They had opened here, at Snagov.

He in turn needed to know...so many things...They told him. How long his "sleep" had been. How Laiota was sweeping the land, hounding the last of Dracula's allies. But his son, Vlad, was safe...still hidden. And Ilona and his other sons were still safe in Hungary.

But Wilk...He had not died in the last battle. He, too, had been taken from the field by the Turks. Wounded. A prisoner now. In the deepest, darkest dungeon of Constantinople. Under torture. Slow. Very slow. The sultan had vowed to "squeeze" his life drop by drop.

Kyril voiced the hope. "But you can lead us again, lord. Imagine!"

Even Dracula had to smile at the thought. But no. "I have a different purpose now. I am not a man. Nor a prince."

He was something beyond both.

"And yet..." he began.

A man would have friends. But he was no longer a man. A prince would have followers. But he was no longer a prince. And yet...What his former friends and followers were to him now was something felt deeply. Deep in the marrow. By instinct. His *brood*.

"Seal the grave," he said.

Let men think that the shallow hole held him.

Cirstian asked, "And then?"

"Then," Dracula said, "there are debts."

On both sides of the ledger. Debts.

It had taken so long. But now the sultan at least had one—one of Dracula's henchmen: Wilk. He was not going to let him go any time soon. Not even to the final peace of death.

In the dark cell, Wilk was shackled spread-eagle on a wheel on a wall. An old, wooden cartwheel. Mounted on its own axle so it could spin. And they would spin it. The jailers. And the torturers. The sultan himself sometimes. They would laugh and jeer and spin it until their victim was sick. Nauseous. Then they would leave him. Smeared with his own vomit. In whatever position the wheel stopped.

He was nearly horizontal now. Parallel to the floor. Wondering what had awakened him. His hair and beard were wild and matted, his body smeared not only with vomit, but also with his own feces and urine. His skin had not touched water for weeks. He was cut and bruised. And burned. And still the torturers, as it were, had hardly scratched the surface. They would keep him alive until the sultan had his fill of revenge. And finally put Wilk on the stake.

But it was not the pain that had awakened him. Not that he was used to it. There was no "getting used" to it. Although, in the dark, in the quiet, the body would numb itself and sleep through the pain. And he would dream. Turbulent dreams. *He was a boy in Poland again. With his father, the old, proud knight. Family prosperous. Happy. Then the Turks or wild-eyed priests would beset them...*

But it was not the dream that had awakened him. Was it the quiet? Dead quiet tonight. Or a voice. Like a voice in thought. A voice that had called him from sleep.

He felt the presence before he saw the green dots. Glowing. Eyes. Glowing brighter. Until the green hue dimly lit the room. And he saw: Dracula.

Wilk muttered a single word: "So."

So it had come to this. Seeing ghosts. Could death be far behind? Yet the torturers had done their work well; he did not feel near death. Or maybe he was still dreaming.

But Dracula came to him and freed him. Snapped the shackles like threads. Lifted Wilk as though he were weightless. Set him down and steadied him. So that Wilk muttered to himself again: "After everything I've been through. *Now* I lose my mind."

"Your mind is as sound as ever," Dracula told him. "I am here."

Wilk touched himself, touched the floor, touched Dracula. He certainly seemed to be awake, and Dracula assured him that he was.

"Well," Wilk said, "if I am not really awake—if I am still dreaming—it's better than being up there." He jerked a thumb to the wheel.

"You are going to go free," Dracula said. As though to prove it, he turned the lock on the door and it bent to open.

"Now I know I'm still dreaming," Wilk said. He shrugged. "Better to make the most of it." He told Dracula, "There are others. Not many. But some were taken with me. They're all around in these cells. Believe me. I've heard them."

"Then they will come with us."

"But how—?"

"Later," Dracula told him. Explanations could wait. "We must make the most of the night."

Still Wilk hesitated. "Some, I'm afraid, are hardly fit to walk."

"Then we will at least give them peace," Dracula said.

Final peace. Quick. Better than being left to torture.

He helped Wilk take his first wobbling steps.

They were at the door when Wilk warned, "There are guards."

"Aye," Dracula said. "But fewer than when I first entered. I will clear the way."

As he did, he silently lamented. The palace was so close. But there was much to do already that night. The sultan would have to wait.

In the room of a Bucharest prison, the lone jailer paced the floor. He was middle-aged and balding. His short frame slouched over a growing paunch. His pacing carried him back and forth, from the door to the single large cell that was his charge.

In the iron-barred cell was a small group of priests. Except for one, they knelt on the hay-strewn floor and prayed, whispering verses in chorus. Endless verses. The prayers of the condemned. Only the one, Father Tibor, lay on a bench against the wall, snoring in a deep sleep.

The jailer wished that he could stop his ears; it was not the snoring, but the prayers. Yes, these priests had helped Tepes. But it did not seem right—executing priests.

The door handle rattled. He thanked God. His relief was coming early. He could find a tavern and soothe his nerves. But his relief usually gave a signal, a sharp rap on the door. There was no rap now. Just the handle trying to turn against the lock. The lock bent before his eyes. The door opened. A black-clad figure. *Tepes!?*

It could not be. But it was. It had to be him: Dracula. Advancing step by step to the jailer's retreat. *But how—? My God!* A cry stuck in the jailer's throat. His hand shook as it drew a dagger. Dracula swiped the blade away. With one hand, he took the jailer by the neck and lifted him clear against the wall.

The priests scrambled from their prayer. The name was on their lips: *Dracula! Dracula?* They instinctively reached for their crosses. At the sight of them, Dracula dropped the jailer and recoiled.

For a moment all was frozen: Dracula shielded by his cape, a low growl rasping from his throat...the jailer sprawled on the floor, quaking, weeping, his breeches stained with urine...the priests, too, quaking, crosses held high...

The snoring from the bench drew one of the priests. He shook Father Tibor awake. The old priest had barely sat up and begun chewing his toothless gums when the other led him to the cell door. Pointing. Shaking his finger at the caped figure.

"Ordol!" he said. Devil.

The old priest asked the figure, "Who are you?" But he glimpsed the face and answered himself: "Vlad Dracula." He broke into a smile. "They said they tricked you and caught you. They said you were dead. But I didn't believe it." He chided his brethren, "See! I told you he wasn't dead. I prayed to God to send him and He did."

Dracula gave a swipe with an arm. "The crosses..."

The priests would not give them up. *Ordol!*, the one insisted. And the others echoed the word.

Father Tibor scolded, "Even if he was the devil, he would be our devil. Do as he says."

The crosses, reluctantly, disappeared under robes. Dracula, again with a single hand, pulled the barred door from its hinges. "You are free."

Father Tibor, beaming now, promptly began to follow. The others hesitated: *Who was this figure they were following? And the guards…outside…*

Dracula prodded them, "You are safe with me."

He turned back to the jailer. The man begged. "I have a wife. I—"

"I will spare you," Dracula said. "But tell them. Tell them what you saw. And tell them…Leave *these* priests alone."

From the fashionable house near the palace, Father Gregor stepped into the night. He paused in the small courtyard, clearing his head with a long breath, with the profuse scents of the garden. In the soft glow of the windows, he could hear the boyars still in their meeting. Now and then among their murmuring they laughed, and he wondered how long their joy would last—how long until other boyars, another faction, was at their throats? No matter, he thought. Boyars—like voevodes—came and went. As long as they served the Church…

A pair of guards awaited him. Courtesy of the boyars. He did not even bother to bid these common guards a nod. He just let them trail him into the streets. His mind was on his master, the metropolitan. The old man would be pleased. The boyars, the new prince, and even the Turk were proving as good as their word. Even better. Not only would the Church go unmolested, it would receive generous endowments. Good for the Faith. Good for the metropolitan. And good for him.

At the mews leading to his rectory, he waved the guards off. He was making the last steps to the door when the voice froze him.

"Rendering to Caesar, father?"

His heart thumped. He knew the voice. Knew it only too well. And he remembered the crazed guard at the jail—his tale of Dracula himself freeing the renegade priests. But it could not be! Dracula was dead.

A shadowy figure stepped into his path.

He gathered his courage. "Who are you? The prince's men are all around—"

"You just sent them off, father. Your cry would be too late."

The figure stepped from the shadows. If there was a cry on the priest's lips, it was stifled by disbelief. Dracula!

He told the priest, "I warned you, father. But you meddled in my affairs. You gambled. You lost." He took Father Gregor by the throat.

The priest managed to rasp a word: "...dead."

"Yes, father. Dead. But here I am. Truly. How? The Church's own curse. You heard the metropolitan pronounce it. Or have you no faith in such things?"

The priest's hand shot into his cassock and drew a blade. He stabbed. He knew he struck. Plunged into Dracula's chest. And yet...

"Ah, father," Dracula said. "Once again you turn to the temporal when you should have turned to the spiritual."

The priest realized. Even through his disbelief. He reached for his cross. The cross could save him from the undead. But Dracula swiped it away, sent it skittering across the mews.

Father Gregor squirmed and just barely loosed the grip on his throat. He groped for salvation: "Die! Leave us in peace! I lift the Church's curse!"

Dracula spoke as though to a naughty child. "Now, now, father. The curse can only be lifted if I repent. And I do not repent."

Even in the closest of his rooms, an inner sanctum of his private chambers, the Conqueror could not bring himself to sit. He had vented his wrath on the guards who had let Dracula's men escape. The guards had died under torture. And to the last they had all sworn: Kaziglu. *He* had appeared. He had entranced them with his green eyes, sent them into a stupor. Kaziglu himself had freed his men.

But Mohammed did not and could not accept it. Could he say that Dracula was alive? Back from the dead? The world would think him plain daft. Could he admit that Dracula had deceived him? Escaped the last battle after all? That the head on the stake belonged to someone else? He had the head—still on its stake—paraded through his capital. Before the people. Before ambassadors from foreign lands. The rotting head. Kaziglu for sure. And dead.

Then the stake—head and all—was tossed into a fire.

There could be no dispute now that Kaziglu was gone.

But...The news had flown from Wallachia: a mad jailer. He, too, had seen Dracula. He swore by all that was holy. Dracula had freed the rebel priests.

And now Father Gregor. Grisly. Impaled on a tree in his own mews. His body forced onto a branch. And the look on his face, they said...

Even in this closest of rooms, the Conqueror found his eyes darting, finding shadows that were not there. What did he believe? The Wallachian bishop warned him now...the curse on Dracula. The Christians believed that Dracula still walked. Undead. Ordol. Devil. Or vampire.

Vampire? Mohammed's empire was huge. It stretched into strange lands where men told strange tales. Vampires? Of course. And ghosts and witches and people who turned into wolves to the full moon.

So many of his subjects swore to it all. Rich and poor. Noble and peasant. So many swore. So what did he believe?

A knock. He jumped in place. He called testily to the door. A pasha entered. "Highness, with all these doings…"

The strange tales of Dracula were travelling fast.

The pasha advised, "Best to be safe. More soldiers."

More guards. All around the palace. Around the entire city.

Mohammed gave the curtest nod to send the man off.

Soldiers. Yes. But for what the Conqueror was coming to believe he needed a special type of "soldier."

The guards saw him but could not move. They were held by the eyes. And the eyes, it seemed—not the tongue—was commanding: *Let me pass.* The guards were about to answer, *Yes*, answer by stepping aside to let him pass, when another small group of men stepped into their midst.

They were not guards. Not in the usual sense. Each carried a book. The Holy Book. The Quran. It made Dracula back away from the sultan's door. From among the group, a man stepped forward. He was not, like the rest, a native Osmanli. He spoke to Dracula firmly. And yet with respect. "No, lord. You may not enter here."

"You have come a long way," Dracula said.

Ibrahim smiled. "Yes, lord, I have. You spared my life. God guided me. And so I have come to this."

So long ago he had come from Africa to carry sword and lance. He had ridden with sipahis and akinjis—even behind the young Vlad—when they took and raped Tirgoviste. He had lamented his brethren's atrocities. Then he had ridden with Hamza Pasha's raiders on the Bulgar frontier of Wallachia. Then, too, he had lamented their deprivations. And Dracula had spared his life.

He was a holy man now. Devoted to God alone.

Dracula gave him a smile, as though between old acquaintances. But behind the smile the green eyes peered fiercely. Boring in.

Ibrahim met them directly. He shook his head. "No, lord. You may not enter here."

Ibrahim's words—backed by the full force of his piety—blocked Dracula like an impenetrable wall. He watched the vampire fade into the night. He muttered a prayer for him. And he also said a prayer of gratitude: He, Ibrahim, had remained a soldier of God after all.

It pained Dracula. Why, he was not certain. In all other ways he was changing—less and less interested in the affairs of men. Mere men. Yet, unseen, watching Ilona in her doorway, he felt a yearning.

It was the same yearning he had felt when he surreptitiously went to see his son, Vlad. A young man now. Truly.

Ilona. A fine woman. And his sons by her both fine sons.

Why not just go to them?

Go to them? Why? If they recoiled from him, and shuddered at his touch, what great pain would that give him? Yet, if they embraced him…what great pain would that give *them*?

Better to let them believe that his legend was just that. Better, when the yearning took him, to simply steal near and watch them from the shadows.

They came through the woods like a flood, a dark flood that occasionally eddied in the shadows of thick foliage only to rush on. They were unnaturally quiet. Only the rustling of leaves and brush. None of their usual howling and barking. As they closed on the clearing, their leader showed distinctly. Bigger and darker than the rest. When he stopped they stopped with him. But always at a respectful distance at his heels.

Cirstian did not know whether to laugh or shudder. "I will never get used to this."

Wilk agreed, "Aye."

A mist began rising from the lead wolf. It thickened and swirled upward, changing the form of the beast like a magician's illusion. The mist thinned. The wolf had become Dracula.

He approached with the query, "All is well?"

All was. Dracula had been tending his "brood," protecting and "feeding" them by his forays into the night. He brought them gold—from his victims. He put the "Fear of God" into their enemies. In fact now his followers could almost travel the land unmolested. In broad daylight. Almost.

At least, they were no longer hunted.

As the three left the woods for a road Wilk gave a low laugh. To Dracula's curious look he explained, "Just thinking. Imagine Laiota's face if you led us again. We could storm Bucharest with two armies: us and the wolves."

There was a quiet laugh all around. But Wilk followed seriously, "Why not lead us again?"

A last appeal.

But Dracula only answered as he had before. He was no longer tangled in the affairs of men: lands, thrones...His nature had changed and was changing still. It was that new nature alone that he would serve. He would survive. Thrive.

Which is what he was about now. At the road, the rest of his men waited in wagons. Kyril, Giorgi, Peter...with the rest of the draguli. They were on a mission for their master. They marvelled at the cold white glaze that colored his skin, and at the hint of fangs protruding from his closed lips. But still they called him lord.

They marvelled, too, at his new powers. The wolves were away in the woods, unseen, but their scent was in the air; the horses were nervous. Yet a single wave of Dracula's hand calmed them.

He looked at the wagons approvingly. They carried boxes. Coffins. They would be spread throughout the land. And beyond. They carried the essential element for his long days of sleep: his native soil.

There were no farewells as the wagons started off. He was of the brood, and they of him. Just as when they had all ridden together as the Dragon and his draguli.

He simply reminded them as they went, "Travel by night."

The land, by day, was ruled by sultan and prince. But by night...

He looked from the shadows of the small window to the waves of the Adriatic. This is where the years had finally brought him. In a very roundabout way. Purposely roundabout. First he had trusted almost no one, then trusted no one in fact. He had shed followers as he went, disappearing when their backs were turned.

For one thing, the sultan wanted him. For what? Who could say? Some said to reward him. But some said...

The sultan's gold would tempt any man. Even the most loyal follower. So Gales had shed his followers.

He even wondered now as the lackey returned from his errand. Surely the lackey was no threat. A tavern drunk who had run an errand for a coin. A common enough errand at that. The lackey did not even know who Gales was.

And still Gales stared past him. Was anyone following along the wharf? There was no one. Only the lackey. Yet when he came to the room Gales's eyes still searched for a hint of betrayal.

But there was no betrayal. The man reported. There was a ship. More than one, in fact, going west. Leaving the Balkan shore for Italy. The first would sail that very night. Others would catch the morning tide.

The man was glad to get his coin. Gladder still at getting two. It was worth it to Gales. Two coins would seal his tongue—get him drunk—all the quicker. By the time he sobered up, even remembered his errand, Gales would be gone. But not on a night ship. Why?, he asked himself. Did he really believe? All the nonsense! Dracula some...ghost. *Incredible tales!*

Gales smirked. What did he believe? He thought he knew. Knew with all the certainty in his reason. But he would not leave his room until the *morning* tide.

He had wound his slow way west to the Adriatic. He would go to Italy— beyond the reach even of the sultan...and the incredible tales.

He had grown into a man of some small skills: tinkering, fixing, laboring. He made a living. He even had a few silver coins in his purse. He gave an honest day's work. He had made honesty his code.

He had travelled the land for better than twenty years. Through all of its turbulence. Through the wars and feuds and lesser evils. There had been a time, in truth, when he was part of the land's troubles. When still a boy. Adopted by a pack that preyed on honest men. He had thought then that his life would be short and come to a violent end. That was the life his adopted "family" knew. A violent end. Sword in hand. A casualty of yet another venture. Still, to a boy, it was somehow glorious.

But then he had been given a chance. A warning. A brush with death. A near brush. A close look at a brutal death. So he had changed his ways.

In truth, the older he got, the more he believed the change somehow protected him. Honesty. His code. And his protective charm. As though it kept the ills of the land at bay. And this charm of honesty, it seemed, worked not just for him, but for so many others who wore it. Simple folk. Peaceful. Oh, yes...tragedy sometimes sought them out. But honest folk somehow lived through tragedy less scathed than schemers and thieves.

Now, at the close of another day, his fortune seemed good as ever. He had found the fountain. There was a time when it was a popular stop, like an oasis just off the beaten track. A fountain with a story. People came to see it. But the vines and foliage hid it now. They even crept into its basin and muffled the sound of the flowing water.

He laughed to himself. Maybe he had just smelled the water, he needed it so badly. He had started in the fields at dawn. It was sunset. He was matted with sweat and dead insects. He actually wore the odor of the crops he had been cutting.

He pulled the growth aside and bent to drink. His foot lighted on something round and he nearly fell. He looked down. Gold?

Gold. And he knew. The fountain's story. His heart pounded and his skin bristled with its own heat as he lifted the goblet. So heavy! A fortune! A fortune!

But this was Dracula's cup.

A fortune!

Dracula's cup.

There was the placard in the dirt. Dracula's warning to any who took the cup. He did not even have to read it. He knew the stories. How many had died.

But Dracula was dead. This cup…

The weight seemed to disappear in his hand. The fountain seemed to disappear around him. He saw…

A road in Transylvania. Long ago. His adopted pack—thieves—had met Vlad Dracula.

Dracula had freed him because he was only a boy. Freed him with the warning: *Never break the law again.*

And here was Dracula's law, still etched on the placard.

But the placard was in the dirt. Dracula was dead.

And this cup…

But was Dracula dead? Or was he—as so many swore and would swear into the centuries—undead?

The sun was fading.

The man asked himself: What did he believe?

He set the cup down. Exactly as he had found it.

He drank Vlad Dracula's water in peace.

0-595-33271-4

Printed in the United States
63920LVS00003B/222

9 780595 332717